It could have been any Saturday with the dog warming her feet, going into the macro file to insert the boilerplate language into her report about how tentative her conclusions were about the subject of the report. The normalcy of it all was, on reflection, deceptive. Then the office doorbell rang. Not usual for a Saturday, she noted in later obsessive reviews of that moment. That Saturday doorbell was something that should have caught her attention, something that got no special attention at the time. She made what she realized retrospectively was her first error. She put Mr. Piggy into a down-stay and went to answer the door.

Rachel was expecting no one. She didn't have to answer the door. A forensic psychologist has the privilege of keeping more usual business hours than psychologists who do therapy. She had closed her dwindling therapy practice for good in the weeks after Sarah's death. She had barely worked at any kind of psychology in the past year. It was Saturday. She had never practiced on Saturday. All of those reasons she recited to herself months later.

Visit

Bella Books

at

BellaBooks.com

or call our toll-free number

1-800-729-4992

MEMORIES TO DIE FOR

ADRIAN GOLD

Bella
BOOKS

2005

Bella Books, Inc.
P.O. Box 10543
Tallahassee, FL 32302

Printed in the United States of America on acid-free paper
First Edition

Editor: Anna Chinappi
Cover designer: Sandy Knowles

ISBN 1-59493-038-4

For my "Anna"

Acknowledgments

I am grateful to the many authors who've written so eloquently about their personal and clinical experiences with incest survivors and to the survivors themselves who've told these stories. I would like to thank the friends who reviewed this manuscript in its earlier forms and who must remain anonymous for reasons known to them. I would also like to thank the cooks and waitstaff at the many restaurants named in this story who fed me while I was working on the first draft of the novel.

There are two real people whose names can be found in this story. Francine Shapiro really did invent EMDR. David Summers really is an attorney in Seattle who has done groundbreaking work pursuing therapists who have sex with clients. Otherwise, as a novel, this story and the people who inhabit it are works of fiction.

About the Author

Adrian Gold lives with her partner in the Pacific Northwest. She has taught students from first grade through medical school, and been a writer of technical materials. She has traveled extensively in Europe and the Middle East. Her passions include reading, riding her bike, practicing martial arts, and cooking and eating great food. In her spare time she is writing the second Rachel Katz book. She believes that the search for intimacy is the ultimate mystery.

Chapter One

After the project ended, Rachel Katz wondered why she had let herself get involved. There were moments, most of them between two and four a.m., when she angrily asked herself what would have happened if she had just said no. The list of what-ifs gets very lengthy when it's dark out and you're alone but for a dog and there are no adults at home in the brain. The no-grown-ups-here phenomenon was the normal state of affairs for her middle of the night obsession-fests.

Once she was hooked and allowed the project to become her new drug to cure the grief, she simply would not stop because the blessing and curse of the mildly obsessive person is persistence. OK, who was she trying to kid, the more than mildly obsessive person, she said to herself at this point. Sarah had teased or harassed her, depending on the day and her mood, about that dogged determination. Maybe if she hadn't been trying to bring some illusion of control back into her life that year after Sarah died, if she hadn't had so much time on her hands, if she weren't looking for something to distract her from the endlessly echoing house, or keep herself safe from new entanglements of the heart, maybe, maybe, maybe. The list was endless of how Rachel might have had an easier time turning down all of the offers to get herself into difficulty. Eschewing the usual anodynes, she took this one. The side effects, she mused later, could be killers.

So much for second- and third-guessing. By the time Sgt. Andrea Cole rang Dr. Rachel Katz's doorbell that April morning, most illusions of control had burnt into a hulk as charred as the car that Sarah had driven to her death. Not quite a year had passed since the night when Rachel's partner had stormed out the house at the tail end of a fight, drunk, and managed to take herself, her car, and three innocents in the next lane off the edge of the Ship Canal Bridge and into the waters below. Rachel's just-starting-to-maybe-break-up rage at her partner had been smashed into a pile of grief and utter disbelief at the turn of events. She hadn't been ready to let Sarah go quite yet. She was certainly not ready to lose her to death, much less that sort of highly public death.

So she was in search of a little control, and this project seemed to have handed her something that felt controllable. The job seemed safe. It didn't require emotional risks, it paid well, it would allow her to satisfy a little morbid curiosity and settle a score here and there. It met criteria, as a psychologist might say about a diagnosis. On dark early mornings barely qualifying for morning status, Rachel remembered all the rationales she had given herself back when she said yes. So maybe she was a little more vulnerable than she was willing to admit when Andrea rang the bell on her office door. Oh, hell, she said to herself again. She was very vulnerable that morning. A year was not a very long time.

She had been sitting in her office, four cerulean walls nearly hidden by piles of books, filing cabinets bursting at their seams, and boxes of tissues that would be moldering if tissues became moldy from disuse. In the last year, she had barely been in the room. Any opened journals in the teetering stack were all dated 1998, as if 1999 had never happened. That year's offerings and most of 2000 were still in plastic shrink-wrap. It was odd that work had become almost unbearable. The office was usually a comforting place for Rachel, the home where she went when she needed to remember who she was—a psychologist, a good one, one who could save lives and testify brilliantly in court and be competent and in control. Not a woman who was helpless in the face of drunks, one who had seen her marriage slide down the tubes and then end in flames and death.

Today she had come to work. She was not in synagogue to say kaddish, the Jewish prayer for the dead that she recited faithfully, daily, for the eleven months of mourning. No matter how much anger had attended the last few years they had spent together, Rachel honored what had come before. Her spouse had died, and damn it, she was going to mourn like a Jewish wife. No matter that Sarah had always mocked Rachel's desire to have a ceremony of commitment, wanting always to keep her options open, unsanctified by even the most homemade of rituals.

The Jewish rules of grief and mourning were comforting in their specificity. They made a safe cradle for the new widow, Rachel had thought from time to time. They told you what to do—when to cover the mirrors, when to sit on the floor and eat eggs, and when to get into the comforting embrace of your synagogue where you could join the rest of the mourners saying kaddish for the ones they had loved, or at least been attached to by the bonds of blood or time. It was like a formal dance, with all the steps plotted for thousands of years.

Now Rachel was free again to spend her weekends writing reports, something that had become an ever larger point of contention between Sarah and her at the end. She was free now to spend as many Saturdays in the office as she wanted. *Oh goodie*, she thought sarcastically to herself. *Free me from my freedom, please.* She just couldn't seem to make her mind stay with the task that she was so free to undertake. She found herself wandering around the room, straightening up the piles, then rearranging, dusting the shelves, moving books from one category to another.

It was an utterly normal early spring day in Seattle, nothing to

3

mark it as a turning in the road. In the skies it was winter, winter being a season that ended sometime in July if the weather deities were being kind. Gray, thin light trickled through a cover of clouds that had been there for too many weeks, never cold enough at sea level for snow but damp enough for months on end to chill her bones and get her into several layers of fleece. Mountains rested invisibly behind the overcast. One hardy kayaker was visible on the waters of Lake Union outside her office window. The too-ordinary weather fueled that day's illusion about returning to life as she had known it.

It could have been any Saturday with the dog warming her feet, going into the macro file to insert the boilerplate language into her report about how tentative her conclusions were about the subject of the report. The normalcy of it all was, on reflection, deceptive. Then the office doorbell rang. Not usual for a Saturday, she noted in later obsessive reviews of that moment. That Saturday doorbell was something that should have caught her attention, something that got no special attention at the time. She made what she realized retrospectively was her first error. She put Mr. Piggy into a down-stay and went to answer the door.

Rachel was expecting no one. She didn't have to answer the door. A forensic psychologist has the privilege of keeping more usual business hours than psychologists who do therapy. She had closed her dwindling therapy practice for good in the weeks after Sarah's death. She had barely worked at any kind of psychology in the past year. It was Saturday. She had never practiced on Saturday. All of those reasons she recited to herself months later.

But there's that obsessive piece, she says to herself in her two a.m. rants, I can't let a doorbell or a phone go unanswered. She convinced herself that it was maybe one of the therapists in the office suite next to hers wanting a quick consult with a senior colleague, or a new client of theirs choosing the wrong door. She should have noticed that Mr. Piggy was waggling ferociously in his vain attempt at staying down. He knew it was an old buddy at the door.

Andrea Cole was visibly taken aback by the sight of Rachel's paled, thinned face. The police officer, tall and muscular, stood awkwardly in the door frame, light shining from the office out onto her light-tan-colored skin and head full of tiny braids twisted together into a bun. The last time they had laid eyes on each other, four years ago, they were having one of those wonderful mutual appreciation experiences called a therapy termination session. After ten years of incredibly hard work, Andrea had gotten sober, and was happy, not in trouble at work, and in love with someone kind and loving. Her life was her own and full of things more inviting than therapy. Rachel vividly remembered that last session. Andrea had done so well, had shown such courage in the face of the childhood memories of abuse that had burst over her head like mortar blasts in the wake of her last drink. Like everyone who had ever been in therapy with her, Andrea had received the letter Rachel had sent the previous fall announcing the closing of her psychotherapy practice. Rachel had assumed that even if Andrea hit hard times, she would never lay eyes on her client again.

And like half the lesbian community of Seattle, a virtual village where word travels very fast, the circumstances of Rachel's lover's death were only too well known. Even if there hadn't been news for two days of the drunken woman who drove herself off the bridge with the others in tow, when you've had one of those long-term committed quasi-marriages that are so revered by lesbians, you're under scrutiny anyway. Rachel had been careful to cover the cracks in their foundation. People outside of her and Sarah's closest circle knew only of the good times, and the double-digit years the two women had spent together. Rachel had wondered in her insomniac moments in the months after Sarah's death whether Andrea or any of her other ex-clients in the department could have gotten into the accident report out of concern or curiosity. She was more than very uncomfortable with what they would have found there.

Sarah's drinking and her temper were two of the cracks that Rachel had covered especially well. The irony of being partnered with a verbally abusive drunk when you were an expert in trauma and substance abuse recovery had not been lost on Rachel. More than one therapist in the lesbian community had seen an exodus from her practice when her human frailties became visible in the wake of a relationship breakup. It was a relief in some ways to know that there wasn't much of a therapy practice for people to leave at the point when the realities of Rachel's relationship hit the gossip circuit.

But to have Andrea show up at the office on a Saturday, in full cop regalia, well, that was a bit too far out of today's expectations, and it showed on Rachel's face before she could pull the professional mask back down. In her confusion, Rachel let Mr. Piggy rush by her and smother Andrea with doggie kisses. The two had a turbulent reunion, with the cop ending up on the floor under a massively waggling forty-pound bull terrier body. Before Rachel could say anything, Andrea pulled herself out from under the dog and jumped in.

"Rachel, I know it's got to be weird to see me here like this but—"

Rachel interrupted her, trying to keep it light. "I guess this must be a pretty serious emergency for you to be showing up here when you know I've quit the shrink business for good." She laughed, feebly. "Or maybe it's Mr. Piggy that you really miss."

"No, it's not about me. I'm good, I'm fine. I'm really happy. I'm here, you know like you used to say, in my cop hat, not my Andrea hat. Look, Rachel, I'm investigating a suspicious death and well, when your name came up, and I'm on the group working the case, well, I volunteered to come do the interview. Because, well, I figure that a cop at the door is, well . . ." Andrea paused, looking for the words.

Rachel finished the sentence for her, still her therapist after all these years, trying to make it less awkward, " . . . is going to remind me of how I found out about Sarah. Yeah. Thanks. You're right."

There was a silence, less awkward now. Something of the old exchange beginning to return, the empathy and connection and care that happen in good therapy, and they had done very good work together, Rachel thought to herself. Andrea had been one of the clients she genuinely missed seeing every week. Some people you wished had never walked through your door. They drove you crazier than they were. Others, you wished you hadn't met as their therapist so that you could have them as friends. Andrea had migrated further and further into the second category as therapy had gone forward. Her absence had been a genuine loss.

So Rachel waited, and Andrea went on. It was another missed opportunity to say no. A month later Rachel would rebuke herself, telling herself she should have just told Andrea to go away, that it had nothing to do with her. But of course, once Rachel knew what it was about, she was hooked, obsessively drawn into the intrigue.

"We're investigating the suspicious death of a woman named Alexandra Price. A researcher at the U—"

Rachel interrupted Andrea again, this time not knowing what emotion to feel. "Alexandra Price? The developmental researcher, the—"

This time it was Andrea's turn to break in. "Yeah, the one who's always testifying that kids can't identify who sexually abused them. That one. It's a little hard for some of us who've seen her at work to not be glad she's bought it, but yeah, her, that one."

Rachel allowed herself to name the emotion. Stunned, she was stunned, and surprised to find herself beginning to tear up. Alix Price had been Rachel's adversary, so it was ironic that they had so much in common. They had been opposite one another in the courtroom repeatedly in the past decade, they had sat on symposia and debated, they had commented on one another's writings, and they had not been kind as time went on. They were gas on flames, an explosive combination.

Alix, despite her WASP-sounding name, had been a classic Jewish beauty, deep brown hair and huge dark eyes in pale skin. Rachel might have been drawn to her had Alix not been so determinedly caustic in their exchanges, and so determinedly straight in her sexuality. "Sexy Lexy," as some of the men at forensic psychology gatherings referred to her, had contempt for anyone who toiled in the trenches of trauma. Rachel, who turned down an academic position in order to soil herself in the muck and mud of trauma treatment, had been particularly deserving of scorn where Alix Price was concerned. Even had they not found themselves on opposite sides of the question of trauma and memory, there would have been little love lost between them. But then there had been that odd phone call. Rachel supposed that some evidence of that had come to the attention of the police. Best to tell of it up front, to control the exchange.

"Well of course you want to talk to me. I must have been in her appointment calendar." Rachel took on a brusque tone. "She called me two or three weeks ago, said she wanted to meet with me in my professional capacity. I tried to dissuade her, I was quite blunt. I told her that we disliked one another too much, even if I were taking therapy clients again. She was insistent, told me that it wasn't therapy, that there was something she needed to run by me and that she trusted me to be rigorously honest with her about it. That she needed it to be in confidence, and that I was the only one she knew would have the expertise she needed. So I said yes, like a dodo bird. She was due to meet with me on Friday. I almost called her to cancel, to say it was a bad idea."

"Which is why I'm here." Andrea began to relax a little after getting out of the flow of client and therapist energy that had surprised her with its return as she walked in the door. She was back into her task as an investigator on the crimes against persons squad. "You're right, your name was in her appointment calendar and, well, you know the drill, you've treated enough cops to have heard about this. Everyone gets talked to. So I thought, like I said, it'd be easier on you if it was me . . ." Her sentence wandered off. Andrea felt odd being in the position of caring for her former therapist's feelings while that same former therapist was right in front of her. She remembered how much shock and pain she had felt for Rachel when the news had come into East Precinct of the identity of the victims of the bridge mess. She had felt so helpless to assist this woman who had been her witness through a decade of pain, of remembering horrors and coming out the other side healed and whole. That helpless feeling was starting to creep back now. Rachel, sensing it, stepped into role and intervened.

"Thanks, kiddo. I mean, truly, thanks. At least we both know I'm having my own little post-traumatic stress episode now." Rachel grinned wryly. "If this had been one of your buds I would have had to fake it, and I'm too old to pull that off anymore. I guess it's my luck that you caught this one. She does live somewhere along the lake, doesn't she? Or I should say, did she? So she's in East Precinct's jurisdiction. But, seriously, Andrea, what happened?"

"Actually, it looks like a suicide." The silence after Andrea spoke echoed. Rachel found herself more stunned. Alix Price kill herself? She would sooner have done Rachel in, that little narcissistic twit, oops, she's dead now, can't think those evil thoughts anymore. "She didn't seem like the kind of person I would see as a suicide risk, Andrea. What in the hell did she do to herself?"

"Oh, you know, the usual girl thing, pills and a lot of alcohol. Her body was found at home by a friend when she didn't show up for their breakfast date." Another silence. Andrea had had her own three runs at that "usual girl thing" in the year just prior to starting therapy with Rachel. The near-success of the last suicide attempt had propelled her into Rachel's office. Her attempt at lightness told the truth about how profoundly it had affected her to see Alix's body, knowing it could have been her once upon a time. "It looks pretty straightforward. But you know, every suicide has to be treated as a suspicious death until we're more certain. So the boss decided to ruin a perfectly good Saturday on the farm with Marsha and the dogs, and here I am. Ruining your morning, too. At least this little guy is glad to see me." She stooped down to scratch Mr. Piggy's brown muzzle.

"Kiddo, sorry, not much I can tell you. If she'd only waited until after we met." Rachel grinned again, this time more broadly. "I mean, I'm a very smart psychologist, but even I can't read the minds of people who haven't sat in that chair yet, much less dead people who haven't sat in that chair yet." With her head, she indicated the "client seat," a huge overstuffed chair of deepest blue leather where Mr. Piggy, after receiving his acknowledgment, had taken up residence.

"OK, fine, you can't tell us about her state of mind, I know. But what did you know about her, and who should we talk to?" Andrea was trying to find a way to stretch out the contact. She hadn't let herself realize until this moment how much she had missed her weekly meetings with Rachel, how easy it was to talk to this short, round woman with her mass of brown curls and endless wardrobe of loud plastic frames for her bottle-bottom thick lenses.

Rachel paused. She had been taking her spirituality even more seriously in the past year of grief, and the Jewish concept of avoiding *lashon harah*, not speaking ill of someone even if it was the truth, was floating to the front of her mind. She had done her share, and then some, of *lashon harah* regarding Alix Price. Not that it wasn't warranted, she had often rationalized to herself. Alix had done her bit to try to undermine Rachel's credibility in the court system simply because Rachel was a lesbian. Rachel had always suspected that her in-your-face Jewishness had annoyed Alix almost as much. So did it count if the person was already dead, since the whole idea was that *lashon harah* was the equivalent of killing someone?

You couldn't kill the dead again, Rachel mused. So she opened her mouth. Another mistake, said the jury of her inner critics.

"Alix was, well, Alix was unique. There, how's that, a nice polite ambiguous word, something we psychologists specialize in uttering." Andrea grinned broadly, and motioned for Rachel to go on, beginning to scribble on her Palm Pilot. "She was extremely productive professionally. U of Chicago Committee on Human Development grad, seven or eight major journal articles published even before she got her degree. Brilliant. I was a year behind her in the program, and the light was blinding, I can tell you. That's one thing even I will give her, the woman was brilliant. She started out studying children's language development and then sort of accidentally wandered into children's memory and their capacity to correctly identify people. Well, not accidentally, because it happens that the way that we remember is tied so intimately to the way that we use language, and our capacity to . . ."

Andrea interrupted her, laughing. "Rachel, you can stop the academic lecture please. I just need some information about the woman, not her research findings. Like, what do people say about her in your world? Who were her enemies, who hated her?"

Rachel shook her head. "I was trying to be a good girl and avoid that gossip shit, Andrea. OK, OK, fine. Information. She was compulsively sexual. She never bothered to make a secret of it, I'm sure that everyone in the special assault unit over at the prosecutor's office knows it. They kept trying to find a way to get it in front of a jury, so it's probably in their Alix notebook." Frequent expert witnesses had dossiers compiled on them by the side they were most often opposite. Rachel had her own notebooks at some of the firms that defended accused sex offenders. "I can list on one hand the men I know in her field who didn't have sex with her—or at least, the ones who claim to have turned her down, at least three of whom I believe."

Andrea grinned again at this aside, motioning Rachel to continue.

"She was married, once, to a guy in the poli-sci department, but that was so many years ago that I doubt it matters anymore. Matt was a nice guy, met him at a couple of conference cocktail parties years ago, always wondered how they ended up together. He was so unlike her. But before, during and after him, when we were in grad school, after we both ended up here on faculty, all the time I knew her, the woman liked sex an awful lot. Or who knows, maybe she didn't like it. But she did it with a large cast of characters. Maybe she pissed somebody off when she got rid of him. Or worse, pissed off his wife. You could track down various old and current inamorata."

"Old and current what?" Andrea stopped taking notes to stare at Rachel, who seemed to be looser and more careless than she had ever known her. Rachel had never talked over her head before, and now she was just running her Dr. Katz mouth. Andrea reminded herself that this wasn't a therapy session, that Rachel was just being a citizen now, not her shrink. Maybe this is how she talked when she's not trying to be helpful. In fact, Rachel was not being helpful at all. This was nothing Andrea and the rest of the unit didn't already know about the late Dr. Price, heck, had known about her a long time before she had turned up as this weekend's latest suspicious death. This wasn't like Rachel to be so unhelpful. She tried again. "Look, Rachel, I'm sorry to be a pest here, but this is all pretty much public record. I guess I have a hard time believing that you don't have some kind of insight into her that the rest of us don't have."

That was the point when the next door opened into misery-land. Much later Rachel would curse her narcissism. She was a fool for wanting to show off, for wanting to take care of a former client, for wanting to be able to do something, grasping for that old illusion of power and control. Damn me, Rachel said to herself. She could have kept her mouth shut. She should have. But she hadn't.

"Well, there are some things she said to me once, in an unguarded and extremely well-lubricated moment at a conference in Italy three years ago." Rachel, Alix, and thirty of their colleagues had been sequestered for two weeks in a villa in the Italian Alps, charged by the National Institutes of Health with creating the definitive document on trauma and memory. A lot of wine had flowed in between the brief working meetings. Rachel, who could fall asleep at the smell of alcohol, had opted out of that phase of the gathering and consequently had been in that peculiar position of the sober person at the party, privy to outpourings that were frequently regretted once the pourer-outer woke up, sober and headachy, the next day.

"She was, not to put too fine a point on it, drunk off her butt. She started to almost literally cry on my shoulder. She told me that she was sorry that she had alienated me. That there were some things in her life that maybe I had guessed at, that she had wished she could talk to me about. That if she hadn't been so mean to me in public, she would have had to follow through and make an appointment with me, because even if she thought all therapists were idiots, I was the best idiot around. And then she passed out. I'm not sure if she remembers saying any of this. She sure didn't get any meaner afterward, so she probably forgot. Alcohol is so good at erasing those sectors of the tape, as you know." Andrea nodded with a rueful expression on her face. She had plenty of her own missing tape segments from pre-therapy days. "And I never pursued it. Figured that it was too weird to follow up on, given our un-relationship."

Rachel lost herself in thought for a moment. She *had* wondered about Alix. The compulsive sexuality. The way in which Alix had grabbed onto the issue of children and sexual abuse, the fervor with which she insisted on the innocence of the accused men for whom she testified, raised funds, and in general advocated. Her scorn for her Jewish roots, even with the map of Eastern Europe painted on her face. Alix seemed to be constantly trying to throw people off the scent of who she was, constantly trying to assuage some kind of deep anxiety. She was brilliant. Yet she could barely stand to be challenged, to engage in the usual push-pull of intellectual debate, or at least, she could barely stand it when it came to the topic of children's reports of sexual abuse. There, she had become fervent and religious rather than empirical.

All of this had tweaked Rachel's curiosity. One of her own clichés was that anything meriting that much emotion from an adult had to be about something from childhood. But what? There were so many possible threads to pursue. And Rachel had no license to pursue. She had had enough people where there was license to keep her fully occupied. Even her persistent need to know what made people tick had been muted where Alix was concerned.

"But that's it, really, Andrea. All I have is a tiny bit of vague disclosure and a lot of pretty useless speculation. Of course there were people who bitterly disagreed with her, but a real enemy, someone who would want to hurt her? Hard to imagine. We're psychologists, remember, creatures of the distanced intellect." They both grinned at that line, remembering not a few sessions where Andrea had yelled at Rachel for not being sufficiently visibly upset by the travails of her client's life. "I'm sorry, really. I feel horrid to hear that she's killed herself. Odd. Very, very odd. But I'm no help." She abruptly changed the topic. "So, anyhow, before you go off, how are you? How're Marsha and the doggies?"

Andrea knew that she had gone as far as she could. Rachel had shifted the conversation, and Andrea never had much luck deterring her former therapist when Rachel had her mind set on something. Maybe Rachel was a dead end. Andrea had been hoping that Rachel would have something wonderful to tell her, would be as great a lead in this strange death as she had been a therapist in Andrea's life. She chuckled.

"So, *nu*, what's so funny?" Rachel queried.

"Oh, I'm just remembering what you said about transference," ventured Andrea. "About how it gave people this golden glow of infallibility and you know, glamour and all that shit. I think half of me coming here today was about transference, like, of course, Rachel, she knows everything, right?"

The two women cracked up laughing, Rachel pounding her fists on her legs in mirth. Transference, ah transference. That strange symbolic process that happened in therapy, where the therapist came to symbolize mother, father, lover, all-seeing, all-knowing. Half the battle of therapy was the transference, the way in which some total stranger, the therapist, became the most important person in the client's life as if by magic, often overnight. Rachel was an expert on what happened when transference went wrong. Her work on sexual misconduct by therapists had been quoted by judges and read back to her from witness stands for years. "OK, so you came here out of transference. What, I was supposed to solve the case?" She grinned, miming looking at a clue through an imaginary magnifying glass.

"Hey, you solved me." Andrea became solemn again. "And

wasn't I a piece of work, trying to hide from myself in large bottles of hundred-proof booze. Maybe Dr. Price was doing the same kind of hide-and-seek with herself?"

The question hung in the air. Rachel decided to let it just float there, because her suspicions about Alix had certainly wandered in that direction. Rachel turned to her desk, came back with a card. "Look, Andrea, I've changed my phone number. After the accident, with all of Sarah's clients calling, I just needed something unrelated to her. Anyhow, here's my card. If you think I might really be able to add something, call me, OK? But I think you're right, you're having a late-blooming attack of transference."

"OK, Dr. Katz, I get the point." Andrea's solemnity had left her, replaced by warmth. "I do miss you. I remember you telling me that therapy would be over when I had better things I wanted to do with my time and, you know, I do. I keep on having better things, more of them every day. I have such a good life now. Marsha loves me, and we're thinking about having kids, can you believe that? We watched that movie on HBO with Ellen and the sperm and cracked up. You know, that could be us in a couple of months, me with the siren on, running sperm from Pill Hill out to the boonies. But I miss coming through this door. I miss Mr. Piglet over there. And I feel sad sometimes that I can't ever come back, now that you're out of the shrink biz for good."

They made their parting noises, and the sergeant left. The door closed. Rachel felt a deepening sadness. Being a therapist had been one loss after another. She got to watch people get whole and healed and then they left, and she hoped for their sakes never to hear from them again, that their lives stayed good. If she met someone at the grocery store or a street fair, it was a gift. She guessed she owed one to Alix for giving her this brief moment of contact with someone for whom she had cared so well, and for so long.

Rachel wondered later why she had ever invited Andrea to call back. Stupid, lonely, seduced by being helpful? She had no idea which one or combination of lousy motives got her closer by one step to signing up for the project. She had thought at the time that she was finding a way to gracefully get Andrea out of the office. Watch what you wish for, she rebuked herself later. Rachel wanted distraction, she got distraction. But at the time, she hadn't been paying attention. Her already shaky concentration interrupted, she walked over to grab Mr. Piggy's leash and collar, determined to walk down to the lake and refocus, and then write the damn report.

Chapter Two

"So then Lambchop chased the sheep all around the field, not herding, mind you, just chasing, having a wonderful time trying to scare the shit out of them like they were squirrels or something. Poor confused sheep. Lambchop was *not* behaving like a proper dog at all in their opinions, if they had any. We were cracking up. And now she wants to herd the cats and us at home. I'm not so sure about this herding class business, but Liz seems to think that it'll be good for her discipline."

Rachel began to laugh hard at the image of her own dog's best canine buddy, long blue merle fur streaming behind her, romping through the fields of rural King County after a pack of bewildered sheep. She smiled broadly at the speaker. "Alice, do you really think that that dog of yours is going to get more disciplined? You are, after all, her mother."

It was Alice's turn to laugh. Rachel gazed fondly across the table at her. Her oldest friend in Seattle, Alice Goldstone had been one of the cadre of people who had held her up in the couple of years before Sarah's death, when the relationship had gone on life support, and then again in the past year when Rachel could barely see straight from grief. Solid, sunny, and incapable of getting anywhere within fifteen minutes of the appointed time, cracking wise in her Bronx accent even after nearly thirty years in the Pacific Northwest, Alice and her partner, Liz, had been there for a thousand too many tearful nights with Rachel. What a relief, Rachel thought, to be back in the banal, talking about the antics of their respective dogs and other things that had nothing to do with misery. Since relief was too unfamiliar, she immediately switched the topic to something more challenging.

"So, *nu*, how is she doing?" Sitting at Café Flora on a surprisingly sunny Friday afternoon, surrounded by other diners cheerfully scarfing down their gourmet veggie fare, Rachel was cautious not to use names, but Alice, having taken over the care of one of Rachel's more fragile clients a year ago, knew the identity of the mysterious "she." Sandra, who had been abused and abandoned by a whole legion of adults before she had started kindergarten, had been one of the longest-running acts in Rachel's trauma practice, and was slowly beginning to show signs of stability when Rachel had abruptly shut down shop. Besides holding Rachel's hand through the seven days of shivah and the succeeding months of mourning, Alice had stepped forward to treat Sandra, not an easy task in the best of circumstances, and even harder because she had just lost Rachel, her surrogate mom. Rachel still worried about her, and was glad for the chance to have free emotional energy to inquire about her welfare.

"Actually, surprisingly well. She has a part-time job now, and a dog. Hasn't cut herself in about three months. She misses you terribly, you know."

"I know, I know, I still feel guilty about it. Somehow I have the delusion that I could have kept on treating her even when I was about as much of a mess as she was."

"Don't," Alice interjected. "I can see the foundation you laid for her. She had some resilience for losing you that she never would have had before. And no way you could have seen her or anyone for therapy last year. Anyway, I thought we were supposed to be talking about easy stuff. You know, dogs, landscaping, not work."

The two women smiled at one another. Alice was a touchstone of sanity, not to speak of one hell of a good therapist. Rachel had had a raging crush on her when they first met, during her internship. Alice had been a senior therapist in the treatment program, a mentor and a friend to her, the only other vaguely visible lesbian around at the time. They had bonded around their common Jewishness, East Coast outlooks, and love for good food, although Rachel, who needed to be everywhere at least half an hour early, would be driven crazy on at least a weekly basis by dealing with "Alice standard time." She had come to be grateful that Alice had kindly pushed her away, and allowed the development of the friendship. No one as obsessive as Rachel would have lasted long as a lover in Alice's laid-back company. But as buddies and family, they did very well indeed. And their dogs adored one another.

Alice, looking up at the doorway into the atrium where they sat, began to frown. "Oh shit, a client. A newish client, even. Is there nowhere in this town that a weary therapist can go and not run into her clients?"

Rachel grinned at her and said, "Just don't make eye contact, she probably doesn't exactly want her therapist with her Oaxaca tacos, does she?"

Alice's frown deepened. "Oh, shit again, why is she walking over here?" Rachel joined her friend in looking up and realized that she, too, knew the short, slim woman in the deep teal designer power suit and stacked heels who was heading over to their table, diamonds flashing from all possible locations, looking about as out of place in the vegetarian haven of Café Flora as a joint of beef.

Joyce Romanski played out the stereotype of high-powered attorney to such a degree that Rachel had often wondered whether she put it on purposely. But in their work together on a series of sexual and racial harassment cases, Rachel had never detected a crack in the persona. She had come to admire Joyce for her intensity and passion as an advocate, and for the inventiveness of her cross-examinations.

She had also been a little relieved about not being Joyce's type, because the attorney had a reputation as a bit of a Donna Juana. Rachel knew she fell outside of Joyce's template for sexual attraction. Plus, Joyce had rules—she didn't break up people's relationships, ever. Her scruples were admirable. It had made them a good working pair, but never close outside the office and courtroom. Joyce lived and moved in the world of the powerful, rarely questioning the values of that venue, while Rachel only traveled there as a sort of visiting alien to give testimony from time to time and upset the power structure when she could.

"Rachel, so good to see you." She glanced at Alice and then ignored her, as if she had no idea who this person—her own therapist—was. Nicely done, Rachel thought. "I actually had been meaning to call you this afternoon. I've got something for you to work on, very interesting stuff. Not our usual type of case. I assume you're back in gear with your forensic work?"

Rachel nodded. "That's about all I'm doing these days. Just trying to see if my brain functions again. I didn't feel like breaking into tears during a cross." Joyce became visibly uncomfortable at the reference to tears. "Well great, good, because I think you're going to enjoy working on this one. So I'll call you, we'll set up a time for you to come down and go over the matter." She pushed off from the table, rejoining a tall, butch-looking woman at a table in the main room of the restaurant.

"Hmm, Joyce's latest conquest? OK, I know, you can't say anything, poor baby. More's the pity, she does provide delightful gossip for those of us fortunate enough to observe the goings-on from a safe distance. Good thing she's started seeing you, she's looking a little stressed out." Rachel teased Alice, who through the whole exchange had been doing her best to appear invisible.

Alice groaned. "You know, Rache, what we need is one of those cloaking devices."

"You mean from *Star Trek*, like the bad guys have to sneak up on the Federation?"

"Well yeah, but we're the good guys. A cloaking device, so that we can be invisible to our clients and still go out and have a glass of wine with lunch." Alice sighed, Rachel commiserated. She knew that Alice would have the opportunity at the next therapy session to process at length just how Joyce felt about encountering her therapist engaging in merely human activities.

That pesky transference again. How many times had she sat through sessions with people who had had all kinds of feelings about seeing Rachel herself at the movies, or at Husky Women's Basketball games, or anywhere in public doing something as normal as drinking alcohol or eating meat. The all-lesbians-live-in-the-small-village phenomenon, she groused to herself. Every act took on potential symbolic meaning for clients and these clients lived on her home planet.

"Earth to Rachel Katz, earth to Rachel Katz, come in please." Alice's teasing voice sounded in her ear. "You looked light-years from here. What, all I have to do is mention *Star Trek* and you boldly go into some inner quadrant of the galaxy?" Both women laughed. Rachel's inordinate fondness for the TV series in all of its incarnations and her tendency to find truth and meaning in the most banal of episodes was legend among her friends.

"Oh, just thinking about transference." A brief silence fell. The waiter, who sported what appeared to be Aztec earplugs in both ears and a long braid hanging out from the end of his beard, arrived with their meals. Rachel realized that she had once again attempted to fit her post-widowhood stomach capacity into her pre-widowhood food choices. Luckily, she was with Alice, who would eat anything Rachel would leave on her plate.

"And speaking of transference, I had the oddest encounter last Saturday." Alice looked up from her pear, arugula, and Stilton on pecan bread sandwich just long enough to make eye contact and nod Rachel onward. "You remember that cop I worked with for so long."

Alice finished the sentence. "You mean the one you sent to our treatment program?"

"Right, her."

"Is she OK?" Alice asked with worry in her voice. "I liked that kid, I thought she had a chance to stay sober."

"Oh, she's fine. But there she was knocking on my office door at noon last Saturday. In her cop role. Investigating the suspicious death, possibly by suicide, of none other than Alix Price."

Alice seemed as stunned as Rachel herself had been on hearing the news. "Wait a minute, that woman isn't old enough to be dead yet! What death of Alix Price?"

"Seems that my former client caught the investigation. Apparent overdose of the usual substances. So she thought that maybe I had insight into my esteemed erstwhile colleague. All of which we decided was transference hangover. All I know is what everyone knows, you know—"

Alice broke in again, "Yeah, that she never met an accused rapist or molester she didn't like." Her normally sunny voice darkened with anger, and her blue eyes went almost black. One of Alice's best friends had sued her father for sexual abuse after memories of horror had surfaced in the aftermath of a car accident. Alexandra Price had appeared as the father's high-priced expert to debunk the possibility that the friend could have remembered the sexual abuse or correctly identified the perpetrator after a delay of so many years. Alice had been in the courtroom as part of her friend's support team and had watched and listened to Price at work. While the friend had ultimately prevailed in court, Alice had quickly come to dislike Alix and what she stood for—intensely.

"She asked me if I knew of any enemies Alix had. And I never did tell her that she could check the lists of half a dozen survivor organizations and find plenty of enemies there. But no one who would act on it. Right? You didn't hold her down and pour pills into her mouth, did you?" Rachel frowned. "Not like the other side." Three years earlier Rachel and several other sexual abuse experts had found themselves on the receiving end of a scary campaign of harassment and intimidation, led by a man named Buddy Lincoln who claimed to have been falsely accused of sexual abuse by his adult daughter. Hang-up calls, ugly picket signs outside their offices, and finally, a Web site with a hit list of so-called "recovered memory therapists," coupled with less-than-subtle hints that the world would be a better place without this cadre of feminists who were planting memories of sexual abuse into the vulnerable minds of middle-class women who were then suing their dear old daddies.

Rachel had been first terrified, then angry, and finally had tried to find it funny. Sarah had been furious at her for drawing the unwanted attention, and for her preoccupation both with the topic itself and with the vicissitudes of the protest. It had been one of the things that had made the last two years of their relationship painful. Just when and where Rachel needed support, Sarah had pooped out, accusing Rachel of being more interested in sexual abuse survivors than in their relationship. Things had died down, but Rachel hadn't stopped looking over her shoulder for a harasser for months, and never quite let go of her anger at that crowd for fueling the flames of her relationship breakdown.

"Earth to Rachel again." This time Alice sounded slightly irritated. "Where is your mind heading off to these days?"

"Oh, you know, the picketers. They're going to be terribly upset at this news. They'll make her into a martyr of the cause somehow. I can see it now, Buddy Lincoln with a picture of Alix on top of his van and a little altar in front. Oh, stop, Rachel, enough of the cattiness, the woman is dead for heaven's sake. Can't you leave her alone now," she berated herself out loud.

"You won't catch me standing up for kaddish for her," Alice muttered. "If, that is, she'll come out as a Jew in her death." Alice, like Rachel, was active in the local Jewish renewal synagogue, which had been a welcoming home to lesbian and gay Jews. And even more than Rachel, she was impatient with people who went around, in Alice's words, "trying to pretend that their grandparents didn't come from Minsk and Pinsk like the rest of ours."

The waiter chose that moment to do his ritual hovering. "Is everything OK?" He glanced down at the barely consumed meal on both plates.

"Yes, fine, we just got lost in conversation. It's delicious, it's always delicious here." Rachel had empathy for waiters—waiters and cooks and all the different jobs that her various clients had held and complained about over the years. Without ever leaving her office, she had an in-depth view of work life in the new millennium and was happier every day that she was her own boss. So she was nice to service people, no matter how she felt. And she did love the food at Café Flora. It was elegant and tasty and even in the depths of her worst appetite loss, she could always tempt herself to eat something by coming there. The waiter smiled and left the two women to their meal.

"So, enough of transference and the late unlamented." Alice brushed a lock of graying blond hair off her forehead and took up the conversation. "I want to talk with you about dating."

Rachel groaned. She had been twenty-five when she met Sarah. Even when she and Sarah had appeared to be heading toward the rocks, she had been motivated to redouble her efforts at reconciliation by the sheer terror of the dating scene. The last few years before Sarah's death had taken a toll on her belief in her own attractiveness. Bed death had descended, with Sarah pulling away sexually and telling Rachel to go find someone to fuck if she wanted to get laid that badly. Rachel, who counted herself among the terminally monogamous of the earth, had just withdrawn into her work and into feeling incredibly frumpy and middle-aged. She hadn't quite recovered from that view of herself. Who, she asked herself frequently, is interested in a plain-looking middle-aged workaholic with mild obsessive compulsive tendencies? And then of course there was the ex-client problem.

"Look, Alice, half the single lesbians in Seattle have probably either been in therapy with me or were in a relationship with someone who was in therapy with me or went to AA meetings with my clients or else haven't had enough therapy and are too crazy." Alice broke out into a laugh.

"Come on, Ruchele my friend." Alice used the Yiddish endearment, slipping effortlessly into the role of surrogate older sister. "You're smart and cute and a mensch. And it's been a year. Enough of this single business already. You know, it's against the rules for such a *shayna Yiddishe maydele* to be alone." The Yiddish words touched Rachel's heart, and the two exchanged crooked grins, remembering the annual High Holy Days debate at their synagogue about a prayer asking the Divine to help the single get into relationships.

"Anyway, Liz met someone really nice in her biostatistics class, and she was thinking that maybe we should invite the two of you over for dinner and see what happens. She's your type, I think. You know, smart, funny, single, on the butch side of the continuum. And new to town, so we're sure she's never been in therapy with you."

Rachel felt the anxiety building in her stomach. She was doing fine living alone. She had a dog to cuddle at night, good friends to talk to and get hugs from. She supposed she could always give in and see a massage therapist if she wanted a little more touch than that. Her libido had gone to visit another planet. Well not entirely, but fantasy and one's own hand worked just fine in a pinch. Who needed the risks and hassle of intimacy? Or of dating? Getting to know someone at fifty was not the same as being starry-eyed and twenty-five.

"Can we make this a little less of a setup? You know, have a large gathering and plunk both of us into it and see if we accidentally converge on the same point? So then I don't ever have to go out with her?" Rachel's voice turned mock-plaintive.

"Vhat, you don't troost your beeg seester?" Alice slipped into her mock Eastern European accent. "You're unlikely to get any less scared by continuing to curl up at night with a good book instead of a good woman. Remember, exposure is the essence of desensitization."

"Yah, yah, I know. Maybe. I'll think about it. But maybe Liz can find out some things. Or already told you some. Like, let's cut to the chase—does she drink?"

Alice knew how painful Sarah's drinking habits had become to Rachel. Jews weren't supposed to have problems with alcohol, but Sarah could, and did, wipe out a bottle of wine in a sitting, and her behavior would deteriorate accordingly.

"No, bubbeleh, Anna, that's her name, is actually in the Program. High double digits. Liz was talking about my work, and

Anna asked her if I knew of some good meetings with lots of sobriety, since she was new to town. Which is how they got to talking, and discovered that they were both members of the family, although it's not like Liz hadn't figured it out already. You know, anyone who carries one of those multi-tools in her pocket . . ."

Lesbians had to rely on a series of codes to find one another in the world, since no one had managed yet to turn lavender. In the outdoorsy Pacific Northwest, it was often hard to tell, since the most heterosexual of married women could be found tromping through in the woods wearing sensible shoes with her hair cut short. Alice and Rachel had had numerous conversations about this confusion of secret code signs when they had first met. Back east, it was so much easier to tell. "So Liz started doing a little pre-screening on your behalf. She figured if she had just moved here from Madison, no way she had ever been in therapy with you, right?"

"Both families? You know how I feel about Christmas," Rachel reminded Alice. Maybe, she hoped, maybe she'll be some nice white-bread American girl, and she could blow it off on cultural grounds.

"Actually, well, no. Not a member of the *mishpachah*. But if this is only practice, then what does it matter, right? Besides, look at Liz." Alice's long-time partner came from Scandinavian Lutheran stock. Seven years into their relationship, she had surprised everyone by deciding to pursue converting to Judaism, and had become a stalwart of the lesbian and gay affinity group at their synagogue. "If I'd had those rules running my heart, I never would have met my sweetie. And Sarah, so she was a *Yidele*, but what did that get you? *Tsoris*, that's what it got you. You could have a nice cross-cultural experience and do a whole lot better, Rachel. I mean, what, you're going to rule her out just because she isn't Jewish yet? So, bubbe, at least meet the woman. Liz has good radar, she says that she's a nice clean girl." The last phrase came out in the mock Yiddish accent that Alice put on when she was quoting her late, beloved grandmother. This had been Bubbe Gittel's highest form of praise, and in the circles of Alice's friends had become a catch-phrase for excellence.

"All right, OK, so invite me to somewhere that I'll run into this Anna. But no promises, Alice. And no pressure, please. Nothing that looks like a pre-date."

Rachel was not entirely surprised to find Joyce Romanski's voice among the messages on her voice mail when she finally wandered back into phone range after lunch. The woman worked fast, in every sense of the phrase. But Rachel was mildly surprised to find that when she called the office, she was put through on the first try. With Joyce it was normally a matter of at least six rounds of phone tag.

"So whatever this is, Joyce, it must be important for you to be so easy to get hold of," Rachel teased. "I mean, the first call? How unheard of. Or maybe you're just taking pity on a poor widow."

"Rachel, this is very serious. Really. It's an extremely delicate matter. Difficult for me. It's about Alix Price." Joyce's voice held no humor and none of her usual slightly condescending tone.

Rachel began to feel as if she was surrounded by the dead woman. Two people in less than a week wanting to talk with her about Alix Price. She made an encouraging listening noise into the phone.

"This is difficult for me," Joyce said again. She paused. "Maybe we had better do this in person? When are you free?"

"Well, my schedule is a lot more open these days than it used to be. You know, not working much since Sarah died. So I could get together with you Monday afternoon, if that would work. Your office? Around two?"

"Actually, Rachel, if it's not an imposition, can you make it this afternoon? This is very important. I'd really rather not wait." Joyce's voice sounded as if it held a hint of tears, a huge surprise to Rachel. What possibly could have led this tough woman to tear up about Alix Price?

"Umm, well, it's not like I have anything in my schedule. OK, I'll come on down. Expect me in about three quarters of an hour—

I have to take Mr. Piggy out for a little walk first, then I'll be on my way."

They hung up. She turned to the muscular brown bull terrier who lay half-napping in the client chair. "Mr. Pig, what is going on with all this Alix Price stuff?" The dog raised his eyes and looked adoringly at her. She was his mother, who could do no wrong, even though he rarely understood the babble of sounds she pointed at him. "Of course, you're no help on this one. So how about a little w-a-l-k, dear heart?" The dog had leapt down by the second word, gave a little bull terrier jump of joy, and headed for the doorknob where his various outdoor apparel hung.

Rachel bundled the dog into the car and drove north around the lake to Gasworks Park. She snapped the expandable lead to the harness and let Mr. Piggy go wild with joy running up and down the hill in the middle of the park while she herself climbed more slowly to the apex. She and Sarah had walked dogs here hundreds of times over the years. It was full of melancholy memories now. She had forced herself to return to the park for the dog's sake, knowing how much the smells and sounds reassured him that everything was normal. But as she stared across Lake Union out at the Seattle skyline, Rachel felt anything but normal. She was off balance. The center of her life was on its side. She hadn't realized how much the relationship with Sarah had anchored her, even in the hardest of times. She had loved Sarah in all the ways she knew, including every single dysfunctional one, and had built her professional life around the core of being securely married. Stability had been more important than happiness, and if misery was the price for stability, she had been willing to pay it.

Now she struggled to find her professional self. Doing some work for Joyce would be good for me, she thought to herself. Create a focus. Even if it was about Alix Price of all people. She stared down from the sundial on the top of the hill at the kayakers sculling across the lake and through the Ship Canal where Sarah's body had been brought up by the police divers. Now would be a good time to have a project to do, one that didn't involve writing the same old boilerplate about her opinions. Maybe Joyce had something interesting for her to do.

Later, much later, Rachel would berate herself over this one, too. She should have asked Joyce just what this was about before agreeing to the meeting. She should have demanded clarification before she got in too deep. She should have said no, period, once Alix's name was mentioned. But instead she took Mr. Piggy around the park, settled him in the backseat of her aging Volvo, and headed down Eastlake Avenue toward the downtown core. Anything to avoid the parking lot called Interstate 5, which by mid-afternoon would already be choked with cars. She felt lulled into a sense of security by the familiar sights out her window as she wound her way to the intersection of Yesler and Second Avenue.

Chapter Three

Joyce Romanski's law offices occupied one of the upper floors of an old building in Pioneer Square, the historic and picturesque district where the original white invaders of Seattle had set up shop and rolled the first of the old-growth forests down the hill. The main drag, Yesler Way, was named after the most rapacious of the mill owners, who of course had become a city father. Patriarchy, Rachel would snort to anyone willing to listen, naming things after the most oppressive white male to chase the indigenous people out. Despite the bad politics of the names in the neighborhood, Rachel had fallen in love with this part of town when she first arrived in Seattle. It was the only part that was vaguely old and quaint. She looked forward to visiting Joyce's office in no small part because it gave her an excuse to spend the hours afterward browsing through one of her favorite bookstores in the known universe, the Elliott Bay Book Company.

She also knew that she could bring Mr. Pig with her into the building, a little harder trick to pull off in the new, huge office towers farther north in the downtown core where most of the big law firms lived. One aftermath of Sarah's death had been an almost pathological inability to be parted from the dog. Mr. Pig was well-trained, and most people found him adorable. Joyce was one of the exceptions. No sentimentalist, she was an equal opportunity detester of furry creatures and small, dirty children. Rachel always brought the dog anyway, slightly enjoying her ability to get under the otherwise thick skin of the attorney. He sat earnestly on the carpet of the elevator, small brown head cocked to one side, eyes on his human, dutifully holding his sit-stay even though elevators terrified him. Rachel thought that in this one, he maybe had reason to be scared. The aged cage creaked and swayed its way up to the fourth floor.

Moving floors violated the bull terrier sense of what the ground should be—solid and immobile. There was something to this viewpoint, she mused to herself. Humans were the tiniest bit crazy, with their willingness to go up in fragile things, assuming they'd get safely to their destinations. Sarah certainly hadn't planned on flying over the bridge railings, she thought to herself suddenly. And just as suddenly, berated herself to stop obsessing about her dead lover. She and the dog stepped out of the elevator and followed the gorgeous Persian rug runner down the hall. Rachel noticed for the umpteenth time how it echoed the teal tones of Joyce's favorite power suit. That woman, coordinating her reception rugs with her suits. Rachel admired such attention to aesthetic detail.

"Rachel, good to see you." Luanne Barnes, Joyce's long-time receptionist, rose from her chair as Rachel and Mr. Piggy came in the door. She was the antithesis of her boss—casual, almost frumpy, warm and engaging. She was a whiz at dealing with the distraught clients, mostly women in sexual harassment cases who were Joyce's bread and butter. She and her husband, who worked as a crane operator on Seattle's busy waterfront, had been among those who brought words of comfort during Rachel's worst periods of grief, had phoned Rachel's friends to learn what to do at the shivah, and then she had stayed away, not wanting to presume on the closeness of the acquaintance. Rachel was amazed at how glad she was to see this woman in her REI-special fleece shirt and jeans. They exchanged hugs, with the dog wiggling between them to be scratched and patted.

"Is her majesty in?" Rachel asked. Luanne raised her eyebrows and pointed. "In her office, tapping her fingers, like you couldn't get here fast enough. I don't know what this is about, but whatever it is, it's thrown her like I've never seen. And she won't tell me what it's about."

Rachel decided that she needed to put her Dr. Katz hat on, fast. "Lu, will you keep the piglet out here with you? You know he loves to play receptionist." Luanne nodded, Rachel handed over the leash, and the dog obligingly settled in under the desk where he could cuddle with his old friend while mama was doing business. He had missed seeing his friends during Rachel's extended period of mourning. Mr. Piggy had always seemed to see the clients as coming to the office for his personal benefit. Rachel headed down the corridor and out of politeness tapped on Joyce's door.

"Rachel, come in, please. And shut the door." Rachel was shocked. Joyce never, in all their years of working together, had shut the door. Whatever Luanne overheard had been fine with her. This was unusual. Alix Price, tears, a shut door, Lu in the dark. Rachel's clinical radar came on full force. She came into the office and plopped herself into one of the mauve leather armchairs. Put on your listening face, Katzie, she commanded herself silently.

Joyce ignored pleasantries and launched into her speech as if waiting to say something would be intolerable. "I said that this was very hard. Harder than you can imagine. Or maybe you can imagine, once I tell you. You of all people will be able to imagine it. Rachel, I need this to be held in confidence until I release you to say anything." Rachel nodded. "So . . ." Joyce took a deep breath, looked out the window. "A while ago, Alix Price and I were lovers."

Rachel felt herself inhaling in shock. Alix Price lovers with

Joyce. With a woman. A non-guy. Rachel had been entirely certain of Alix's terminal heterosexuality. Talk about not showing up on the radar. And with Joyce. No wonder Lu could know nothing about this, she realized. Luanne Barnes was in the short list of people who would be toasting Alix Price's death. Price had testified for the man accused of abducting and raping Lu's beloved grand-daughter. She had managed to skillfully cast doubt on the girl's identification of the defendant. The family later learned from the prosecutor's office that had it not been for the DNA evidence, the jury would have been unable to convict. The child had never com-pletely recovered from the trauma. From what Rachel had heard, she was still in treatment at the Harborview Trauma Center and being homeschooled. Lu had not since been able to say Alix Price's name without spitting.

Rachel ran through this line of thought, then gulped hard a few times. She put her Dr. Katz face tightly back on, pulled inside her-self into her professional listening mode, and motioned Joyce to go on.

The attorney's voice wavered. "Her bisexuality was a closely kept secret. I wasn't the first woman, or the last, I think. But there it is. We met at a bar association banquet years ago, and one thing led to another, and you can imagine how I feel right now. And you know, I can't talk to Lu about this, given the givens." Rachel nodded. "She would feel completely betrayed." Joyce paused and patted at the tears that were mixing with her mascara. Her face suddenly crumpled in grief, her mask of composure dissolving.

Rachel felt herself warming to Joyce for the first time in their long association. She had always seen the attorney moving effort-lessly from conquest to conquest, never risking her heart in the process. But this was heartbreak, compounded by the secrecy that had been imposed on the relationship by Alix Price's own deep closet and by Joyce's divided loyalties. "Joyce, I'm so sorry. To lose someone you cared for . . ."

"And who I cannot acknowledge as a lover. It's like the bad old days when people had to pretend to be roommates or just good friends. Ironic, no? Joyce Romanski, lesbian flirt, of all people having a closeted relationship. But I promised her, and I'm not about to break that promise now except for this one thing. Luckily I broke down a few months ago and found my own therapist. Someone who has to keep the secret. I'm seeing your friend Alice, you know. Pretty good at what she does."

Rachel was almost as shocked to hear Joyce admit to being in therapy as she was to know the reason for that uncharacteristic step. Joyce, the official tough person bothered by nothing. She wondered for a moment, how in the hell had Alice been dealing with Joyce's feelings about Alix, given her own contempt for the woman? Her admiration for Alice's clinical skills deflated as Joyce went on, "Even she doesn't know yet who the woman was I've been so upset and confused about. I never used her name, kept protecting her even when and where it shouldn't have mattered. Guess I'll have to tell her now. So I'm in what, the early stage of grief, whatever you people call it. I haven't even seen Alice since this happened, I've been so busy dealing with the fallout."

Ah, thought Rachel, that explains Alice's surprise at the news of Alix's death. She wasn't putting it on, she really hadn't heard yet. Rachel had done her friend a favor, allowed Alice a chance to ventilate her own feelings before she had to put them aside and be emotionally present for Joyce. It was going to be enough of a surprise to learn the identity of Joyce's mystery lover, much less be empathic with Joyce's grief. Poor Joyce. Her therapist and her receptionist both hated Alix and for roughly similar reasons. She forced herself to turn her attention back to the lawyer just as Joyce said, "But Rachel, the reason I've called you is she made me her personal representative."

Rachel knew that Joyce could count on her to comprehend the legal terminology associated with death. The PR, better known as the executor, was the person who carried out the wishes of the will and guided the estate on its way through probate. Been there, done that, she thought to herself. Quelle miserable task.

"And it's in that capacity that I'm talking to you, Rachel. I

34

simply cannot and will not believe that Alix Price killed herself. The coroner's verdict came in this morning. Suicide. I don't believe it. I won't accept it."

Rachel nodded. "You know, that was my response when the police came to my door on Saturday . . ."

Joyce interrupted. "Your door? What were they doing talking to you about Alix's death?"

"Well, since you're the PR, I can tell you. A few weeks before she died, Alix had called to make an appointment with me for a personal consultation. I had tried to dissuade her, but she was insistent that there was something that she needed to talk to me about, not incidentally that I have any idea what. That appointment was due to occur just after her death. Yesterday, in fact. My name was in her datebook, so I got a visit from Seattle's finest and said the same thing, that I couldn't imagine Alix Price killing herself, and I had no idea what she wanted to talk to me about."

Rachel noticed that Joyce had ceased to listen a few sentences back. Her blue gaze drifted past Rachel's face, to a point on the wall somewhere. Rachel knew she was watching a descent into memory, as Joyce's skin tone changed and her pupils contracted. She waited. This felt so completely familiar, this listening and observing mode. Maybe she had made a mistake giving up doing therapy. It was so easy, so natural to observe people in this way. She shook herself from her own reverie just as Joyce came back to herself, suddenly aware again that she was in the room with another human being. Rachel grinned inwardly; her own well-tuned detectors were working, letting her know about the subtle shifts in another person's state of mind even when she wasn't paying careful attention.

Joyce rallied herself. "So you see, Rachel, the notion that Alix will go down as a suicide is intolerable to me. It wasn't who she was, no matter how embattled she was feeling to do this. We hadn't been in touch a great deal over the last few months. I'd been in trial, she was giving speeches back east. Contact with her was increasingly harder for me to manage. But when we did talk, she never once did something that made me worry about her. I loved her more than I let myself know until I started to look at it in therapy. I knew I couldn't keep her, I knew she was in no position to make a commitment to me or ever be open about our relationship, but at least we were still able to be friends. She was a tough person, Rachel, tough like I am, a fighter. I can do something about this blot on her memory. I want to hire you, on behalf of her estate, to conduct a psychological autopsy. To find out what really happened. It had to be an accident."

The urgency in Joyce's tone was compelling, as was the offer. A psychological autopsy would give Rachel the luscious opportunity to collect gossip about Alix Price and be completely legitimate about the whole sordid enterprise. The goal of a psychological autopsy was to gather information about an individual's state of mind in the months and weeks before their death in order to determine whether or not the picture best fit what was known about suicide. Most psychological autopsies were conducted for insurance companies that were trying to avoid paying out a policy on account of a suicide. Sometimes they followed workplace murder-suicides in an attempt to learn what the killer's trajectory had been and accurately predict and prevent the next outbreak of violence.

But a few were done for grieving families who simply could not accept the possibility that the person they loved had killed her or himself. Rachel had done perhaps two dozen in her entire career, making her one of Seattle's more experienced practitioners of the arcane assessment form. In fact, she was the person who had explained the concept to Joyce years previously when the topic came up tangential to a case they were working on. Her willingness to share information with everyone and their sister was coming back to haunt her. Joyce would never have had the bright idea to have the assessment done if Rachel hadn't planted the seed.

The professional conducting the autopsy was free to ask anyone anything about the dead person. Even small bits of information could be telling as to a person's state of mind, not to mention more overt things such as giving away prized possessions, which was one of the classic red flags of someone about to attempt suicide. This offer was dangerous territory, Rachel knew. She was too excited by the idea, she could tell. The proper stance of dispassionate interest had never even made a token appearance on the scene. So Rachel made a feeble attempt at talking Joyce out of it as a bow to her conscience. Later, she wished beyond all belief that she had succeeded in dissuading Joyce, or failing that, had just said no and passed the case along.

"Joyce, this is going to be terribly expensive. The estate is going to end up investing in the middle five figures at least to make this happen. I really doubt that Alix would have wanted to enrich me, of all people, that much. What's the point? Alix doesn't have family, or a spouse."

Joyce interrupted her, angry. "I thought you of all people would understand this, Rachel. For God's sake, stop and pay attention. She had family. Her friends and students were her family, even that idiot Buddy was her family. She had a professional reputation, a legacy in her work. And I can't, no, I won't, allow her to be labeled something she was not, to have her contributions dismissed because she was simply one of those crazy psychologists who kill themselves. People can hate her for her work in life, but not despise her for the manner of her death. If you won't take the case, fine."

Joyce's tone fueled Rachel's interest. "No, Joyce, OK. I just thought that in the interest of full disclosure, you ought to know. This is going to be expensive and lengthy. I might find out in the end that Alix probably did kill herself. That's a big risk, my friend. You know there was less than love lost between Alix Price and me. I don't really care why she died. I'm not happy she's dead, mind you. She was a lot more interesting alive, and a lot smarter than most of the people on her side of the arguments, so at least it was a fair fight between us. I'm just indifferent to the way she got there."

Joyce stared out the window again. "You know, it's like when they took the Kingdome down." Seattle's ancient domed stadium had recently been imploded to make room for a new, taxpayer-funded fancy home for a football team owned by one of the world's richest men. "One moment she's this unavoidable thing on the landscape, dwarfing everyone around her. Maybe you think it's an ugly thing, but it's present, tangible. And then poof, she's gone, she's rubble. I don't want her to be rubble, Rachel. I want some kind of terrible accident, not suicide. It's good that you don't give a damn. It'll make you more open to the facts. I really need you to do this."

Rachel was noticing that as Joyce became uncharacteristically emotive and self-disclosing, she was herself drawing back further and further into her professional demeanor. Too many rules of the working relationship were breaking down. She decided to cut things short before Joyce mistook her for a real therapist. Another mistake, she said to herself later. If she hadn't been in such a hurry to calm Joyce down, she might have thought for two seconds and said no.

"All right. I'll take the case. I suppose you're right that it doesn't hurt that I wasn't her buddy, huh? This way you can be sure I'll be keeping objective, I've got no investment in the outcome. Alix would be pleased, getting Rachel Katz to act like an objective scientist. She sure ragged me about that, how unscientific and subjective I was.

"So here's the deal. We need to draw up a contract. I need you to sign a blanket release, as the PR, for me to talk to everyone and anyone. I'll need a list of her physicians, her friends, her colleagues, anyone you know about, Joyce. Names, phone numbers, e-mail if you have it. Her password for her e-mail, too, I should read that."

Joyce seemed to snap suddenly back into her lawyerly self. "Fine. Right. A contract. Yes, we should do that. The police still have her appointment calendar. I think I can get them to release that to me now that they've closed the book on her. You might have to get university MIS to help you on the password, though."

"Did you know who her friends were, Joyce? It would really help me to get in the door if they got a call from someone they thought of as Alix's buddy. I mean, anyone who was friends with Alix . . ."

"Knew that she respected you, Rachel." Joyce finished the sentence in a completely different vein than Rachel had intended. "We talked about you a couple of times. She knew how much I relied on your testimony in my work. She used to tell me that she was sorry that things had worked out so that you and she couldn't be friendly. I wouldn't be at all surprised if the other people in her close circle had a similar viewpoint. You were sort of a fixation of hers, you know. She could never understand how you managed to pull it off, being you and still credible in the courtroom. It drove her a little bit crazy sometimes. You intimidated her."

Rachel sat and digested this new information. Alix Price had respected her? Been intimidated by her? Talk about information inconsistent with the observed phenomenon, she thought. Heck, she missed this one. Rachel was usually sensitive to subtle cues and chided herself for letting her ego get in the way and cloud that sensitivity.

"I'm sad to be hearing that now for the first time, Joyce. That she respected me, that is. I respected her, too. And that wasn't a secret. I'm glad she knew that. But I still think it would help if you could open a few doors and help me in sorting who's worth talking to and who's just noise. So who did you know of her bunch?"

"There were a couple of the guys in the department that she introduced me to. Of course, they just thought we were working on cases together, but they know who I am. You know George Lewis?"

Rachel's nose wrinkled in mild disgust. "Joyce, this is already getting to be a lot harder than just doing a psychological autopsy. We have the psychological equivalent of the smelly rotten corpse here. I get to talk to all of the psychology jocks at the U who've ever pissed me off. Yeah, I know George. Good old George wouldn't know a gender issue if it were wearing pink fuck-me pumps and hit him over the head with them." Joyce snorted, restraining her laugh, which only egged Rachel on. "Mr. I'm such a sensitive guy, why do you women hate me. Mr. I'm such a scientist, worship at the altar of my utterly useless but very well-designed studies. Do I ever know him."

Joyce's snorts escalated into laughter. "Well, my dear, you've had to encounter worse than George in your forensic work. If you can interview some of the perpetrators you've talked to in the last few years, you can interview George about Alix. He was her closest friend in the department. So you'd better interview him."

"You'd better call him if you want to make that happen, Joyce. George thinks I'm unfit to call myself a psychologist, you know, not strictly scientific enough. Don't have twenty peer-reviewed studies to attach to every sentence I utter."

Rachel shook her head in mild dismay. George Lewis was prominent in a movement within the field of clinical psychology to stop psychologists from doing therapy unless and until they could prove with repeated lab research that every intervention being done was absolutely effective. Of course, the research was only ever done on young, white, middle-class college students, and didn't precisely apply to the battered, raped, and terrorized children who grew up into her adult clients. But George and his friends were adamant that psychology had lost its way in a cloud of messy, woo-woo, non-scientific arble-garble, and he was on a crusade to bring it back to its white, middle-class roots. He and Alix had been allied in their views of trauma treatment as the worst example of this kind of fuzzy thinking. He had once said while turning down one of Rachel's good friends, a leading sexual assault expert, for tenure, "You can't randomly assign your subjects to the 'rape' and 'no-rape' conditions, so you can't really study the effects of sexual assault." No wonder he and Alix Price had been such good friends, she thought to herself.

"So OK, there's Georgie-boy. I can breathe deeply and handle him, you're right. And he probably knows the rest of the crowd in William James Hall who might have something to say. Could even convince her RAs to talk to me, do you think? In my not so humble opinion."

Joyce's snorts had completely turned into guffaws as Rachel swung into her comedy routine. "Graduate students know much more dirt about faculty members than the faculty can ever imagine. My buddy Aaron O'Neill was a second-year student the year that Alix came back from sabbatical in Princeton and told me that she flirted with him by sitting on top of the photocopy machine in the department office, legs spread, while it went back and forth. I mean, jeez, Joyce, how could Alix do stuff like that? I mean, there are easier ways to put people off the scent of one's bisexuality, aren't there?" Joyce shook her head. Apparently she had had some similar questions for Alix. "But anyway, on the more generic question of grad students—if you could pry a few of those loose for me I'd appreciate that, too."

Joyce pulled out a legal pad, blue, Rachel noted approvingly, in tune with the color scheme, and began to scribble. "Actually, I know the name of a student who's been working with her on a study of children who make false accusations of sexual abuse. Ilona Hegevary. She did her undergrad work in Hungary and came here to work with Alix. Alix told me once that they played racquetball every Thursday. I'll bet that she'd know which other students were close to Alix. Then there's a couple of women on the faculty she was pretty connected with. The cognitive psychologist, you know, the one who does research on memory and suggestibility, I can't remember her name right now, but you know her, the one with the floppy hats? She and Alix were collaborating on some kind of study, although I think they'd had a falling-out in the last few months. Loftus, right, that's her name. You might want to talk to her, too, Rachel."

Rachel's mind began moving fast and furious. She had to develop a plan, not just randomly wander around collecting a gossip database on Alix Price. She needed to strategize about who would be in a position to know Alix's state of mind, and what factors she would organize the inquiry around. Develop a decision tree. There had to be some clear indications of suicidality that could emerge in talking with people—or not. The task was becoming more contained, less emotionally driven. She was back in the groove, thinking like the good diagnostician that she was. Dr. Katz took over from Rachel again and issued more orders.

"All right, Joyce, this is a really good place to start. Let me tell you what else I need off the top of my head. Access to her medical records. Maybe her doc just told her that she only had a month to live or something. You'll have to do a specific release for those, that's the rules under the Health Care Act, oh, you know these ropes, Joyce. And her bank and checking accounts. I want to see if there was any evidence of coercion or extortion going on. Phone records, too, please. I'll need the key to her house, and if there's an alarm, the code, please. Sometimes a person communicates their mood by how they keep the house up. Sometimes there's just a smell, a certain je ne sais quoi, that gets me on the right track." Rachel realized as she said the last sentences that she could have been talking about herself and the large colony of dust monsters that had grown up in her usually spotless home in the months just after Sarah's death. That someone might have wondered about her state of mind if they wandered into her house when she was out. Still maybe could. She pushed the thought aside and put herself back on task.

"I knew I was right to engage you for this, Rachel." Joyce looked more relaxed than she had during the whole interview. "Frankly, dear, I can count on your enormous desire to dot every i and cross every t. No matter how you felt about Alix Price, you feel one way about the quality of your work, don't you?"

Rachel shrugged. "True. Disgustingly true. That's why I dropped out of sight after Sarah died, you know. I knew that I couldn't use work to cope this time, and I didn't want to live with a legacy of screwups on top of the death of my partner. That would have been like having two deaths in my life. But I feel like I'm back on track now, and this is as good a place as any to start. Anyway, Joyce, how do you want me to communicate with you about this?"

"Nothing in writing, please, until such time as I request it. I know you want to tape your interviews. I really, really wish you wouldn't. But I'm going to write up the contract so that I'm engaging you as an investigator and can make this all work product." Rachel nodded. Attorney work product, anything that attorneys used to inform their actions in a case, was as strictly privileged as the direct communications between attorney and client. Making her work into work product would protect it from prying and curious eyes, although it was inevitable that the people she questioned would talk to one another, given that they were all a part of Alix Price's life. "I'd like weekly verbal reports in person, not by phone, when that's feasible. But do you have to bring that animal with you when you come?"

"The animal, as you call him, is my family, Joyce. He has a name, even if it is a corny name. And a personality. And Lu adores him. Since you're going to have to break this news to her at some point, you can offer increased bull terrier visits as a consolation prize for her having to rethink Alix Price. I think you can survive having a few little muddy pawprints on your Karastans."

"Not Karastans, real antique Persians!" Joyce went into high dudgeon mode.

"I know, I know, just teasing. Your leg should feel longer." Rachel grinned broadly. Joyce was the only person she knew who took herself at least as seriously, if not more so, than Rachel herself. She shifted gears. "OK, on another note, who was that cute butch number you were having lunch with at Café Flora? I must say I approve of your taste."

"She's one of the assistant coaches for the new WNBA team, the Storm. Met her at a fund-raiser for the Women's Funding Alliance." Joyce referred to the local feminist version of the United Way which underwrote the work of feminist abortion centers and interpreters for abused deaf women, among other projects deemed too politically radioactive for mainstream charities. Rachel had been a long-time active donor to WFA, and had sent a large part of the proceeds of Sarah's life insurance to them, trying to make some good out of the loss. "I was surprised not to see you there."

Rachel nodded. "You know, I was really doing the Jewish grieving rules pretty strictly. No parties and social events for the first eleven months, not even for a good cause. Which turned out to be a good thing. Back in January I could no more have managed to be socially appropriate than spit. I was still bursting into tears at the drop of a backward gimme cap. I just sent money instead. So, a jockette, huh? Didn't know you went in for the physical type."

"Actually, she's quite bright, and that's enough of your elitism about athletes." Joyce grinned broadly now, and Rachel found herself surprised. They were having a femme-to-femme conversation like they'd never had in more than a decade of working together on cases.

"I surrender, Joyce. She did seem awfully cute. And anyone good enough to be a coach for a women's pro basketball team has to have plenty of smarts. But enough of this talk about girl-watching. I'm resisting going back on the dating market pretty strenuously myself. This case is going to give me a marvelous excuse to delay things further. Your therapist, bless her, is nudging me to get out there again."

Joyce laughed hard. "Rachel, you'd better watch what you wish for. I happen to know for a fact that there are a couple of women who weren't exactly sad to know that you were available. I told them I'd let them know if I knew you were considering yourself open for business. So you're going to find yourself having to really resist, trust me." The two women stared at one another, shocked at where the conversation had gone. Rachel had never thought of herself as anything but plain and somewhat off-putting. Sarah had reinforced that belief, conveying to Rachel the message that the latter was lucky that the former had taken pity on her and deigned to be involved for so long. The notion that there were women, plural, interested in her who had actually so intimated to Joyce Romanski was a shock. And the shock helped her to avoid analyzing her decision to go forward, until those morning emotional morbidity and mortality conferences she began to hold with herself after it had all ended.

Chapter Four

The group of people sitting around the table in the faculty club could have been aging baby boomer university faculty from any one of hundreds of schools. There was a mold and they had been sprung from it. The three men were all doing battle with hair and waistline. The one woman had long ago given up on the hair front and starting tinting her gray streaks an interesting shade of reddish blond that went a bit oddly with her skin tones. Her stringy leg muscles were evidence of the temporary triumph over post-menopausal weight gain. They had all seen fifty a little while ago, and none of them were thrilled about it. Universities are a place of perpetual youth, where even fifty-year-olds still get summer vacation and spring break and are free to throw temper tantrums once they have tenure in hand.

But the important thing that afternoon over the Thai tofu and the veggie burger with Brie was that they were alive, and Alix Price wasn't. They had just returned from the memorial service sponsored by the university, where the one with his back to the stunning view of the mountains, George Lewis, had delivered the main eulogy. George rested his hands on his small pot belly beneath his unruly beard, and sighed loudly.

"Have any of you heard from Joyce Romanski?" The two other men nodded; the woman shook her head and looked slightly mystified. None of them were forensic psychologists. Represented around the table were a therapy outcome researcher, a specialist in inter-group dynamics, a sports psychologist, and an expert on learning styles. Calls from lawyers, even ones who were known to be friends of the relatively dear departed, were not part of their normal life experiences.

"I saw her at the other service, George," Thaddeus Taylor chimed in. "She mentioned that she would be calling me about this psychological autopsy thing. I'm very disturbed by the whole idea. Then to find out that she's hired Rachel Katz."

The woman of the group widened her eyes. "That kook? Excuse me guys, what could she possibly contribute to this sorry situation? Alix had nothing to do with trauma, for heaven's sake." She winced a little at the thought.

"According to Joyce, Rachel is very well thought of forensically. She's worked with her a lot, says that she's just dynamite with juries." George was trying to deal with his own conflict over what was happening. Joyce had been very firm with him. Alix's large bequest to the department for an endowed chair would be cut by half if her insurance company went with the suicide verdict. It was in his best interest, and the entire department's, to cooperate with Katz. Even if they all thought of her as something of a lightweight, she was the one Joyce had hired, which meant, as Joyce had made clear to George, that it was as if Alix herself had reached out from the grave and hired Rachel. "She is expert in this psychological autopsy business. Joyce tells me that she's very professional in her role, that we'll all be treated with respect. Anyway, it's not us she's interested in. It's what we observed in Alix."

"I still think this is all such utter bullshit, George." The third man at the table spoke up. Deep black eyes hid behind extra-thick

46

lenses. Paul Cunningham was the sport psychology guru, the kid picked last on the team who was now the darling of professional athletes who would pay him enormous sums to assist them in getting over their bad streaks on the playing field or life problems off it. "It has nothing to do with whether Katz is a flake or not. Actually, I had some dealings with her during that last incident, and I was impressed, and rather surprised. I thought she'd take my head off. But she was actually pretty helpful in arriving at a resolution." Paul was referring to an extremely well-publicized case of alleged date rape by one of the local football stars. He had been the player's psychological consultant. Alix had been working with the victim's legal team, and had assisted in negotiating an outcome that kept everyone out of court, Paul's client out of prison, and most of all, the outcome out of the news. "You could all stand to reassess your views of her. But what I think is bullshit is any attempt to make Alix out to be other than a suicide. Look, people kill themselves. We hate it when it's one of our colleagues, it reminds us that we're vulnerable, too."

The other three at the table breathed deeply. Paul made more money than all three of them put together, thanks to his consulting business, and he saw actual clients of a sort. He intimidated them, and they were a little contemptuous of him, for both of those reasons. But then again, he actually knew something about suicidal people, which was more than George, Thad, or Ilene could say.

George leaped in again. "Paul, it seems like we aren't the ones making the decision. Joyce has a fiduciary duty to the estate to preserve its assets." Now the other three suppressed their groans. George had recently finished probate on his mother's estate and fancied himself something of an expert on the ins and outs of personal representative-hood. "If the verdict of suicide is allowed to stand, the estate and its beneficiaries are going to be out of a major chunk of change. So she's just doing her job, like lawyers do. I really encourage you to talk to Katz if she calls you. I'm going to meet with her tomorrow, in fact."

Thad Taylor restrained his sneer. "George, I have the sneaking

47

suspicion that you're one of those beneficiaries. What if what I have to say isn't going to help that hypothetical group of people?"

"Just say what you know, Thad. Only don't embellish. It's not like you have any clinical skills." The group laughed. Thad had become an expert on therapy outcome in grad school because he seemed incapable of getting outcomes from any of his clients. He was perversely proud of the whole thing, claiming that this made him the most objective researcher possible. His colleagues enjoyed tweaking him with this well-known bit of history from time to time.

"Fine. But you owe me one, George. The next time it's between your favorite candidate and mine for a new position . . ." He left the rest of the sentence to his colleagues' imagination.

The offices in William James Hall had been built during the late phase of the Johnson administration. Johnson, miffed at the antiwar chaos on campus, had engineered a cut in the federal funds for the building. Everything had to be shrunk in half, including the offices of tenured full professors like George Lewis. Rachel was aware of feeling mildly claustrophobic when she sat down across the desk from him. The tiny room was almost a cubicle, and it was overflowing with articles, books, and stacks of raw data waiting to be analyzed. The screen saver on the computer was the most tranquil note in the whole jumbled scene, with spaceships moving slowly through the galaxy. It was an awkward moment. George Lewis had been one of the people who had egged on Buddy Lincoln when he was picketing outside of Rachel's office. And there was his role in keeping her friend Deb from getting tenure with his stupid remarks about rape. Rachel told herself she was feeling fine about this. George, after all, was the one with butter on his head and Rachel acted like it was all fine. She reminded herself she had a job to do and swung into full Dr. Katz mode.

"George, thanks for seeing me so quickly. I know that Joyce called you, but I'm going to give you a copy of the release of information from her. You'll see that it indemnifies you against any liability arising from your participation in this interview. And this is my interview consent form. If you wouldn't mind reading and signing it?"

She pushed the papers gently across his desk. He fumbled in his pocket for a pair of reading glasses, gave the papers a cursory review, signed the consent form, and handed it all back to her. "So what do you want to know? I don't think I have much to say, Rachel."

"Let me decide about that, George. There are so many factors, and if you simply try to give me your preconceived ideas, then I may not get what I need. So here's where I'd like to start. In a broad, general way, what changes did you observe in Alix Price's behaviors in the six months prior to her death?" Rachel, ever the careful interviewer, didn't give George the option of saying that there were no changes. Everyone's behavior was always changing, usually in banal ways. You streaked your hair or took up yoga. It didn't mean anything in the abstract. But the puzzle pieces could come together. Suicidal people had trajectories that could be traced backward from the time of their death, often for more than a year. The signs and symptoms might mean little to those observing them, especially when taken in isolation. But she could pull it all together.

She remembered the woman whose suspicious death she had investigated three years ago. The subject of the inquiry had a lifelong and well-established fear of heights. To the surprise of all of her friends, not long before her death she had taken up rock climbing. Her body had been found at the bottom of what most climbers considered to be a safe, easy cliff. Rachel's careful study of the dead woman's statements to others, and especially an interview with her climbing instructor, revealed how she had commented that she had finally gotten over her fear of dying. Her friends had seen this as evidence of some kind of spurt of personal growth, but the no-fear-of-death line was a huge red flag to Rachel. People who had decided to die stopped fearing it. Further investigation led to a clinic out of state, where the woman was in treatment for the fatal effects of a diet drug she had taken. No one knew about the drug, or the pulmonary hypertension that had followed. But the probably suicidal leap that the woman had taken, dressed in her climbing gear to try to throw people off track, became more and more obvious to Rachel as all the data bits converged and became a clear picture of a dying woman trying to take control of the where and when of her death. She knew she would have to do the same thing with Alix Price's life.

For the next hour she took George Lewis through a careful tour of Alix's last six months as he had seen them. For someone who had supposedly known Alix well, George seemed to have little insight into her feelings and minimal knowledge of her daily life. His answers were so persistently superficial that Rachel found herself wondering whether he was purposely concealing something. No, Alix hadn't seemed depressed. No, she wasn't particularly anxious. As far as he knew, no romantic relationship of any import had failed recently. And so on. But a few subtle things stood out, the kind of hints that resisted even the best attempts at subterfuge. When she left, she found herself mulling over a couple of the more offhand remarks he had made to her.

"One thing I did notice. She was always out of her office on Thursday afternoons. I had no idea this was happening until some of the undergrads in the developmental psych class began to complain to the department that she was never around after class for questions. Not that she had to be around outside of office hours. But she was just away. I asked her about it and she changed the subject. I guessed that she was maybe seeing somebody. But maybe not, come to think again. She was always pretty open about seeing somebody. And she stopped wearing perfume. Alix was one of those women who had just loved perfume. Wore it all the time, she did." Rachel remembered that only too well and was taken aback by George's intelligence. She had unpleasant memories of following Alix onto a witness stand and becoming disoriented by the scent left behind. "Anyhow, she just stopped. Thought that was odd, but what do I know. You know, women change this stuff, don't they?"

Rachel wanted that appointment calendar. Something was happening on Thursdays. Rachel began to generate hypotheses—secret volunteering at the local homeless shelter and didn't want to ruin her reputation for cold-hearted rationality? Not likely. The perfume? Alix was proud of her expensive taste in perfume. Rachel had heard her go on about how much she had spent for the stuff while they were both at the meeting in Italy, how she could get it only by special order for years before a distributor opened up in Washington. Rachel wondered why Alix would stop wearing perfume, but more importantly, what it could possibly have to do with her state of mind. She dismissed the idea, chalking it up to George losing his sense of smell. People get sick of perfume and George was so thick, she thought, it's astonishing he managed to notice the perfume at all.

She decided that she had other things to worry about. This information was preliminary. She could file it and let her brain mull it over, see if anything emerged from the formless mush of not much information that George had given her. That was her strategy, to outline the task, get data, throw it into the hopper in her brain, and let it ferment. There was the problem of her own real life to look at. Alice and Liz had invited her to dinner tonight with a "small group of friends," Alice's message on her voice mail had said. Which meant that this Anna person from the biostatistics class was no doubt going to be there. Rachel felt torn between purposely dressing in her most frumpy sweats and going home, shaving her legs, and getting into casual femme finery. Ah, the joys of feeling fifteen when you're fifty, she groaned to herself. Maybe I'll just come as I am. Rachel Katz, boring forensic psychologist who hated statistics. Maybe that'll keep the temperature down.

Home was a 1920s Craftsman bungalow just west of the university in the much-coveted Wallingford neighborhood. She had bought the house in the 1970s when prices were still depressed and over the years had carefully remade it into the home of her dreams.

Sunlight came in through skylights on Seattle's rare sunny days, and lilacs and a Japanese red maple that she had planted in the year before Sarah's death were coming into full leaf. Flowers in every conceivable shade of blue and purple bloomed everywhere in her yard. Weeding and digging had become excellent diversions from emotion over the years. The house felt too big with just herself and Mr. Piggy taking up the space. But she loved the place, and, as she often groused to her friends, these days she couldn't afford to buy a fixer-upper in the industrial zone what with the current hot housing market, much less her own home, whose value and taxes had grown by leaps and bounds. All around her people who worked at one of the area's high-tech firms were buying houses at inflated prices, and then never being home to enjoy their huge investments. Rachel had been home a lot in the past year, away from the office, grieving. She had been surprised to see how few people were around during the day.

She walked into her house feeling slightly bereft and wandered up the stairs into her closet in search of the right outfit for meeting the woman she didn't want to meet. Her ambivalence about this encounter was sufficiently powerful that she found herself considering calling Alice to plead some kind of illness. Dating sickness, she thought to herself, the symptoms of which include sweaty palms and regression to age fifteen. Yuck. She was trailed by Mr. Piggy, who was equally bereft. She barely noticed him at first, further evidence of her utter preoccupation with the coming gathering. Rachel had not yet become accustomed to coming home to no human, even after almost a year. No one glad to see her, but also no one angry that she was invading the quiet of the house, as Sarah had often been at the end.

The dog was, of course, thrilled to see her. The trip to the university had been minus bull terrier. The day had grown too warm to safely leave him in the car, and non-service dogs were not welcome in university buildings. Only animals that were being studied and tortured, she thought grimly to herself, proud of never having run a single rat on the way to her Ph.D.

"Oh, Mr. Piglet, I know, it was terrible, a whole two hours without your mother. Well, I have good news, baby boy. We're going to visit Lambchop." The dog twirled in circles, making little leaps. Lambchop was his dog sweetheart. Like the separated lovers in the old shampoo commercials, the two dogs would make bee-lines for one another whenever they met at the park or in the neighborhood.

She stared in her closet. Nothing. Miles and miles of nothing to wear. She decided to stay with her current costume, one of a long list of black skirts and teal sweaters, and just go before she could think about it any more. She turned to the dog. "So let me put your coat on." She fastened an embroidered blue harness around his stout middle, and attached the expandable leash. "OK, slow down, don't pull me down the steps." She thought in passing about some research she'd heard at a conference about single urban women and their pets, how the former talked incessantly to the latter, as if there were an actual intelligence hearing and respond-ing. She sure did fit that profile, she thought.

The two went out of the house and up the street. Alice and Liz lived on the other side of the Good Shepherd Park, rows of apple and cherry trees situated on the grounds of what had once been a Catholic home for wayward girls. Now the huge old stone struc-ture housed yoga classes and the local NOW chapter, as well as an organic gardening group that kept the grounds fragrant with herbs and flowers year round. The statue of the Good Shepherd, lamb in arms, still stood guard over the park, the site of many solitary tear-filled walks in the past several years—tears of rage and frustration before Sarah's death, and grief afterward. The beauty was evoca-tive of all kinds of emotion. Even when she began her sojourn there completely numb, Rachel would often find herself with wet cheeks as the scents of lavender and honeysuckle snuck into her brain. The dogs frequently met there in the mornings, and the warming weather made it a good night to walk over. Inviting the piglet was a stroke of genius on Alice's part, Rachel thought. It was one thing for her to churlishly turn down a dinner invite. She believed that humans could tolerate rejection, but depriving the doggie of a play date with his best buddy is another thing entirely. Rachel figured she could stand meeting this Anna person. It was only dinner, right?

The door of Alice and Liz's home was a deep shade of purple. It was the first sign that anyone entering was in for a less than calm experience. Alice and Liz had comical, eclectic taste—their backyard was full of found objects masquerading as plant stands, including a good-sized collection of former toilet seats in a riot of colors. The house itself was jammed full of antique oak furniture and various objets d'art that the two women had collected on their travels all over the world. Rachel had long coveted a couple of pieces of art glass from Finland that had the place of honor on the mantelpiece, joking with Alice and Liz that if the pieces ever disappeared, they would know where to send the cops to find them.

Usually, walking through this door was a chance for Rachel to relax. But this evening she was aware of mounting tension as she cut across the grass in the park. How in the hell was she going to pull off meeting this woman without acting like a complete idiot, or worse, an entirely didactic prig. And why should she care? she asked herself. She didn't want to meet her. But she worried nonetheless. Rachel knew that her default mode when stressed was to lecture and that while her colleagues found this astonishing, especially since she could cite chapter and verse of original sources when making her point, most other people could politely stand it for only so long before yawning and disappearing. Maybe that was a good thing, thought Rachel. She would bore this Anna to tears, and that'll stop Alice from ever doing this to her again.

The door opened, and she was nearly bowled over by a barking mass of flying fur. Lambchop had seen her beloved Mr. Piggy coming from the window, and was so eager to get to him and begin their romp that she ignored the inconvenient human in their path. Rachel was temporarily discombobulated, trying to keep hold of her dog's leash and avoid falling over or tripping over her long skirt when a hand appeared from behind her and steadied her on the elbow.

"It appears these two dogs have some prior acquaintance," a pleasant alto voice said from just above her ear. Rachel turned and was momentarily lost in a pair of hazel-green eyes looking down on her from what seemed like half a foot up. The eyes were framed by gray hair, cut severely short, and set in a square face with prominent cheekbones. The face topped a tall, muscular body, clad in black jeans and a deep indigo shirt. She was struck dumb by what she saw.

"I'm Anna Sigurdson. You must be Rachel Katz. We're supposed to not know that Liz and Alice are fixing us up tonight." The woman grinned, the wrinkles at the corners of her eyes grinning with her. "You certainly fit the description."

"What, you mean terminally clumsy?" Rachel attempted to get herself back in control of the situation. "Yep, that's *moi*, the girl who can trip on flat ground." She tried to collect herself, falling back on humor, the Jewish last resort in times of stress or terror. Or sexual arousal, she noted in the back of her mind; that seemed to be happening here too, oh dear.

"Uh, no, actually, Liz said that you were this cute, short, what's that word she used, she said it was Yiddish for, uh, being rather voluptuous . . ."

Rachel broke in. "Zaftig. Also *moi*. I don't know about the cute part, but zaftig and short, definitely." She found herself nervously trying to make the most superficial conversation possible. "You sorta resemble what I've been told, too."

"Which is . . ." Anna grinned at her again. The woman was persistent, that was clear immediately.

"Butch. Visible from ten paces as a member of the club." Rachel was surprised by her own bluntness. Now this woman would be truly put off, and she could relax.

"Well, that's true. I was never one of those women who had people guessing. Now you on the other hand require serious gaydar." Rachel noticed that Anna seemed anything but put off. Rachel only hoped that she didn't think she was flirting with her. Alice should have said something about how she looked to prepare me a little, Rachel thought to herself.

55

As Rachel steeled herself to form a rejoinder, Alice popped her head out the door, feigning a look of innocence. "What are you two doing, hanging out in front of my house and causing a scandal. Rachel, get your dog under control and get your butt in here. Hi, you must be Anna, come on in, too."

Rachel called the dog, who, temporarily satiated in his desire to chew on his friend, came trotting into the house, followed by Lambchop who was trying hard to grab his flag of a tail in her teeth. Anna asked, "Do these dogs always do this?"

"What, you mean act like long-lost lovers? Oh, yes. We call them the virtual litter-mates. They met when they were just little babies and spent a few nights in one another's company and now they're truly in love. It's a real bonus that one of my best friends' dogs is my dog's best friend. Do you have animals?" Rachel thought she handled that nicely—got the conversation off of herself fast and onto that favorite lesbian topic, animals. They walked side by side into the living room, still talking.

"Not at the moment, no. My old Weimaraner died about a year ago. I knew I was coming out here and wasn't sure how hard it would be to find housing with a dog. And it would have been disruptive for a new pup to just get used to a place and then be yanked into something entirely different. So I figured I'd wait to see what Seattle offered. Then grad school happened, and ate up all my time, so no new dog yet."

"Alice told me that you came out here from Madison. I almost ended up there in a teaching job years ago, but the prospect of more Midwest winters just didn't do it for me. Are you a Wisconsin native?"

Good, good, more banal conversation, Rachel said to herself. Nice boring distanced banal questions.

"Actually, I'm from everywhere and nowhere. Grew up in a military family. My father was in the Air Force, a flight surgeon. I've lived on most continents and in some of the most God-awful middles of nowhere in the U.S. Fairbanks, Alaska, for example. Talk about cold winters, it made Wisconsin seem tropical. I just did my master's in Madison. I'd been working in public health, HIV prevention, in Boston for about ten years before that at Fenway Clinic. And I did the lesbian living-on-the-land routine in Vermont before that. You know—"

Rachel broke in, "You mean serious tofu and woodstoves and processing all decisions? Eeek. No thank you very much. How did you survive that?"

She didn't notice that the two of them had sat down on the couch in Liz and Alice's periwinkle blue living room. The conversation had taken wings despite Rachel's reservations. " 'Survive' is a good word, actually. I had just gotten sober about a year before I moved onto the land, figured it was a good way to make sure that I wasn't anywhere close to a bar for a while. So between early sobriety and having to cut through the ice on winter mornings, I'd say 'survival' is a very good word, indeed. It was actually good for me. But it sounds like it's not your kettle of tofu."

"You know that Woody Allen quotation, 'I am two with nature.' That's me. Camping to me is a motel without room service. Wood is for making furniture. Heat comes out of the vents in the floor. Although I must admit to an inordinate love of tofu when it's smothered in sesame sauce from the food co-op. I guess I can retain my dyke credentials that way, huh?"

The two women laughed. Rachel was taken aback. They were actually communicating. This was not a good sign. She was planning to remain aloof, reserved, and uninterested, and here she was having an actual conversation with this Anna person. Rachel told herself that it was too late to turn back, that it would look more than a bit odd, suddenly reverting to cold and professional. It was just a conversation, she said to herself.

It was past eleven when she finally left. Alice and Liz had indeed invited over another couple, Siony, an accountant, and Elaine, a computer systems analyst, both of whom Rachel already knew well enough from previous social events to feel at ease with. That had evened out the intensity starting up between her and Anna. They had talked and talked about everything and nothing, getting further and further into the middle outer circles of one another's personal lives. And there was a spark, a definite spark, for Rachel. It was those eyes, she thought. Hazel green eyes, she was a sucker for those eyes. But there was something about the woman, too. A certain calm solidity that seemed immensely appealing, as well as a nice wry sense of humor. Both ranked high on Rachel's list of must-haves.

Anna had asked if they could exchange phone numbers, "maybe go for a walk with you and that dog," and Rachel had said yes. Walking across the park under the night sky, watching the clouds come in over the moon, smelling the lilacs blooming in the cold night air, Rachel found herself wondering how in the world she could ever allow her heart to open again. Sarah and she had been in such trouble for so long. She was painfully aware of how much the edge of her grief had been taken off by the relief and the anger that were present in equal measures. She was so wary of anyone else. Sarah had been loving and good at first, so initial assessments were useless. And more to the point, Anna was an adult, full of baggage. At least she and Sarah had been youngsters when they had started out together; their baggage was a joint effort. Rachel wondered if this was a warning sign. She asked herself, what does it mean that she's in her late forties and single?

Rachel admitted to herself that she was lonely. She hadn't made love with anyone in almost fifteen years—that was how long bed death had visited her before real death did. She didn't know if the equipment even worked anymore. She didn't know if she could take off her clothes in front of a new lover, especially with all the sags and stretch marks of her fifty-year-old body. She was scared, Rachel thought to herself. It was far easier to hide out behind the facade of overwork again and just haul out the erotica books and the sex toys. Or cybersex, that was an idea. Anything but allowing someone into her life again.

She checked her voice mail when she came home. A message from Joyce Romanski. "Rachel, Joyce here. I'm having Alix's appointment calendar and address book messengered over to your office tomorrow morning, so be there, please." Great, Rachel thought with a measure of sarcasm. Now Joyce was telling her where to go and what to do. Fine, good, it was the distraction she wanted. She went to bed, and tossed and turned unhappily for several hours, leading Mr. Piggy to jump off in disgust and get into his own usually neglected dog nest in the corner. She finally drifted off, feeling glad that at least she didn't have to deal with any humans the next day.

Chapter Five

The phone rang at eight-thirty. Rachel had been sitting in her study, drinking cocoa and reading the *New York Times*, staring at the violet walls of the room, trying to have what she thought of as a normal morning, alone and quiet with only the NPR announcers' voices in her ears. She checked the caller ID, which read Private. It could have been any one of her friends, all of whom blocked their phone numbers, so she picked up.

"Is this Rachel?" She was uncertain who the voice on the other end belonged to, so grunted in assent. "It's Anna Sigurdson, you know, the one Liz and Alice are trying to fix you up with, the one who rescued you from death by dog last night at their door." The voice on the other end held a note of laughter. "Do you have a couple of minutes?"

"Uh, sure, a couple of minutes. I mean, it's not like the paper is going anywhere without me. Let me turn the radio down." Rachel retreated into sarcasm, trying to get some distance. What was this woman doing calling her so soon?

"I was wondering what you're doing on Saturday night. I remember you mentioning last night when we were talking how much you love folk music, and I noticed that there's a performer at the Ballard Firehouse, Mary Julia Ryan, a local folksinger I heard on NPR who I think you'd like a lot, and well, nothing ventured, as they say."

"Is this a date you're asking me on?" Rachel parried. She wanted to have the terms set right away.

"Well, no, not a date in the sense of afterward we're supposed to make out or anything." Anna laughed harder. "More like a prune, if you're looking for the fruit in question. Or a banana? Just two middle-aged dykes going out to hear music that will remind them that they're not young anymore. Or you could see this as a good deed, helping a newcomer find places to have a good time."

"I think I could handle that, good-deed-doing, I mean. Very much in my line, to do good deeds." Rachel berated herself internally as she talked, noticing her rambling, unformed sentences. The woman was going to think she was a nut. But why should she, Rachel, care, she wasn't going to date her, right? Oh, shut up, she finally said to herself. "Shall we meet there?" Rachel was trying to find ways to avoid being alone in a car with Anna. Cars created too much proximity, she thought. Too much chance to accidentally make physical contact. "And at what time?"

"Oh, the show starts about eight. So how about a little before that? We could try to get a good table. I'll be the one looking lost. Where is this Ballard place, by the way?"

"You just keep going west from my neighborhood until all the drivers get very slow." Ballard's slow drivers were a local cliché. The neighborhood was indeed slower and quieter than many in Seattle, although it also housed the Fisherman's Terminal from which rowdy crews went off to the waters of Alaska. Like everywhere else in town, it, too, was beginning to succumb to gentrification, with the row of folk and blues clubs being the leading edge of the wedge. The dot-commers came to Ballard to hear music and started to buy houses.

"Hey, with your last name you should fit right in, it's

Scandinavian central out there. They celebrate Norwegian independence day. Which I guess is good unless you're a Swede, right?"

"Actually, the family is Icelandic, about three gens back, that's where all that alcoholism comes from. But hey, I get the picture. No one will wonder what I'm doing in that part of town, eh?" Anna laughed again. She seemed to be a cheery soul, Rachel thought. Too cheery, maybe, one of those terribly pink-cloud grateful AA types? That would have been another good reason to not get involved. Rachel thought of herself as a typically East Coast Jewish cynic, someone who took everything with large grains of kosher salt and who wore black as her favorite color. Although it might be interesting to keep company with someone cheerful for a while. Sarah had been determinedly acerbic and unsentimental. Rachel realized that she was getting uncomfortable staying on the phone too long with her thoughts running in directions she did not approve of. There was no future here to consider, she told herself. Just going to Ballard to hear music, that's all.

"Look, Anna, I've got to go, I'm expecting something to show up at my office this morning and have to haul over there." She forgot that she'd told Anna how free she was not two minutes earlier.

On the other end of the phone, Anna sighed almost inaudibly to herself. Liz had warned her that Rachel was extremely skittish. There were good reasons, she knew. Anna had arrived in town just before Sarah's accident, and could imagine how painful it was for Rachel to be in the spot of being fixed up. She'd at least had time, plenty of time, since the end of her last relationship, and she and Carola were still friendly.

But Anna's attraction to Rachel had been immediate and powerful. Rachel's deep brown eyes kept coming back to her mind, not to speak of the curves of her figure. So womanly, that was Anna's erotic type. And smart, too. Someone who wouldn't be scared off by Anna's own hard-edged mind. Someone who knew about sobriety, if she was friends with Liz and Alice, so there wouldn't have to be lengthy conversations about why she didn't just try to drink in moderation. She decided not to remind Rachel of her small faux pas.

Rachel took the verbal initiative again. "So I'll see you Saturday, just before eight. Oh, yeah. I'm chemically sensitive, so in case you're one of those women who loves her perfume, could you leave it at home, please?"

"Didn't you notice I was a little bit butch? Not the perfume and makeup type, I assure you." Anna laughed even louder. "Not to worry, Rachel, I'll be clean and scent-free. I assume a little deodorant is still OK with you?"

"Yep, I'm one of those urban women who believes in deodorant and all the other accoutrements of polite living. Just as long as it doesn't smell too strong. I kind of like the smell of unvarnished woman." She had stopped herself, realizing her side of the conversation was approaching flirting. "Seriously, it seems like everyone asks me that question. I guess I should be glad that folks take it that seriously. Anyhow, Anna, I didn't give you very good driving directions." She proceeded to offer a concise, crisp verbal description of how to get from the Madison Valley, where Anna lived, to Ballard, where the performance was happening. Rachel prided herself on her capacity to give directions well. The daughter of a scientist who had trained her to be precise in her observations, she was not going to be a woman who got lost easily.

After she hung up the phone, Rachel sat glaring at the wall. She was brought back into the present by an insistent paw on her lap. There was a dog attached to the paw, with a look of yearning on his face. She patted her knee, and the bull terrier leaped into her lap with one spring, turned in a circle, then settled himself down. She leaned into his sturdy body and sighed. The last thing she felt like was going into her office to await the package from Joyce. But maybe the address book would give her some information about where Alix Price had been spending her Thursday afternoons.

It was drizzling. It's Seattle, so it has to be damp. She reminded herself as she often did that this was precipitation that one did not need to shovel, and that this was why waterproof clothing had been invented. Mr. Piggy had uncharitable feelings about getting wet. He huddled and shivered in his fleece cape, digging in his heels and making it difficult for Rachel to get him down the steps and into the car for the short trip to the eastern side of Lake Union.

When the doorbell of the office finally rang, and she opened the door to admit the messenger with bicycle helmet perched jauntily atop her purple hair, Rachel noticed that she had managed to pass two hours online very productively reviewing the literature on suicidal risk in professional women. One of the reasons why Alix Price's presumed suicide was so credible on the first pass was that professional women were so much more at risk to kill themselves than were others, although women in general made more unsuccessful attempts than men did. Those stats were changing, she thought grimly. Younger women were shooting and hanging themselves at ever increasing rates, making suicide an equal opportunity experience. Not exactly what we fought for in the women's movement, she mused. She knew that she fit a risk profile for suicide herself, the recent death of a spouse from what might have been suicide if the contribution of alcohol hadn't been so clear, depression, and being a professional herself. Lesbians had higher suicide completion rates, too. Getting rid of gender roles meant less of whatever was protective about femininity. But that possibility had never really tempted her. Even when life was painful, it was the preferred alternative. Which was partly why she couldn't imagine Alix taking her own life. She knew that the woman had been as obsessed with her own interests as Rachel was with hers.

So it was a relief to have the appointment calendars and address book to go through. Guilty pleasure, she thought. How often does anyone ever get to do this, go through the books of someone with whom we regularly crossed swords? So let's look at Thursdays. What was happening on Thursdays?

Thursday afternoons were busy times in the life of the late Alexandra Price, Ph.D. As Rachel had suspected, the initials "IH" featured prominently in the one o'clock hour. Racquetball with the research assistant, so what was the big deal, why so secretive about a nice safe game of racquetball? Unless, of course, Alix had been using the cover of a racquetball date as a code for a different kind of high-intensity workout. But an hour and a half once a week just didn't make sense for a lover. Too calculated, even for Alix, she thought. And then there was the next thing—a time block from three until seven, or sometimes eight, every Thursday evening, with the letters TX marked in. The T Rachel could play with—Thaddeus at the university, Ted someone, but what about the X? Xavier? Ximeno?

She sat and stared at the appointment calendar. It was one of those expensive high-end leather ones, with the ring binder paper that could be slipped in and out. Gorgeous, soft, almost edible deep purple leather, something Rachel herself might have picked out if she would have allowed herself to spend three hundred dollars on an appointment calendar. Luscious, she thought. Alix had a luscious calendar. Forget about the calendar, think about the contents. Who in the hell was TX, she asked herself.

Then it hit her. It was as clear as the nose on her face. TX, as in "tx," the common abbreviation for therapy or treatment. How many times had she written "continue tx as per status quo ante" on session notes. But this was improbable, given who was under investigation. Alix and therapy? What in the hell would Alix Price be doing in therapy? Not that she hadn't needed it, Rachel thought. But Alix had proclaimed her devotion to the unexamined life too many times for Rachel not to have taken that stance semi-seriously. Nah, not possible. Maybe physical tx, she mused. That can go on for a while.

She decided to work her way back through the calendar to see if there were earlier entries with more information. Joyce had thoughtfully included the pullouts from the previous year. There might have been a first appointment—and there was. On a Thursday in November, two weeks before Thanksgiving, Alix Price had noted an address in her calendar for a three p.m. meeting. The address was 1910 East Cherry, Suite 305. Rachel sat back in her chair. Wait just a fucking minute, she said to herself. This address was familiar, very familiar. Some other psychologist practiced at that address, someone she had sent records to somewhere in the not terribly distant past. Rachel should have known this, but the missing name was part of the fallout of perimenopausal memory lapses, she thought. She should know this. She used to be able to grab names out of the air like a magician. Now she had to hunt like normal people through the misfiled folders of her brain. Who in the hell is on Cherry? she thought. She leafed through to the back of the calendar, in search of a phone list. Rachel found it ironic that Alix organized her life in a way similar to her own—it was easy to find things, because she knew where to look. The phone list was behind its own neat tab and Rachel scanned through the names.

The phone list itself was a revelation. The names in the first two or three pages included not simply the usual suspects, defense attorneys and researchers at other universities, and activists in the false accusations world. There were also listings for someone who Rachel knew to be a spiritual healer who worked with body energies and for several other similarly New Age sorts of people. Maybe Alix was doing some kind of debunking research with them. Alix was, or rather, had been an active member of several groups whose mission in life was to prove that the unprovable was therefore impossible, hoping perhaps that this would lead the general public to give up their beliefs in angels, divine beings, and organized abuse of children, among other things. Not to mention past lives. So that sort of made sense, Rachel thought. Hope springs eternal in the breasts of the terminally rational. There were also the names and home phone numbers of several powerful, prominent men, at least two of whom had been linked with Alix at one time or another. She was more surprised to find those sitting in plain sight in the address list. Alix apparently hadn't imagined the possibility that a stranger would be looking through her book before she had the chance to alter it.

It was under the listings for G that the name finally popped out at her. Joel Gibbs, that's who it was at that address on Cherry. Figures. If Alix Price were going to ever see a therapist in Seattle, then Joel Gibbs would have been the perfect choice, all of Alix's drunken comments in Italy set aside. He was definitely Alix's type of therapist. He was a loud member of the heavy empiricism faction. His main delight in life seemed to be in taking potshots at other more prominent and successful colleagues, especially if they were women. He was frequently embroiled in conflict with one or another mental health professional in town. All one had to do was mention his name in a group of psychologists and the groaning tales would begin to spill out about his latest excursion into obnoxiousness. But no one ever accused him of stupidity—he was certainly smart enough to take on an Alix Price.

Rachel and he had had civil dealings for the most part. He did only a small amount of forensic work, normally working on the defense side of the street. But he operated in a different orbit more of the time than not. They had faced off once or twice in employment law cases, where he would do his best to minimize terrible things that had happened to people in dangerous work settings. There was no warmth between them, but the cases had been straightforward enough to have kept Joel from finding a reason to climb on one of his various soapboxes with Rachel. He wasn't a trauma specialist, just your basic cognitive behavioral guy who treated a lot of garden variety anxiety and depression. He was consequently someone who could be counted on to disbelieve transference and thus neglect the possibilities that the rich symbolic layers of the therapeutic interaction offered to therapists and client alike. Perfect for Alix, she thought again. Just perfect. Someone who would require no insight whatever, and would function like a mind mechanic, giving someone a tune-up.

What was odd to Rachel was Alix having sessions with Joel that were lasting two, three, and four hours in the last three months. Cognitive therapists did not do marathon sessions. They stuck to the fifty-minute hour like barnacles. Maybe they were doing some kind of in vivo desensitization work, Rachel conjectured. In vivo, the Latin term for "in life" was something that behavioral therapists occasionally did as part of the treatment of phobias. The person with the fear of heights would be accompanied by the therapist to a high place, where standard interventions such as relaxation and desensitization would be used right on the spot. Exposure therapies worked and had lots of research to back them up. Maybe Alix had a hidden phobia that no one knew about. That would make sense of some of her well-known outrageous behaviors, especially the alcohol use. Phobic people often tried to self-medicate with alcohol.

In any case, her speculations didn't matter, really. Rachel would find out exactly why Alix was in therapy, because she would of course set up a meeting with Joel Gibbs. If anyone had known whether Alix was sufficiently depressed to kill herself, it ought to have been her therapist. She grabbed her state psychological association directory to look for Gibbs's number and dialed.

Voice mail answered. Rachel winced at the grating tones of his voice. How the man kept a therapy practice she didn't know. Nothing about him engendered trust. Then again, there were not a few therapists who were unattractive as human beings on all variables—voice, personality, appearance, you name it—and they still seemed to keep busy. Transference strikes again, she said to herself. If there was a way to bottle that golden glow it gave people, we could sell it as an aphrodisiac. She punched in the pound key, hoping to skip over the lengthy dissertation on the outgoing message. It worked. She spoke after the beep, purposely taking a somewhat formal tone to assert her authority.

"Joel, hi, this is Rachel Katz. I'm working for the estate of Alix Price, who I believe to have been your patient. In that capacity, I'd like to set up a time to interview you about her state of mind prior to her death. Please be assured that there is no action contemplated against you. I am conducting a psychological autopsy. If you'd call me back with the number, I'll fax over a copy of the authorization to release information from her personal representative, Joyce Romanski, and then we can go ahead with setting up a time. I'll look forward to hearing from you."

She left her phone number and hung up. The day had been

productive. It was almost noon, and she had managed to spend most of the morning making money the easy way. Time for a break. She looked over at the corner, where the dog was asleep in the client chair. He was always good for some time off. Maybe a little jaunt to the Arboretum; it was bound to be pretty there this time of year. The azaleas might be blooming. The drizzle had let up while she was working, and the Seattle weather phenomenon known as a sun break was happening. "Seize the sun break," she muttered to herself. And she was, for once, dressed for walking in the possibility of mud, no skirt, just a pair of old jeans and hiking boots. Almost incognito, she thought to herself. Then she could go to lunch.

Rachel was barely aware of her tendency to talk to herself at such length. The past year had been spent so much in her own company that she had begun to have protracted discussions with herself and with the dog when necessary. She knew, dimly, that she was developing a habit of eccentricity and withdrawal. She was determined to ignore the trend. She was fine, she told herself when the nagging voice appeared in her ear. Considering what she had been through, wasn't she doing well to be showing up at work again and plunging into projects? She was skillful at ignoring distressing psychological data about herself and her life when she wanted to.

It was a trait acquired from her mother, who had managed for years to pretend that her own history of childhood abuse and subsequent adult depression and suicidality hadn't really happened. Rose Katz had put on a happy face for her children and husband every day after her return from the psychiatric hospital during Rachel's sixth year until she found herself relieved to be taken by a swift colon cancer when Rachel was in her early thirties. She remembered how oddly her mother had responded to the news that her biopsy had come back positive. It was as if she had been waiting for someone to finally let her off the hook. The last ten months of Rose's life had been revelatory for her daughter. Rose had dropped the mask of phony cheer and become real, alive, and vibrant in a new way as she was dying. Rachel and her mother had finally had intimacy just as Rose left the planet, and Rachel had been able to make sense of her own attraction to the field of trauma at last. It had been hugely sad to finally have her mom and then lose her like that.

So of course she wanted to work with trauma survivors. She had been her mother's support person from as young as she could recall, and that was her on-the-job training for being a trauma therapist. The "vacation" that Mommy took for months after her younger sister was born had been six months in an old-style mental institution, complete with shock therapy. Rachel's own rage and sadness at how her mother had been malpracticed upon had fueled her move into the forensic arena where she could take on the modern-day equivalents of the psychiatrists who had ignored her mother's trauma history. With her move to action, she had managed to ignore completely her own tendency to shove her life under whatever cover was handy.

But this early noon, Rachel was thinking of anything but her family history and her tendency to deny her own distress. She was too busy denying the denial. She suited up the dog, stuck a journal in her oversized bag to read over lunch, started the engine, and crossed Eastlake to catch the road into the Arboretum. The entire route was lovely—the street's residents had planted the tree-lawns with flowering cherry and crabapple trees, and all of them were in full bloom, making passage down the street like a procession through a bower of pink and off-white. She allowed herself to revel in the sensory experience, driving on autopilot until she arrived at the main artery through the Arboretum. She turned to her left and drove to the parking area along Portage Bay where infestations of Canada geese were beginning to show up with their cute hatchlings. Mr. Piggy loved to chase geese, and since the birds had acquired the status of nuisance, leaving large mounds of slimy green goose poop everywhere they went, it was no longer politically incorrect to let one's dog chase after them. Since he stayed safely on his leash, Mr. Piggy could have his fun without Rachel worrying that either of them would get into trouble with Animal Control.

She decided to leave the car and walk up to the main Arboretum path, where all of the cherry and plum trees were in bloom and the azaleas were indeed beginning their multicolored flowering. The path was sparsely populated. Although on weekends there were hordes of children and dogs running up and down the muddy green, on a weekday noon it was relatively quiet. Rachel lost herself in thought, so much so that she was entirely unaware of the figure bearing down on her from a side path.

"Rachel, Rachel Katz, that's you, isn't it?" She came to attention with a start. It was that woman, Anna. Oh, shit, Rachel said to herself. She wondered if Liz and Alice had introduced her to some kind of stalker. First the phone call, now this. She stiffened. "Oh, hello, Anna. I wasn't paying attention. I know it's a cliché, but fancy meeting you here . . ." She trailed off, uncertain of what to say next, intensely uncomfortable with her mixed responses. She didn't want to feel attracted to this tall hunk of butch loveliness, but the nerve endings were definitely standing up in all the wrong right places even as she felt annoyed at having her reverie interrupted by Anna.

"It is odd, running into you like this. I almost didn't say anything when I saw you. Welcome to my retreat center." Anna made a sweeping bow, a la Walter Raleigh with cape. "I come here during the noon hour to meditate and walk. It's so close to the campus and my house, I can just bike on over here in good weather. When the rain let up, I decided to come on over, even without the bike. But what a treat to encounter you and, what's-his-name . . ."

What's-his-name was enthusiastically licking Anna's face as she knelt down from her considerable height to pet him. "Mr. Piggy. Also known as the piglet, Mr. Pig, or sweetie pie, depending on the day and angle of approach." Rachel segued right into her ironic mode, shields up. "He seems to be thrilled to see you again. My

71

dog is useless as a protective device. Everyone is his new best friend."

Anna was quiet. She couldn't tell if Rachel was trying to insult her or whether this was just East Coast Jewish-style humor. She had regularly gotten into trouble during her time in Boston for taking too seriously the sarcastic, meant-to-be-funny cracks of Jewish friends and coworkers. Two years in Madison and almost a year in Seattle had made her skills at coping with this kind of verbal banter rusty. She opted for the positive interpretation, reminding herself again that Rachel had reasons to be skittish. "So the question is, is his human thrilled to see me? Or at the very least, not unhappy to see me?"

Rachel felt herself melting inside and cursed herself for responding to this total stranger this way. She told herself to be a mensch, at least not be rude. This was probably a very nice woman who happened to make Rachel throb inside. It wasn't *her* fault. Rachel admonished herself to slow down with the wisecracks.

"Definitely not unhappy, Anna. Just a little shocked, is all. I guess that the statistical likelihood of running into you here approaches that of my winning the lottery. I don't buy the tickets very often, and I don't come here very much, either. But if it's your regular hangout, then I'm the one who should be accused of following you around, not the other way."

She paused, realizing that she had just given away her thoughts. She was completely knocked off guard and making it abundantly clear to Anna that she had no social skills.

Anna politely ignored the implied meaning of Rachel's remark. She rose from petting the dog and made the decision to join Rachel in making light. "As someone currently pulling down a four-point-o in her biostatistics class, I can concur with that statement. It's not every day that I encounter someone who thinks in statistical likelihoods. Sounds like you're pretty familiar with Bayesian theory."

Rachel breathed a sigh of relief. This was going to adhere to the banal and distant, good. Maybe there was hope for this woman to leave her alone after all. "I was introduced to it in grad school, which is a little unusual given that it was the seventies when almost no one used that paradigm. But as a forensic psychologist, it's come in extremely handy for developing hypotheses in difficult assessments." She unconsciously slipped into her pedantic, teaching voice. Anna observed, amused. Liz had told her that Rachel would disgorge data bits with only the slightest of encouragement, some of which she had also seen over dinner the previous night.

"It's become very popular in my particular field of interest. But most social scientists have never encountered it, so they think I'm speaking in some kind of foreign language. Look, Rachel, I'm just heading out of the park, and it looks like your boy there is raring to go up the path." She gestured to Mr. Piggy, who was now at the very end of his expandable tether, sniffing cheerfully at something under an azalea bush. "I won't keep you two. I'll just see you Saturday, OK?" She smiled and began to head down the path to the road. Mr. Piggy, noticing a loss of audience, turned and trotted after her. She reached down and petted him again. " 'Bye, little guy. Maybe your momma will give us a chance to get together and play sometime. See you, Rachel."

She left. Rachel stood in the mud, fuming. She couldn't believe she said yes to Anna. She was a month out of mourning and knew nothing about this woman. Clearly, it was her hormones talking. This was not the pleasant, relaxing trip to the Arboretum that she had planned. She shook herself back to the present and told herself to walk, move, anything rather than getting caught in her endless obsessions. The dog provided the motivation, pulling on her persistently as he spotted geese in the near distance. She commanded herself to focus, to think about Alix Price, to take stock of what she had learned so far.

As she and the dog moved past the weeping cherry trees, Rachel barely saw the blooms on either side, and she added up an imaginary set of columns in her mind. On the suicide side, the only clear indicator so far was that Alix had apparently been in therapy. People who went to therapy had problems, and people with problems sometimes saw killing themselves as the only solution to those dilemmas. But so far, absolutely nothing else argued for that point. So how had a lethal dose of downers and alcohol ended up in Alix's system? On the accidental death side, there was Alix's well-known tendency to knock back plenty of booze, although that also sort of went into the suicide column. People who had problems with alcohol were higher risk for suicide, too. But where had the pills come from? The pharmacy records hadn't arrived yet. She had to bug Joyce about that, she made a mental note to herself.

It was at that point that the dog yanked her out of her reverie by taking off after a duck. "Stop now," she shouted. He ground to a halt, hearing the distress in her voice. "Sit. Stay. Good boy." She let the leash snap back in, walked over, and petted him. "Time for us to head back to the car, I think. Momma needs to get some food into her, soon. Momma is getting weird, don't you think?" The dog wagged and lifted his face in her direction. Food, he knew that sound, what a nice sound it was. Sound meant yummy things. Where was the food?

"No, silly dog, not here. As if you understand me. The great pathetic fallacy, that the dog understands what I'm saying." The two wandered back toward the parking lot. Rachel put him into a stay while she carefully arranged cloth over the car seats. Pig's feet were muddy, and even her old Volvo deserved a little care. She let him into the car, then sat in the driver's seat, brooding. Those pills, she was stuck on those pills. She rummaged in her pack for her cell phone and punched in Joyce's number.

"Luanne, it's Rachel Katz. Yes, the boy is with me, I'll give him a pet for you." She listened carefully for any signs that Lu knew about Alix, and detecting none, used caution. "Listen, is Joyce around? I'd like to talk to her, please. About the matter we discussed the other day." Joyce was on the phone almost immediately. "Rachel, hello, what have you learned?"

"Well, it's a lot of nothing, but some interesting leads which I'll fill you in on when we get together. Did you know that Alix was in therapy?"

The initial silence on the other end of the phone was telling. "In therapy? No. You knew Alix's attitude toward therapy and therapists better than I did, Rache. Are you certain?"

"Well, not completely. But the information is suggestive." She went on to explain to Romanski what she had found and put together that morning. "Leaving completely aside whatever the mysterious something was that she had approached me to talk about, if she went to see a therapist she must have had a very good reason indeed. Maybe the kind of reason that could lead to suicide. But still, it's not convincing. So I was wondering, have you had any luck at getting me a copy of her pharmacy records? I'm intensely curious about where those pills came from."

"Not yet, no. I may have to get into my best litigator mode and threaten them." Joyce's voice held a hint of amusement, even glee. She loved threatening large corporations, it made her very happy. Rachel knew this particular characteristic of Joyce's and was slightly pleased to have given her an opportunity to exercise it.

"Well, good, Joyce, you do that. Because you know Alix was a pretty heavy drinker—no surprises about how she got that much booze into her. But I really need to know where those downers came from. And did you get the tox report back yet? As in, do we finally know what the downers in question were?"

"That's another missing piece. Good thing you're so thorough, Rachel, I'd probably have dropped all of this between the cracks. I didn't think it would make much of a difference. And as your friend Alice keeps pointing out, I'm in grief, which is supposed to be my excuse for being distracted and forgetful."

Rachel ignored the personal comment and went on with her inquiry. "For the psychological autopsy it's very important to know things like where pills came from. If a doc prescribed them that means something different than if she got them illegally. Getting a surreptitious lethal dose of meds is a factor on the side of a possible suicide and, well, you get the drift. I do need to know."

Joyce sighed. "Maybe I wish you weren't so thorough, Dr. K. But it's not as if I didn't already know that about you and that you

75

didn't warn me that any outcome to this process was possible. So what are you going to do while you're waiting for that information?"

"I have a call in to the guy I think she was seeing, and I've left messages with most of the other people in the psych department who you thought would be valuable to track down. Talked to George Lewis already, yielding minus nothing so far. I'm going to meet that RA, Ilona, tomorrow after her classes and a couple of the other faculty early next week. She doesn't seem to have had a lot of other people close to her. But if I can get to the therapist sooner, I might just be able to cancel some of that out, save the estate a bunch of money. You know, this still feels odd, Joyce. For me to be tromping through Alix's life."

"I'm sure you can deal with those feelings, Rachel." Joyce's tone had become businesslike again, or maybe angry that Rachel hadn't responded to her flash of vulnerability. "I'll work on the pharmacy and tox records, you just keep me posted." She hung up, abruptly.

Rachel decided to check her voice mail. Three new messages, said the cheery voice. The first grated on her ears, even though she had wanted to hear it.

"Rachel, it's Joel Gibbs. Terrible about Alix. Yes, fax that release over to me, then I have some things to tell you." He left a fax number and hung up. Oh goodie, Rachel thought to herself sarcastically. The idea of spending time with Joel repulsed her. She retrieved the next two messages—attorneys, wanting her to call them right now about cases. The word was out, Rachel Katz was back at work. Oy, she said to herself, so much for a gradual reentry into the work world. But she couldn't live on the proceeds of Sarah's life insurance much longer—there were bills to pay.

She shut off and stowed the phone. Sushi, she needed sushi, her favorite un-kosher food. She pointed the car in the direction of the International District, visions of succulent unagi in her head.

Chapter Six

Ilona Hegevary stood at the door to William James Hall. She was tall and thin in a way that made her look almost waiflike, if one were to ignore the sharp golden eyes and the sharper mind that danced inside. No waif there, but a clear, inquiring intelligence. Her hair was a deep coppery red, her skin tone the pale white that was so typically associated with red hair, but minus the freckles that one would see when the hair and skin came from Celtic rather than Magyar stock. She looked older than the average grad student, appearing to be somewhere in her midthirties. Rachel was not entirely surprised. Students coming from the former East bloc tended to be further along in life when they were able to complete their degrees. The researcher's clothes were European style, too black, tight, cut well to show off the woman's figure. Rachel couldn't help noticing what a beautiful woman she was about to interview. "Oh, shut up," she said to herself, after thinking that she was reduced lately to slavering over every semi-decent woman who crossed her path.

"Are you Dr. Katz?" The words came out in a faint accent, reminding Rachel of her grandmother's voice. Strong, no hesitation, the auditory equivalent of the flavor of chicken paprikash. This might be a graduate student, but definitely not someone who felt less powerful than a full-fledged Ph.D.

"I'm Rachel, yes. You must be Ilona." Rachel extended her hand in greeting. She had enough European friends to know that this formal gesture would feel right to the Hungarian woman. "Thanks for making the time to speak with me. Where will you be most comfortable having this conversation?" She let her voice trail off, opening the way for the other woman to take the initiative and set the tone of how deep they would go. Even a supremely confident grad student was not going to feel entirely at ease in this situation; the more choice she could offer her, the better. It wasn't like interviewing those pompous asses of the George Lewis variety, she thought to herself. This woman had been dependent on Alix, but like many grad students, she also was in a position to know details about the personal life of her faculty mentor that were invisible to peers. More than one faculty member in any department in this university had cried on their students' shoulders, taken refuge in their arms, and in general taken advantage of the indentured servant nature of the relationship between research assistants and principal investigators.

"Rachel, is it? You Americans continue to amuse me with this instant first-name basis. So much faux familiarity, wouldn't you say? I would really prefer as much privacy as possible for this interview, if we may." The word "privacy" came out with the British pronunciation. Rachel nodded. "We could meet in my office. I actually have quite a bit of space, and since I'm still running Alix's lab, I can let us into her office as well, if you'd like."

Rachel was pleased. Access to Alix's office had seemed difficult to obtain. George Lewis had hemmed and hawed and in general been non-forthcoming on the topic of when and if she could get into that space. Now here was someone offering to allow her in, in fact to sit in there and soak up the atmosphere. Perfect, she thought.

"I really appreciate that. I've been wanting to have the chance to look through Alix's things here at work. So if you don't mind . . ." She trailed off again, indicating that Ilona should lead on. She followed behind her into James Hall, and up three sets of stairs, Rachel blessing her own recent fixation with getting fit enough that she didn't have to pant on the last flight.

"As you can see, we have, well, had, I suppose, a very nice setup here." Ilona opened the door to a suite of offices. Rachel had had no idea that anything so spacious existed in James Hall. Through a door in one of them she could see a view of water to the south. Very nice indeed, she concurred silently. Not the usual faculty rat cage. "Alix had brought in substantial grant monies, so the department was able to dedicate a fair amount of space to her and her research team. Knocked down a few walls to make this suite for us. We're trying very hard to complete the projects that were in process when she died. As the senior RA, I've had to shoulder the lion's share of the task. It's the least I can do for Alix, though. After she did so much for me."

At this point the redheaded woman surprised Rachel by bursting into sobs and collapsing in a heap in the nearest chair. Rachel was temporarily taken aback. This cool, polite woman, oozing with European savoir faire, turned into a quivering heap of grief in front of her. Time to haul out the old clinical skills, she thought. She knelt down beside the chair, and tentatively put an arm around Ilona's shoulders. The younger woman sagged into the arm and began to cry even harder. With her free hand, Rachel rummaged in her bag for tissues. The sign of being a grown-up, she had often said to her friends, was when one began to carry tissues in one's purse. By those standards, she was very adult indeed. Masses of tissue emerged.

"Here." She thrust the tissue under Ilona's nose, the latter stopping her sobs long enough to blow heartily into the white mass. Rachel stayed silent, letting her reassurance remain physical only, creating the emotional and intellectual space into which Ilona's own ideas and words could emerge. Whatever she might learn in terms of information about Alix Price, she was learning something incredibly precious—how Ilona had felt about Alix. The tears told volumes more than words might.

The words, though, were not long in coming. "I miss her profoundly, Rachel. I cannot even express how I feel in English, this cuts so deeply." Ilona took another breath, then spoke hurriedly. "And I know I can tell you this, because Alix told me that you were one of us." Rachel's mind punctuated that "us" with an amused question mark. Stuck on the "us," Rachel reminded herself that she was getting paid to listen, not to enjoy finding out about the secret life of Alexandra Price.

"Alix and I were lovers," Ilona continued. Oy, thought Rachel, another one. "We met at a conference in Stockholm three years ago. I had never encountered such a brilliant mind. We were going to spend the rest of our lives together. We could be colleagues, I would be the junior P.I. on her grants, no one would have ever suspected that we were other than close research collaborators." Rachel nodded. She knew of upward of a dozen such "collaborators" who turned out to be collaborating in the bedroom, too, although they had all been women of an older, pre-liberation generation. One of them had been Alix's advisor at Chicago, maybe where Alix learned her hiding strategies. Rachel forced her mind back to Ilona's account.

"Her affairs with men were such a good cover, and they meant so much nothing to her, you understand what I mean? It would have been so easy. I'm so afraid now. I don't know what I'm going to do without her. I don't know if I can stay here much longer, once my student visa expires. She was going to get me a green card as a special talent. Then I come to try to find her because she is late for breakfast, and she is lying there. She is dead. It was grotesque. How can she be dead?" Ilona collapsed into sobs again.

Rachel groaned inwardly. The back-off-and-make-space strategy wasn't working. She would have to do a spot of psychotherapy in order to get this woman into any shape for answering her questions. No one had bothered to mention to her that Ilona was the friend who had found the body. Andrea and the rest of the cops had been as distracted from the possibility of a female lover as Rachel herself had been. She would have to get back to Andrea on this, she said to herself, then turned her mind back to the reality in front of her. Having access to the person who was apparently Alix's most current lover—or at least one of them, she thought, Alix not being known as a model of fidelity—was not exactly a problem, even if she would have to restabilize Ilona before she would make coherent sense. Au contraire, ma chere, she thought to herself, this could be a gold mine.

"Can you tell me more about your relationship, Ilona? I don't mean to pry, but the more I know, obviously the easier it's going to be for me to fulfill my obligation to the estate and help determine an actual cause of death. And you may have known something about her state of mind prior to her death."

"Well of course we didn't live together. It would have looked odd, you know, a graduate student living with a faculty member. Very poor form. We had to be very careful. We had a regular standing date on Thursdays, we told people we were playing racquetball. And breakfast on Friday mornings, sort of a research meeting. Other times, when she was free. But Thursday was our special time together, one we knew we could always count on. There is nothing so lovely as making love in the light of the day. And yes, before you ask, I knew there were others. Alix wasn't willing to be sexually faithful, she didn't believe in fidelity. Thought it was nonsense, that people simply had to trust one another in the moment. That was challenging for me at first. But it was the price of admission, as you Americans like to say, and I was willing to pay it."

"Did you know anything about her therapy relationship with Joel Gibbs?" Rachel, anxious for information, ignored the first rule of conducting psychological autopsies, to let the interviewee set the agenda. Enough of the continuing soap opera of Alix Price's love life, she thought. The woman was a master at stringing girls along, she decided. Very smart, gorgeous women like Joyce, this Ilona—lovely, feminine, highly accomplished women who were willing to settle for much less than they could have gotten anywhere else, in order to have the privilege of being Alix's lover.

Clearly there were sides to Alix Price that Rachel had never been able to see. She was regretting her blindness. And wondering how much of their mutual antagonism had been unconscious protection on both of their parts. There could have been attraction there, Rachel thought. Maybe they were both protesting too much. She pushed the thought aside. Her mind was wandering far afield. She forced herself to pay attention. That's what Joyce Romanski was paying her to do, not to have posthumous sexual fantasies about Alix Price.

"Not very much, actually. I was quite worried about that. She wouldn't tell me why she was meeting with him. She started to cut short our times together because Thursday afternoons were the only times he had available to see her. I'm surprised she let me know she was consulting a therapist, to be frank. At first she seemed lighter, happier than I'd seen her in the whole time I knew her. But the last few months, not so. Something seemed different. Not that she was depressed, not at all. But things were odd. Their sessions became longer. I begged her to tell me what was going on in her therapy, but she could only say that what I didn't know couldn't hurt her. I promised I'd be close-mouthed, but she was insistent. Said that no promise of keeping a confidence was reliable unless there was a legal reason to back it up, and as I had no such legal requirement, she'd prefer I had nothing to let accidentally slip. I had to respect that boundary, Rachel. You've been in relationships, I'm certain you know how it is. One sacrifices the nonessential elements to obtain the core. For me, the core was knowing and loving Alix, being able to work with her, to learn from her. I didn't require knowledge of her therapy or the remainder of her life."

Rachel sighed. Alix Price conducted her life like a series of noninterlocking boxes. Each one led to its own borders then stopped abruptly, as if the other boxes simply did not exist. She decided to go back to the question of what Ilona had observed.

"All right, Ilona. Let's back up a little bit, shall we? If you don't know precisely why Alix went to see a therapist, perhaps you observed something? Had some working hypotheses?" Rachel consciously and intentionally switched to the language of psychological science. If she could get Ilona into her usual comfort zone, the younger woman might relax and begin to remember things that her current level of anxiety and grief were blocking. As Rachel often told therapists when she lectured to them on trauma and memory, it isn't that memories are lost or repressed that makes them appear unavailable to conscious knowledge. Rather, the optimal conditions for retrieval and recall are absent. Anxiety, any kind of high emotional arousal, as well as its opposite, emotional shutdown and numbness, were two of the most common culprits in the creation of non-optimal conditions, and both of them existed in abundance in the psyches of people who had been traumatized. Rachel wanted Ilona to remember well, and getting her back into her professional self would help the process. Finding Alix dead had to have been terribly traumatic.

Ilona breathed slowly and deliberately a few times, then straightened up in the chair and unobtrusively pulled away from the comforting arm that she had sought only moments ago. Good, thought Rachel, she's turning back into an adult now.

"Of course I had hypotheses. Would you care to first know the data upon which I based them?" Her arrogance was back. Rachel welcomed it, and she nodded. "Hold that thought for a second, Ilona. I need to make a record of what you tell me." She reached into her bag, pulled out her tape recorder, and hit the button.

"You know Alix was a connoisseur of fine wine," Ilona began. Rachel nodded, barely suppressing her sarcastic commentary about just how much of a connoisseur the late Dr. Price had been. "Well, somewhere last summer, in the months before she started to see that Gibbs fellow, I noticed that she was drinking a bit much. She usually held her liquor well, like a European. You know, we drink a good deal more by volume, but there's a real premium on not turning into a drunken fool. It's not that Alix turned into a fool, mind you. Just that I noticed that when we spent time together in the evenings, not during our regular date, that she was drinking more."

Ilona paused and looked upward as if consulting a sheet attached to the inside of her forehead. "Also, she stopped wearing her scent." Rachel started internally. This was the second comment on the end of perfume. This one, she took far more seriously. "You know, she wore men's scent, something very old-fashioned from Caswell Massey, I believe. It was expensive stuff, they didn't make very much of it. She said it was what her father had worn, that it reminded her of him. But then she just stopped, and didn't want to talk about it.

"And something was troubling her, although it might have been transient. The only information I have is sketchy at best. One night I slept over at her house, it was a weekend, no one was likely to be dropping by unexpected. We could do that sometimes, spend a whole night together, rather than simply hide behind working late on a project. That night she must have awoken me half a dozen times. Nightmares, shouting, screaming, coming up out of the bed with a start, talking in a little girl voice as if she were a terrified child. I soothed her back to sleep, the next morning she claimed to have absolutely no recollection of the whole thing."

Rachel was intrigued. Marked behavior changes, starting therapy, quitting the perfume, nightmares, drinking more heavily. "Ilona, did she ever say anything about what was troubling her?"

"She dropped some hints. At one point we were working on a paper for the upcoming forensic psychology symposium, you know, the one that was in New Orleans in January." Rachel nodded. A conference she had skipped, unable to tear herself away from home and her dog in the midst of her grief. "It was a critique of the whole repressed memory crowd and their justification for presenting their stuff in court. Well, of course you know how she felt about that, you're one of that crowd, I know. Hope you don't take this too personally."

"Don't worry about me, please, Ilona." Rachel's voice held a hint of acid. "I knew where she stood. It was professional disagreement. I have those all the time. Go on, please."

"We were working on this paper. She had been terribly enthusiastic about it when we first submitted the proposal. But she started to balk and procrastinate. She was drinking that evening, was a little tipsy, I thought. Nothing too unusual for how she'd been lately. Then she surprised me by saying that this one had better be good, because she had the funny feeling it might be the last one in a long while on that topic. Then she clammed up, tight, got angry with me when I tried to get her to elaborate on that cryptic remark."

Rachel disguised her surprise. A *last one*, the kind of remark people made when they knew they were going to be dead soon. She had to practice the art of disguising surprise regularly on this job. "What do you think she meant?"

"I have no idea. But I began to get the impression that she had lost her heart for this line of inquiry. She turned down at least a dozen solicitors who called her to testify in cases for falsely accused men this year. I'd never seen her turn down work like that before. She loved it, gloried in it, and here she was saying no. She wouldn't talk about it, though, reminded me that one of the ground rules was that we respected one another's privacy, and that this was private. She wouldn't have tolerated that sort of prying from me."

Rachel's mind was racing a million miles a minute. Alexandra Price had made her reputation, as well as a large hunk of money, from her work in the field of memory and child sexual abuse. For her to be pulling away from it, or even vaguely considering pulling away, had to mean something very important. But what? Those damn boxes again, she thought. Alix was apparently a master of keeping secrets.

"Ilona, what else can you think of? Even small things might make a difference."

"You must know that I've been agonizing over this myself. If it was suicide, then I missed something, missed it horridly. And if that is true, I don't know how I can forgive myself. If it was an accident, well, then, I am still left with my grief. What would you like to know?"

"Ilona, it's incredibly important that I keep things open-ended here. You know, suggestion and all that. I tell you what, though. It sounds like you have the key to Alix's house . . ." She let her voice drift off, trying not to betray too much enthusiasm for the idea.

"Well, yes, that's how I got in and found her. What of it?" Ilona tensed up, as if she were being accused of something wrong. Rachel reminded herself that this woman had grown up in a totalitarian state, where even innocuous acts could be made to seem suspicious. She attempted a benign smile of reassurance.

"Oh, not a problem, no. I was just wondering if you would be willing to let me in sometime. To sniff around, literally. Sometimes I see something that sticks out, something that the people in their former life can't notice because it's become too familiar to them for commentary. I could probably get a key from Joyce, but this would be quicker and easier."

Ilona sat, saying nothing for a few moments. Her face flushed and paled again in sequence. "All right. But I don't want to come with you. I don't want to go back there again. I know what the behaviorists say about exposure, but I can't expose myself to that house now. Too painful. All of this is too bloody painful. Here." She dug into her black leather bag, came up with a ring of keys, sorted through them. "This is the house key. The alarm code is 0404. Her birthday, you know."

Rachel felt chilled. Sarah's birthday, too. Not a difficult number to remember.

"Thanks so much, Ilona. You know, you're likely to recall some other things after I leave. So here's my card—please don't hesitate to call me if something comes to mind. And Ilona . . ." She hesitated, then plunged in. "Look, you probably heard, I lost my partner tragically last year. I know something of what you're dealing with. If you just want to talk—talk, you know, or if you'd like a therapy referral to someone who takes the student insurance . . ."

Ilona first bristled, then teared up. "You Americans. You think

86

that because we have similar experiences that we'll open our hearts. You, how do you say this, crack me up. But thank you. I'll give it some thought, OK?"

They shook hands. Rachel left, brain churning, ignoring the chance to go through Alix's office now that she had a better offer. If she was going to get into Alix's house, she had probably best let the cops know. No need to have an unpleasant episode with some patrol guy from East Precinct who didn't know her. When she got back to the car, she dug the phone out of her bag and dialed the number for Andrea Cole's desk. Still have it by heart, she crowed to herself.

"Cole here." The familiar voice answered on the second ring.

"Andrea, hi, it's Rachel Katz." She heard the intake of breath on the other end of the line, so spoke quickly. "Listen, I'm calling about Alexandra Price. Her PR, Joyce Romanski, has hired me to do a psychological autopsy. Can't believe it's a suicide."

"Well, well. You can't get rid of that woman, can you?" Andrea was relieved enough by the details to tease her former therapist a tad. "So why are you telling me this?"

"Because I have the key to her house, and will be in it sometime soon, and I don't want one of your overzealous buddies to show up and haul me over to East Precinct. I thought I'd give you a buzz and get the word into the system."

"No problem, Rachel. It's not a possible crime scene anymore, you know, so unless one of the neighbors called it in, I doubt you'd get a cop showing up anyway. But just in case, we can't have the former therapist of half the women cops in this station being hauled down here, right?" Andrea laughed. The numbers weren't quite that high, but she knew there was a time when at least three of her coworkers had been dodging each other in Rachel's waiting room and in the AA meetings they were all attending.

"Right, can't have that." Rachel was laughing, too. "Listen, I don't know when I'll be there, probably sometime next week. But do you want me to just buzz you before I do go over?"

"Not a bad idea. I'll get the word out anyway, just in case you get the sudden urge to do something." They both laughed. Resisting the sudden urge to do something had been one of Rachel's pet admonitions to Andrea early in the therapy, when the anxiety of not knowing the truth about her past had fueled not a few impulsive actions on Andrea's part. Oy, Rachel thought, clients often sounded like their therapists.

The two hung up. Rachel looked down at her watch. Four-thirty. Perfect time to hit the health club. Maybe Cori would want to join her for a nice long swim.

Corazon Diaz was Rachel's other very close friend. Unlike Alice, who mirrored her East Coast Jewish background almost to a T, Cori was Chicana, from Texas, the oldest of a good-sized Catholic family. Straight, and married to one of the nicest men that Rachel knew, Cori had met Rachel through their mutual membership on a contentious committee whose unhappy task it was to try to make the local psychological association more welcoming to people of color. Rachel had known from the start that the committee was an attempt by the then-president of the association to deflect criticism rather than a strategy for real change. She had fought her way onto the group, determined to give it teeth rather than have it be another token effort that would discount how exclusionary the association truly had been. As a lesbian, Rachel was only too familiar with how subtly the old-boys-and-girls networks in psychology operated to keep out people whose former position had been only as subjects of study, not as colleagues.

Cori had been taken aback by Rachel's apparently genuine commitment to inclusion, what Rachel jokingly called her "best little antiracist white girl routine." A tentative friendship had formed then, nurtured by a mutual love of swimming and coral reefs and by the respect that Rachel and Cori came to have for one another's skill in dealing with difficult professional issues. The two women had, over the course of the years, developed a deep connection, discovering surprising similarities across their enormous apparent differences. They joked that being the eldest daughter of a research scientist, which both of their fathers were, was a more powerful molder of personality than ethnicity or geography, so striking were some of the parallels. Back when Rachel had had an appetite, they had frequently cooked together, sharing the spicy foods of their respective ethnic cuisines.

"Hey there, girl." Cori's voice still held a hint of Texas twang. "So you want to go get wet? Can you wait about an hour, so I can finish up this article I'm working on?" Cori was a prolific writer. Unlike most psychologists in private practice, she had found the time to churn out several books on the topic of trauma and ethnicity, not to speak of the reams of articles in professional journals. Rachel had no idea how she did it. Her own publication rate was modest in comparison, although still respectable for a non-academic.

"Sure, anything to assist you in making your CV even harder to fit into book length," Rachel teased. "Do you want me to pick you up?"

"That's a good idea. My eyes are going to be so blurry from sitting at the computer that I'll be a menace behind the wheel. Why don't you come by around six, OK?"

They hung up. Rachel sat in her car, considering what to do—go home, walk the dog, think about whom to interview next, revise the assessment plan.

When she swung the Volvo into Cori's driveway an hour and a half later, her friend was waiting out front, short black hair sticking up in gelled spikes, brilliant amethyst eyeglass frames perched on her face. Cori's color scheme was the opposite of Rachel's—bright jewel colors, fashion forward outfits and hairstyles, gold chains and large aquamarine brilliants hanging from her neck and ears. The stylish eyeglass frames were the one point of convergence, and Cori had been the force driving Rachel out of her rimless specs and into the arena of frames-as-décor. Cori was tiny and small-boned and could pull off wearing things tight and short and still look elegant as all get out. Cori was gorgeous, Rachel thought. Glen was a very lucky man, and he knew it, she mused. She reached over to unlock the passenger door.

"Girl, you are looking positively radiant. Are you in love?" Cori rode into the car on a wave of energy.

"Well, no, nothing like that. Just a couple of kind of exciting professional things. One, I'm doing a psychological autopsy on Alix Price."

"Oh, my God. Really. Alix Price, of all people, Rachie girl, no wonder you're looking aroused." Cori let her shock show. "The things you must be hearing."

"And can't say, of course. But yes, it is very interesting. Very, very. Anyhow, that's not what I'm excited about just now. After I called you, I got a message at home from Avi Silver that Pearl Legrand had to poop out of being a discussant on the symposium on integrating trauma and forensic work at the SPST meeting, and was I maybe free to sub for her at the last minute, since the conference was so close? And you know, Cori, for the first time in a long time, I felt excited about work again. So I called and said yes. Even though it's this weekend, and I'll have to cancel some stuff out. But it's in San Jose, it'll be an easy flight down there. Maybe it'll be fun to see some of the old crowd."

The Society for the Psychological Study of Trauma was Rachel's professional home base. She loved the annual meetings, the chance to see friends from all over the world and tell war stories, occasionally from actual wars, about the work they were all doing. The small group of forensic trauma people who came to the meetings was a tight-knit band, and she had been regretting that her grief had led her to miss getting a proposal in for this year's meeting. In the midst of everything else, going to the meeting had dropped off her inner radar screen. The phone call from Avi had been a real treat. She could go to San Jose, have a legitimate reason to cancel getting together with Anna, and see some of her old buddies.

"Isn't that nice?" Cori's tone held a bit of a tease. "You and JoAnn Ducey at the same conference and you single for once. Oh, I wish I could be there to watch."

JoAnn Ducey, a trauma specialist from Massachusetts and one of the few other very out lesbians in the SPST inner crowd, had

90

made no secret over the years of her interest in Rachel. Cori, who frequently came to the SPST meetings, had attempted to bring this to Rachel's attention numerous times, only to have Rachel pooh-pooh her on the grounds that no one was going to come on to someone as married as she was. Rachel had finally had to concede the correctness of Cori's analysis in the past year when JoAnn's e-mail messages to her had been direct as to her wishes.

"Cori, this has nothing to do with my saying yes to Avi. Zero. Maybe less than zero. Could even be a negative factor. I mean, OK, yes, she's very cute, and has a nice bright mind, but jeez, the woman does not know the meaning of the word no, does she? I don't know what this fixation on me is. Flattering yes, but come on, Cori, you know me."

"Yes, Ms. Oh-so-conservative when it comes to matters of the flesh. Rachel, you're not in mourning anymore, right?" Cori had been the ride to synagogue on several occasions when Rachel had spent a Friday night in tears on her couch, and she was well oriented to the rules of the Jewish grief rituals. "So you could flirt back, couldn't you? Well, couldn't you?"

"I suppose I could." Rachel reluctantly cracked a smile. "Cori, what it is with you and Alice, is this a plot or something? Your inner Jewish mother taking over?"

"Yes, a plot to make our friend happy. Or to at least have a sex life, which is close to the same thing, right?" Like Alice, Cori had been privy to the absent nature of the sexual relationship with Sarah. More risk-taking than the rest of Rachel's friends, Cori had been urging Rachel to ditch Sarah, or if not that, take a lover, for years now. "It would be about fucking time to get laid, not to put too fine a point on it. You could do like everyone else and have a fling at a conference. You could do a lot worse than Jo Ducey."

"I suppose. You know Alice is trying to fix me up with a classmate of Liz's. I was supposed to go out with her this weekend, now I get to cancel out. But I'm not, I repeat, not going to have any flings with anyone at this conference. And why aren't you going, huh?" She tried to shift the focus back to Cori.

"You know why. Because it's our anniversary, and Glen is taking me to Victoria." Glen and Cori had one of the good marriages. High school sweethearts who had met again when she was in grad school and he in an MBA program, they had managed to form one of the tightest and best bonds Rachel had ever seen. Glen was an actual feminist, not just one of those overly sensitive guys who thought that if they cried, you would forgive them their sexism. A hulking Texan who looked and sounded like a good ol' boy, Glen Bishop was actually a rabidly progressive community organizer who had been asked to leave his religious-run college when he tried as an undergrad to organize the janitorial staff. Rachel teased him sometimes about being an honorary lesbian, and he knew it was a huge compliment.

"So I won't have you to push me into Jo's bed. Good. Because I'm not going to be going anywhere near there."

The conversation hit a pause just as they rolled into the parking garage. The two women segued into less loaded chatter as they headed into the health club and got into their suits. Cori couldn't resist one last word. "I mean, look at you. You've lost all this weight, you're all nice and fit from swimming, you're looking gorgeous. Who wouldn't want to haul you into bed?"

"Cori!" Rachel was indignant. "Enough already. I am a frumpy middle-aged woman who swims. Gorgeous, no, Cori, you're hallucinating. Or you're biased. We are going swimming. I am going to a conference. I am not having sex with anyone except myself any time soon."

Chapter Seven

It appeared to have been a case of protesting too much and too hard. Four nights later Rachel found herself shaking her head in amazement at the turn of events. Jo Ducey was lying in bed, stripped to a T-shirt and undershorts next to Rachel, who was in a similar state of disarray. Jo's mouth was on Rachel's left breast, avidly sucking and licking her nipple through the thin silvery fabric of her bra, and Rachel was allowing herself to be taken along by the intensity of the physical sensations running through her.

She had been determined that this was not going to happen. She had left the pool with Cori after a long, hard swim, called Anna and canceled their get-together, and felt a huge sense of relief at the notion that she had once again put off the problem of going out on an alleged date. Mr. Piggy had been safely left with Alice and Liz, both of whom were less than thrilled at her blowing off the date with Anna. She flew down to San Jose, remembering how much she had loved traveling in the years before Sarah's death. It had taken her away from her quotidian life, given her brief moments of respite from the turbulent atmosphere at home.

And she had been having a lot of fun being back in the swing at the conference, chatting, catching up with people, letting herself fall back into the warm bath of acceptance that she found among her peers in trauma work. The symposium had gone well. Rachel was a master of the erudite sound bite, and she had outdone herself this time. She had been cogent and funny and moving. People had come up afterward to tell her how she had pulled the whole thing together beautifully. She felt full of herself.

So she had probably had a bit of a buzz on when Jo Ducey had showed up at the cocktail hour that night. Not from alcohol, but from the heady feeling of being happy, truly happy for the first time in what seemed like years. She knew, if she could muster the objectivity from where she presently lay, that she was probably looking pretty interesting to Jo just at that moment. And Jo didn't look half bad herself. A long, tall woman, tight jeans packed around a firm butt and well-developed muscles showing through the sleeve bottoms of her snowy white short-sleeved oxford cloth shirt, the four pierces in her right ear sparkling with graduated diamond studs, the physical type that made Rachel a little weak in the knees. Rachel had made the decision to just go with whatever was happening. Going out for dinner at a little sushi joint that Jo knew in San Jose was not going to bed with her, right?

But the sushi had led to sake, the one thing Rachel would drink because she had the illusion that it didn't make her drunk. And the sake had led to loose talk about why sushi was Rachel's favorite food. "Because, you know, Jo, you must know this, that the best maguro"—referring to a fleshy red variety of tuna belly—"reminds me of the smell and taste of a woman. And isn't that a kick, to sit in public and enjoy consuming that. Appeals to the exhibitionist in me." The flirting talk had escalated, double entendre after double entendre. More sake had been drunk. When Jo offered to walk Rachel back to her room, gallant butch that she was, Rachel had not turned her down, ignoring her inner knowledge of what would come next.

Rachel had stepped inside the door and turned to thank Jo for the lovely evening when the other woman, taller and stronger, pushed her way inside and took Rachel in her arms. And kissed her, hard. Rachel had resisted not a bit. She kissed back, tongue searching the soft inner surfaces of Jo's lips, teeth connecting and sparking, allowing herself to melt into the feelings of sexual arousal, tasting the other woman's mouth, sucking hard as if to swallow her up, thirsty and hungry. She reached upward to wrap her hands around Jo's head and neck, caressing them, feeling the muscles in Jo's shoulders and upper arms, pulling Jo's mouth even closer, as Jo's hands cupped her buttocks and lifted her upward so that their breasts touched under their clothes. It had been a very, very long time since any woman had kissed her with such passion, and she didn't want to stop.

It was a short distance from the doorway to the bed where they lay now. Jo had lived up to her butch appearance, taking charge sexually in a way that both thrilled Rachel and somehow left her off the hook for what was happening, feeding her diminishing denial about the fact that she was, indeed, about to have sex with Jo. She shut down her inner observer, who had been yelling at her to stop for several minutes, as Jo had unzipped Rachel's skirt, pulled off her sweater, and thrown Rachel's clothing into a corner of the hotel room as she steered Rachel onto the bed and gently yet firmly pushed her back into the pillows. She nibbled on the hollow of Rachel's neck, then began the process of attaching herself to Rachel's nipples.

Rachel noticed herself moaning. She had been for a very long time in a wasteland sexually, with no nourishment but her own hand and imagination. Even the thought of Jo's mouth and hands moving south of their current position sent spasms through her. She thought for two seconds about safe sex, and then let it go. She knew she was disease-free, she figured Jo would have said something if she weren't. Damn the torpedoes, the feeling of Jo's mouth on her nipple was just too good to interrupt with a conversation about latex. She opened her eyes and looked downward to the sight of Jo's face, eyes shut in ecstasy, pulling back from her breast before burying her head of short, soft blond hair in the cleft between the two mounds. There was something powerfully erotic about that sight, the other woman's boyish yet unmistakably female face being swept away and softened by the taste of Rachel's breasts.

Rachel pulled Jo's head to her, hard, and wiggled her body upward so that her thigh came to rest between Jo's legs. She could feel the incredible warmth coming from Jo's crotch, an almost palpable swelling and a dampness seeping through the cotton boxer shorts that the other woman wore, swelling and heat and damp that mirrored precisely what was happening between her own legs. She reached down to Jo's waistband in the back, began to pull up the sleeveless tee. "I want to feel you," she whispered.

"Not yet. Not yet, Rachel." Jo raised herself up, so that she loomed over Rachel, face taut with lust. "I kind of like to be in charge, you know. Especially with such a powerful woman. I want to take you."

Rachel shuddered with anticipation and delight. Her own sexual fantasies had long included such a scenario. In her sexual heart of hearts, Rachel loved to be dominated and mastered sexually, to have a partner who would take charge. Sarah had found the whole thing nonsensical and politically reprehensible, even when she had been willing to have sex with Rachel, and had insisted on a completely equal exchange. What Jo was offering had only been the stuff of dream and fantasy for Rachel until now. She shut down her fears, and nodded. "Yes. Go ahead, Jo. Take me how you want. Safe word, we need a safe word . . ." She trailed off, because as she had been speaking Jo had moved one of her hands down Rachel's belly and under the hem of her panties, which were now soaking with the juices of Rachel's arousal. Rachel was distracted.

"Don't worry, we won't go there. I just want to fuck your brains out, Rachel Katz. I've been imagining doing that to you for years now, make you scream with pleasure, not pain. You aren't going to need any safe words with me." Rachel gave in to the sensations emanating from her vulva and shut down the last pieces of her mind which were desperately trying to get her attention and get her up and out from under Jo Ducey.

The next hour or so never made it into memory in a sequential fashion, proving conclusively what high levels of arousal do to memory storage. The subsequent day, there was a series of inner video clips, each one of which had the power to make Rachel blush and grow wet again. One clip of Jo taking off Rachel's bra, and cooing in admiration at Rachel's voluptuous breasts, then removing her shirt to reveal her own small, girlish breasts, finally allowing Rachel the incredible feeling of another woman's breasts against her own. Rachel remembered thinking, "I can die now, and it would be OK." She had missed that intimate skin-to-skin contact more than she had known. It felt so good, like nothing else in physical experience. Another memory video of Jo's mouth and tongue on her clitoris and labia, licking gently, then harder, sending cascades of energy down her nerve endings, so that at one point her entire body felt like a gigantic clitoris, awash in arousal. And the best video clip of all, one that Rachel replayed endlessly, of Jo's large, firm hand entering her, pushing gently at first, searching for the tight muscles to push against, then harder, over and over, seeming never to tire, finally hard enough that Rachel came in a rush from the exquisite sensation, part pleasure and part pain, that rushed upward from the contact between the core of her and Jo's insistent, intelligent hand. Herself, screaming, hand jammed into her own mouth to deaden the sound so that the people on the other side of the wall would neither be entertained nor tempted to call hotel security.

Jo would not let Rachel reciprocate. She held Rachel in her arms after Rachel had exhausted herself on her umpteenth orgasm of the night, stroking her gently, kissing her neck and ears. But when Rachel moved to bring her hand down to Jo's vulva, the other woman stopped her. "Look, Rachel, I'm just a bit stone on the first pass with someone. So let's leave things where they are." Stone butch, Rachel mused. A woman who would give tremendous pleasure to another, but whose need for control was large enough to be resistant to being taken by her sexual partner. Fine, if that was how Jo wanted it, Rachel had thought, and fallen asleep for a while.

She woke to find herself alone. Jo must have let herself out. Rachel ran the shower and stood under it for a very long time, allowing the hot water to run down her body where the nerve endings were still firing furiously from the first sex Rachel had had in, how many years was it? Too many, by any count. That was when the inner voice came on, loudly. Rachel asked herself what in the hell did she just do? What kind of stupid horny teenager did she fancy herself to be? Rachel let that woman fuck her silly all right, silly to let Jo fuck her at all, no matter how gloriously she did it. What was she thinking?

The whole experience gave her a sudden burst of sympathy for Alix Price. Was this what it had been like for her—brief, intense couplings at conferences that rang all the bells of your nerve endings and left you feeling hollow and foolish? Rachel dried herself off and looked at herself in the mirror. Nothing different from that morning—still a woman with wide hips and a rounded belly, large breasts sagging slightly from their own sheer weight. Nothing to show that sex had happened, that her body had been opened and taken. She brushed her teeth and got back into the bed, this time between the covers.

She couldn't tell if it was the rebound effect from the sake, or her still-aroused central nervous system, or just general overall emotional discomfort that made the night so long and restless. Finally around six, she gave up, dug through her suitcase for her swim clothes, and, wrapping herself in a robe, went down to the hotel pool, which was advertised to be open twenty-four hours. At least a half hour or so of lap swimming would calm her down, she thought to herself.

An hour later, she hauled herself onto the pool's edge, exhausted in body but clearer in mind. OK, that had been fun, but that was going to be it, she had decided. Jo had left her with some exquisite memories, but she was not going to allow it to go further. She had done her presentation, and she could play hooky from the conference for the rest of the day or just stand by on a earlier flight and go home. She didn't have to stick around to deal with the ramifications of having had casual sex with a colleague she was going to see for years to come at this meeting.

As she was thinking this, the colleague in question appeared at the door of the pool room. "I thought I'd find you here when you didn't answer the phone in your room, Rachel. Remembered how you told me once that you got up early at these things to grab pool time before the crowds showed up. I wondered if you wanted to do breakfast."

Rachel felt herself blushing. For God's sake, Rachel said to herself, the woman had her hand up you last night. It wasn't like Jo didn't know what Rachel looked like with most of her clothes off. She glanced down to see her nipples hardening against the shiny black lycra of her suit. Damn cold air, she thought, and looked back up to see Jo observing the same sight.

"Uh, Jo, good morning. Breakfast, well, I guess. I should get a little more dressed than this, don't you think?"

"Do you want an honest answer or the polite one?" Jo's grin seemed slightly wolfish. "I wouldn't mind having you for breakfast, which would suggest somewhat less dressed than this, frankly. But somehow I have the feeling you might want something more substantial than that."

Rachel knew that she was blushing furiously. She tried to take matters in hand. "Jo, last night was lovely. And it was a serious error on my part. I had a great time, and I don't want to do that again. So if you're proposing breakfast because you think that feeding me makes me an easier lay, please save yourself the time and energy. I don't know what I was doing last night. Well, a little honesty might help. I do know. I was horny, and you were quite hot. And I don't let women pick me up at conferences and fuck me." She surprised herself with her bluntness.

"So if you don't let women do that, then who the hell was the one I had under me last night?" Jo retorted. Her face flushed with anger or disappointment, Rachel wasn't sure. She clearly wasn't happy with how things were going.

"That was me, making a mistake. Not about you, Jo. You were lovely, really. But I'm still an emotional mess from losing Sarah. I don't care how long it's been since I had sex last, I should have told you no and sent you to your own room." She could feel the water drying on her skin; she felt chilled. "Excuse me, I have to grab the robe, I'm going to start to freeze. Jo, I'd love to do breakfast with you. And that's all I'm going to do. If you're up for that, then give me about twenty minutes, and I'll meet you down in the lobby." She brushed past the other woman, then turned back to look quizzically at her. "So, are we having breakfast?"

Jo sighed. "I guess that's what I can get. Damn, Rachel, you are maddening. Absolutely maddening. I'll see you in the lobby."

Rachel breathed a sigh of relief in the elevator. This felt back under control. She had had a fun experience, and then she was going to put an end to it. No mistaking sex for love, not even really great sex. Which, now safely back behind her barriers, she could stop and admit. It had been truly great sex, the kind she had dreamed of endlessly. Too bad she had reverted to being a grown-up, she laughed to herself. It would really be better this way, to make it a mistake and try to rectify things with Jo. After all, she did only see her once a year. Maybe, having finally gotten Rachel into bed, Jo would back off, the thrill of pursuit dampened by the reality of acquisition. It was done, she told herself firmly, very done.

It was two days later, home in Seattle, that the undone nature of the sexual encounter with Jo Ducey began to announce itself in the form of a horrid itch, followed shortly by a greenish discharge, both centered in Rachel's vulva. A quick trip to the feminist health center and an exam at the capable hands of Fern Nguyen, the nurse practitioner, yielded unpleasant results. Jo had given her a nasty case of trichomoniasis. Great, thought Rachel, so much for what happens when you ignore safe sex. One of the very few things that one woman could easily give to another, and she had gotten it. Yuck. An STD, just what she always didn't want.

Fern clucked at Rachel about her failure to look for the latex, then prescribed a course of Flagyl. "Now you know this stuff is pretty deadly, Rachel. It has to be, to kill those nasty parasites you've got swimming around in there, but it's got the potential to make you very sick indeed. So no booze, please. The combo of alcohol and Flagyl is guaranteed to make you barf." Rachel grinned. Fern was so blunt, so unpretentious. It was part of what she admired about her, aside from the woman's incredible skill and knowledge as a primary care provider who had helped to pioneer independent nurse practice, and had founded a health clinic where she worked. Even though Rachel could long ago have afforded private care, she still went to Aradia out of loyalty to her feminist roots and gratitude to the clinic's careful attention to the realities of lesbian health care.

"You know, Fern, the one time in a year that I drink anything, I end up in bed with a very nice woman, and now look what I have. So I don't think you'll catch me drinking or fucking any time again soon, not to worry." She laughed ruefully. Now she was perfectly safe to go out on a date with Anna, wasn't she? No sex until the trich cleared up. She was going to be on the Flagyl for at least the next three weeks. She noticed how pleased she was feeling with Jo for giving her this little gift. It's almost like she wanted to have negative consequences, she thought to herself. Like having a bad outcome from casual sex was a good thing. Kept her in line.

Back at her office, she dashed off an e-mail to Jo with news of the trich, and a quasi-humorous suggestion that the woman carry latex in her pocket the next time. Fern had explained to Rachel that it was entirely possible for someone to be an asymptomatic carrier of the damn thing, and she decided to take that charitable approach to the whole matter. It had been fun, she had a nasty bug, the end. It would make it easier to propel Jo away from her in the future. With luck, the other woman would be too embarrassed to come on to her again.

The voice mail was full of messages. Three from Anna Sigurdson, proposing various times to get together again with various tempting activities to go with them. OK, Anna, I'll go, she thought to herself. She was safe from her now, so she could go out with her. One message from Joel Gibbs, confirming that he would meet with her two days hence at his office. Why did Alix have to choose him for her therapist, Rachel thought. Couldn't it have been someone Rachel liked better? She could think of a dozen male therapists in Seattle she'd rather be spending the time with— some of them were even dear friends in their fashion. But Joel it was. OK, fine, she'd see Joel and see what light he could shed on Alix's demise. There was a message from Joyce wanting to schedule her weekly update. And one from Ilona Hegevary. "There's someone I think you should talk to, Rachel. Give me a call, let me tell you about it." This was followed by an unfamiliar phone number. Not the same one Rachel had called her at earlier. Then a message from Cori wondering how the conference had gone. Oy, red face time, she thought. How was she doing to avoid that encounter? Two from lawyers wanting her to evaluate their clients. Life was going on. She sat down at the desk to return calls.

In the middle of the afternoon, a messenger showed up with more goodies from Joyce. This pile of paper included, at long last, the tox report on Alix Price. Rachel read it with growing interest. A blood alcohol level of point-three. My God, Rachel thought, she was loaded. That amount of booze alone could have done her in and upped the possibility that she was looking at a stupid mistake here. But the rest of the tox report caused her to pull up short— extremely high levels of barbiturates and opioids. Rachel couldn't imagine what was going on, and who was prescribing this stuff for Alix.

Further down in the pile she found a partial answer—the pharmacy records. Joyce had been very efficient. Alix had a long-standing script for oxycodone, in very high doses, from a physician who was well-known to Rachel as an expert in pain management. Hmm, evidence of chronic pain, Rachel said to herself. That's one for the suicide side of the chart. People with pain problems were at terrible risk. But also one for the accident side, especially because they were prescribed, and it was entirely possible for a person to lose track of how much they'd taken and accidentally OD. At that high a prescribed dose it was entirely possible. But where were the downers coming from? The rest of the pharmacy record was silent on the matter of the barbiturates.

The rest of the record was interesting, if lacking in investigatory value. There were very recent scripts for Buspar, an anti-anxiety medication, and for a low dose of Trazadone, an antidepressant whose chief benefit was that it knocked you out, hard. Anxiety and sleep problems, OK. There was a long-standing prescription for birth control pills, several different types of asthma inhalers, and blood pressure medication. Alix Price had not been the wellest of women, Rachel thought. Asthma, blood pressure problems, sleep disturbance. Not a pretty picture. And apparently chronic pain. But no barbiturates. And they were clearly in the tox screen. Alix had come by them somewhere.

She once again made up the imaginary spreadsheet in her mind. Recent behavior changes, anxiety, sleep problems, chronic pain, increased drinking. The balance sheet still hung in a state of ambiguity. While Alix's death was looking more and more like a bad accident, it could have been the same kind of accident that Sarah had had, one so fueled by alcohol and misery that it skated right on the edge of suicide. No one who knew Alix seemed to think that she was about to kill herself—not Joyce, not George Lewis, not Ilona, not to mention the hordes of casual observers. She needed more data. Joel Gibbs was going to be the best source of that. She sighed, audibly enough that Mr. Piggy perked up his ears and tilted his head with concern. She hated having to give Joel so much power in this situation, but he was the therapist and the one most likely to know. Even therapists who didn't believe in transference elicited it, after all. Their clients told them things that no one else, even those closest to the client, had ever heard. Rachel knew this from both sides of the room. Her own therapist, eons ago, had been privy to secrets that no one else knew, or ever would. So it was probably true that Joel Gibbs knew what Rachel needed.

She pushed the mass of paper away and rubbed her eyes. Call

Anna, she said to herself. Rachel figured she'd try to set up something easy and fun—Anna doesn't bite. Leaving a message on Anna's voice mail wouldn't be nearly as hard as having Jo take her clothes off, Rachel thought.

She had her message all set to go when a live person answered the phone. A live Anna, to be precise. "Oh, hi, Anna, it's Rachel Katz. I was expecting to get your voice mail."

"So should I hang up so you can leave a message?" Anna teased, gently. She was pleased that Rachel had called her back. The canceled date had been a huge disappointment. She understood wanting to take a professional opportunity as it arose, but sensed that Rachel had probably been more willing to fly halfway down the coast simply because it got her out of a challenging situation.

"No, silly woman." Rachel was relaxed, to her amazement. The encounter with Jo really had done her good. "Look, I'm really sorry about pooping out on you. I think I'm just a little ambivalent about this dating thing."

"A little ambivalent? A little? Come on, give me a break," Anna replied. "It's not like I can't see how hard this is for you. Of course you're ambivalent. So I'm really glad you called, given how ambivalent you are. Like, maybe you might be willing to actually go out with me sometime, Ms. ambivalence?"

"Well, yes. I think so. I think it would be good to do something where we could actually talk to one another. You know, not have entertainment to help us avoid contact."

Anna could hardly believe what she was hearing. Rachel Katz the ambivalent was proposing doing something that would allow for connection to develop. She cautioned herself not to sound too eager.

"I hear you're a great fan of Café Flora. And I just live around the corner, back behind Bailey Boushay." Anna referred to the AIDS hospice that dominated and had transformed the neighborhood around the restaurant, making it a center of queer life. "I'm not a vegetarian, but I love their food. Are you free any night this week?"

"Tonight and tomorrow, and well, every night this week, actually. It's not like I have a booming social life. In between being a therapist and having been in seclusion for the past year, I'm a free woman. And I never turn down a meal at Café Flora. Alice must have been filling you in on ways to get to me, the fiend."

"Then let's be a little spontaneous. I'm fresh out of statistics problems to solve. How about we meet there around seven? I'll be the one with the pleased expression on her face. I really am looking forward to getting to know you better, Rachel. I'm glad you seem to want to get to know me."

"Whoa, Anna, please hold the kudos. I'm still ambivalent, OK? I'm just trying to stop being in such terminal avoidance. I have to start somewhere. So yes, at seven. I'll be the one looking cautious."

They hung up. On the other end, Anna grinned broadly. She didn't know what it was about Rachel, but there was something that kept her in careful pursuit.

Rachel, for her part, got back on the phone and called Ilona Hegevary. This time she did get a voice mail, with a woman's voice that wasn't Ilona's. "You've reached Suzanne's voice mail. Please leave a message." Odd, Rachel thought. She decided to be circumspect.

"Hi, this is Dr. Katz. Ilona Hegevary left this number for me to reach her. She can call me back tomorrow between ten and twelve at the following number." She left her office number, then paused and gave her cell phone number. She thought to herself, why not? Ilona was a good source and good sources got the cell number.

Rachel was back at work on the pile of Alix Price records when her cell in her purse began to ring. No one ever called her on her cell phone. She picked up.

"Rachel, Dr. Katz?" It was a hesitant voice with a Magyar accent. "I know it's not between ten and twelve tomorrow, but I thought I'd try, since it appeared that you had rung not too long ago."

"Ilona, not a problem. I'm glad you called me back. I was away at a meeting so I didn't get your message until today. I didn't want to leave you hanging. What's come to mind?"

105

"Well . . ." The woman hesitated. Rachel breathed slowly and deeply, allowing herself to shift into a waiting and listening stance. No psychological autopsy was helped by impatience or urging on the part of the investigator. Friends and family of the dead were always, and understandably, reluctant to speak, to expose the secrets that they had protected in life. Ilona seemed on the verge of divulging something new, and Rachel was not going to muck it up by rushing things.

"I have been contemplating how I could assist you. And thinking that I know of someone who you might want to speak with. Do you have sometime?" Ilona's English sounded formal, almost stilted, which indicated to Rachel that she must be quite nervous. Rachel looked up at the clock. It was half past six. She should be leaving for dinner already. But heck, she was ambivalent, right? This wasn't a therapy session, she could be a little late for dinner. "Yes, I do, go ahead."

"Few people knew this, but Alix had seen a massage practitioner for many years. She was a little nervous about people knowing it. It seemed out of character for her, she said, not scientific. But she was in terrible pain a lot of the time, and the massage was one of the only things that seemed to help. I think she may have confided in this woman."

"What leads you to that theory, Ilona?" Rachel slipped back into the language of psychological science, wanting to open up her listener as much and as subtly as possible.

"How she was when she spoke of her. As if this woman were some kind of mother figure. Somewhere about a week before she died, she told me that she and Emma, that's the woman's name, had had a very important conversation. That she was grateful that Emma was in her life. So I know that they talked. Maybe it wasn't about anything that matters to what you're doing. I did a psych abstracts search on psychological autopsies." Rachel groaned silently when she heard that and thought, so much for the blank slate approach to interviewing. "Seems that even small, apparently meaningless bits of information can make a difference between a

106

judgment of suicide and one of accidental death. Perhaps it was simply some new approach to treating Alix's neck pain that made a difference. But I thought—"

Rachel finished the sentence, breaking her own rules of listening. "Evidence of good news might rebalance the spreadsheet. You're right, Ilona. Is this Emma, hold on a second, let me look at Alix's phone list"—Rachel grabbed for the address book—"Emma Forche? Is that who you're talking about?"

"Right, Forche, a French last name. Alix once told me that the woman's family had come from Alsace. That's her. You know what the research says, sometimes the data bits that arrive in our minds unexpectedly are the ones to which we need to most pay attention. This one has been troubling me. So here it is. Do with it as you think best."

"Ilona, thanks so much." Rachel's voice held a note of effusiveness. "Are you doing OK, by the way? I worried about you after I left last week."

"I'm staying with a friend. A woman I've come to know through my folk-dancing class, very sweet. She's taking good care of me. Is sending me off to see a therapist of her acquaintance. Peg Stone, do you know of her?"

Rachel smiled. "Yes, very well. I supervised her for her post-doc hours. She's incredibly competent and smarter than most of us put together. She's good at grief. Your friend did you quite a favor." The two women exchanged further pleasantries, then hung up.

Rachel looked at her watch. It was five minutes to seven and that was good—no way would she be the one sitting in Café Flora waiting for Anna to arrive. Nothing like cultivating a new habit of being late.

Chapter Eight

Dinner with Anna was fun, Rachel reluctantly admitted to herself. Freed by her itching crotch from the risk of being sexual, she had relaxed and allowed herself to take in Anna's openness, her decency, and her wry sense of humor. She could, too, let herself notice once again how compelling this woman's physical presence was to her. The iron gray locks of hair hanging into her hazel eyes, the strong high cheekbones, the evidence of hours in the gym pumping iron in the visible muscles in her upper arms—all of it drew Rachel in. She found herself sitting at the table wanting to reach over and take one of Anna's equally muscular hands into her own small, soft ones, to touch and caress it. A highly sexually charged thing for one lesbian to do with another. Hands are sex organs for lesbians, especially butch women like Anna. Rachel knew that stroking Anna's hand would be the equivalent of allowing someone to stroke her naked breast in public. So she practiced restraint and focused on the conversation instead.

"So what happened after you finished grad school," Anna was asking her. They had been exchanging the top layers of their respective autobiographies, and Rachel had just completed a blow-by-blow of her mad dash through her doctoral program.

"I had interned out here, at the state hospital, part of the time on their mentally ill offenders unit. Which got me into forensics pretty early on. Most psychologists would rather face a firing squad than an attorney with an array of questions. But it felt so much like living in my family, you know, the constant interrogation and having to stay one step ahead of the game in order to survive, that I just fell into it backward. After growing up with a father whose mantra was 'show me the data,' it was easy. And of course, I was only the fourth or fifth dyke in town to have a practice. Alice was the first, you know. She's the mother of us all. No wonder she thinks she can push me around in the dating department." Rachel guffawed, and Anna joined in.

"I've noticed that she is, how can I put this delicately . . . ," Anna began.

"One of us very pushy Jewish broads from back East? Yep. That's why I love her, she's *mishpachah*. Family, in Yiddish, you know. And she was the supervisor on my other rotation, at the treatment center. When I decided to stay here instead of going back to Chicago, she really encouraged me to set up shop. I had a job at the university for a couple of years, but I decided early on that I wouldn't want to put up with the bullshit and politics. So I left the hollow halls of academe . . ."

"Don't you mean the hallowed halls," Anna teased.

"No, very, very hollow, girl. Left them to do this practice thing. And the rest, shall we say, is history. I'm going back to work now, after, well, you know. Sarah's death threw me for an enormous loop. I'd been with her since I was in grad school. She was the love of my life, no matter how hard it got. I couldn't do therapy to save my life after she died, don't know if I can now, to be honest." Rachel found herself straining to keep her voice light. "But I've got this other gig, so it keeps me busy and Mr. Pig in dog food."

Anna sat back in her chair, watching and listening. Rachel was so sad underneath her veneer of charm. She wanted to pull the smaller woman into her arms and rock her, make her feel safe. Anna told herself that she had to be careful, that she didn't need to go on another rescue expedition. She was looking for a nice, sane grown-up this time around, no more wounded birdies. Anna thought Rachel was cute, smart—sterling qualities that certainly could take her in. But then the words were out of her mouth, leaving Anna wondering if she'd gone temporarily insane.

"Rachel, would you like to come see my little place before you head home? It's just around the corner here, I could show you the pics of my late lamented dog. How about it? I promise no back rubs, OK?" The two women laughed. Back rubs, the original lesbian come-on. Here, let me give you a nice back rub, something easy to accept that could naturally lead further if a hand happened to slide from back to breasts.

"Sure, why not?" Rachel, safe behind the barrier of her STD, felt open to all possibilities. "I'd love to see your place."

They signaled the nearest waitperson, an adorably butch young woman with a dark cowlick whose eye Rachel had caught more than a few times while eating at Flora's. The check handled, they walked out the door and down Madison to the traffic light, chatting as they went.

"So now it's your turn, Anna Sigurdson. Or should we say Sigurdsdottir, isn't that how your ancestors would have done it."

"You know, back during my womyn-with-a-y period, I tried that out." Anna's comment referred to a time in the seventies when lesbian separatists tried to rewrite the spelling of anything that had the words "man" or "his" in it. *Womyn, wombmoon, wimmin*, had all had their vogue. "Didn't fit, so I went back to the original. Besides, if I were following Icelandic traditions, it'd be Philsdottir, or maybe Gwensdottir, doesn't quite ring right. So, my turn for what?" Anna was flirting.

"To tell me how you got from that women's land in Vermont to a doctoral program in public health in Seattle. A long distance any way you measure it."

"Do you have about six hours? Because that's how long it'll take."

The two women had crossed the street and now were going up the stairs of a small house nestled back from the street, framed by tall, deep purple rhododendron bushes.

"Well, not six. But at least one more." Rachel stopped to take in the mass of purple all around her. "Great flowers, Anna. Did you buy this place or are you among the oppressed renters of Seattle?"

"Yep, I'm a homeowner. I came into an inheritance just before I started grad school. A trust fund from my maternal grandmother. Contingent on my staying sober for twenty years. I guess she never thought I'd make it. The damn thing was huge from sitting and just earning money for so long. I'd practically forgotten it, then I get this letter from a law firm in Maine, telling me that if I could demonstrate that I had met the terms of the trust, that money was there for me. I had just been accepted into the program here, was renting a nasty little place closer to the U. So I got myself an agent and bought this place, figured it was a good investment with the rents and housing prices the way they are here in Seattle. This way I can have a dog when I'm more around to raise another pup. I'm glad you like the rhodies. They were a real selling point for me."

The women walked into a living room alive with color. Quilts hung on the walls, kilim rugs covered floors and draped over furniture, Mayan embroideries hung framed over the mantel. Deep, rich colors flowed in waves everywhere in the small room. Rachel drank it in. The room was alive and its beauty moved her. She felt knocked off balance and tried to put the lid back on by falling into interviewer mode.

"Are you a collector?" She turned to Anna with a huge smile opening up her face.

"Ah, yes, the fabric art." Anna decided to be a little disingenuous. She had guessed right that Rachel would instantly be taken by her collection. "I didn't start out to be, but I woke up one day and discovered that I had become one. The work of many women's hands. I feel surrounded and protected by the energy of all of the creators. Now I'm intentional about it. If you ever get to see my

111

bedroom, you'll see the quilt and hangings I commissioned from this incredible woman in Santa Fe. And the leaded glass windows to match that I found here." The bedroom remark flew by casually, but was noted by both.

Anna was barely keeping herself speaking coherently. Something about seeing Rachel framed against all of the rich color brought out an intense desire to take the other woman in her arms, but not to comfort her. Rachel's dark beauty was impossible to ignore in these surroundings. What was possible to ignore was her inner voice, warning her against sheltering another wounded woman. She stepped closer.

"I know I promised no back rubs. But I'd like to put my arms around you, Rachel Katz. I want to feel how you would feel in my arms."

The audacity and directness of Anna's approach stunned Rachel. She had become aware of the growing sexual energy in the room, but was busily pretending that it wasn't there. To have Anna voice it so clearly was something out of the ordinary. Most women beat around the bush. This was getting to be a habit, women coming on to her. She wasn't sure she didn't like it. She breathed deeply, and looked up the half-foot into Anna's eyes.

"I don't know what we're getting into here, but can we just do this very slowly please . . ." Her words disappeared into Anna's gray polished cotton shirt front, where she found her cheek pressed against the small mounds of breasts and taut muscle underneath. Oh shit, oh dear, Rachel thought. She felt incredibly turned on. She didn't think she could handle the intensity of her desire. She wanted to want to push away, and she didn't. Her overwhelming arousal made her feel like she was becoming the slut queen of the lesbian community. Rachel told herself to stop thinking, just experience, and her mind ran busily on. She noticed Anna's hand stroking her hair.

"Anna. Look, I'm feeling very attracted to you. But this is nuts. I don't know you, you don't know me. I think we should back off a few paces, please."

Anna backed off no paces. "Rachel, no. I'm going to claim my right to overcome the reluctance of the fair maiden. So just allow me this for a few more minutes, all right? Then you can go home and be as ambivalent as you want. I'm not ambivalent. I want to find out what's underneath all of those teal sweaters of yours. To find out more of what's in that sharp, funny mind."

Rachel sighed and pulled back. "Anna, this is very complicated. You know, I'm just barely out of mourning. And, well, I did something on the very high end of the stupid continuum last weekend in San Jose." Anna waited, not commenting. "I let someone pull me into bed. She'd been pursuing me for years, and I guess my horniness got the better of me. So I paid for that, big-time, with a nasty little STD. Nothing that won't clear up in time, but I have a bit of a chastity belt on for the time being. There, I said it, wasn't so bad, was it?" she said for her own benefit.

Anna's face changed color slightly. "It's not like I thought you were a virgin, but I'm a little disappointed, to be honest. I guess it's nice to know that even the great Rachel Katz"—at this Rachel began to hoot, and the atmosphere lightened considerably—"can do truly silly things. Hey, been there, done that. At least you were indoors, right? My version of this happened at Michigan, at a music festival, so I not only got a roaring case of bacterial vaginosis, I also got a butt full of mosquito bites. Be grateful it's only an STD." She laughed and relaxed her hold on Rachel. "Look, Rachel, I really do like you. So could we at least make out? You know, pretend to be sixteen. Nothing below the waist, remember that rule?"

Rachel hesitated for a moment. What in the hell was she doing? Last week in bed with Jo Ducey, now in Anna's living room being invited to a make-out party? Was this some kind of divine joke, heaps of sex after years of absolutely nothing? She didn't know, but if it was a joke, it was very amusing indeed. Not being one to waste the gifts of the goddess, she took Anna's hand and pulled her over to the nearest couch.

"OK, let's audition your kissing technique. I can learn quite a lot from . . ." The sentence was never completed. Anna's mouth came down on her own and stayed there for a very long time. The photos of the late lamented dog never came out of their album.

Rachel arrived back home in Wallingford very late. Mr. Piggy was anxiously peering out the front window. It had been years since he'd been left home alone for that long. She kneeled to pet him and be doggie-kissed as she came in the door. He sniffed her pointedly, as if to communicate his awareness that someone else's smell was on her.

"Well, Mr. Piggy, your mom just had an adventure. She is getting to know a very nice woman. I'm glad you seem to like her, piglet, we might be seeing more of her." She was aware of the difference between how tonight's encounter felt and the one in San Jose. Tonight she felt full, alive, in herself. Something right was happening. Anna had indeed kept things above the waist, and Rachel had rarely been so aroused. A real champion of lovemaking, she mused about Anna. And a nice woman. Solid, grounded, Watch out, Rachel, down girl, she muttered to herself. Rachel liked Anna, she was sexual dynamite, but she barely knew her. Rachel knew it would be prudent to slow down, not that prudence was being very attractive just this moment. It wasn't the time to be auditioning women for the next act of Rachel Katz, married lady. Dynamite is explosive, she reminded herself. Don't blow up.

She sighed and headed for her bed. The bedroom was Rachel's pride and joy, a huge master suite that she had created in her remodeling frenzy. But the room had been empty of love and affection for a long time. In the years before her death, Sarah had spent most nights snoring drunkenly, or woozily watching the TV, ignoring Rachel. In the year since Sarah's death, only the dog had joined her there. Maybe Anna would visit, Rachel mused. She imagined that silver hair looking gorgeous against her deep purple sheets. Heck, if she could color-coordinate her sex toys with her sheets, she could do the same with her lover's hair. She laughed at herself, stripped, donned her nightshirt, and staggered into the bed, exhausted emotionally from the evening's encounter. Her sleep was restless, marked by dreams of watching Sarah fading into the distance, unreachable, Eurydice to her own female Orpheus.

When she met with Joyce Romanski the next afternoon, Rachel was aware of her own slight nervousness. Several weeks had gone by, and what did she have to report? Very little. Some detective you are, said the inner voice. All she knew now was that Alix had one more woman as a lover than she knew about when she started this. And that she was in chronic pain, and had a masseuse. Not a lot of data, although suggestions of a direction where the information led. But Rachel knew that Joyce wanted and needed an update. She prepared herself to cope with the lawyer's disappointment.

"Here's the scoop. The information isn't pointing in any one direction so far. I've learned that she was seeing a therapist. I'm going to meet with him tomorrow, in fact. Did you look at the pharmacy records?"

"Actually, I did. I recognized a few things, the birth control pills, but what are Oxycodone and Trazadone? Or Buspar? I know I've seen this stuff in records, but just for the moment it sounds like some kind of alien substance to me."

"Oxycodone is a painkiller. Similar to Percodan, pretty powerful and potentially quite addictive, and lethal. I'm sure that it accounts for the opioid level in the tox report from the medical examiner. The Trazadone is an antidepressant, and apparently she was using it for sleep. It's really quite effective as a non-addicting sleep medication. Buspar's for anxiety." Rachel didn't tell Joyce that she had had firsthand experience with the last two of those drugs and knew only too well whereof she spoke. "I've seen them in psych records quite a bit." Rachel tried to remain nonchalant. "So anyhow, Joyce, it appears that Alix was dealing with some kind of fairly serious chronic pain. Did you know anything about that?"

"Umm. In fact, yes."

Rachel groaned inwardly. Of course, the one person she hadn't interviewed or even thought about interviewing was Joyce herself. As one of Alix's former lovers she ought to have been on the must-see list. But Joyce had a large ax to grind, Rachel thought to herself, and couldn't be trusted with what she would say. She turned her attention back to the room.

"Yes, I knew she had this terrible neck and shoulder pain. It was like there was always something digging into her neck. I remember one time when we were together, and just as she was, well, how can I be delicate about this, just as she was about to come, her neck began to hurt so badly that we had to stop what we were doing. So what does that have to do with anything, Rachel?"

"I'm doing a sort of spreadsheet, one column for factors that argue accident, one for suicide, one for unclear. And chronic pain goes into the risk for suicide category. But habituation to a narcotic, combined with drinking, goes into the accident category. Access to the means for suicide, like a narcotic, goes into you can guess which. She was troubled, Joyce, very troubled." Rachel weighed her next statement carefully. She had to tell Joyce sometime, better not to create the impression that she had withheld information. "Ilona, her research assistant—I don't know how to say this, except directly—was one of her lovers."

Joyce blinked hard and colored. She waved at Rachel, who had paused, to go on.

"OK, if you're sure. Anyway, she told me a few things about recent months. That Alix was drinking more, becoming visibly affected by it, which we both know wasn't typical for Alix. That one time when Ilona spent the night, Alix was having nightmares and waking up screaming. That there was some kind of shift of focus happening in her work. None of that lands squarely in one column or the other. So the picture is as ambiguous and inconclusive as it ever was. But maybe by tomorrow I'll have some idea."

"Why's that?" Joyce snapped at her. Rachel recoiled at the intensity in the lawyer's voice and face.

"Because I'm going to meet with her psychotherapist. Turns out she started seeing this guy back last fall sometime. Joel Gibbs, I think you know him. Wasn't he defense expert in that sexual harassment case out of Northwest Airparts a few years back? You know, the guy who said that being thrown twenty feet off the ladder in the strut shop at Northwest Airparts wasn't traumatic? That one." She could hear noises of assent coming from Joyce as she looked down at her list for a moment. "He's the guy she was seeing. You've got to give it to her, Joyce, she stuck with her beliefs in everything. The guy's Dr. Cognitive-behavioral." Joyce raised her eyebrows slightly, signifying incomprehension. "They think it's all your thoughts—*je pense donc je suis miserable.*" Joyce, who spoke passable French, laughed at this twist on the old Descartian cliché. "I still have no idea what she was seeing him for. But he's a competent guy. He should have a pretty good handle on her state of mind. So my guess is that after I see him I'll have a better idea of which column she lands in."

Joyce was silent, a highly atypical state of affairs for the otherwise intensely verbal attorney. The news of a therapist seemed to be the most difficult for her to encompass, even harder than hearing about Ilona's status in Alix's life, Rachel thought. Her analysis was confirmed when Joyce began to speak.

"Alix in therapy. That I never would have surmised. I guess that one of the risks of commissioning this psychological autopsy is discovering that I didn't know her as well as I thought I did."

"Too right, my friend. This assessment is giving me a metaphor for Alix's life, Joyce, if it's any comfort to you. A series of non-interlocking boxes. She kept everything, and everyone, in their own box. And herself in the tightest one. Whatever was giving her nightmares, she refused to let Ilona know about it. Told her . . ."

Joyce finished the sentence. "What I don't know can't hurt her. Right?" Rachel nodded. "She said the same thing to me on more than one occasion. So I guess that this is just one of your boxes. I had no idea she was so troubled, none." Joyce shook her head, as if to shake off a fog. I just handed her another loss, Rachel thought to herself. Nice work, Katz. The attorney went on. "I had vaguely suspected that the grad student might have been another one of her lovers. She was Alix's type. Very feminine, very smart, all that."

Rachel knew that Joyce was talking about her own characteristics and held back from commenting.

"The other thing, Joyce. Ilona gave me the key to Alix's house and her alarm code. I just wanted to run it by you before I actually went in. I don't know what I might find, but you never know. Sniffing around, sometimes there's something in the air. Is that still OK with you?"

Joyce barely hesitated. "Of course. If it doesn't give you the creeps to be walking into the place where she died . . ." Her sentence trailed off, and her eyes teared up. She grabbed a tissue from a box on her desk and loudly blew her nose. Rachel kept a respectful silence, remembering the many times she'd had similar waves of emotion hit her at the most inopportune times. Joyce shook herself off again and rejoined the conversation. Her voice had the sound of a tight larynx, the result of tears pushed back.

"Yes. Go look at her house. Do you have the address?" Joyce used the banality of the transaction to bring herself back under control. Rachel had to admire Joyce. When she was that raw herself, she showed nothing resembling control. Joyce's skills at keeping a poker face, honed in the courtroom, served her well in her grief.

"It looks like it's somewhere over in Madrona, is that right?" Rachel prided herself on being able to tell the location of an address anywhere in Seattle from the street number and directional signs. Fortieth Avenue, an address in the mid-teens, signaled the old houses, lake and mountain views, and quiet elegance of the Madrona neighborhood. She had known that Alix lived in one of the expensive lakeside neighborhoods, Leschi or Madrona. That's why she was in Andrea's precinct, she reminded herself. Then she pushed aside her mind's tangle of tangents and refocused on the discussion.

"Yes, overlooking the lake. I never knew why she needed such an enormous place. You know, she bought it after she and what's-his-name split up. It's big enough for a family of ten. Which I should know." Joyce grimaced. Rachel knew that the lawyer had grown up in a huge Catholic family in the suburbs of Cleveland, where her father taught philosophy at a small Jesuit university. She had once told Rachel that she had almost ended up a nun before she had realized that "my lack of vocation for the sacrament of marriage had nothing to do with a vocation for the religious life, more a vocation for some of those very cute sisters in the religious life."

"I'll probably go over there after I see Gibbs, then. He's on Pill Hill," she noted, referring to the Seattle neighborhood one rise up from the downtown core that had more hospitals and medical offices than any of the other six parts of Seattle combined. "So I'll be on the other side of the Ship Canal already. I've already let one of the detectives know that I might be there, so we won't have to worry about arousing the cops."

Rachel hesitated before bringing up the next question. "Joyce, have you told Luanne yet? This is very odd, working with you on a matter that she knows you're keeping her out of. It has to be affecting you if it's affected me, which it has."

Joyce grimaced. "I know. I keep putting it off. Maybe this week sometime . . ."

Rachel nodded. "I hate to butt in, but it would help if I could deal normally with her. I think the longer you wait the angrier she'll be that you withheld from her."

Joyce nodded. Her face conveyed a resignation to the necessity of yet another painful task falling out of Alix Price's death. "I'll let you know when I tell her. Soon, I promise, soon. Maybe I can discuss how to do it in my session tomorrow with Alice." Joyce's tone turned slightly acid at the last remark, reminding Rachel of what a bitter pill it was for the attorney to find herself actually needing the services of a therapist.

The conversation ended in a round of appointment-setting for the next report meeting. Rachel collected a protesting Mr. Piggy from an equally reluctant Luanne and walked up Main to the lot where she had parked the Volvo. She sat in the car and went over her list again. The masseuse, she needed to call the masseuse.

Emma Forche's phone exchange put her somewhere in the same general area of town as Rachel's home, north of the Ship Canal, west of the freeway.

She noticed her aversion to making the contact and scolded herself for her unscientific attitude toward this part of the endeavor. Prejudiced, she told herself, she was prejudiced against this woman just because of how she makes her living. She, of the supposedly open mind. Rachel, scientist's daughter, had managed in her nearly thirty years on the West Coast to maintain her East Coast skepticism about massage and all the rest of the cornucopia of alternative health treatments that were everywhere available in Seattle. She had it filed in her brain along with herbs and aura reading, the kind of thing that no right-thinking person would do, even though several right-thinking people of her acquaintance did. In this last year she had flirted with the idea of getting a massage for herself, just to have some regular physical touch, but had managed to avoid it.

This classification scheme had conveniently ignored the reality that her beloved Cori went regularly to a psychic or that Alice and Liz saw something called a Hellerwork practitioner and had been furiously urging her to do the same since well before Sarah had died. So her friends partook of this *mishugass*, that didn't mean she had to. It felt like more of a stretch to imagine Alix Price going for massage, although the chronic pain made some sense of it. Rachel had never given much thought to the possibility that her own avoidance of all of this supposedly irrational stuff had anything to do with her tendencies to ignore her feelings and become numb to her body, two of the strategies that she had employed for years to cope with Sarah's withdrawal. She would call her when she got back to the office. No need for haste. The car's engine turned over, and woman and dog headed north toward Eastlake.

As expected, voice mail answered the call—a calm voice with what sounded like Bach playing in the background. At least it wasn't any of that New Age crap, Rachel thought. Bach was an encouraging sign. "Hello, Ms. Forche. My name is Dr. Rachel

Katz. I've been engaged by the estate of Alexandra Price to investigate her state of mind prior to her death." Rachel hesitated for a moment. What did one call the customers of a masseuse? She settled for the generic: "I understand she was a client of yours for a number of years. If you believe that you might have information that would assist me in this investigation, would you please call." She left her office number. No need to give out the cell number. But this was one more i to dot, and she was determined to do it.

She sat back in her chair after hanging up, and leaned back, looking at the sun that suddenly beamed in her office window. Should she call Anna? She had had the desire to reconnect all day long, and had pushed it aside with a combination of work and the fear that she would appear suddenly too eager after all of her talk of ambivalence. What if Anna's reaction to their encounter yesterday had been to realize that Rachel was too screwed up, running around at conferences having sex with women and getting nasty diseases? She went back over the details of the latter part of the evening in her mind, trying to find a hint of how Anna had really felt.

Oh, stop, she said to herself. She needed to stop being so bloody obsessive. Where were her clinical skills? She knew how Anna felt, and the only reason she didn't end up getting to see her custom-designed quilt was that she had conveniently saddled herself with an STD. All Rachel had to do was think about where Anna's lips had been. Rachel sighed with the return of arousal and a tingling in her breasts as she revisited Anna's lips playing over them. These were better reruns even than the encounter with Jo Ducey. There was something about Anna, all right. So call her, Rachel told herself, don't be one of these women sitting by the phone waiting for it to ring.

She punched in the number and this time was disappointed to get voice mail. After several weeks of chance encounters and real humans at the end of the phone, now of all times to get the recorded voice of Anna Sigurdson. She hesitated. She could not leave a message, and Anna would never have to know that she was

121

Chapter Nine

Joel Gibbs's office looked a lot like its occupant. Stark was Rachel's initial thought. Academic rather than clinical. She was perpetually curious about the insides of other psychologists' offices, believing that the décor and the location said something about the inhabitants. Sometimes her colleagues surprised her. A visit to the inner sanctum of an acquaintance who practiced fairly strict psychoanalysis yielded a treasure trove of art, the kind of intense sensory stimulus that she hadn't imagined would appear in the realm of strict boundaries and therapist reserve. Joel's office was in contrast austere, more what she would have expected from an analyst. His walls were beige, barely enlivened by black-and-white photographs hanging on a few of the walls. Even the rug on the floor was in earth tones, she observed. She thought to herself, oh well, people weren't coming here for art appreciation. At least everything was in impeccable taste. Maybe this was Joel's way of protecting his privacy.

"Joel, I really appreciate your taking the time to meet with me. I've been hoping you'll have the information I need to put this picture together, finally. I guess that I'm a little like the rest of the world, I somehow think that a person's therapist will know just enough more about them than even their nearest and dearest."

"I think you've come to the right place, Rachel." Joel seemed to preen. She was right, his needy little ego would sit up and beg for the kind of flattery she had just laid on. Oy, the man was so transparent. But so apparently eager to help, which was not completely what she had expected. His client had, after all, possibly killed herself. She would have expected at least a hint of defensiveness, particularly knowing Gibbs's reputation as someone who sparred with colleagues. But he seemed open, friendly, not what she had anticipated. She chided herself, not for the first time in the investigation, to put aside her preconceived notions and simply listen to what the man had to say.

"You know I'm doing a psychological autopsy on Alix, at the request of her personal rep, Joyce Romanski. You remember Joyce, she deposed you in that case a while back . . ." Rachel stopped short. She didn't want to remind the man of humiliating defeats. She watched carefully. Joel's color changed ever so slightly, but her apparent rapt attention to him did its work.

"Yes, I remember Ms. Romanski. A bit flashy, don't you think? Can't imagine why Alix chose her as the personal rep, but oh well. Not that we didn't talk about her will, mind you. Just that Ms. Romanski's name never came up during the time we worked together. I had no idea Alix even knew the woman, to be frank."

Rachel's ears perked up. Will-making was one of those things that suicidal people often did just before they knocked themselves off. Joel had to know it, but she decided to act as if this were an innocent passing remark. Risky to pounce too soon on the signs of any one hypothesis, she reminded herself. Premature cognitive commitment is always dangerous in an assessment, even more so when so much was at stake.

"Well, Joel, what can you tell me about Alix's therapy experience?" She deliberately kept her question vague and open-ended. Joel would talk about whatever he thought was important; she just had to give him a little free rein.

"As you know, Rachel, I'm an expert in the treatment of anxiety disorders. Even did a little presentation on it at the last Association of U.S. Behavior Therapists conference. On the same program with Beck." Rachel nodded, playing the part of the respectful colleague, all the while thinking yeah, right, probably in the same program book with the famous Aaron Beck, inventor of cognitive therapy, but on the same program? Ha. She turned her attention to Gibbs again, who seemed thrilled and pleased to have her as his audience.

"I had known Alix tangentially for many years. George Lewis, you know George, introduced us. George and I are old friends, we did our post-doc training together, did you know? When the Federation of Falsely Accused Parents was holding their conference two years ago I was one of the people who gave papers on the need for stricter controls over what therapists do. Terrible stuff, those recovered memory therapists. I hope I'm not hurting any feelings there, Rachel." His voice took on a snide tone. Rachel, simply because she worked with trauma and was able to document cases of actual delayed trauma recall, had been lumped into a category created by the FoFAP of recovered memory therapists. She thought it was all so much baloney, even though it had been the apparent impetus for Buddy Lincoln's picket brigade surrounding her office two years ago.

"Not at all, Joel. And you know, my feelings really aren't an issue here. I'm much more interested in your observations of Alix. You were, after all, the only clinically skillful person to get a close look at her before her death. Her colleagues and students are helpful, but they aren't practicing clinicians. And you are. You were her clinician." Rachel swallowed the urge to tell him what a self-important twit he was, and went back into her admiring colleague mode. After all, maybe the guy could genuinely help her with this autopsy. She would be grateful to him if he did have something useful to tell her that might tip the balance sheet into clarity from its current and chronic state of ambiguity. And this was all her countertransferential stuff anyway, she told herself. He reminded her too much of her father, which meant that she needed to back off. Gibbs went on.

"Alix knew that I was firmly in the empiricist camp as a clinician, and what my specialty is. So when she called me for therapy, I was pleased, albeit a bit surprised. After all, she seemed so high-functioning. But I was quite honored that she would consider me for treatment."

"When was this, Dr. Gibbs?"

"Oh, call me Joel. We're colleagues, after all, none of this formal stuff. I really want to help you with this, Rachel, be a collaborator as it were. Let's see, here's her chart. She started to see me in September 1999. And before you ask, I'm sorry, there aren't any notes. Alix immediately exercised her rights under our state Health Care Act to have no records of her sessions. She was an intensely private person and had no desire to create a paper trail of any kind."

Rachel sighed. The Uniform Health Care Information Act was a boon and a bane to mental health professionals in Washington State. It made life more simple in one direction, allowing mental health professionals to make emergency contact with other care providers and family members in case of a crisis in a client's life without going through the formalities of obtaining a signed release of information. But it also allowed clients to refuse note-taking for a session. For someone like Rachel, who had an excellent auditory memory and had always tended toward short session notes, this made little difference. But for many therapists who were used to taking notes as a session went on, it was maddening. And for herself in today's role it was a pain in the butt. She would have loved to have the notes. She would have to settle for Joel's recollections. Oh well, something would be better than nothing, she reminded herself. And it could be a very good something. He seemed to know his late client well.

"Can you tell me what she was coming to see you for?"

"Of course. You know, Alix had been working with FoFAP for several years, almost since its founding. Had become quite personally close to Georgina and Tim Gains, the people who started the group when their son accused them of such heinous crimes. Spent a lot of time with Buddy, you know, Buddy Lincoln, the local group coordinator. Heard so many devastating stories of families ripped apart by false accusations.

"Rachel, it finally got to her." Joel's eyes gleamed. With tears? Rachel wondered. Clearly he had strong feelings for his dead client. Which of course he would, she reminded herself. Any therapist would. "Alix never was clinically trained, didn't have the skills at detachment that you and I learned. Got quite overwhelmed. Began to have intrusive thoughts about what she was being told. Images of fathers being confronted in therapists' offices. Tormented her. Nightmares. Made it hard to do her work."

Rachel sat, mildly fascinated. In the field of trauma work, it was not uncommon for therapists and front-line workers to get something called "secondary post-traumatic stress disorder." Hearing too many stories of disaster and horror could cause nightmares, terrible thoughts and pictures in the mind's eye, sleep problems, the whole syndrome associated with the mind's response to terrible events. The empathy of a therapist could become the opening through which the images of their clients' trauma marched, those traumas becoming the therapist's own. Secondary PTSD was a serious problem in the trauma community. It caused seasoned, experienced people to drop out of the work because they were dreaming dreams of their client's rapes and beatings and combat experiences.

Could Alix have developed some kind of weird, twisted secondary PTSD from hearing the stories of people who claimed to be falsely accused of sexually abusing their children? It made some immediate intuitive sense to Rachel. Some of those people really had been falsely accused, even though she was fairly sure that the bulk of them were perpetrators hiding behind the convenient shield of a national movement. To be accused like that had to be traumatic. And Alix had indeed immersed herself in the FoFAP world, in just the way that trauma therapists might plunge themselves into the painful realities of survivor clients. Immersed herself more, given that she had no rules about boundaries to protect her.

"To make a long story short, she came to me because she knew that I could treat these obsessive symptoms." Rachel sighed inwardly again. Obsessive symptoms, right. Forget about the trauma component, of course. But hey, it was a legitimate way of thinking about it, she said to herself. Just because she was so enamored of trauma as a topic didn't mean that everyone else had to see things that way. She shut up her inner dialogue, ignoring the obsessional quality of her own responses, and nodded politely to Joel to go on.

"We started right in with exposure and response prevention. Are you familiar with those, Rachel?"

She was, but decided to feign a little ignorance in order to draw him out. "Not really, Joel. You know my interests haven't run in that direction. I'm more of an EMDR kind of shrink myself." She tossed off the letters signifying a powerful treatment for trauma symptoms, Eye Movement Desensitization Reprocessing. Its inventor, Francine Shapiro, had incurred the wrath of the behavior therapy world by developing something that worked like magic, even though no one was entirely sure how. Rachel was certain that Joel would be among those who looked down on EMDR, although she'd never heard his views on the subject. She hadn't been able to resist the little thrust.

"Oh, really?" Gibbs raised his voice and eyebrows. "I think I'd heard that. I don't know much about it, except what Zona and Perlmutter have to say." He let drop the names of well-known behavior therapists who were staunch opponents of the technique. "So I guess I'll have to explain to you what I was doing with Alix."

"Yes, please, Joel. That will help me quite a lot." Rachel thought to herself that she couldn't tell who was the worse fake in the room, Joel Gibbs with his growing bombast and self-importance, or herself, pretending ignorance of a topic she was quite familiar with. But whatever works, she thought.

"The idea is that when people have obsessive thoughts, they begin to try to stop from having them. So they start to avoid the things that they imagine bring the thoughts on, try to avoid having the thoughts and push them out of their minds. Eventually a person's whole life comes to revolve around avoiding the obsession. Which then can lead to compulsive behaviors, which can be quite debilitating. It's a terrible disorder, OCD is. Vastly misunderstood."

Rachel noticed that as he warmed to his topic, Joel relaxed, became more open. The bombast gave way to engagement. She could detect a strong vein of genuine compassion when he spoke about people suffering from obsessive compulsive disorder, or OCD. Public understanding of the disorder had improved greatly in the wake of an award-winning movie in which Jack Nicholson had brilliantly portrayed an OCD sufferer. But many of the symptoms made people as unlikable and difficult to handle as the movie character had been, and for most of the lay public, compassion wore out quickly to be replaced by annoyance. Joel, on the other hand, seemed to truly relate to the pain of obsessive-compulsive disorder. There weren't many therapists who had the patience to work with highly obsessive people. Maybe there were deeper layers to Joel Gibbs that she had never been able to imagine.

"So the goals of treatment are twofold, really." Joel went on with his lecture, clearly in his element now. "First to teach the person to tolerate the obsessive thought. That's the exposure component. We do this in a number of ways, largely through helping people to learn to relax and breathe deeply when the obsessions occur. We also do some mindfulness work. To learn to simply observe the thought, without judging it or fleeing from it."

Rachel nodded. Trauma treatment also used exposure therapy at times. One of the experts whose name Gibbs had dropped earlier had famously developed highly effective exposure therapies for women who'd been raped. The therapies were tough work for the client, requiring repeated reliving of the trauma until the experience lost its emotional edge and became simply another chapter in life's book, but they could make a world of difference to the trauma survivor. Learning to encounter the facts of the trauma in a safe and supportive environment until the huge emotional arousal of terror went down could make a genuine difference for sufferers of post-trauma problems. She began to feel a grudging respect for Gibbs. He seemed to really know his topic area, and she always admired competence.

"The response prevention component is a little trickier with obsessions that don't involve well-developed compulsions. In Alix's case, beginning to avoid certain things and situations. For example, stopped wearing her cologne. Said that being reminded of her father had become too painful in light of all the grieving fathers she was dealing with. Started to pull back on work. Refused a bunch of court cases. Was really cutting into her income."

Rachel, listening, noticed that something was different in how Joel was speaking. What was it? She attended closely and finally hit on it. When he spoke about his work, or the model of therapy, or anything except Alix Price, Gibbs used complete sentences. But when it came to Alix, the pronoun referring to her dropped out. The sentences lacked an actor. Odd. Maybe it was too painful for him to talk about his dead client. Perhaps he had to work to have some emotional distance from Alix. He had seemed to like her quite a lot. She decided that she was the one being obsessive-compulsive, and dropped the matter.

"So we were also focusing on trying to get her to bring those behaviors and some others she was dropping out back into her repertoire." Phew, thought Rachel, a pronoun at last. She was making a big deal out of nothing.

"Working on getting the full range of behaviors back. Took an unexpected turn for the worse at the end of the year. Went for a family reunion of some kind, people nasty to her. All this stuff about families breaking up got going again. So I suggested that we do some longer sessions, perhaps some in vivo work."

"You know, Joel, I had been wondering about that. I noticed in her appointment book that her sessions with you were getting longer and longer. And it kind of made sense that this might represent some sort of in vivo. Knowing that you're such a strong proponent of exposure modalities."

"Yes, precisely. I advised her that we could speed the process up by increasing the exposure and having her practice it in session with me, rather than simply imagining the things she was avoiding. So we upped the session times. It was urgent to get her back to her work. So many families being hurt, and her not able to help them as long as this was going on. Started feeling more hopeless in February."

"Who did?" Rachel interjected. This no-pronoun thing was getting a little confusing.

"Alix. You know, her, she did." Joel seemed a bit flustered at being interrupted mid-monologue. "Started to feel more hopeless. Normal part of treatment, that symptoms get a little worse before they remit. I told her so, tried to normalize it for her. Didn't believe it, began to get depressed, too. So I did some cognitive therapy for depression with her in addition to the exposure and response prevention for the OCD. I also referred her back to her primary care physician for some medication."

"Did you know that she was also taking quite a large dose of pain meds, Joel?" Rachel was curious about the absence in Gibbs's monologue of any reference to Alix's chronic pain.

"You know, to be honest Rachel, no. As I said, Alix was a very private person. Mentioned that when these obsessions happened, started to feel an increase in neck pain. I thought that this was simply a sign of increased muscle tension, it's pretty common among people with OCD. So I assumed that if we got to the root of the problem, that the tension would decrease. Didn't tell me that she was on pain medication. What was she taking?"

"It's not that important. Just curious, is all. I imagine it's your usual practice to obtain information about the medications a client is taking. It's like one of my grad school profs said, before you do psychotherapy, you need to be sure that what you're treating isn't being caused by some chemicals being prescribed by the idiot on the other side of town. With all due respect to physicians, mind you. They just don't think very much about psychological side effects of things. Makes our job harder."

"As you know, Rachel"—Gibbs's tone grew a shade more frosty—"you can't know what your clients won't tell you. And she didn't tell me."

"Oh. So it must have come as quite a shock to hear about it, huh?" Rachel worked hard to make her tone as conciliatory as possible. This couldn't be easy for him.

"It? You mean her suicide?" Gibbs was taken aback by the question.

"No, I mean her taking pain meds. And let me rewind here for a minute. You said suicide. Sounds like you're pretty sure that that's what it was. Why?"

Gibbs's face fell; his breathing became slightly ragged. He was visibly upset. Poor guy, thought Rachel. This has to be so painful for him. No one loses a client this way without having it strike a blow to self-esteem. And he apparently cared about Alix as a good therapist should. He had to be grieving her in his own way. His voice became full of emotion.

"Why am I sure? Because when I look back over that last month, I can see some signs that I might have paid more attention to. I wish, oh, I wish I had. As I said, she was more symptomatic. Kept making these remarks about wishing she could just get out of this pain. Didn't sound serious, brushed me aside when I tried to probe. Talked about revising her will, giving money to FoFAP, 'just in case something happens to me' is how she put it. But when I asked her if we had any reason to worry about her doing something foolish, she told me not to worry, that she had faith in this treatment. Had read all the research, knew it would work in time, just had to apply herself to it. I did confront her about what she was saying. I guess I shouldn't have believed her, Rachel. I feel so sad about this all."

By the end of his recitation, Rachel thought she could detect tears in Gibbs's eyes. The pieces were certainly falling into place.

Terrible chronic pain, painfully mounting call-them-what-you-will obsessions or intrusive thoughts, hopelessness and increased depression, a tendency toward too much booze, and worst of all, easy access to lethal pills. Alix Price could well have killed herself.

"And you know, Rachel," Gibbs went on, interrupting her tallying up of the internal spreadsheet, "something I didn't think much about until after her death. Her father was a suicide."

Rachel sat up in her chair. One of the biggest predictors of a suicidal person's lethality was the suicide of a parent. She had talked at least half a dozen women out of taking this step when she was practicing by reciting this statistic and asking them if they wanted to sentence their own child to such a fate. Why in the hell hadn't Joel Gibbs thought about that, for goodness sake? Then she scolded herself, thinking she should have some empathy for the guy, for heaven's sake. It was too easy to second-guess in a situation like this. He was helping her, for crying out loud. She leaned toward him, oozing empathy and sympathy.

"I know what you're probably thinking, Rachel. That I should have given more weight to that factor. Well you know, working with anxiety disorders, I don't see many people who are lethally suicidal. I'm just not as up on this stuff as some people are. My clients are generally high-functioning folks. Plus, it's not like I'm especially focused on people's life histories. I'm pragmatic, I just want to know about the symptoms and how we can relieve them. She only mentioned it in passing, after that awful family reunion.

"After she died, I ran a lit search and a whole bunch of things popped out at me. Her father's suicide was one of them. Didn't know if the pain was particularly bad, but that certainly had to be a factor. That talk about making her will. I just thought it was good sense, she had made a bundle in tech stocks and didn't have any heirs, so of course it was a good time to get her affairs in order, and who better to discuss it with than your therapist, I suppose. She flew so much in her work, you never know what will happen to you. I guess she knew a couple of the people who died in that plane crash, so I thought that was the catalyst for the will talk."

Rachel nodded in assent. Seattle had been terribly shaken by the crash of an Aleutian Airways plane off the California coast. Almost everyone on board had lived in the Seattle area. A couple of the dead had been faculty at the university It would make sense that this had gotten Alix thinking about wills. If she had been the therapist, she might have made precisely the same interpretation and missed completely the possibility that this was another step toward suicide as the only choice available. And if you didn't think much about suicidality, you might not have thought that those crash deaths were another stone in the bag around Alix Price's neck, pulling her further into the waters. Rachel felt a genuine, unforced rush of sympathy for Joel Gibbs. Pretty clearly, he'd done his own version of the psychological autopsy and realized what he had missed. That had to be painful for a therapist. And she had to admire his honesty and integrity. He could have left all these details out, after all.

"Joel, do you think there's any chance this was an accident? That maybe she just miscalculated what she was taking that night?"

"I've thought about that a lot, Rachel." Gibbs appeared almost a parody of a man thinking, his brow furrowed. "She was a pretty careful person, not sloppy. It doesn't seem to fit her. I guess I'd rather it were an accident, but there are so many factors here, not just the ones we've talked about. She was really afraid of losing her professional identity if she continued to be unable to deal with this topic. So that was another piece that I think fits into the suicide picture. And oh, yes, there was something that happened at her family reunion, did I mention that?"

"I'm not sure you went into the details. Could you tell me about that?"

"Apparently one of her cousins was ragging on her about her involvement in FoFAP. The woman was one of those recovered memory harpies, claimed that she'd been abused and that Alix was hurting people. Screamed at her, Alix told me, right in the midst of the family. And it seemed that people were siding with this woman against Alix. She told me that she felt like she'd landed on an alien planet. Here she thought that her relatives would be proud of her for her work, saving so many other families from heartbreak, and all they wanted to do was hassle her."

"Sounds like she experienced quite a lot of losses." Rachel was beginning to think that she had all the picture she needed. There were now many more points in the suicide column of the spreadsheet than in the accident side. It seemed like such a relief to see some clarity emerging from the muck and fog of Alexandra Price's last months of life. Pain, multiple losses, depression, hopelessness, making a will. All seemed to add up. Although there was still the nagging question of why kill herself? Why, if she had so much support from so many people, had Alix Price just given up? The woman had seemed so persistent, so energized. Maybe the prospect of being unable to continue in her crusade had been larger than Rachel could imagine. Ultimately, most suicides were mysteries, because the survivors could always see options that were invisible to the tunnel vision of the actively suicidal person.

"OK, let me play devil's advocate with you for a minute, Joel."

"Nothing would please me more, Rachel. If someone could convince me that this was all a terrible accident, I'd still mourn her loss, but at least I wouldn't blame myself for missing the clues."

"All right. You think all of these pieces add up to suicide. But she had plans for her life. Her research assistant found her because she was going to meet the woman for breakfast and never showed up. She was set for two symposia in the next month, and there are at least half a dozen court cases that she had taken on, some she was already in the middle of. Would the Alix Price you knew, and I did too, abandon all that in midstream just because she hurt so much? She seemed a lot more resilient than that."

Gibbs frowned, as if in concentration. "Hmmm, that does make some sense in support of the other hypothesis. But I don't think anyone else saw her as I did, in tears, telling me that she just couldn't make herself do this exposure treatment, even if she knew that without it she would never get better, never go on with her life. No one else knew how painful this was for her. That's what convinced me, all other things being equal." He sighed, his face fallen.

"Joel, this has been extremely helpful." Rachel began to think that she had enough information. It had been nearly an hour.

"I'm so glad to be of help. If there's anything else I can do, please let me know."

"If you can think of anyone else I should interview, that would be helpful. Let me tell you who I've talked to so far." She listed the names of George Lewis and several other faculty from the university, Ilona, and the woman who had been Alix's personal trainer. "Oh, yeah, and I've got a call in to the masseuse that she was seeing, Emma somebody." She looked down at her list. "Emma Forche. Ilona Hegevary seemed to think that she would be a good person to talk to, although what she can add at this point I have no idea. We've been playing phone tag about when to meet."

"I never heard her mention this massage person. Everyone else is familiar to me. Seems like it would be a massive waste of your time to talk to someone who you know isn't going to have much to say. Why bother with a dead end? If you give me a little time, I'm sure I can come up with some much more productive people for you to talk to, if you really think that will be necessary. I'd really like to help."

"You know, Joel, I sort of think that it'll be a waste, but I'm going to do it anyway. Interview that massage person, that is. I guess I'm a little OC myself." He laughed politely at this statement. "I just can't complete a task until I'm sure that I've covered all the bases. Ilona, her research assistant, was pretty close to Alix, she worked with her every day, and she was the one who came up with this name. Frankly, on my own I wouldn't have thought to pursue that lead. But I'd love to hear your ideas about other people to talk to."

"I'll see if I can remember the names of any of her family members. Maybe they'll have some ideas. Maybe she said something about killing herself to them when they ganged up on her. And I think you should seriously consider interviewing Buddy Lincoln. He was like a father to her."

The notion of intentionally having contact with Buddy Lincoln made Rachel want to wipe the imaginary slime from her body. But he's right, she said to herself. One doesn't get to choose who's in the life of the person one's autopsying. She took a deep breath and realized that there was something nagging at her by its absence. Alix, the woman with many lovers. Where were they in this equation? Rachel berated herself for having neglected to follow this line of inquiry earlier and pushed forward. "One more thing, Joel. Did she tell you anything about relationships? Anyone she was involved with?"

Gibbs smirked, jarring her. Or at least she thought it was a smirk. Maybe this was how he smiled. "I suppose you knew that Alix was a woman of a very open mind where sex was concerned. Terrible that so many people judged her for it. Sexism, I say. A man can do it, but a woman is supposed to be in love. Well, no need to lecture you about sexism, I imagine." Rachel wearily nodded her head. What a wonderful cover for sexual compulsivity, clinging to the banner of equal opportunity to behave stupidly. She refocused on Gibbs, who hadn't noticed her shift in attention, so taken was he with his own narrative.

"She mentioned that she was seeing Ivan Lindsay from time to time." Gibbs dropped the name of a local criminal defense attorney, infamous for his theatrical appearance and his highly creative courtroom strategies. Alix had been an expert witness for him on several occasions, Rachel knew from her friends in the prosecutor's office, testifying that crime victims could never accurately identify their attackers.

"Didn't I read in the *Times* that he just got married to Susan Conners?" Rachel asked. The latter was the anchor of one of the local evening news shows, blond and elegant. The wedding had been local gossip, given that both parties had been married to other people until quite recently.

"Well, I had wondered if his sudden decision to choose that

Conners woman had something to do with her suicide," Gibbs said. "They got married just a few days before she died, didn't they?"

Rachel did the calculation in her head. She would have to check to be certain, but if this were true, it might be a case of a last straw falling on Alix's head. Even a woman who didn't believe in commitment or forever might feel jilted and humiliated when her lover very publicly married a different woman. Especially when that woman was feeling depressed and experiencing a mountain of loss already. It didn't seem entirely likely, given Alix, but suicide was funny. Sometimes the oddest things constituted that final straw.

"But otherwise, no, not much I know about her relationships. As I said, that wasn't the focus of treatment. We don't wander all over the map wasting people's time in this approach, you know." Gibbs's self-satisfied dig at long-term therapy missed its mark. As Rachel thought to herself that at least she knew who was important in her clients' lives, Gibbs interrupted her self-congratulatory and defensive reverie. "I tell you what, Rachel. Why don't you let me know when you're going to meet with this massage person. We could get together afterward and go over what you've got. I'd really like to help resolve this for everyone."

Rachel hesitated for a moment. It wasn't the usual way to do a psychological autopsy, to include one of the witnesses in the process of adding up the numbers. After all, everyone in the dead woman's life had some investment in the outcome. But Joel Gibbs was a special case. He was a colleague, even if not a close one. He knew a lot about Alix Price, as well he should. She admonished herself to not freeze him out of the process just because she hated the way his voice sounded. He was a psychologist and Alix's therapist. He could help. It wasn't going to kill her to work with him.

"Fine, Joel. That's really sweet of you to volunteer yourself in this way. Not many folks would be so forthcoming. I tell you what. Once I've got a time pinned down with Emma Forche, I'll let you know. Then maybe we can plan to put our heads together once I've had the chance to sit down and carefully go over all the data.

Oh, yes, and one other thing. Do you have any idea where Alix could have come into a large stash of barbiturates?"

Gibbs was visibly shaken by the question. "What do you mean, a large stock of barbs? What does that have to do with anything?" His tone became truculent, almost aggressive. It was another jarring change. He must have been surprised, Rachel thought. Some people get aggressive when they're surprised, she reminded herself.

"The tox report from the medical examiner's office says that along with a very high blood alcohol and a huge dose of opioids, which I'm going to assume are her prescription pain meds, she was also full of downers when she died. I've been through her prescription records, and there's no sign of anything that even has a barbiturate content. So for the life of me I can't puzzle out where she might have come by that. I thought you might have heard something."

"You know, come to think of it . . ." Gibbs pondered the question. "Most people didn't know this, but she had a cat that she just loved to death. Cat had a seizure disorder. Maybe she had phenobarb from the vet? Just a guess."

Rachel felt another puzzle piece fall into place. She'd had to give the same medicine to one of the dogs who preceded Mr. Piggy. It was human quality stuff. Vets got it when it was past the expiration date for humans, but that didn't mean that it wasn't a barbiturate and that, in combination with the rest of the toxic cocktail Alix had swallowed, it wouldn't add to the deadly nature of the mixture. Taking her cat's phenobarb could in no way be classified as a mistake. That had to be purposeful.

"Whoever would have thought to look at her cat's pharmacy records, huh? I didn't even know she had a cat, Joel. I'm actually going over to her house tomorrow, to do a walk-through. I suppose if I'd done that earlier I'd have run across the pill envelope from the vet myself. But this is very helpful. You're a veritable font of information. Just what I had hoped."

Gibbs smiled. He seemed pleased, but nervous. Rachel decided that it was really time to get out the door. She was beginning to go into information overload herself, a good place to call things to a halt. "Listen, Joel, you have my number if anything comes up. And I'll give you a buzz about getting together once I've scheduled this meeting with Emma Forche. Thanks again so much for your assistance. I'm going to ask Joyce Romanski if the estate will reimburse you for your time. After all, this was a professional relationship you had, not a personal one."

"Ha-ha, yes indeed. Not personal. You know, Rachel, it's one of the nice things about being a behaviorist. We know that there's nothing to this transference clap-trap, that therapy is just a business transaction aimed at helping people change their actions. So I'd appreciate that."

Rachel was bothered by what felt like the gratuitous nature of Gibbs's last remark. What did transference, or the lack of it, have to do with their discussion? It felt as if Gibbs were trying to score one last point before she headed out the door. Too bad. She had almost started to like and respect the guy, even feel some sympathy for his loss of Alix, and then he had to go and sneak in a dig about something that he knew, heck, every therapist within shouting distance knew, was a pet peeve of hers. Oh, well. She wasn't doing the psychological autopsy to win friends and influence people, she reminded herself. She was here to find out what happened to Alix. Stick to the task, Katzie, she said to herself.

"Thanks so much." Rachel rose and walked toward the door, followed by Joel Gibbs. She left, closing the door behind her.

Chapter Ten

"So then he sat there going on about what a wonderful behavior therapist he was and how he didn't have to deal with transference. My God, Alice, the man is practically a parody of himself."

Rachel Katz and Alice Goldstone were sitting around the fake fireplace at The Bungalow, one of Rachel's favorite underappreciated neighborhood joints. It was easy to miss if you didn't know what it was, perched above a busy main street in a renovated old home. Although ironically the place specialized in wine, leading Alice to joke that they were probably the only devotedly non-wine-drinking customers ever to come through the door, the appetizers were tasty and large enough to make a meal, especially for Rachel's shrunken stomach. She munched contentedly on sheep cheese, redolent of smoke and grass, while conducting a postmortem on her encounter with Joel Gibbs. Alice knew Joel better than Rachel, having interned together with him, and held him in somewhat lower regard than Rachel did.

"I'm a little troubled by one thing you said, Rache," Alice interjected. "You know, that bit about how he did a lit search on suicide because he doesn't encounter it very much?"

"Yeah, what about it? Seemed like his own obsessive-compulsiveness in action to me, what's the deal?"

"Well, I don't think it's true, the bit about not having experience with suicide. Maybe he feels embarrassed about this, but I've heard from a couple of folks that he's had a run of clients completing suicides. Let's see, what did Leona tell me?" Alice crinkled her forehead, eyes darting up. Leona Adams was one of the other therapists in Alice's group. She did a practice that overlapped anxiety disorders and substance abuse, helping people who'd started to use drugs and alcohol to calm the terrors within switch to less lethal and more legal antianxiety compounds. Like Joel Gibbs, she was something of a cognitive behaviorist, because, as she had once told Rachel over tea at a conference, "it works. And heck, I'm a pragmatic sort." This line, Rachel reflected, seemed to be in the explanatory repertoire of all cognitive behaviorists.

"So what did she tell you already?" Rachel felt impatient and curious.

"What she told me is that he had a woman client kill herself about two years ago. And that at the time, she'd heard a rumor about another one somewhere a few years before that. I remember her saying that it was a little unusual in an anxiety disorders practice, but apparently not unheard of with really severe OCD. So I wonder why he did that shtick with you about not knowing about it."

Rachel paused and considered. That was odd. For a colleague to purposely disclaim knowledge of a topic that was almost of universal concern among therapists was strange and had struck her so at the time Gibbs said it. But what to make of this odd prevarication, she had no idea and not much energy for considering what the explanations might be. She decided to default to her newfound sympathy for Joel Gibbs.

"Maybe the poor guy is feeling a bit red in the face about it. I mean, jeez, Alice, three completed suicides in your practice? That's a lot. Even the borderline experts don't get as many casualties as that. Maybe he ought to look into believing in transference. Something in the nuances of what his clients are telling him that seems to be going over his head."

"Or probably banging up against his thick skull. Rachel, I swear to you, this man is so thick. Smart, you know, he had to be to get into grad school, but thick. Oy veh. He's as concrete as, well, I don't know, as concrete as concrete. Metaphors desert me."

"So anyhow, even with all of his pompous crap, he did manage to shake loose a few more useful data bits." Rachel was trying to give the man his due. He had helped to fill in the picture pretty well. "Poor Alix was a lot more of a mess than any of us gave her credit for. And to have Joel Gibbs for your therapist, that's got to be the slimy icing on the poison cake. But you know I actually felt sorry for the poor *schmendrick* at the end. He's hurting just like anyone would. So maybe not as concrete as all that."

Alice shook her head. "So enough of Joel the non-magnificent. I hear that you and Anna had a hot date last week. Tell, *bubbeleh*. Your beeg seester vants to hear all the sordid details." Alice reverted to her fake mittel-European accent, trying to make the topic a little lighter for her friend.

Rachel blushed. The memory of her evening with Anna was still a source of pleasure, but she was nonplussed by how far she'd let things go. And this after her determination to stick to just going out to dinner. "Well, we went out. And we went back to her house. And we made out. The end."

"What do you mean, the end? Excuse me, I've been married for a long time now." At this the two women broke into peals of laughter. "I deserve to have a little harmless titillation in my boring old life. So give, girl, give. Ve heve vays uf making you talk."

"Fine, all right. Here's the punch line. I succumbed to a full-court press by Jo Ducey at the SPST meeting." Alice groaned. She knew and did not approve of JoAnn Ducey, largely because she had dated her briefly herself when they were both in grad school in Boston. Part of Alice's motivation to intern in Seattle was to put as much distance as possible between herself and her former girl-friend. "So I didn't insist on latex, and she gave me a nasty case of a nasty bug. Trich, to be precise."

"Rachel!" Alice's voice rose in alarm. "That creep, how could she do that to you? I will kill her, truly I will. Anyone who messes with you is toast, serious whole-grain bread toast."

"Calm down, Alice. Look, it's not her fault. She was asympto-matic, she had no idea. And I didn't do anything to protect myself. So anyhow, I'm taking Flagyl." Alice wrinkled her nose in mock disgust. "And obviously, I'm not having sex with anyone. Or at least I thought as long as I was defining sex as below the waist, I wasn't having it with anyone."

Rachel paused. She felt shy all of a sudden. Why was it so hard to tell her closest friend about what had happened with Anna? She had gone on, in detail and at length, about the end of sex in her relationship with Sarah, and both of them had traded details of their sexual adventures when they were younger. So what was the problem? She took a deep breath.

"Anyhow, Anna invited me back to her house after dinner to see photos of her former dog. And I don't know, we got there and she just, well, how do I say this. She acted like I was the juiciest tidbit she'd laid eyes on in ages and like she was a starving person. So we made out. Stayed above the waist. Not that that made a bit of dif-ference. Apparently, my breasts have become a major erogenous zone. Alice, she's good. Really good, it's scary how good she is. Like she walked right out of my fantasies. And it's not just the sex. It's the person. We talked a lot before we got to her house, and she's walking right into my heart. It's scary. I'm not, really not ready to fall for anyone again. I don't know if I'll ever be ready, my heart got so hurt by Sarah, for years before she died she hurt my heart. Anna feels dangerous to me."

"Dangerous?" Alice's voice rose in tone. "Tell me about that, *bubbeleh*."

"She feels too much like the possible real thing. She's smart, she's sober, and if what happened the other night is a preview of coming attractions, she's sexual dynamite. She seems to have a good soul. And that, my dear friend, is dangerous. I could fall for her, and then what happens? Then my nice safe retreat inside myself is like the houses of the three little pigs, blown all down. Makes me want to run as fast as possible in the other direction."

Alice's demeanor softened as she listened to her friend. She knew that Rachel was telling a painful truth. It hadn't been easy for Rachel to allow Sarah into her life when they first met. She had always been skittish about intimacy and vulnerability, a lasting legacy of growing up with an emotionally shut-down mother and an angry, critical father. In some ways, Sarah's emotional and sexual withdrawal had been easy on Rachel because they allowed her to hole herself up in the world of her work and the less emotionally laden, and thus less threatening, relationships with her friends.

"Hey, kiddo, I know. And that's a part of why Liz and I are pushing you. I know that you'll stay alone and sad for the rest of your life just because it's easier not to make yourself so visible. You could do a lot worse than Anna, you know."

"I do know. Which paradoxically makes it harder. If I allow her to keep pursuing me, then I allow her to really see me, to know me. And she's someone I could take pretty seriously. Come to love. And there lies so much pain. Oh, Alice, this is so bloody complex. So much easier to just work. Or to dish the dirt about the likes of Joel Gibbs."

Alice sighed. Her friend was a piece of work sometimes. She loved Rachel and worried about her. "Listen, Rachel. Just stay in the present for a moment. You know, the here and now, that thing we're always telling our clients about? You don't know what'll happen with Anna. Or whether falling in love with her will inevitably hurt. All you know right now is—what?"

Rachel shivered and hugged herself as if to ward off a blow. "I know that I feel incredibly attracted. That when I see her I want to smile and then flee in whatever the opposite direction might be. That spending time with her was fun, inexplicably. That talking with her both soothes and excites me."

145

"So that's all you need to know. I think it's time to do a refresher course in mindfulness work." Alice grinned at her friend. Mindfulness meditation was exactly what she and other trauma specialists prescribed for their clients. She knew that this comment would annoy Rachel enough that she might just get off her stuck place and do something to change her emotional life. Rachel grimaced, then stuck her tongue out at her friend.

"Whatever. Anyhow, don't you want to hear some more about Alix Price? I'm going to get to look over her house in a couple of days. See if there's anything that'll tip the balance for me one way or the other. Although after talking to Joel, I think that I know what I'll find."

"You know, I'm a little bored with Alix. Can we talk about someone else? A live person. You, maybe, or me? Your sister-in-law, my nephews, anyone about whom I don't have more than mixed feelings? I've done my fair share of hearing about the late Alix in the last couple of weeks, dontcha know?"

"Oh, yeah." Rachel was silent for a moment. She guessed that Joyce had finally come out with who the mystery woman was. She decided to stop making Alice's life complicated here. "Sure, I'll be glad to talk about more appetizing topics. Would you like to hear about the latest in adolescent angst, Katz family version?"

The conversation subsided into the more commonplace territory of nieces and nephews, with Rachel regaling Alice with the tales of her sixteen-year-old niece Zelda's latest forays into early heterosexuality. As they talked Rachel was aware of being slightly detached, observing herself participate in the exchange while her mind continued to play over the question of Anna Sigurdson. The terrible truth about being a therapist was that it allowed her a carefully titrated dose of something that resembled intimacy. It had always been just enough that it sustained her without threatening her façade. She had always known it, had struggled with it, and then as the relationship with Sarah had gone cold, had resigned herself to it, prizing stability and inertia over the risk of pain and loss. And then she got pain and loss anyway, she chided herself. Like she'd told a zillion clients, there is no way to control life enough to protect oneself against that. Even bargaining away passion and intimacy didn't work in the end.

She was still wrapped in her inner self-scrutiny when she and Alice hugged good-bye with promises to share a ride to synagogue the next morning since Liz had a weekend class to attend and couldn't join them. The sounds and smells of 45th Street were only barely at the edge of her consciousness. In the distance, the freeway gave off a noise like a quiet ocean. She was content with life as it was, with the quiet routine of walking the dog to the corner bakery in the mornings, with doing a little work here and there. Sarah's death had left her richer financially, the beneficiary of a hefty life insurance policy even after she had donated large chunks of it to charity. Work was optional if money was the sole consideration. But it was non-optional as her protection against the possibility of a new relationship. She could become a very wealthy solitary woman.

The caller ID was lit up when she arrived home. Three "private" calls. One from Joel Gibbs. Curious, she thought, in light of the evening's revelations. The dial tone was stuttering. She toyed with just leaving it all there until the morning. It was one of those how-could-you-be-so-bloody-obsessive moments that came to the fore later on when it was the middle of the night. She dialed in her code.

One message from Anna, asking if they could get together sometime soon. "I hope I didn't scare you off, Rachel Katz. That's the last thing I want to do. So call me, e-mail me, communicate, I don't care how. I want to see you again." Rachel stood balancing glee and perplexity. Did this woman know what she was getting herself in for?

There was no second personal message, just Gibbs's grating voice. "Hello Rachel. Just checking in, wondering if you've set up a time with the massage woman yet. Call me back when you have a chance."

Rachel was drawn to put a new spin on Gibbs's alacrity to be helpful. If he really had had so many suicides among his clients, perhaps his attempts to offer something to her were a part of working through whatever feelings of guilt and loss he would have had. She decided to be a little more charitable with Joel Gibbs, the poor man. She dialed back and left a message on his voice mail to the effect that she and Emma Forche were playing phone tag and thanking him again for his assistance.

The third call was a surprise. Luanne Barnes, sounding stiff and tight and uncomfortable. "Rachel, I think I need to speak with you about something related to your investigation in the death of Dr. Price. Please call me as soon as you can." She left a home phone number in the 253 area code, the southern suburbs of Seattle. Rachel dialed it, but no one answered, so she left a message in return. Joyce must have come clean, she mused, but why did Lu want to talk to her? She would have to wait to satisfy her curiosity.

Later she sat curled in her overstuffed chair, a deep purple fleece throw hugged around her shoulders, the dog a comforting weight in her lap. This wasn't so bad, she told herself. Her house was quiet and pleasant. She had Mr. Piggy for body contact. Why subject herself to the messy, murky, emotional morass that was intimacy? She decided not to call Anna back yet. She fell asleep over her mystery novel.

Going back to synagogue on Saturday felt odd. It had been almost a month since the end of official mourning, and Rachel, with a little help from the ghost of Alix Price, had managed to make herself too busy and too preoccupied elsewhere during that month. It was as if *schul* had become so enmeshed with the experience of Sarah's death that it was no longer the comforting, safe home that it had been for her. Good thing that Alice nudged her to come, she thought, waiting for the latter to drive by and pick her up. It was ten minutes past the appointed time, so Rachel knew she had another five or so to wait. She wandered, desultory, through her house, straightening up things, shifting piles of mail. She thought about calling Anna that afternoon. Maybe a little safe outdoors something, like a dog walk? That would keep their hands off each other.

The sound of steps coming up to her front porch brought her out of her reverie. "I'm here, I'm here," Alice's voice sounded through the door. "So come on, already, we're late."

Rachel quickly kissed the dog on the nose, cued the alarm system, and ran out the door. "Of course we're late, Alice. You're driving, so we're late, so what else is not new under the clouds," she teased. "Just please don't drive any faster to make up for it, OK? It's not like *schul* is a therapy appointment."

In fact, Rachel mused as the car headed over into the Ravenna neighborhood where their synagogue was situated, Alice's free and easy use of the concept of time was right at home in synagogue. People attending Congregation Or Chadash wandered in during various parts of the service, left to have conversations outside in the hall, and in general tolerated huge individuality in the ways in which people engaged in their devotions. There were a few parts of the service that were well-marked for group participation, but this New Age Jewish renewal congregation resembled the Orthodox *shteibels* of New York more than it did the polite suburban Conservative congregation in which Rachel had grown up. It figured, Rachel thought. Half of us are refugees from those *shteibels*, and the rest are boomeranging back into Jewish life from flirtations with atheism, Hare Krishna, and Trotsky. She liked the free-form nature of things there. It loosened her up, got her outside of herself enough to look at things larger than her day-to-day life. Since one of the group activities was a silent meditation, it also forced her to slow down and pay attention in a setting where no one was available to distract her.

Driving into the parking lot, Alice was chatting away about her latest call home to her parents, who had just returned from a cruise. "You know, if I didn't know those two were in their eighties, I'd swear they were younger than me. They play so well together."

Rachel grinned, warmed by the energy of Alice's description of her parents. Sol and Frieda Goldstone had become parental figures to all of Alice's close friends. Happily retired from their careers as New York City schoolteachers and embarked on their second careers as travelers and Democratic Party activists, they were the kind of energetic, socially engaged old people that Rachel hoped she would herself become. Missing a mother, and with a father who had permanently cut her out of his life for the sin of being a lesbian, Rachel glommed onto other people's parents, hungry for that kind of unconditional love.

"It's not like you don't take after them, kiddo. You and Liz do that playing thing very nicely yourselves."

"Yah, yah, but we take ourselves so seriously sometimes. Those two, well, they've always been able to find themselves funny. I guess that was a good thing . . ."

Rachel broke in. "You mean, considering how they made their livings?" The elder Goldstones had worked in the toughest of ghetto schools, committed to bringing to the latest generation of kids in poverty the kind of teaching that had propelled them, children of poor Russian-Jewish immigrants, into the college-educated middle class. Sol, who should have gotten his doctorate in physics, but had been cut off by the financial needs of his immigrant family, had taught gifted classes in high school, sending his students off on scholarships to prep schools and fancier colleges than he could have ever imagined and to the degrees he never got. One of his former pupils was in Congress today, a favorite lobbying target. Another was on the short list for a Nobel. Frieda had taken the other end, teaching first and second graders, little ones who increasingly came into class never having heard English spoken. Some of the stories they had told Rachel during visits to Seattle had made her shake her head in amazement at their persistence, compassion, and sense of humor.

"Right. Makes doing trauma therapy look easy, I always say. So enough already, look, there's Chana and Dovid with the baby."

Across the parking lot, a couple in their late thirties were doing the task of unloading an infant from their minivan and settling her into a stroller. The pair, with their old-fashioned Hebrew first names, were among the refugee-from-strict-Orthodox-families contingent at Or Chadash who occasionally dazzled the rest of the congregation with arcane bits of knowledge that each had gleaned during their rigorous religious educations. Chana and Dovid's daughter was four months old, born on the cusp of the new century. The two looked perpetually exhausted these days. Rachel and Alice walked over to meet and greet.

"How's the goddess Shoshi doing?" Rachel joked with the younger pair. Shoshana was, like most children in this congregation, extremely wished and planned for, cooed over and attended to. Her parents had been through a year of infertility treatments together before finally achieving this pregnancy, and Rachel had been one of their support people. She had been relieved that they were well into the pregnancy when Sarah died and her ability to offer support went flying over the bridge with her. She had barely made it to the baby-naming ceremony three months ago.

"Do you really want to hear the latest on how she's beating all of her developmental milestones?" Chana, who was a pediatric nurse at Children's Hospital, teased the two psychologists. "I somehow doubt it, but bear with me."

"OK, OK, so you're proud. Is she already talking in three-word phrases?" Alice jumped in, tweaking Chana's understandable tendencies to mark Shoshi's development against the norms.

"Actually, I was telling Chana that she had to find something that Shosh was normal at soon, before we got into the habit of expecting too many great things from her," Dovid added as he hauled the last of the baby paraphernalia out of the van. "I'm voting for color sense, what do you two think about that?"

The four adults hooted at that proposition. Dovid was a professional artist whose day job was teaching at Cornish, the small local private arts college that had once famously been home to John Cage. He, of course, had a marvelous color sense, something that had made his childhood in a rigidly observant family where art was a devalued sacrilege a long series of challenges. To suggest that his adored baby daughter could be mediocre in that arena was a perfect metaphor for the depth of his love for the child. Rachel's eyes teared up with the bittersweetness of it all. She was always moved, deeply, by the unconditional love of parents for their children. Her own family had been a series of tests and hurdles, opportunities for her and her siblings to disappoint their father, who was always ready to toss one or the other of his children over the side of the family boat if they displeased him. Chana and Dov were the parents that children deserved, she thought to herself. No wonder Rachel got so much pleasure being around them and was so thrilled that they got to get pregnant.

"So what did she do, already?" Rachel decided to let the new parents off the hook. "Come on, I want to hear some serious bragging. And let me take that, what is it, not a diaper bag, looks like provisions for a week on the road." She reached over and relieved Dovid of one of the pastel bags hanging from his shoulders. Chana launched into a description of Shoshi's skills at turning over and reaching for objects while the four adults headed up the path into the building that housed the synagogue.

The first part of the service was in full swing when they walked into the sanctuary. The rabbi was off at a retreat, so the congregation had reverted to its earlier ways of being led by a member. Not quite letting the lunatics run the asylum, Rachel mused. She had been one of those lunatics at the beginning, parlaying her knowledge of Hebrew and Jewish culture into a leadership role when the synagogue was just a group of people, dissatisfied with the establishment, meeting in one another's homes to rewrite the prayerbook in non-sexist language and integrate bits of Buddhist lore and left-wing diatribe into the Hebrew phrases. Probably the only synagogue in Seattle where they say a prayer for the success of worker's rights before we do mindfulness meditation, she had joked to other people. Over the years as the group enlarged she had fallen further back into the distance, and in her year of grieving had had little to give. She missed being up there leading services, she realized. Maybe it was time to get back involved again.

As the Torah service drew near, her friend Nancy, co-chairwoman of the ritual practice committee, came down off the bimah, eyes scanning the congregation. They lit on Rachel, and she hurried over.

"Hey, Rachel, so good to see you back again. I wondered if eleven months had burnt you out. Hey, we need someone to do *cohen aliyah*, are you willing?"

The service of reading a weekly portion from the Torah, the first five books of Hebrew scripture, involved giving various people turns to "come up," have an *aliyah*, say the blessings and participate in the *mitzvah*, the commandment of Torah reading. The order was fixed. First *aliyah* went, when possible, to a *cohen*, a person whose family traced its descent from Aaron, the brother of Moses and the first high priest. Rachel had read in the past year that someone had done a DNA study of people who, like her family, claimed cohen descent, and damned if the DNA wasn't the same. Her family name, Katz, was the Hebrew contraction for the words "righteous priest." Even if she hadn't been repeatedly told in her early years that her family was ritually special, her name would have been a dead giveaway. Rachel had avoided going up for an *aliyah* during the last year, too. She wanted nothing to rejoice at.

"Yes, of course. Thanks, Nancy. The timing on this couldn't be more perfect for me. Thank you." Nancy hugged her and headed off in search of other volunteers of the correct varieties for the next *aliyot*. Rachel tried to focus herself, to make some inner space for connection with whatever it was she used to feel when she went up for an *aliyah*. The Divine, maybe, or the history of the Jewish people. She was always struck, during her participation in Jewish ritual, by the fact that all over the world for thousands of years other Jews had said and done what she was saying and doing. She might not take the words of the prayers very seriously or literally, and God was a highly suspect theoretical construct, but it felt huge to her to be saying them along with the rest of the Jewish world. Her father might hate her, she thought to herself, but somewhere that morning he was probably in synagogue saying the same words, maybe even going up for *cohen aliyah*. And at that place, there was a relationship between them. She didn't want to think too hard about how she clung to that thread.

Absent a rabbi to offer a sermon after Torah reading, the service went quickly to its conclusion. At the end, after the announcements about needing petition workers for the new universal health care initiative, the congregation rose, hands joined or around shoulders, to sing a parting song—"*Oseh shalom bimromav*, Oh Divine Being, make peace in the world," the song of the Jewish peace movement, as well as lines from the prayer for the dead, beseeching the Divine to bring peace among and to all of creation. Rachel had always loved the song, but this morning it took on a particular power, moving her to tears as her fellow congregants sang, clapped hands, and in general raised their collective energies. Peace, yes, she could use a little of that. A lot of that, if the truth be told. The fatigue of the last year settled on her shoulders like a shawl made of rocks. No wonder Alix Price killed herself, Rachel thought. If she was anywhere near as tired as Rachel . . . She caught herself in her thoughts and recoiled. She didn't know that Alix killed herself. All she knew in that moment was that she felt terribly weary.

Alice noticed a shift in Rachel's energy, and the tears in her friend's eyes. She tightened the grip around Rachel's shoulders. "Hey, *bubbeleh*, are you OK?"

Rachel sniffed quietly. "Yeah. And no. Just sad. Noticing that I could use some peace. It's been a hell of a couple of years, girlfriend."

"Ain't dat da troot," Alice responded, accentuating her Bronx accent. The two hugged. They joined the crowd heading into the social hall for the post-service reception, known as an *oneg shabbat*. This week's was being sponsored by two men, a couple who would be having their union ceremony the next week just before Passover, with the myriad dietary restrictions that took over their culinary lives. She wanted one of those the next time around, Rachel mused. A union ceremony with the chuppah and the broken glass and being carried around on chairs by the crowd. Renewal, Reform, and Reconstructionist Jews allowed their lesbian and gay pairs to have something resembling a marriage, and she was going to take advantage of that, damn it, she thought. If there was a next time around, she wanted the whole thing. With a really great dress. She quieted her inner monologue and joined the group in loudly singing the prayers over bread and wine that preceded the reception.

In the car on the way home, Alice noticed Rachel was still quiet. Her friend worried her. Sarah's death had been hard, harder because the grief had not been pure. Rachel had been so angry at Sarah that it had been a real strain to keep the bitter edge off her grieving. And Alice had wondered just how much Rachel's loss of Sarah had triggered internal spirals into all of Rachel's other unprocessed losses. Rachel's father had refused to bend during the time after Sarah's death and offer comfort to his daughter. Her siblings, who had never liked Sarah much, had shown up, but were too obvious in their relief at the absence of their sister's annoying partner to wholeheartedly support her. She knew how skittish Rachel was about intimacy. It had been a part of her own decision to not allow Rachel's crush to go forward. As much as she loved her, Alice would have gone crazy repeatedly coming up against Rachel's inner walls. What a time for her to have those walls be full of holes, Alice thought.

"Rachel, what're you doing for the rest of the day? Are you up for going shopping with me?"

Rachel thought it over for a few seconds. Shopping with Alice could be a challenge. Alice was a careful, deliberate decision-maker. Long after Rachel was ready to be done and out of the store, Alice was still weighing her options. It would, on the other hand, give her an excuse to avoid calling Anna back. She opted for honesty.

"Here's the deal, Allie. I could call Anna and see if she's up for an unplanned get-together. Or I could go shopping with you. Or I could stay home with Mr. Piggy and isolate. So you can imagine where I'm leaning."

Alice grinned. "In that case, I am following you into the house and staying until you've made a date with Anna. The woman really likes you, Rachel. And Liz and I approve of her. And according to what you said last night, you had a very good time after dinner. So there's simply no options, are there?"

"Hey, I was being honest. What is this, punishment for being upfront?" Rachel's voice held a laugh, her mood shifting out of gloom. She wasn't feeling punished at all. She just needed that extra push to get on the phone with Anna, and she knew it. "I don't think you have to follow me in."

"Oh, yes I do." Alice laughed hard. "I'm your big sister, and I know what you'll do if I don't sit there and watch you punch the numbers into the phone."

"And what's that, pray tell. And since when did I have a big sister?" Rachel was rolling with the joke now.

"You'll get in there and start to obsess about whether you really want to see Anna. So you'll walk the dog. Or check your voice mail. Or wash dishes. Anything else except call her. I know you, Rachel Katz. So come on, let's get in there and pick up the phone."

The two women ran up the steps giddily and came tumbling in the door to an uproarious puppy greeting. Mr. Piggy was so glad to see his momma happy and so glad to see his Auntie Alice. But where was Lambchop? He stuck his head out the door, nose in the air. The two women's laughter escalated. "Hey, at least someone in this household isn't ambivalent about love, right, Alice?" Rachel cracked.

"Well, even if that's true, you still have to call Anna before I'm leaving. So either you have me camping out here in the living room, or . . ."

Rachel smiled. "Or I get on the phone. OK. Watch me."

She stepped into the study and picked up the phone. With luck, Anna will be out somewhere, Rachel thought, then she could get Alice off her back . . . Her inner monologue was interrupted by Anna Sigurdson's live voice on the other end.

"Anna, hi, it's Rachel Katz." She stopped dead in her tracks, uncertain of what to say next. Alice yelled from the other room,

"Hey, Anna, hi, it's Alice. I told this brat that I wouldn't leave the house until she called you."

Anna burst into laughter on the other end of the line. "Is it that bad, Rachel? Did I scare you so much that you have to be force-marched into calling me?"

"No, seriously, Anna, it's not that, it's just, well . . ." Rachel, usually articulate, ran out of words again. "I was just, well, uncertain. You know. But I was gonna call you, truly, really. The other evening was lovely. That Alice just thinks she can push me around, is all. She didn't believe me . . ."

Alice broke in again. "No, she was gonna wash dishes instead. Of course I didn't believe her. I know this woman, Anna. She needs to be pushed."

"Jeez, what is this, I'm being ganged up on by everyone. OK, hi, Anna, it's me, the queen of reluctance. Would you like to come walk Mr. Piggy at Gasworks with me this afternoon? There, are both of you happy now?" She feigned a pout in Alice's direction.

"Hmmm, let me check my ever so busy social calendar. Let's see. I have nothing, nothing, and nothing, plus a whole stack of lit review that I did this morning because I was up early pining for your company and couldn't sleep. So I think I can squeeze you in. After all, I do like that dog."

Rachel didn't know whether to feel flattered or terrified by Anna's joking response. She decided to go with the light interpretation. "I'm honored you can squeeze us in and agree with your taste in dogs. How about you give me time to get out of my go-to-synagogue duds and have a little lunch, and the boy and I will come by your place."

"Actually, Rachel, it makes a lot more sense for me to come over to yours. You do live, what, five or ten blocks from the park, don't you?" Rachel groaned silently. She had been trying to keep distance by keeping Anna out of her house. But the woman was right, it was ridiculous to drive herself and the dog over to the Madison Valley and then all three of them back again to lower

Wallingford. "And I can bring lunch. We can have a picnic. A little takeout from Madison Market OK with you?"

"Fine, you're right. Better to have you come here. And yeah, let's see, what do they have there that I like, uh, how about some sushi? And let me give you my address." Once again Anna got to be impressed by Rachel's concise directions. "Turn left at the erotic bakery. If you pass it, you've gone too far."

"I would say that it's probably gone too far itself, hasn't it, Rachel?" Anna ventured the joke, and Rachel laughed. Good, thought Anna, she's not that uptight today. This woman was such a challenge, she was beginning to wonder if it was worth the effort of the chase. It's not as if Anna hadn't met some other quite attractive women in her time in Seattle. She'd gone out to coffee after AA meetings, and to post-exam pizza dates, attended the over-forties lesbian drop-in, and had had more than one chance to pair up with some very interesting people. So what was it about Rachel Katz that kept her engaged? The odd combination of what felt like a huge amount of personal power and gutsiness, combined with a vulnerability and sadness that tore at Anna's heart whenever she got within hailing range of Rachel. Plus, the woman's looks. There weren't very many zaftig Jewish maidens in Seattle, she thought. And she sure did like that zaftig, didn't she? Anna turned back to the conversation.

"I think I'll just hop on over now before you can change more than your clothes, Rachel. Unless the Montlake Bridge is up, expect me over there in, say, no more than twenty minutes. That should give even a serious femme like you time to decide which casual outfit to change into, right?" The tease was deliberate and hit its mark.

"My God, am I that obvious?" Rachel volleyed back. "I guess I'd better race up to the closet . . ."

"Oh, no, don't go into the closet on my behalf, please," Anna teased on the double entendre.

"As I was saying," Rachel huffed in mock offended dignity, "I'll race up to the clothing depository room, how's about that, and find something suitable for dog-walking and picnicking amid the geese. See you." She hung up the phone somewhat abruptly, and turned to Alice.

"So have I been a good girl? Can I be left unsupervised now, Alice? Or are you going to stay around to make sure I actually get out the door with Anna?"

"Come to think of it, that's not such a bad idea." Alice relaxed internally at the teasing footing that the two found themselves back on. Maybe she had been a little pushy. But she was worried about Rachel. "Unless you can't stand another few minutes of my company?"

Rachel laughed. "Of course, stick around, help yourself to what's in the fridge. Here I am, failing at my job as a good Jewish hostess and not feeding you within five minutes of you coming through the door. I'd better watch out, I'll lose my membership card."

Rachel headed up the stairs, unbuttoning her dress as she went. Why was Anna so willing to persist, she wondered? She was pleased, in a backward way, to have the attention. And it was different, after years in which she had been the one doing the work of a relationship, to have someone else constantly taking the initiative. But what was wrong with Anna that she was willing to persist in the face of such blatant ambivalence? Yes, we had a good time the other night. But so what, she could probably have a better time sexually with any one of a score of other women in town. It fell outside the realm of Rachel's imaginings that Anna could simply find her sufficiently compelling that there was no need for the latter to possess a fatal flaw. Rachel's sense of herself as attractive had been more damaged than she realized. So she continued to try to parse Anna's actions as evidence of an error in progress as she changed into her jeans and an unavoidably flattering indigo blue fleece top with the University of Chicago logo discreetly embroidered across the middle.

Chapter Eleven

Anyone watching the two women sitting on the grass at Gasworks Park that afternoon would have noticed the intense energy that was flowing back and forth between the two of them. Anyone, that is, except Rachel Katz, who was in the middle of the energy field—and oblivious. As Mr. Piggy wandered in the twenty-foot radius of his leash, which Anna had found a way to stake securely into the ground, Rachel and Anna were engaged in a lively debate about the merits of social constructivism for understanding gender, including that ever-popular favorite, the question of how many genders there are anyway. Anyone listening would have never guessed that this was a courtship ritual.

References were being cited, principled stands made, Rachel forgetting her anxiety and ambivalence as she flung herself into her element. Intellectual debate, in which she could even occasionally double back and devil's-advocate her own positions, was so delicious to her, so nourishing. She felt completely solid and at home on this ground. Her father, for all of his tendencies to rejection, had forced her to learn to hold her own in verbal repartee, and she had no doubt that she could do so. She was shining, lost in the process of intellectual spin.

Anna was mildly amused, and highly aroused. Whatever uncertainties Rachel had demonstrated in their prior encounters, none of them were visible now. There was nothing personal happening, and Rachel was thrilled, she could tell. Anna liked intellectual exercises like this one as much as the next Ph.D. candidate, but Rachel was positively glowing, which made her all the more attractive to Anna. This was why she was staying in pursuit, she told herself. This mind at play. There might be, and there were, plenty of other attractive single lesbians in Seattle, even ones with Rachel's looks, but not too many of these minds available. Her own last two relationships had foundered not in small part because, after the initial thrill of great sex and new infatuation, there had been so little to talk about. She had suffered from that lack, and even been punished for being "too elitist" by her last partner, who could see no value in playing with theories when there were social injustices to be righted, right now. It was requiring a good deal of self-control to stay physically at enough of a distance to be decent in public, she thought to herself. Rachel seemed to have read everything, often knowing the authors personally, and to have thought long and deeply about the ways in which gender configured itself in the world. For Anna, a butch lesbian who had spent years coming to terms with her position somewhere on the edges of gender, it seemed like a feast for the mind to find someone who had taken the question so seriously, and was so cute, too.

Anna reminded herself not to be too taken in by Rachel's wonderful mind. She could forget some of her other criteria for potential partners in the headiness of this all. Her father had been brilliant—a brilliant drunk who would recite poetry and lines from plays. A man who, on the front end of his binges, had been full of wonder for the beauty of the world, and on the hind end had been angry, critical, and abusive. Anna could detect the edge in Rachel's remarks, the way in which she moved easily to judge. She wouldn't want to be on the receiving end of that.

Rachel left her intellectual spin long enough to notice that Anna seemed a little disengaged. "What, am I boring you already?" she joked, uncertain of whether to be glad that Anna's attention was elsewhere, or to feel peeved that she was no longer the object of this woman's desire. It was kind of fun being pursued like this. She just had to watch out and not take it too seriously. Sarah had been fascinated at the beginning, too. Rachel thought darkly to herself that now she fascinated all the girls. At first they were all so impressed with her huge brain hard drive. Then they got tired of being around a walking encyclopedia. She sighed.

"Not boring me, no. Quite the opposite. More, well, you've got me thinking a lot about what I find attractive in you. About the perils of being attracted."

"Ah, at last, a little uncertainty on your end," Rachel almost crowed. "You've been making me nervous, woman, with all of this pursuit and persistence. I mean, it's lovely, it's flattering, but my experience is that once someone gets to know me well enough, the glow fades quickly. And heck, I can't be the one carrying all of the ambivalence for the both of us." Her voice sounded brittle, her chipperness at this pronouncement faked. Rachel was well-defended against the desires of her heart, but in that heart she had often wished that someone, someday, would simply fall in love with her and stay that way, would want her unconditionally, whole-heartedly, without reservation. She had convinced herself that this was a regressive fantasy and lectured herself often during her relationship with Sarah about the value of a mature acceptance of the limits of adult love. But she had been enjoying what felt like Anna's unalloyed attraction.

"You know, it's not really you I'm uncertain about, sorry to disappoint you." Anna's grin was wry. "I'm falling in love with the way your mind works. And I'd be less than honest if I didn't say that that scared me. You're so damn quick, and you suffer fools so badly, Rachel. And I'll be one of those fools sometime, you can count on it. I only scored seventy-five on my Miller Analogies . . ."

"Only, come on, what are you talking about?" Rachel castigated Anna playfully. The Miller Analogies was a pr-grad-school test. Rachel knew that Anna's score was well above what most people could achieve. "That's one hell of a high score."

"Yeah, but what was yours? Come on, give, it's time for some truth."

"Umm, I could pretend that I don't remember. But you've probably guessed that I can recall what I scored on every standardized test since fourth grade, huh? OK. I had a ninety-five. But it doesn't really count, I'm extremely verbal and read a lot, and—"

Anna interrupted. "That's precisely my point. I'm smart, really I am. Not brilliant, though. I also blew out God knows how many brain cells before I got sober, and those you don't get back. I've never been a fast reader, and girl, if you've really read all those sources you quote, it sounds like you swallow words like candy. No, don't answer me yet. I want you to listen, please. Liz told me that you pretend not to be as smart as you are because you think you'll scare people off. That you're trying not to intimidate. Well, I'm not intimidated, but I'm abundantly aware of the risks of getting involved with someone whose mind goes so much faster than mine. My dad was as smart as you are, and I adored him. And he was as critical as I think you can be. And that devastated me. I'm too old to get torn up like that again. Once in a lifetime was enough, don't you think? I've managed to spend my life being careful not to get too close to such brilliance. But here I am, falling for you. So I'm sitting here trying to remind myself that I'm an adult and can protect myself, and you're not my father, and that being drawn to your mind isn't one of these moth-to-flame routines. That protecting myself by going for duller minds just left me bored. There, I've said it, you can rebut me now."

Rachel sat silently for several minutes, digesting what Anna had said to her. If she allowed herself to listen clearly, to move her own ego and terror out of the way, she could hear Anna's declaration of interest and desire. Anyone telling you how afraid they are of getting hurt by you is telling you how open they already are to you, of their willingness to create the relationship in which that hurt could

163

happen. She knew that, both as a student of human behavior and as someone who had kept her own heart shielded for much of her life for entirely similar reasons. She needed not to be flip with Anna this time, and she chose her words carefully.

"Anna, you give me a tremendous gift with your honesty. So let me be honest in return. You're right. I'm terribly critical, largely out of self-protection. If your dad was a zap artist, well, all I can say is that my father left me with a permanent hole in my heart. And my mom was AWOL until just before she died, no help on that score. So I protect myself, until I forget, and I don't. I didn't with Sarah, and when she started to hurt me, I went into default mode, worked harder and became nastier. It's up, big-time, these days, that urge to be critical and judging. I want to find everything wrong with you, every little nit to pick about you so that I can keep my heart protected. I could fall in love with you, and then where would I be?

"So all I can tell you is that you have some control in the matter. That one way to be sure that I'm critical of you is to hurt me. To scare me. To let me know how badly I've failed you at whatever it is I'm trying too hard to do right. Because, girl, and this is the truth, once I'm in, once I give my heart, I'm in and gone, and I'll do whatever it takes to make it work, and to make it worth your while to stay. I'm a danger to myself that way. If you're Ms. Wrong, and I give you my heart, then criticizing you is the only way I have of keeping that hole in me from feeding on your judgments and swallowing me up."

There was another long silence. The topic of conversation had moved so fast from the heady intellectual realms into the truths of the heart that neither woman was quite certain what to do next. The weight of verities spoken hung in the air between them. Rachel was aware of the distinct desire to run, hide, cover herself, take back the intemperate words she had just spoken. Her eyes filled with tears.

"Sweetie, what's wrong?" Anna leaned forward and took one of Rachel's small fine hands in her own large strong ones. "You're crying."

"Oh, it's nothing. Just . . ."

Rachel's attempt at a façade crumbled in the warmth of Anna's solicitous regard. She began to sob, freely and loudly, causing Mr. Piggy to cease his search for goose poop and rush over to his momma prepared to deliver consolation in the form of stinky tongue-swipes. The flurry of keeping his poop-laden tongue from her face broke the solemn mood.

"OK, there, I'm back to normal. The pig did his job, distracted me." Rachel pulled her hand back from Anna's and wrapped both of her arms around herself protectively. "I'm fine, really I am, I have no idea what just got into me."

Anna looked distressed. "Bullshit. Excuse me, Rachel, and I know this is presuming on awfully short acquaintance, but that didn't look like fine. And I have the feeling that you know precisely what you just got into. I mean, it's OK to tell me that it's too soon to tell me, you know? But please don't pretend around me. I'm not a psychologist, but I'm not insensitive."

Rachel was taken aback. Usually people were more than thrilled to be given an out from her feelings, and she normally conducted her emotional life alone, in private. What was up with this woman that she wanted to know what Rachel felt?

"I'm sorry if I was offensive. I know you're not insensitive, hell, Anna, that's part of the problem here. You are sensitive, and nice, and turn me on, and I could get hurt, damn it." She yelled the last few words. "Do you see, I don't want to get hurt? I'm fine as I am, I'll be just fine if everyone would just kindly leave me alone." Her decibel level continued to mount. Tears began to spring up again. "I was fine before you walked into my life, Anna. I'd had my relationship, and it was over and that was fine, don't you understand?"

Anna reached back for Rachel's hand again. "Yeah, so fine that the oh-so-composed Dr. Katz is yelling and crying in public. Very fine, I get it. Like, I don't have to worry nearly as much about me getting hurt as I have to worry about how I could hurt you, huh?"

Rachel went into minimizer bunny mode. "No, no, seriously, I'm not fragile, Anna, it's just that, oh shit, I don't know. I don't have the energy or the desire to keep up this front with you. I'm not fragile, not. It's just that once I let someone into my heart, they can hurt me terribly. I don't have reservations, and I don't hold back. So it was fine to be alone because I have my friends who love me and who aren't quite so far into my heart. And you do, too, have to worry about me zapping you. I'm not nice, and I know it. Just ask any two attorneys in town, they'll tell you how not nice I am. Conjure up Sarah's ghost. It'll tell you what a controlling bitch I can be, how secretive and withholding I am."

"I'd actually rather ask Liz. She told me what you did for Alice when her dad got sick."

Sol Goldstone had had a serious bout with colon cancer just after he retired from teaching. He was long in remission now, but when he'd been in his acute phase, and Alice frantic with worry and flying back and forth across the country almost weekly, Rachel had just stepped in and handled Alice's practice for her. She'd given Alice as many of her own overstock of airline miles as Alice would accept, helped Liz out with the shopping and the dog, and in general had just showed up to try to make the hard time a little easier.

"But that's what you do for a friend who you love. Or at least it's what I do. It's not about being nice, it's just about being there."

"Call it what you want," Anna retorted. "Nice, there, I don't think I care, really. It's that you did it. You've got to control your PR people, Rachel." Here Anna cracked a huge white grin. "Because they're making you sound nicer than you want to be. And remember, I lived in Boston for ten years. I've been around you closet nice people before, pretending to be tough and critical. But I want to get back to this matter of your heart, please. Seems like if I'm going to keep on being persistent and understanding, you ought to let me know about what I'm trying to be understanding about, doncha think?"

Rachel sighed loudly. "I think you've actually got it all in front of you right now, my dear. You know, I'm like that cliché of the shoemaker with the holes in the soles of his own shoes. I've managed to avoid doing much therapy work myself all these years. Good excuses, like any decent shrink in town is my friend. And not-so-good, like I'm terrified that if I finally go into that hole inside me, I'll never come back out. So when I'm safely defended,

I'm pretty happy and good. I simply don't know how to defend against anyone I fall in love with. Ergo, my ambivalence, ergo my well-honed defenses against falling in love. I'm a complicated critter that way. Sarah turned out to be my dad all over again, and I hung in there doing my little reenactment of the drama, trying this time to make it right and earn the love I wanted. All the while knowing that what must be earned by the loss of self is no prize. And this must sound familiar to you, huh?"

Anna's face was solemn. "More than you know. Except I didn't have the choice to avoid doing the work on that hole in me because it was so full of booze that I would have died. And it's not as if I haven't been a lot cautious myself along the way. I'm surprised at myself for hanging in with you. You feel too compelling to be safe for me. But too compelling to walk away from. If we keep seeing each other, it's not simple. And you know, I've done simple. Carola, the woman I was with before, is a lovely person, without a complicated bone in her body or thought in her head. She was so good to me and for me. But I went stir-crazy after a while with all that calm and simplicity and made her unhappy, too. I guess I'm never going to get over my need for color in my life."

"Like the inside of your house, huh?" Rachel ventured an interpretation.

"Right you are. Like my decorating choices. I want the intense energy of women's creativity around me. I think I've learned, finally, that I'll have to find calm somewhere other than in an intimate relationship, because calm there just makes me want to fall asleep. Literally and figuratively."

"Uh, Anna, can I do a little process check?" Rachel was becoming acutely aware of her growing discomfort with the direction the conversation was heading. "We seem to be talking as if we're agreeing to consider the possibility of maybe pursuing—"

Anna interrupted, laughing, "Girl, if you put any more conditional terms into that sentence we're going to be in the realm of speculative fiction. Are you trying to tell me that we're having a discussion about what could happen if and probably when we get more involved?"

"Uh, yeah, kinda sorta possibly that." Rachel teased.

"Well, Ms. Kinda Sorta Possibly, that's fine that we're having this discussion. We do seem to be doing things a little back-assward here."

"You mean, first we had that heavy make-out session, and now we're talking about the perils of intimacy?" Rachel kept teasing.

"Uh-huh. Exactly. And so now I am about to propose something along the intimacy lines. Sexual intimacy, to be precise."

"Wait just a minute, Anna. I was under the impression that this was a hypothetical discussion, you know, just considering possibilities and laying out information for the other person to digest."

"If this is hypothetical, then we're taking the notion that all reality is socially constructed to a pretty absurd level, Rachel. I'm about to be serious, so pay attention."

Rachel sat up. Anna looked directly into her eyes and reached out and held both of her hands.

"Here's the thing. You know, I was a safer sex educator for forever. Used to put on safer sex parties for dykes. So I know more than almost anyone about how to be sexual with someone who has an active STD and not pass it along."

"Oh shit, Anna, are you going where I think you're going?" Rachel's own level of arousal, which she had been carefully keeping in check, began to assert itself.

"Well, where I'm going is this. I still have my plentiful supply of latex goodies. Gloves, finger cots, even a couple female condoms, plenty of dental dams. So I was thinking, well, I'm not sure 'thinking' is the word. You know I want to make love with you. That's not a secret. And I know you've been hiding behind that trich you so conveniently caught. So I finally said to myself, Anna Sigurdson, how many hours did you spend teaching women to have safer sex? You could do a little demo with Dr. Katz here, lord knows she needs to learn some of what you have to teach—"

Rachel interrupted, laughing hard. "Oh, so this is all about doing a good deed and making sure that I don't catch anything the next time, say, somewhere in the next decade, I allow a woman to pick me up at a conference. Gee, how altruistic of you, Anna."

"Hey, I try to help." Anna was doubling over with laughter. "So what do you say? Will you let me make a date with you for a little private safer sex demo?"

"This all feels so incredibly cold-blooded and intentional, Anna. Making a date to have sex. Probably preferable to doing the swept-away-oh-my-God-I-didn't-mean-it routine, huh? Can I think about this for a bit? Because my first impulse is to ask you why you didn't bring the damn latex thingies with you today, you know. And to tell you that there's a wonderful condom shop over by Wallingford Center, just up the road. Not that I've even been in there, mind you. But I think I should be considering this alone, without the distraction of your eyes and your hair and your hands and, well, you get the drift, I hope."

Anna felt pulled. So Rachel wanted to have sex with her. Good. But wanted to think about it. Shit. The woman was a little maddening—but it was information she filed away for later consideration. If this was the audition-for-partner phase, then was this type of indecision written into the role in her script? She hoped not, hoped it was just the phase they were in, of her reeling out the line in Rachel's direction, hoping to keep her long enough on the hook to bring her in. It had to be a phase, she told herself, and Anna eased out the line a bit.

"You sure you don't want to take a visit to the condom shop? We could just look, you know. Not buy anything. It was just a proposal."

"Anna, dear." This time Rachel was the one who reached out for hands, then lifted her hand to draw it down Anna's cheek and across her surprised lips. "It's a lovely proposal. I think it's one I want to take you up on. Just not today, OK? It's already a little closer than I can handle. I have to integrate what we just talked about for a little while."

Anna's eyes closed as Rachel's fingers traced the lines of her face. This was purely wonderful, she thought to herself. Who needs to play with latex—Rachel's touch on her face out in the wind and sun was a whole erotic high itself. She told herself to back off. It was good, there was time here.

Chapter Twelve

It was Sunday evening when Luanne Barnes called Rachel back. Rachel had been home, re-rereading a favorite sci-fi book, when the phone rang. "Private" again. Rachel thought that it was time to get one of those things on her phone that refused anonymous calls so her friends would make themselves known. She picked up the receiver, and the identity of the caller was not quite expected.

"It's Luanne Barnes, Rachel. I'm sorry to disturb you at home like this, but . . ."

"No apologies necessary, Lu. You said you had something to talk to me about?" Sensing an odd hesitancy in Lu's voice, Rachel let her own words trail off in the air, inviting a response.

"Yes. A very hard thing to talk to you about. Is this a good time?"

Rachel sighed inwardly. In the past, any time would have been a good time. She was always in search of distractions in the form of work. She got spoiled this last year, she mused to herself. But here was Lu on the phone. "Of course, Lu. Please, what's this all about?"

"You know how I feel about Alix Price." A cold, firm statement, then silence. Rachel held her peace, and Lu finally took up the conversation. "I hated her. I really wished that she could suffer the way that Jordie has suffered. I was glad when I found out she was dead."

Rachel nodded on her end. No surprises here. "So . . ." she said into the phone.

"So, Ed hated her, too. More than me, maybe. He was so close to Jordie, and she can't even let him hold her anymore. So . . . so . . . So anyway, Friday afternoon Joyce told me that she was representing Alix Price's estate. That they had been friends. I'm still digesting that one, Rachel. How could Joyce have been friendly with that woman?" Hmm, Rachel thought, so Joyce didn't come out for Alix to Lu. She made another listening noise to keep Lu talking.

"I told Ed about it when I came home. I was so upset and confused and furious at Joyce. And of course I told him that she had hired you to do this, what did she call it?"

"Psychological autopsy, Lu."

"Right. The autopsy. And then Ed told me something. And I knew you needed to know it. So here he is."

The phone clunked down. Rachel could hear the argument in the background. Lu was saying, "Talk to her now, I told you, it's safe." Ed's voice was farther from the receiver, his words unclear but his tone clearly distressed. Rachel waited. Then Ed spoke into the phone.

"Dr. Katz. This is strange, let me tell ya. Is it OK to call you Rachel?" Ed Barnes was slightly formal, respectful. They had only met when Lu had brought him with her to the shivah. He had seemed a decent guy, she remembered. What in the heck was going on here? she wondered. "Please, Ed, whatever makes you more comfortable."

"OK, Rachel, so here's the deal. I'm so glad that fucking bitch is dead. You know that, what the fuck, that's not the problem. The problem is, well . . . OK. You know, after the trial and all that bull-shit she said about how Jordie couldn't really say who the perv was that, you know . . ." His voice broke. Then he went on.

"So, I was furious. My little grandbaby, such a happy kid, and now this, and then this bitch getting up in her fancy suit to tell people that Jordie was, what, too stupid to know what had happened. I couldn't stop thinking about it.

"So I thought, ya know, this woman has to suffer. I knew this wasn't the first time she'd done this to some sweet kid, the prosecutors told me she did it all the time. I kinda got hung up on the idea."

Rachel sat silently aghast. Oh, please, don't let Ed Barnes tell me that he killed Alix Price, she thought. She did not, not, not want to be a part of destroying Luanne's life any more than that rapist already had. She breathed, deeply. "So what happened, Ed?"

"So what happened is, I started following her. I guess you shrinks would say I was stalking her. I watched what she did, where she went. Hung out in that stupid coffee shop where she went all the time. I kept trying to get a handle on her. Ya know, I've got a ton of vacation time, I've been using it. Felt good, like I was gonna do something, protect the next kid from that bitch. I was studying on how to make her suffer. Not die, ya know. But suffer, like my poor baby is suffering. But then I guess maybe someone beat me to it. Or she did. I don't know. That's what Lu says I gotta tell you."

Rachel's relief was palpable, so much so that she almost forgot to get the next bit of information from Ed or, for the moment, to question his assertion that he had no hand in Alix's death. "Ed, I'm so glad you didn't kill her. You and Lu have lost so much already. But there is something—"

"I figured it out after I read her obit, which, by the way, we celebrated here with quite a round of toasts. May she roast in hell, the bitch. Anyway, here's the deal. I guess it was the night she died. I was outside of her house, trying to figure out how to get in. Ya know, I'd been watching the place for a while. Anyway, this guy comes up the walk, rings the bell, she lets him in. No big, she's let-

172

ting people in all the time. So he's there for a while, and then he leaves. Then the lights are out, kinda early for her, she's one of those late-night types usually. But no big. I hung out for a while, then I went home. Didn't want Lu to know what I was doing. She woulda creamed me, ya know."

Rachel sat and thought. A man visiting Alix Price on the night of her death. Not an unusual occurrence. Not something that necessarily meant anything. Something smelled about this whole confession. She pressed on.

"Ed, why haven't you gone to the police with this information?"

"Yeah, right, Rachel, like I'm gonna go and say I was stalking the bitch so that's how I saw some guy visit her house. Sure. I may not have a Ph.D., but I am not stupid, trust me." The anger in his tone was intimidating.

Rachel reared back and began to mollify the man, trying to keep him on the phone and talking to her. "Ed, I'm not trying to suggest that you're stupid. I can see your point, really I can." His reaction surprised her. One moment helpful, the next moment practically shouting at her. Proceed with caution, Katzie, she said to herself. "Look, can you tell me anything about this man?"

"What the fuck do I know? A guy, dressed like a lot of you other yuppies. Not too tall, dark hair, you know, it wasn't very light out. It's not like I was looking at him, ya know. Looked like she knew him. Like she wasn't all that happy to see him—no hugs and kisses for that one, I'll tell ya. Some kinda goddamned BMW kinda car." Ed was proudly union, and proudly drove American-made cars only, his feelings about imports apparent in his disdain for distinguishing between the types. "Not much special about that guy."

Rachel inhaled. "Ed, you know I need to share this information with the investigating officer. This is a lead they need to follow up on."

If Barnes could have come through the phone and choked me, she thought later, I'd be a dead woman myself. "Whaddaya mean, share this information with the police. Fucking share nothing, you damn fool! What are you, some kind of idiot? I thought talking to

173

a psychologist meant it was confidential. Shit. You can't do that. You can't."

Rachel shook from the force of his rage. Why such secrecy? She calculated fast and furiously how to handle this situation. She raised her voice and went into alpha dominant mode.

"Ed, slow down. Now. I am not your therapist, so you have no right to confidentiality. I'm sorry, I had no idea you thought that. I will have to share this with Joyce, you know. I'm working for her. And I'm fairly certain she'll want us to share this with the police. Ed, if you've done nothing wrong, you have nothing to hide. So you followed her. She never made a complaint, they can't charge you with stalking if no one ever complained." She felt herself working to get him, and the conversation, under control. She could hear Lu in the background, crying. What in the hell was she doing to these people? she thought again. All they ever did was have a molested granddaughter cross the path of Alix Price. She paused, and Ed spoke again, slightly quieter.

"I don't like this, Rachel. I thought you were on our side. Heck, I thought Joyce was on our side. Come to find out she was friends with the bitch. Right now I don't know what side is up." Rachel breathed slightly easier and went for the empathy, trying to de-escalate the exchange.

"Ed, I really am sorry. I was as mad as you were at Alix Price for what she did at that trial. But this is a whole separate thing. Joyce needs to know what happened. She has a legal responsibility to the estate, to the heirs. If the police think that there was someone there that night, they might reopen it, reconsider the suicide verdict. I know you hate this, but you have to prepare to talk to them. Look, if you don't feel safe doing that alone, I can ask one of my other lawyer friends to go with you. Elliott Citron, he's someone the cops are a little afraid of." Citron, a top-of-the-line trial lawyer, began his career as a public defender, some of whose indigent clients Rachel had evaluated pro bono back in the old days. He owed her one. And his specialty today was suing the police department. Wouldn't hurt Ed to have Elliott at his side.

"Fine, do what you have to do." Ed's tone was sullen but quiet. "I never shoulda told Lu about this. Let fucking well enough fucking alone. But no. Too many years working for lawyers . . ." His sentence trailed off.

"Ed, you did do the right thing." She hoped he was making this up. She hoped there was nothing more to this. She hoped he did go home that night. "Listen, do you want to tell me anything else? Should I talk to Lu?"

"Yeah, I'll put her on." The receiver clunked down again, then Lu's voice, clearly teary.

"Rachel, I'm really scared. I can't take any more, really. First Joyce friends with her, now this. What if the police think Ed did something?" She began to cry quietly.

Rachel was horrified. Such good people who had offered her comfort in her time of grief, caught up in the mess that was Alix Price's life and death. She couldn't help and might really hurt. "Lu, sweetie, I don't know what to tell you. I told Ed that I'll ask Elliott Citron to stand up for him if the cops want to talk to him. But you know I have to tell Joyce. I just do."

The crying petered out. "I think I'm going to call Joyce and tell her I'm taking a few days off," Lu said. "I need to think this all through. Rachel, do you know a good therapist down here in Kent? I think that I need to talk to someone who can keep my confidences—and nothing against you, but I know you can't do that."

Rachel darted off the couch, phone in hand, and returned with the psychological association directory from her home office. She gave Lu two names and numbers of women who had done internships with Alice, about whom Alice had spoken highly. The conversation limped to a close, and she hung up, grateful it was over.

Rachel barely slept that night, her sleep interlaced with visions of Ed Barnes in the defendant's chair. What had she gotten into, doing this damn psychological autopsy? Why hadn't she and Joyce left well enough alone? Until now, it had been getting increasingly clear that Alix had probably killed herself. And now this. She couldn't conveniently pretend that she'd never heard it.

It was two days later when Rachel drove up to the former home of Alexandra Price. Situated on the edge of a bluff overlooking Lake Washington, the house seemed almost palatial. Alix Price had done well financially, and her choice of dwelling announced it to everyone. But what could one person do in such a big house, Rachel asked herself, deliberately ignoring the irony of the question given her own accommodations.

The front garden seemed to be tidy and well kept. Someone had trimmed hedges and cleaned out the flower beds, which were full of late spring perennials, tulips, and pristine white daffodils. Mt. Bakers, Rachel suddenly remembered. White, like the mountain. Sarah had been a fanatic about flowers, poring for hours over the bulb catalogs. Rachel was shocked by the sudden intrusion of memory. She pushed it aside and came up the walk, letting herself into the house and punching the alarm code that Ilona had written on a piece of paper into the keypad. The beeping noise of the system stopped.

Rachel stood still and closed her eyes. She took a deep sniff of the air in the house. It smelled, what, not empty. It smelled anxious. It smelled like someone scared had been living in the house, she thought. She had no way to quantify this perception. She only knew that the houses of people smelled to her of their feelings, and she relied upon this information to assist her in knowing the person whose smell was left behind.

Opening her eyes, she glanced to both sides. A formal living room on the right, a dining room on the left. Each was carelessly, albeit expensively, furnished. Rachel could tell that, just as at Joyce's office, the rugs on the floor were real Persians, not the mid-priced copies she herself owned. The furniture, leather and teak, was haphazardly scattered, the colors bland and lacking in life. Nothing hung on the walls. Something that looked like a cat toy sat forlorn on a corner of the rug.

"You were camping out here, Alix," Rachel said out loud to the house. Her eyes teared up. Alix Price didn't seem to have had a sanctuary in her home. Hold on, she cautioned herself. It might be less bleak upstairs. If there was a cat toy, maybe there had been a cat.

It wasn't less bleak. As Rachel roamed through the house, she was repeatedly struck by the absence of a defined style or presence. The kitchen was full of expensive pots hanging from a frame above a huge, restaurant-style Vulcan stove and green marble countertops. But the expensively made pantry cupboard was almost bare. There were only a few spices in the rack. No further evidence of a feline presence, at least in the pantry shelves. It didn't seem as if Alix was much of a cook, even though she owned all the gourmet equipment.

The upstairs of the house was, if possible, even more desolate. How was it that neither Ilona nor Joyce had remarked on this? Rachel wondered. The bedroom was the only spot of life, and even that was somehow sad. Incongruously, it was decorated in bright primary colors, almost like a child's room. It jarred Rachel to see this, the site of so many real and alleged adult sexual couplings, decked out as if for a five-year-old. The only photo was of a nondescript gray long-haired cat perched on what looked like Alix Price's desk at the university.

She began to systematically look through the contents of drawers in the bedroom. People were predictable, she mused, so Alix would probably predictably keep the things most important to her somewhere close to where she slept. The bedside table was by now no surprise. Along with a box of condoms—colored ones, Rachel noted in passing—there was a silk pouch that, when opened, revealed a large silicon dildo, also colored light blue and shaped like a dolphin. Rachel had seen some of these on the shelf at Toys in Babeland, the local lesbian owned and operated sex toy store, so the shape of the dildo itself was not surprising. Now knowing of Alix's bisexuality, the presence of the dildo was no surprise either. The Velcro handcuffs, which Rachel knew were used in bondage games, were consistent with the picture of a sexual adventurer. Half-used bottles of sexual lubricants and a bunched-up pair of panties completed the picture. For all that Rachel had thought Alix a libertine, there was even more to that facet of her than she could have imagined. She held the panties to her nose. The stink of semen was unmistakable, even if it had been decades since Rachel had her own encounters with the stuff. A keepsake of the saddest kind, she thought.

The surprise was not in the contents of the drawer. It was in what was under a pillow, stuffed between the mattress and the headboard. It wasn't *The Story of O* or something by Anne Rampling. Quite the opposite. A well-thumbed copy of *The Courage to Heal*, a book that some referred to as the bible of the sexual abuse survivors' movement. A collection of first-person accounts of abuse and recovery by women who had lived through the horrors of childhood sexual abuse, it had been the lifeline for thousands. Rachel had bought a dozen copies over the years, each one replacing one that had left the office with a client, never to return.

Rachel knew that Alix along with others from the advisory board of the FoFAP had been hugely critical of this book, claiming that simply reading it could cause women to develop horrific false memories of abuse and falsely accuse innocent old men. Rachel had scoffed at these assertions, joking sometimes that if reading books could suggest things, then her clients' steady diet of uplifting volumes carted out of her office should have cured everyone in weeks, if not days. Finding out that Alix owned the book was not surprising. Finding it in this most personal of hiding places was. Of course Alix had the damn book, Rachel said to herself. Her critique of it was based on too close a reading. But what was it doing behind the pillows?

She allowed the book to fall open on its own. It rested on the section on dealing with memories. What to do when you're inundated by the terrible pictures of what happened when you were little, how to cope, how to get through, including some strong admonitions not to kill yourself. Maybe Alix had thought, in her desperation over her painful visual intrusions, that some of the techniques in the book might help her? Or maybe she was just looking for the minute errors made in any self-help book, the better to skewer it further. Rachel could feel the questioning tone in her inner voice. She was sure that Alix had read the book carefully in order to trash it, so she had to have remembered the helpful stuff. But it was out of place in this bedroom. Unless the woman sleeping in that bed was very troubled indeed. Another indicator that all had been going badly for Alix Price, another vote in favor of a verdict of suicide. After talking to Ed Barnes, Rachel wanted it to be suicide more than ever. Anything to spare that family another loss.

She knew that Alix's body had been found in the tub, scented candles all around, as if she had downed her dose of drugs and alcohol and gotten into a bath. Maybe she had fantasies of being like drowned Ophelia. Or perhaps she was like the woman treated by one of her professors in grad school who had told that therapist that she couldn't possibly kill herself, she would soil the sheets. Maybe Alix hadn't wanted the release of her bowels and bladder after death to soil the sheets, Rachel mused. It could have been that she was just confused and disoriented, taking a bath to relax with just that little bit too much downer in her, just enough to depress the breathing functions of the hindbrain. Rachel reminded herself to hold off on any decision until all the information was in. She was skating awfully close to premature cognitive commitment. Ed could have killed her. The mysterious guy could have killed her. Or none of the above.

Rachel gingerly walked into the bathroom. It had been professionally cleaned. No way anyone could know that someone had died in here. The scent of candles lingered in the air. She turned to see a row of them lined up on shelves over the toilet tank. The bathroom told her nothing to tip the scales of the autopsy. Alix, like Rachel herself, seemed to love fancy soaps, Rachel noted as she went through the drawers. Roger et Gallet sandalwood, La Rioja black soap, gels, and loofahs everywhere. But nothing that said whether that last bath had been meant for solace or as a grave.

As she walked out the front door of the house, Rachel was

pleased to see Andrea Cole, dressed in her non-uniform uniform of slacks and a long straight coat and standing at the end of the walk. "Well, Sergeant, I hope you don't plan to arrest me for breaking and entering," Rachel joked.

"No, not at all. You told me you were probably coming by here this morning, so I thought I'd drive by to see if I could catch you. When I saw my favorite bull terrier in the car, I knew I was in the right place. So what's the scoop, oh wise Doctor Katz?"

Rachel knew that Andrea's joking covered her mild discomfort. She beamed back at her former client. "This was one sad woman, Andrea. The house is barely inhabited except by a lot of expensive furniture and what looks like a ghost cat. Did you see one when you were out here that day?" Andrea shook her head, and Rachel continued. "But other than that, I'm not sure yet, I—"

"Have to chew on it. Let it digest. I know, you and your eating metaphors." Andrea chuckled and Rachel felt slightly miffed. She hadn't realized how much her clients memorized her personal clichés. That was transference at work again, she knew it. The utterings of the therapist became golden, to be hoarded and brought out by clients to soothe or encourage or admonish them- selves. She wondered why she was always so jarred by her encoun- ters with the manifestations of this phenomenon. It wasn't as if she ignored it when she was still seeing clients. But it troubled her, she realized, to be so powerful, so big in the psyches of others. No wonder people like Joel Gibbs were happy to pretend it simply didn't exist.

"I'll probably have a report out in a couple of weeks, Andrea. I have one, maybe two more people to interview, and some more records to sift through. And I've got a deposition in another case coming up, so I have to back-burner this temporarily and get prepped for that. It's been nice knowing you were out there on the case if I needed to call on you, though." Rachel prepared to walk down the street to her car. It was clear from this exchange with Andrea that Luanne had said nothing to Joyce, which meant that telling the tale of Ed's stalking of Alix would be her job. In any

180

event, the police still had no idea about this important new fact. It made Rachel uncomfortable, withholding important information from her former client, but at the moment, her loyalties, and the privilege of confidentiality, lay with Joyce Romanski.

"Actually Rachel, that's not the only reason why I'm here. I've been trying to get up my nerve for this, so I figured that if I put it into the context of something familiar, like you always said"—the two grinned again at the therapeutic cliché—"then I'd be able to pull it off. This is a little awkward, but, here goes. Marsha and I are going to have a commitment ceremony in the summer."

Rachel broke in. "Far out, Andrea. I always knew you'd make a lovely bride."

Andrea ignored the teasing and went determinedly on. "We've talked about this, and we've decided that we want you to be one of the people who speak at the ceremony to bless our union. You know, we both know, that without you, without the work we did together, I wouldn't be alive, much less able to be in a relationship with someone who loves me, who's good to me. And Marsha knows that, too. You're one of the mothers of this relationship, Rachel. We want you to be a formal part of it. Will you, please?"

Rachel was dumbfounded. There was nothing in the APA ethical guidelines to tell her how to respond. She had on occasion attended clients' rites of passage, from adult bat mitzvahs to graduations from college, even a couple of art show openings. But the leap from sitting anonymously in the audience to being in front, speaking, seemed cavernously large.

"Can I think about this, Andrea? I'm enormously honored. But I think I need to talk to my consultants about this, OK?"

"Come on, Rachel. You're not going to be my therapist again. You don't do therapy anymore, right? So you can't muck up my transference any more than it already is, right? And I'll formally release you in writing to break confidentiality so that you can say how you know me, if that will make it easier. Just don't find some rule to hide behind. This is the culmination of everything you worked with me on, Rachel."

Andrea's vehemence was convincing. "All right, how about probably yes, and I still want to think about it, and talk to a couple of people about it. How soon do you need to know?"

"Sooner is better. We're having a fun time planning this. I mean, here I am with a family full of church ladies who are going to just shit at sitting through this thing. My momma's gonna make 'em show up, it's her baby girl's wedding and the aunties won't be allowed to miss it. And Marsha with her family who think that God is a concept invented to enslave the masses." Andrea's partner came from a long line of socialist rabble-rousers and union organizers who were thrilled to bits at their daughter's transracial relationship, but appalled that Andrea believed in God and attended the local affirming Baptist church with Marsha an occasional companion. "So we figured, what the heck, throw in a little bit of everything that matters to us. A little gospel, a little Emma Goldman. And you matter to us, Rachel. You can be our rabbi, how about that?"

"You put it that way, and you make it irresistible," Rachel parried. "I mean, I've always wanted to get up and preach."

"Like you didn't from your therapist chair, right." The banter loosened up as Andrea relaxed, having delivered her message, and Rachel fell into the easier undertones of their exchange. Andrea got a chance to play briefly with Mr. Piggy before being called away by the screech of her portable two-way. Rachel patted the seat of the Volvo, inviting him to jump back in. The visit had been another mark in the suicide column, she thought as she drove up the lake shore.

Chapter Thirteen

The view from the conference room at Shultzman and Kline was breathtaking. All around one could see the Sound and the mountains. Rachel always looked forward to being deposed at the large downtown corporate defense law firms. They all had palatial suites of offices high in the towers of the business core with views to die for. So what if going there meant several hours of being grilled by an attorney for the other side of a case? She figured that at three hundred and fifty dollars an hour, plus the views, it was worth the time and trouble. At least this wasn't a federal case, she thought. The U.S. Attorney's office, befitting its role as the servant to taxpayers, had conference rooms that didn't just lack a view. They were windowless, to boot. Rachel had spent way too many hours in one of those windowless rooms when she did the Salmon case early in her career. She wasn't unhappy to be up here in the corporate-lawyer clouds.

The court reporter looked familiar. "Have you taken my dep before, Kay?" Rachel queried.

"Yes, remember, in *Clarke v. Northwest Airparts*. That case with the transsexual person." Rachel nodded. The woman/man who wanted to use the women's room before the final removal of her/his male genitals. What an interesting one that had been. Talk about deconstructing gender. "And besides, all the court reporters know you, Dr. Katz. You're so funny. I told the gang I was going to report you today, and I had to fight off the competition. Where've you been lately, by the way?"

Kay Tollefson was pleasant and friendly, as were so many of these hardworking, vastly unappreciated toilers in the dark mines of the legal world. Rachel decided to be a little open. "My partner of twenty years died, very suddenly last year. A car accident. So I've been a little out of commission in the last year. You know, even with these views to soothe you, a deposition can be pretty grueling."

"I'm so sorry to hear that. I shouldn't have asked . . ." The court reporter turned, began to busy herself again with her apparatus.

"Don't apologize. It's kind of nice to know that I stand out in your mind. I mean, you folks report so many depositions, hear so many psychology experts."

"True, but not too many with your sense of humor. And actually, not too many who take the time to talk to us like we're people and not an extension of our reporting machines."

The conversation faded away as the two women went back to their respective preparations. Rachel glanced up as the attorney who had engaged her in the case came into the room, hauling a huge box of files behind her on a rolling luggage cart. Deborah Smiley had been an Olympic rower before she went to law school, and she still towered over most of the people in any room, looking incredibly healthy and wholesome. The sweetness of her looks camouflaged one of the brighter legal minds in town. She had become a specialist in disability discrimination more than a decade ago after adopting a daughter from India who had cerebral palsy, and as she put it, being sent to the new planet for the parents of kids with disabilities. A few years after learning what life was really like for people with disabilities, she had transformed herself from a real estate attorney to a leading voice for access and accommodation.

S & K was the law firm that Rachel and several of her friends had voted least likely to ever hire her for a case. It represented, among other corporate giants, Northwest Airparts, a huge aircraft manufacturer. Try as it could, the company had been unable to overcome a corporate culture of white old-boy networks. It had recently settled a mammoth class action lawsuit with African-American employees. Disabled employees, smaller in number and not organized as a group, fared no better there. Today's case had to do with a woman who had developed multiple sclerosis after working at Northwest Airparts as a stock clerk for nearly fifteen years. Following the federal and state guidelines, she had requested some, to her, minor accommodations that would have allowed her to stay in the job. The company had refused, gave her poor work evaluations as her impairments became predictably more pronounced, and then terminated her. Which had led to a huge depression, which was why Rachel was in the gorgeous conference room, riffling through her files, getting ready to testify.

Deborah's face looked serious and composed. "Ready?" she asked Rachel, knowing full well what the answer was.

"For sure, Deb. This one is so easy, so straightforward."

"I worry about those, you know. Too straightforward, I keep thinking."

"Well, I looked for hidden explosive devices in her life. But Madelyn"—referring to the client in question—"is one of those people who actually had a good life before this all happened. Remember I told you it was one of the shortest evaluation sessions I've ever done with the plaintiff. A good childhood, a great husband, the whole shebang. Too many witnesses to that reality to even imagine it wasn't so. So, of course, no internal protection to cope with becoming a member of a despised minority group in middle age."

Deb's face took on a wry smile. "Unlike that daughter of mine.

185

Talk about the holy terror little activist from hell I'm raising. No one's ever gonna mistake her for a nice shy girl in a wheelchair, not her, oh no." The voice of the proud and weary parent. Were all parents tired all the time? Rachel wondered, thinking about her weekend encounter with Chana and Dov.

Rachel smiled back. "Especially not if she whizzes past them as fast as she did me the last time I was at your place." Deb had her law office at home. It was entirely accessible, which made it perfect for her clients with mobility impairments. Lakshmi, who was a star of her wheelchair basketball team, had come roaring into the office while Rachel was last there consulting, to crow and be made much over with her latest school report. "A four-point-o, Mom, way cool, huh? Tell Dad he owes me a trip to the Wizards game store." Lakshmi was a devoted fan of an elaborate card game called Magic, whose creators, the Wizards of the Coast, had a game center near the university. "Hi Rachel, bye you guys," was Rachel's recollection of the exchange. A small whirlwind, emanating intelligence and determination. So much for the influence of genes on personality, she mused to herself. Lakshmi was the very emotional image of her mom, without a single strand of DNA in common. Maybe genes of the soul, if there was such a thing.

The two fell silent at the sound of voices outside the door of the conference room. The voices were followed by the speakers, two impeccably groomed white men in probably expensive suits. Jim Travers and Arnie Keefe were representing Northwest Airparts on the case. Rachel had been deposed by Travers before in a sexual harassment matter. She knew him to be deceptively friendly, one of those litigators who confuses his victims by leading them to believe that he was on their side, before going in for the kill. At this stage in her career, Rachel knew better than to take seriously either the mock friendship that some opposing attorney proffered, or conversely, the mock hostility, often full of overt lesbian-baiting that some others had as their preferred cross-examination strategies. That last wouldn't happen here, she knew. Keefe was a gay man, who in his other life had worked with Rachel on a couple of ballot initiatives. This was a job for everyone sitting at the table that day, and the cross-examination tactics were just the dance that lawyers did. Her job was to say what she knew and how and why she knew it.

For years, she had had to explain what depositions were to her friends, who treated the forensic realm as a dangerous foreign country to be visited rarely, possibly never if one had the choice. Then the scandal around Clinton and Lewinsky hit the news, and no one ever again wondered what it was she was doing when she told friends that she was "off to a dep" that day. Cross-examinations under oath, depositions were essential way stations on the road to the successful conclusion of a lawsuit. Each side used them to collect data that would guide the attorneys in strategic decisions. A good deposition by an expert could make or break a case. She had come to enjoy the chess game aspect of depos, trying to figure out from the questions being asked the direction that the other lawyers were going, and then, as she thought of it, planting herself in their path and refusing to let them through.

The trick that day was going to be separating out the almost normal depression that happened in the lives of everyone who had MS, according to the research, from the tearing, wrenching grief that Madelyn Kestin had suffered when her beloved employer, to whom she had been loyal and faithful, first denied her help in staying functional at work, then, as she put it, "threw me out like so many rags." Like many working-class Seattle area residents, Madelyn's family had a whole work shift of Northwest Airparts employees among its members. Her parents were both retired from the company. Her brother, a cousin, and her husband had all worked there. Her entire friendship network was full of Northwest Airparts employees and their spouses. She had crossed picket lines during machinist strikes, booked her travel to make sure she flew on company-made craft, and was a real flag-waver for the corporation. She still could hardly believe what had happened to her.

This was the linchpin of Rachel's analysis of the problem. Betrayal and helplessness were two big factors in Madelyn Kestin's depression. Her relationship to the company had not simply been employer and employee. She saw herself as part of a family, one that would of course care for her when she became affected by her MS. The accommodations she had requested seemed minor to her—more flexible starting and quitting times to account for the inconsistency of her ability to balance, extra breaks because of the tearing fatigue that accompanies MS, a work site closer to the restrooms because her bladder was no longer predictable. Nothing major.

When her manager's response had been to tell her that no accommodations would be made, she had only tried harder to keep up with the normal demands of work. This, in turn, according to the neurologist whose many records Rachel had carefully read and annotated, had created extra stress, which made the MS worse and more disabling. When Northwest Airparts finally terminated her because she was coming in late, needing to leave early, and using every moment of her sick time for regular visits to the physician, the charge was absenteeism and abuse of sick leave. Madelyn was horrified, hurt, and depleted. Her neurologist, furious, was the one who had urged her to bring this action. Her indecision about whether to sue the beloved former employer had almost cost her her chance, the lawsuit being filed only days from the end of the statute of limitations. This, too, went into Rachel's analysis. Madelyn was not looking for a way to get rich. She just wanted her job and her relationship with the company back, and she had explored every avenue to that end short of suing.

As Rachel saw it, this woman already experienced too many losses. No more camping, backpacking, whitewater rafting, or playing soccer with her kids. No more being able to trust her body to do what it had done for years—simply get up and walk, have energy and balance and predictability. Relapsing-remitting MS, the form Madelyn was diagnosed with, was less debilitating than some of the highly publicized cases, like that of the cellist Jacqueline Du Pré. But it left people in a difficult limbo of unpredictability and cascading losses as new parts of the brain lost their protective coat of myelin. There were some treatments around now, but they only slowed the progress of the disease. So at least she should have been able to preserve her sense of herself as a contributing person in her family and her workplace. And have those great health benefits, Rachel thought to herself. Northwest Airparts employees had killer health benefits, perfect for a person with a chronic disabling condition. She shuffled the file one last time.

"Dr. Katz, so good to see you." Jim Travers offered his hand, and Rachel rose slightly to shake it, firmly. "We've missed you around here."

"Hey, you guys must be getting the company to clean up its act, is all I can say," Rachel quipped back. "And you know, I do work for the defense side from time to time—no rule against hiring me."

"And break your perfect record with us? No, I don't think so." His tone changed as he turned to the court reporter. "Are you ready to swear the witness?"

Rachel welcomed the ceremony of swearing to tell the truth. It served as the ritual that helped her into what she thought of as her "deposition zone" where she became sharply focused, attentive to every nuance of each question, wanting to be certain that there were no trick wordings being sent her way. For the next few hours, her breathing would become shallow, her sense of time and her body remote, as she applied herself to the task of being cross-examined. She usually came out of a deposition spent, starving, and hyper from the strain of being perfectly attuned for hours on end.

Several hours into the proceedings, Travers suggested a break. Rachel stood up, shook herself, and walked out of the conference room to the foyer, where the law firm graciously provided a spread of soft drinks, tea, coffee, and very tasty cookies for the occupants of its conference rooms. There was a porch deck, high above downtown. She grabbed some tea and two cookies, and walked out into the air, followed by Deborah Smiley. Her face was living up to her name.

"Rachel, you're being your usual dynamite self in there. Better than usual, in fact. I loved it when he asked you about depression in MS."

"And then I cited that article that came out last week. Boy, was he not prepared for me to know that one. I loved the look on his face when I swooped in with the citation."

"And that bit where you interviewed the women from her whitewater rafting group. They sure had left that stone unturned, or at least their expert did."

Predictably, the defense lawyers had hired an expert who seemed to know very little about the topic at hand. Angelo Horner's specialty was people with chronic lower back pain. "I guess they figured that low back pain and MS were similar enough, you know, both something in the body, right?" Rachel quipped. Horner's evaluation of Madelyn Kestin had been cursory at best. He had neglected what Rachel considered an essential component of such a case, talking to the people who had actually known the plaintiff well, long before the thing had happened that sent them into a lawsuit. He had opined that Madelyn had always been depressed and that nothing the company had done had made things any worse for her emotionally. And that she was failing to make a good adjustment to her MS, because she was insisting on staying employed rather than facing reality—evidence, said he, of a serious underlying personality disorder marked by grandiosity and feelings of entitlement.

Rachel had spent several hours talking to the rafting group. These women had been friends since high school and had seen Madelyn more times and in more challenging situations than Rachel or the other expert ever could have. They told her about Madelyn before her MS, and more importantly, Madelyn after the diagnosis and before her employer had snatched hope out of her hands. "The MS part was hard," one of these women had told Rachel. "But you know Maddie, she just went out and got herself educated and taught all of us and told us that we should expect her on the raft until it wasn't safe for us anymore. Not her, us. Taught us to laugh about adult diapers and why she couldn't tolerate the heat. That's my girl Maddie, doesn't know the meaning of 'I can't.' But after this stuff with the company. I just don't know. I never knew that something like that could happen to people. I mean, there are laws, aren't there?" The indignation in the friend's face and voice had been palpable. Welcome to the planet of the disabled, Rachel had thought, someplace that anyone among the temporarily able-bodied, their family, and friends, could be sent to visit in a heartbeat.

"I get the feeling that no one's heart is in this one, Deb. Maybe it's just my optimism, maybe I'm projecting my own lack of enthusiasm for anything these days, but Travers and Keefe seem off their game."

"You might have something," she replied. "Jim does seem a little low-key even for him. I wouldn't mind if this one settled out, although Maddie's raring to go to court and have her say. I'm seeing how bad this is affecting her."

Deb explained that Dr. Jonas, the neurologist, double-degreed in medicine and physiology, board-certified in two specialties, and a mother hen to her MS patients, had been on the phone almost every day nudging Deb to get the stress out of Maddie's life.

"So go back in there and get 'em, woman," Deb said. "The facts aren't in dispute, so a lot of this is hinging on the size of the damages."

The two headed back into the conference room. The defense attorneys had been chatting, and fell silent as Rachel and Deborah came back. "Are you ready to go again, Dr. Katz?" Travers inquired.

"Absolutely. Although I sometimes wonder what you folks put in those cookies . . ." She let the sentence drift off, amusement in her voice.

"Let me remind the witness that she remains under oath," Travers intoned, and the court reporter began to press the keys of her machine again.

It was at the point when Travers said, "I have only a few more questions, Dr. Katz," that Rachel found herself suddenly and unexpectedly caught up in a wave of emotion. Grief. She nearly panicked, wondering what she was doing about to break down in tears in the midst of a deposition. She breathed hard, looked out the window at the cloud formations, and realized that she had just finished talking about Maddie Kestin's husband's devotion to her and how difficult it had been for him to understand her as she became more and more depressed. How the depression, more than the MS, more than anything else that had happened to this couple over the years of their marriage, had challenged his ability to stay in the relationship. How he'd told Rachel, when she interviewed him, of his guilt and shame at being unable to tolerate Maddie's silences, her irritability, the disappearance of her libido. "We had a great sex life, you know, Dr. Katz," he had told her, a little red-faced, but comfortable enough to make such an admission after more than an hour with the psychologist. "Even after the incontinence started to be a problem. We just joked about developing an interest in, what is that fetish called, golden showers. We were doing what we both do best, make a whole meal from the lemon, not just lemonade. You know, I love her. She's my girl, she's always been my best girl since we were in high school. But now she feels like she's gone, a long long ways away, and I don't know if she'll ever come back."

And that, thought Rachel, is why she was feeling grief. All this stuff about relationship loss was a bit much for her, still. She pinched herself on the calf beneath the table and tried to focus her attention on Travers.

"Dr. Katz, do you have an opinion to a reasonable degree of psychological certainty as to the proximate cause of the major depression you diagnosed in the plaintiff?"

The formal boilerplate language helped Rachel to reconstitute. Such nonsense, the terms of legal reality. The simple question is, what did it?

So she answered, "Yes, I do have such an opinion," then sat and waited. Rule number one of a deposition—don't answer the question you weren't asked. It was a game, and she knew it, but it was always better to play by its rules.

"And what is that opinion, Dr. Katz."

This was where she could do the paragraph out loud. She launched into it. "My opinion, based on the materials I reviewed, the interviews I have described to you today, the psychological testing, and my review of the research, is that the proximate cause of Madelyn Kestin's depression was the company's denial of her accommodations request combined with her termination from employment. That as a result of these experiences, she experienced a profound betrayal of trust and a loss of the relationship of trust and loyalty to her employer that she so highly valued. That this betrayal, in turn, led to feelings of helplessness, and that this helplessness, in its turn, led to depression. That there are no other circumstances in her life aside from her MS that are possible risk factors for depression. And that the evidence is clear from multiple contemporaneous observers, both lay and professional, that Ms. Kestin's MS was not initially accompanied by depression. The depression only enters the scene when she is betrayed and abandoned by her work family. When Northwest Airparts fired her."

There. That was it. All of these hours of looking at psychological tests and rehashing her conversations with Maddie and her husband LaMarr and her rafting buddies and Dr. Jonas, all of the citing of citations, all came down to this. Would that her current project, the deconstruction of the death of Alix Price, were so easy, she thought to herself.

"One more question, Dr. Katz," Travers said. "Can anything make this better?"

That was easy. "Madelyn Kestin wants to be back in the workplace again, a contributing person. She wants to do what she can do, which is all of her job, with the few accommodations she needs. That would make all the difference in the world, Mr. Travers. For her to get her work home and work family back. For her to have the chance to be the competent contributor she's been all her life.

Oh yes—and for the company to apologize. Maddie isn't someone who holds grudges. Without that, all the therapy and medication in the world will never get her back to where she was."

Travers, across the table from her, was silent. He looked through his papers, turned to whisper *sotte voce* to Keefe. He looked back and said, "No further questions." Rachel turned to Deb Smiley, who in turn said, "No questions." Rachel glanced at the court reporter and said, "Reserve signature," which meant that she was going to read the transcript line for line, correct it, and sign it before it went into the formal record.

The room busied with five adults repacking papers into boxes and briefcases and the court reporter reversing the setup procedures for her machines. Deb was the first out the door: "I have to pick the kid up from computer class, talk to you later." Keefe and the court reporter exited. Rachel was slowed by her thoughts and found herself alone in the room with Travers, who rose from his seat and abruptly said, "I don't think you know this. My wife was diagnosed with MS about two months ago. So I guess I'm glad to know that there are some great resources out there for her."

Rachel was slightly shocked at this personal disclosure from the attorney and reacted from her default therapist mode, with empathy and concern for the man whom she had defended herself against for the last four hours. "That must make this matter very hard for you."

"Harder for my wife, actually. You can imagine I'm not popular at home these days," he responded ruefully. Since Travers's wife was also a partner in the firm, Rachel could only guess at the heat being applied. MS was more common in the Seattle area than anywhere else in the country and seven times more likely to occur in women than in men, so the apparent coincidence of Travers defending a case with a plaintiff who had MS and having a wife develop MS were less of an odd juxtaposition than Rachel might have expected. Small world syndrome strikes again. Rachel was glad to know the source of the halfheartedness of Travers's cross-exam of her, though. She betted that Sue Anne Travers was getting great accommodations from S & K. The firm was known to be a wonderful, fair employer, unlike the corporations who hired its services. Maybe they learn from all their clients' mistakes, Rachel mused.

On the way down the elevator, she pulled out her cell phone and checked voice mail. There was a message from Emma Forche, still in phone tag. The woman was almost as unavailable for return calls as Rachel was herself, she thought. Another from one of the faculty at the university who had been out of town when she was doing interviews there, volunteering his time for the next week. OK, Thad, she thought. Your turn, and I bet you can hardly wait. Joel Gibbs again, insistent. "Did you have that appointment set up yet?" Jeez, the man was getting on her nerves. And one from Anna. "Hi there. It's your friendly safer sex educator, calling to arrange a tutorial. I'm going to be free over the weekend for an intensive seminar. Give me a call."

Rachel noticed the warmth spreading through her at the sound of Anna's voice. She was aware of her conditioned response—she heard the woman's voice and her genitals salivated. Rachel reminded herself to think before she acted, to wait a few moments before she called back. And she firmly told herself not to make a detour to Toys in Babeland on the way home. She walked out of the elevator into the building lobby on automatic pilot, steering by sheer kinesthetic memory toward the garage elevators, suddenly realizing that she had to remember what floor she'd parked on. There were just enough old Volvos in Seattle that she could easily spend, and had at times spent, half an hour or more hunting through the floors of parking garages in search of the one metallic blue one that was hers.

As she slid into the driver's seat, the deposition zone trance left her for good. She shivered, suddenly chilled. The ravenous post-deposition hunger hit. Anticipating the onset of low temperatures, she pulled the extra jacket that she had brought out of the back seat, wrapped herself in it, and turned on the car, hoping that the heater would come to life more quickly than usual. Food, she needed food, she thought. She was downtown, surrounded by possibilities, but nothing easy to get to. She told herself to just go home, she would find something on the way.

Out on Third Avenue the traffic was in its typically heavy pre-rush-hour mode, fleets of articulated buses crowding the curb lanes. She started to turn north, in the direction of Wallingford, when the urge hit her. Go down to the waterfront, she thought. She hadn't been there in ages; she could grab a fish taco and walk and get the deposition out of her head. And think about Anna, about Alix.

She turned right rather than left, went down the eight blocks to the intersection of James and Yesler, and turned right again. There was always good, cheap parking under the Alaskan Way viaduct along with the usual assortment of sleeping homeless folks. She found a metered spot, pumped quarters in to protect herself from a ticket, and leaving her briefcase locked in the trunk, headed west across the trolley tracks to the waterfront.

Late spring was too early for tourists. The broad sidewalk was almost deserted in late afternoon. Even the lineup for the ferry to Bainbridge Island was sparse. The rush-hour ferry commuter crowd hadn't gotten in line yet. A perfect place for Rachel to take her grief and chill and hunger. At moments such as these, her feelings of invisibility fell on her.

Since Sarah's death, Rachel had had a series of experiences in which she became aware that no one knew where she was. She could disappear, she thought. She could walk into the bank and take her money, go home and get the dog, step on the ferry, and just disappear. No one would notice for days on end. After more than twenty years of having someone know where she was almost every moment of every day, Rachel's life had become lost to scrutiny. There were moments when she loved it. The feeling of freedom, of having no one to whom she was beholden for her time, was profound. Not seeing clients made it even more freeing.

But there were also moments—and this was one of them—when the sense of alienation, of walking around clothed in a veil of invisibility where she was connected to no one human, was also profound and painful. We only know we exist in interaction, she thought. Look at the research on how children remember. The memories that stick are the ones that we share. And no one shared this moment with her. In interpersonal space, Rachel stopped existing for a moment.

Clutching her jacket around her in the slight breeze, she walked south, past the ferry terminal, stopping at a food stand along the way to buy a salmon taco. Only in Seattle, she thought, not noticing the tang of the sauce. Food was fuel at this point in a deposition day, better to cram in something with plenty of protein and deal with niceties later. She came to a temporary halt at the park that stretched down one of the piers. A homeless woman, shopping cart full of belongings, occupied one of the picnic tables. Rachel plopped herself down at another, staring out to Elliott Bay, watching the next rain system blow in from over the Olympic Mountains to the west.

Rachel wondered if Alix felt sometimes as she did, wondered if Alix had moments in that huge old house of hers when she knew that no one knew that she existed. Did she feel like the tree that fell in the forest with no one around? Is that why she fucked everything in sight? To be visible, to validate her existence? Is that why she was dead? Rachel missed Alix. She didn't even like her when she was alive, but now she felt like Rachel's most intimate companion, more present in her thoughts than anyone.

The words of a k.d. lang song came into Rachel's mind—"I've been outside myself so long . . ." That could have been the theme for her last couple of years, Rachel mused. She wondered if Alix had felt outside herself, too. She was becoming convinced that the death had been no accident. This kind of deep alienation was a directional marker to self-obliteration. At these moments, even Rachel felt a little tempted.

The food finally kicked in and started to do its work. Rachel noticed her body warming and the pangs of hunger subsiding. The day seemed to brighten, even as the sun sank closer to the horizon.

Rachel decided to chalk up her existential angst to low blood sugar. What a drama queen she was. She vowed not tell anyone about this little episode. It was bad enough to burst into tears in front of Anna and worse that she was humming morbid song lyrics to herself and thinking that they were profound commentaries on her life and existence. She wasn't invisible. She wished she was but wasn't. She was ready to go home and take her dog for his walk. Rachel rose, and as she passed the homeless woman, stopped for a moment. "Hi. Are you OK?" she asked. Here was someone who was invisible, she thought.

The woman blinked, as if she thought Rachel was a hallucination. "Are you talking to me?" she demanded, defensive.

"I just wanted to know if you were OK," Rachel said. "You looked like you could use someone to ask."

The woman shook herself in disbelief. "Ya know, dearie, I think you're the first citizen to ask me that in I don't know how long. Actually I am OK, thank you. Got my stuff, got a bed at Lutheran Compass, got a line on a job soon. Got a safe place to hang for the moment. But thanks for asking."

Rachel walked back to her car. What in the heck was that about? she asked herself. Was she turning into some kind of strange person who talks to homeless women? What's next, pigeons? She shook her head, failing to notice that at least a few passersby were looking oddly at the well-dressed woman who was talking to herself, almost out loud, getting into a beat-up old Volvo. She fired up the engine, turned onto Western Avenue, and headed north past the Market and onto Highway 99, toward home. She could call Anna, she thought with some delight. She would schedule that little private safer sex lesson. It was not a gap in her education she could sustain. She quietly laughed to herself, thinking this was one good way to know she was not invisible.

Chapter Fourteen

"I had been wondering whether anyone would ever contact me," said the calm alto voice on the other end of the line. Emma Forche, in person, or at least on the other end of the phone, at last. Rachel realized when hearing her directly rather than on voice mail that Emma Forche sounded older than she had imagined a massage practitioner might be. Hard work for young hands, she had always figured. The two women had finally found a time when they could talk on the phone, after repeated unsuccessful phone tags. Her response to Rachel was surprising, too. "Actually, Dr. Katz, I was wondering when you were going to call me. I was glad when you did."

"To be entirely frank, it took me awhile to even consider that you might have something to tell me about Alix, Ms. Forche. Her therapist didn't think it was a very good idea. But I'm thorough, and at least one of Alix's friends was sure that you'd have something to tell me, so here I am."

"You can call me Emma, Dr. Katz. Unless you're more comfortable keeping this formal."

"No, not at all. And I'm Rachel when I'm not in court. Which we aren't yet."

Rachel found herself wondering at this initial verbal jousting. She had truly expected that Alix's masseuse would have little to say about her state of mind. But it seemed that she had something that she had been waiting to talk about, to judge from her first words to Rachel. The banter about nomenclature only served to reinforce the impression. Rachel felt a current here, but flowing where?

"Alix told me a great deal, Rachel. You know, there are some of us in the massage business who do more than ease aching muscles, and I'm one of them. So when I heard from some of my other clients who were friends of Alix's that you were asking questions about her last few months in this existence, I knew that you would have to come to me at some point. But what I have to say, I want to say to you in person. I do better communicating when I can see and read the other person's entire physical self, and this is going to be one of the least easy conversations I'll have any time soon. So when can you come and meet with me?"

Rachel pulled out her appointment calendar. "I'm free all of the afternoons this week and next, Emma. Does any of that work for you? And just where exactly are you located?"

Emma was free late that Friday. She gave directions to a funky remodeled office building in the Fremont area. That explained the phone prefix—Wallingford and Fremont shared phone exchanges. Rachel couldn't help admitting to herself that this, at least, fit into her image of massage therapists as the last hippies on the planet. Fremont was perfect for the stereotype. The neighborhood, across the water from her office, proclaimed itself the "Center of the Universe" and held summer solstice parades annually that featured nude bicyclists, stilt walkers, and women with live snakes around their foreheads along with the more usual assortment of latter-day twentieth century–style colorful characters replete with piercings, tattoos, and hair in colors not found outside of a dye bottle. It was

200

home to a genuine sixties-style coffeehouse, a plethora of retro and recycled clothing stores, and a shop that specialized in exotic scented products. The emblem of the neighborhood was an odd statue titled "Waiting for the Interurban." Concrete commuters waited for the trolley that never arrived in the company of a dog with a strangely human face. It was a local sport to decorate the statue to commemorate holidays or personal transitions. Across the way from this retro-sixties entity lay the local headquarters of a software firm, twenty-first century meeting the sixties with élan. Geeks in jeans could be seen crossing the street to the oh-so-politically correct food co-op for healthy takeout. Rachel was fond of Fremont and didn't mind the idea of a trip there. It would give her a chance to browse some of her favorite antique junk joints, even if the interview with the massage therapist turned out to be less than fruitful. And the food co-op had good takeout. Maybe she could start eating a little more healthily.

She punched in Anna's number after hanging up from Emma Forche. This time, she wanted Anna home and answering the phone. The fates did not disappoint.

"Anna here."

"Hey, is this the famous safer sex educator? It's your pupil, calling to schedule a safer sex tutorial." Keeping it funny made it safe and manageable.

"Oh, girl, I was sure I'd put my foot in it that time. Are you really OK with my proposal?" Rachel was pleased to hear the slight pleading in Anna's voice. She was beginning to enjoy the femme fatale role. Something about coming clean to Anna with her fears had shifted the dynamic. Less ambivalence, more clarity. She was going to allow the pursuit. She might even pursue back.

"Very OK indeed. This is one class I'm not gonna miss. Might even need to have regular refresher courses. You might find that I'm a slow learner." Rachel impressed herself with her audacity in flirting. This was fun, she thought.

"Well, let's start with a beginner class and we can assess your skills. I have Saturday free. It's an intensive, so you'll need to schedule several hours." Anna kept in character and kept the joke going. She had to be a little nervous herself, Rachel thought. It didn't hurt either of them to have this fiction to protect themselves.

"Do I have to wait until Saturday?" Rachel mock-whined.

"Unlike some people, I have to go to real classes this week. Write a paper. Work on that Ph.D. that someone else had the good sense to earn a little earlier in life. Sorry, Rachel, I'm really not very free until Saturday. And I want to make this a good experience for us both, not try to cram it into some evening when I'm pooped from a day at school. I could do a little get-together on Wednesday, though, if you'd like. You know, dinner, something a little more low-key. Give you another chapter in the saga of Anna."

Rachel sighed. Attraction to a responsible grown-up came with its own problems, not the least of which being that responsible grown-ups fulfilled their responsibilities no matter how attracted to you they were. Oh, well, this was what she wanted, right? "Dinner Wednesday sounds good. I promise to keep my hands to myself."

"Hey, you don't have to do that," Anna teased. "Just nothing below the waist, remember?"

The two women bantered a bit longer, agreeing to meet two evenings hence at the Noodle Ranch, a funky pan-Asian joint in Belltown, then signed off. Rachel headed up the stairs to change out of her deposition outfit and into dog-walking gear. It was going to be a long wait until Wednesday. Even longer until Saturday.

Heading out the door and down the steps with Mr. Piggy, Rachel hesitated. He'd been home by himself again for such a long time. Maybe she should have given him a treat, something more than a walk around the neighborhood. She looked down at the dog, who had his head cocked with eyes on her face. "Whaddaya think, puppy dearest? Do we want to go someplace exciting for our w-a-l-k?" His talk wagged, a whip propelled by sheer energy. "OK, let's go to Gasworks. You had fun there with momma and Anna last weekend, didn't you?"

She settled the dog on his pillow in the front seat of the car. This thing needs to be washed, or vacuumed, or something, she thought critically. But then there would just be dog hair again, so why bother. Because she was obsessive compulsive, she retorted to herself, and she liked things clean. She shushed her inner voice and headed south.

She was enjoying the view from the top of the hill, letting the dog roam freely at the long end of his lead, when she heard human panting behind her. She turned, wary. The park was relatively free of people, and Seattle was safe compared to Chicago, but her city girl instincts still kept her a little on edge. She relaxed when she saw the head of Joel Gibbs appear at the top of the trail.

"Wow, this seems to be a habit," she joked to Gibbs.

"What do you mean a habit?" The man's voice was suddenly defensive. Then, as if hearing himself and noticing the vague welcome from Rachel, he smiled.

"Hello, Joel. What I mean is it's getting to be a habit that I take the dog for a walk and run into people I know. I didn't realize you came here. I though you lived in West Seattle somewhere."

Gibbs seemed mildly uncomfortable. "Oh, I was just meeting someone for lunch up at Arnie's." He gestured with his head at the restaurant in the building across the road from the park entrance. "Sharon McLean, you know her, don't you?" He named a well-known local cognitive therapist. Rachel liked Sharon a lot. Unlike many of her colleagues in cognitive therapy, Sharon was an integrationist who actually looked at non-conscious process in her work. Rachel had attended a workshop she'd presented on treating women's depression, and found it impressive for its combination of pragmatic cognitive ideas with feminist insights. She couldn't imagine why Sharon would give up precious time for Joel Gibbs, although it was entirely possible to imagine why Gibbs would want to lunch with Sharon. She was also drop-dead gorgeous and smart.

"Yes, I know her well. Great woman, great therapist. We all can learn a lot from her." She couldn't resist the dig.

"Yes. Well, we were meeting to discuss a program I'm developing. And then I had some time after lunch and I thought, why not have a little walk. And surprise, here you are. With your dog. I didn't know you had a dog." Gibbs's nervousness had not decreased since the encounter began. He seemed if anything more uncomfortable. Rachel thought it was odd. His social skills deficit this time, not hers. She had nothing to say to the man. She had come to the park to be alone, not to interact. Her silence seemed to nag at him, and he persisted.

"Ah, Rachel, I've been wondering if you've met with that massage person yet." Gibbs's faced screwed up with the effort of getting his words out. Rachel wondered what it was with this guy. How obsessive compulsive can one get, she thought. She made the stupid mistake of telling Joel that she would let him in on the final decision-making process, and he proceeded to haunt her repeatedly about when she was near the last step.

"Joel, I told you I'd tell you, OK? What gives, seriously? I mean, it's not really standard protocol for me to include someone else in on this part of the decision making. I know this process has to be agonizing for you, but I'm doing you a favor, you know?" Rachel was annoyed enough to be blunt.

Gibbs stood his ground. "Well, yes. But you said you would let me know. I'm relying on your word as a colleague. So even if it is a favor, I assume you'll follow through."

Rachel shrugged. She was annoyed and fought hard to hold on to her compassion. "Look, Joel, trust me, OK, I'm not gonna leave you out of this. I swear, you are looking more OC by the moment yourself." Rachel was irritated enough to allow the gratuitous insult to slip out, and she didn't care. "Here's the deal. I need to interview Thad Taylor. He's finally in town and available. That's my priority. You didn't think that Emma Forche was very worth my time anyhow, so I've put her sort of low on the list. I wouldn't have talked to her at all if it weren't that Ilona Hegevary was so insistent."

Joel paled, but Rachel wasn't looking. Mr. Piggy was demonstrating entirely too much interest in whatever was buried in a clump of grass down the hill, and she tugged at his leash. "Leave it, Pig. I said leave it. No snacking on garbage. I don't buy you expensive gourmet organic dog food so you can eat garbage at the park." She laughed, then turned back to look at Gibbs, who now seemed somewhat more relaxed. Maybe he just felt awkward, approaching her like that, she thought. She needed to give the man a break—after all he ran the way up the hill to say hello, and she acted like an ice queen. "I sound just like my mother, going on about my kid eating junk. Anyway, as I was saying, what is the big deal with you?" She held back from asking him why he hadn't told her that he had treated a client who committed suicide a couple of years ago. It was bad enough to have Joel Gibbs appear out of nowhere during a dog walk and spoil her alone time. She didn't have the energy to get into a pissing match with the man, which she was certain would ensue once she brought up the withheld information.

"Not a big deal, Rachel." Gibbs seemed to flutter. "I'm just anxious for you to be done with this thing so that we can put poor Alix to rest. I think I knew that this Emma person was the end of the line, so I just want to know that the end really is in sight. That's all. This is pretty hard for me, too. I was her therapist, after all." He stopped abruptly, waiting for Rachel to respond.

"Well look, Joel, I will let you know. And now I really need to give this boy the rest of his walk, OK? I'm kind of prickly today, don't take it personally. I'll call you." Rachel skipped the usual pleasantries in her hurry to get down the hill and away from Joel Gibbs. It was one thing to run into Anna accidentally. In fact, there were a whole lot of other people she wouldn't mind running into here in the park. Half of the rest of the psychologists in town, some lawyers, even. But Joel Gibbs—she didn't think so. Even liking him slightly better than she had at the start of this whole autopsy, she still didn't feel quite comfortable with the guy. She guessed his tendency to go after colleagues bugged her. It was simply odd—she never saw him or ran into him and then this.

Rachel dismissed it. Spurious correlations, she thought, just the chance of circumstances and humans seeming to have meaning to their arrangement. If Rachel wasn't on this case, then it would mean nothing that she accidentally ran into a colleague in the park.

Joel Gibbs stood on the sundial at the top of the hill watching Rachel and the dog descend. His teeth were clenched, and his hands balled into fists. If Rachel had bothered to look back, she might have found the sight of him a little perturbing. She might have thought that he was angry at how she had brushed him off. But Joel was outside of her consciousness even before she went around the corner and under the hill on the way to the south side of the park where the dog could forage for goose poop. Gibbs stayed, watching, well after she had left his view.

Thad Taylor had amazed Rachel by making himself available the next afternoon. He asked if they could meet at her office, explaining that he wasn't planning to go in to his office at the university until the next week and didn't want to signal availability to his grad students until then. "You remember how it is, Rachel," he said wearily. "When you're running a research team, everyone wants a bite out of you. So I'd rather make them think I'm still in Banff." She ascertained that he wasn't allergic to dogs and gave him the directions to her office. "Just turn right rather than left at the Red Robin," she said, naming a landmark burger joint, "and go down the hill. It's the building between you and the water."

Taylor was an attractive man, Rachel mused as he settled himself into the client chair. Medium height, slight of build, with piercing blue eyes and hair that had once been black now going to gray. He had a good reputation among the grad students for being a caring mentor who made sure that his protégés went into the world with enough good publications to ensure the academic jobs they wanted. And best of all, she thought, no one had ever suggested that he was hitting on students. While George Lewis was on former-grad-student wife number, what was it, four or five at this point, Thad was known as a very married man whose wife, with her own degree in social policy studies, was fairly high up in the state Department of Human Services.

Which was why she was surprised when Thad Taylor said, "So if you're talking to everyone she slept with, I guess you have to talk to me, huh?" This autopsy was just full of surprises, Rachel thought as she composed her face. First Alix Price is having sex with women. Then she's in therapy. Then she has a cat. Or had a cat. Now Thad Taylor the most married was telling her that he had sex with Alix Price?

"Well, Thad, actually, I just wanted to talk to people who knew her well, not necessarily the ones who knew her in a Biblical sense. I have to say I'm shocked."

"You should be. I am. I've been avoiding you. It's not just that I was in Banff." He looked out the window to the lake, avoiding eye contact. "I've been married since I was twenty-one. And aside from Alix Price, I have never gone outside my marriage. I'm not proud of myself. And I frankly don't care that I'm supposed to be in such distinguished company." His grin was rueful. "It was not what I wanted to do, and I did it. So what else do you want to know?"

Rachel felt a rush of compassion for the man. Thad Taylor didn't respect her very much, she knew that. But he had made himself vulnerable to her, and he didn't have to. Alix Price's death was breaking open secrets all over town, she thought. So how to handle this? She reached over and put a hand on top of his, startling him.

"Thad, I admire your honesty. You really took a risk in sharing this with me, and I assure you that it won't go beyond Joyce Romanski, who is the representative of the estate. And it's not you I'm interested in, you know. It's Alix. And how she was in, say, the six months before her death? Let's say during fall and winter quarters. Did you see much of her then?"

Taylor blushed. "Uh, actually, yes. I guess I'd better just do this and get it over with. We were at a conference on teaching psychology down in Santa Cruz the end of last summer. Which is where this thing with her started. You know, the usual script. We had some drinks, we were having fun, one thing led to another, she kissed me, and I wasn't thinking.

"And then I was hooked on her, really hooked. Like, teenager-in-love hooked. I couldn't stand not to be with her, and of course she wasn't at all interested in that. I was just another quick fuck for her. I guess she put up with me for a couple of months and then let me down, as gently as she could. And by the time fall quarter started, we were just colleagues again. It was surreal, Rachel. But in the meantime I did some serious damage to my marriage. Marissa and I are seeing a couples therapist because I said and did some stupid things while I was sniffing after Alix."

Rachel felt slightly impatient with the confession. Fine, good, she thought, Thad led himself around by the penis, I'm sorry to hear. But what about Alix?

"So what did you observe in her?"

"Well, you know, we had always been friendly. She seemed to be this very energetic person, pretty happy, pretty up. Sometime this fall, though, I don't know, she seemed to change. I noticed that she wasn't wearing her perfume anymore, and when I commented on it she nearly took my head off. She was spending hours closeted with that research assistant of hers, Ilona what's-her-name. She seemed to have lost weight. We went out for lunch one day, when was it, October maybe, maybe early November. Anyhow, we were sitting there in the Union Bay Café and she was belting down the wine like there was no tomorrow. It shocked the shit out of me, frankly. She was no drunk, and she was acting like one." Taylor shook his head at the memory.

"So I confronted her," he continued. "Asked her what in the hell was happening, told her that I was worrying about her, and so was Paul. Who, before you ask, is not someone who had sex with Alix, because I asked her, and she told me that he had the good sense to turn her down." Rachel was amused at this aside. She had wondered about Paul Cunningham until the time she'd spent working with him on the date rape case. His good sense was a good case of the well-disguised closet. If his sports stars had known Paul

208

was gay, they would have stayed away in droves. She wasn't about to out him to Thad Taylor, but she was tickled by Paul's achieving this reputation as a man of rectitude and self-control. His lover, a very closeted member of the clergy, would appreciate it, she thought to herself.

"So she told me to put a sock in it. That she was just having some normal ups and downs, and wasn't she allowed to be a woman going into menopause like other women. Backed me off—hard and fast. And gave me the choice—change the topic or end lunch. So I changed the topic, and we had an absolutely useless discussion about the new software for multivariate analysis. Gossiped about the department and who the next chair of clinical would be. Talked about Phil Zimbardo running for APA president. And then she kept her distance from me. I was still feeling bad enough about the affair that I guess I was relieved. That's when I told Marissa who I'd had the affair with. Which, I should tell you, made things a lot worse. I thought she wouldn't care if I did it with someone who wasn't serious about me. She was so damn mad that I, what did she say, 'fucked the class whore,' I guess she felt even more devalued because Alix wasn't someone special and pure."

Rachel could tell it was a strain for Taylor not to talk about himself. His information about Alix certainly converged with everything she already knew, but he added nothing new. Alix seemed to have drawn back from her usual networks of people that fall and winter. Odd for someone who had loudly proclaimed her disdain of therapy and lesbians, that the two best sources so far had been her therapist and her lesbian lover. Oh, well, thought Rachel, so things are seldom as they seem. Alix Price was skim milk masquerading as cream, all right.

"Thad, did you observe anything else about Alix that might be pertinent? Even something that seems really dumb?"

He scratched his head. "OK, dumb thing. Maybe two weeks before she died, I saw her come tearing into the building. She looked like she was on fire. I stopped her in the hall to say hello, and she was practically levitating, she was that angry, Rachel. I thought the better of it and just did the hello bit and went on down the hall. Something was biting her butt that day. Then half an hour later she was at the door of my office. Asked me if I knew if Marissa knew anyone with the psychology board. I told her, wrong department, they're in the Department of Health, not the Department of Human Services. She turned around and left. So I'm guessing she was mad at the board again." Alix had had her hand slapped a couple of times by the psychology board because, even though she was unlicensed and untrained for clinical practice, her advising to the local FoFAP chapter verged on doing therapy. Thad's interpretation made sense in light of that recent history.

"Anything else, Thad? Just take a little time, let your mind go blank and see if anything floats to the surface." Rachel gave Taylor a standard post-hypnotic suggestion for enhancing recall. Nothing ventured, she thought. He sat silent, staring out the window at the lake again.

"I don't think so, Rachel. I guess I'm just relieved to have this over with. I'm very sad that Alix is dead. And I'm horrified to admit this—I'm a little relieved. Marissa got a lot less mad once Alix was dead. I love my wife. Alix alive was bad for my marriage. Not that I would have done anything to her, mind you . . ." His voice trailed off.

Now isn't that silly, thought Rachel. A second man suggesting that anyone but Alix Price had killed Alix Price. First Ed Barnes hinting at the visiting stranger. Now this. Thad must be feeling awfully guilty to come up with that one.

"Not to worry, Thad. There are exactly two possibilities here, and neither of them involve you doing anything. I'm just glad you came clean with me. What you said was helpful." She gave him her standard parting line, asking him to call or e-mail her if anything new came to mind, and then showed him out to the door.

After he left, she sat alone in the deepening shadows. Alix Price had left so many wounded people behind her, she mused. Lovers whose lives were tossed about, a therapist who was so defensive about his work with her that he could hardly see straight, Lu and

Ed Barnes in more terror and pain, secrets in little boxes everywhere. Alix was more a piece of work than Rachel ever thought.

She glanced at the clock. Nearly five. The dog had been dozing quietly in his nest the entire time Thad Taylor had been in her office. She roused him from his slumber, got him into the car, and headed homeward. She needed an evening with a good mystery novel, she thought. Something by Laurie King or Patricia Cornwell, something to take her mind off Alix Price. And off Anna Sigurdson too, she reminded herself. Tomorrow evening was still further away than she wanted.

When Wednesday evening finally came, the anticipation made it feel awkward for the first time. Here she was sitting across the table at Noodle Ranch from Anna, picking at the grilled fish in grape leaves on her plate, feeling slightly foolish for the level of exposure she'd fallen to in the last two encounters. So now she'd cried on her shoulder and told her that she could hardly wait for her to come over with her latex goodies and fuck her, Rachel thought sarcastically. Wonderful. Just what she always wanted, to be so exposed.

Anna sensed Rachel's discomfort. Two steps forward, one and a half to the side, she thought. Rachel the skittish returns to the scene. She had been enjoying Rachel's bout of increased openness, but knew that the predictable next step would be precisely what was happening now. Silence, vapid chatter about the women's basketball team, retreat. Oh, well. This would take time. The spring rolls were delicious—she turned her attention to them, hoping that a reduction of focus would relax Rachel a bit.

Rachel finally decided to take the initiative. "Uh, Anna. Uh, you're probably noticing that I'm a little, uh, what shall I call it, a little . . ."

"Reserved. Pulled back. Freaked out. Any of the above." Anna tried to keep her tone light. "I get it that you were a little more out there with me last time than you had planned."

Rachel cast her eyes back down to the fish. "Uh, yes. Out there. Uh, maybe this idea for Saturday night is, uh, well, too much too soon. Maybe. I don't know." She fiddled with the fish, picked it up with her chopsticks, dropped it on the plate, picked it up again, and stuffed it into her mouth. Clumsy fool, she thought to herself. She couldn't even use chopsticks in front of this woman.

"Rachel, listen, hey, will you just cool out for a moment." Rachel was struck by the tone of Anna's voice. She sounded not as entirely understanding and supportive as usual. Oh shit, have I screwed this up, too, she thought. Oh, shit. Stupid girl, Rachel, always trying to be in control and now look what happened. Her eyes teared up. This was getting to be a habit. See Anna, then cry.

Anna noticed the tears. "Rachel, what did I say? Are you OK?" She dug in her pocket for a tissue and passed it across the table. In the crowded restaurant, no one noticed the minor drama happening at their table.

"I'm sorry, Anna. I didn't mean to be such a twit. I'm just so scared, is all. And you're right. I exposed myself to you, and that's not like me. I want to be in charge here, to be cool and distant and not give a damn how gorgeous you are. Not let you know how gorgeous I think you are, for that matter. Just be suave about the whole thing. And here I am raining all over dinner, again. You're gonna be real tired of this real fast, aren't you?" Rachel's voice had taken on a slightly beseeching tone. She looked up at Anna, eyes wet, visibly longing. Anna felt the blast of her intensity, out of the blue. The woman was explosive, that was for sure, she thought to herself.

"Rachel, if you need a little more distance, if you need to postpone our little workshop, that's OK. I've made a decision about you."

"And what's that?" Rachel felt frightened. A decision?

"That I want you in my life. That what I've seen so far makes me think that you're worth sticking around with. And that there's time. That we have plenty of time. So if you need to take a day, or a week, or a couple of weeks, or however long, to work out what feels right for you, I can just hang out here. When you get done figuring this out, I'll be standing here."

Rachel drew her breath in. This was as close to a declaration of love as she had heard from anyone else in a very long time. "And what if, when I get done figuring it out, what if I figure out that you're not the one? That no one is the one, that it's gonna be me by myself all alone? I don't want to break your heart, Anna. You seem to have such a lovely heart. I don't want it on my conscience."

Anna smiled. "Rachel, in case you haven't noticed, I'm a grown-up. I'm fifty-one years old. I've been around the block at least as many times as you. More, actually. It's my heart, and if I want to risk it on you, I will. So if you break my heart, I'll survive. And I'll have known you, even a little bit, in the process. Which makes it all worth it. How many women have the privilege of really knowing Rachel Katz, huh?"

Rachel felt herself relaxing. "So if I want to spend the evening talking about something completely, well, cerebral."

Anna chimed in. "You mean, like HIV risk in lesbian populations? Like my dissertation proposal? I'd love to, thank you."

Rachel grinned, back in the saddle. "Is that what you're gonna do it on? Far out, very far out. Tell me about your research design."

Anna smiled back. "Not so fast, little one."

Rachel bristled with fake umbrage. "Just who are you calling little? Excuse me?"

"You, oh short woman." Anna teased back. "In case you haven't noticed, you barely come up to my chin. Which I find adorable, but you gotta get outa denial about this, Rachel. You know, hi my name is Rachel and I'm short."

Rachel laughed. She was back, connected. Anna didn't expect her to put out, emotionally or any other way. Tonight, she could just hang out and be.

"So as I was saying, not so fast. Yes, we can talk about the design of my study, because I'm pretty sure you'll have some great ideas for me. But before we do, I just want to be very clear. You're becoming special to me, Rachel. I want to be that for you, too. I

213

treasure the times you open up with me. And I'm not standing here with an emotional crowbar demanding more, OK sweetie?"

Rachel melted under the warmth of the endearment and ventured a step out of her emotional fortress. "You know, Anna, you're getting to be kinda special to me, too. Every time I think of your eyes and your hair, I get shivery all over. You've been so kind. It astonishes me that someone who barely knows me could be so kind. It seems like my major scared rabbit routine hasn't chased you off. So thank you. And now can we please talk about your dissertation proposal? Because I've hit the limit of emotional risk tonight, I think."

"OK. Here's my basic idea." Anna launched into the synopsis of her proposal, and Rachel, now relaxed and happy, leaned forward and listened. When the two women left the restaurant later that evening, Anna, ever the gallant butch, walked Rachel to her car. Her goodnight kiss was surprisingly passionate. Rachel reeled, was caught off guard and instantly aroused. "Good night, little one. I'll see you Saturday. And we can decide how we want to do this class, OK?"

"OK. Good night, Anna."

Chapter Fifteen

As she was heading out the door on Friday afternoon, Rachel realized that she had forgotten her promise to call Joel Gibbs and let him know what was happening with the investigation. There was a moment's hesitation. She kept thinking that she really shouldn't be involving one of the interviewees in this process. But she had said she would call him, and he was bugging her with his messages. He was awfully anxious, poor guy. Oh what the hell, she thought, no harm no foul, just call the guy. She detoured to the phone in her kitchen and punched in his number.

"Hi, Joel," she began her voice message. "It's Rachel Katz calling about two-thirty Friday afternoon. Just wanted to let you know that I'm on my way to meet with Emma Forche now. So I'll call you again when I'm done with her to make a time for us to get together to go over the data. I really appreciate you volunteering to help out like this." And then maybe she could suss out whatever is going on with this business of his supposedly not knowing much about suicide, she thought. Too odd, it's just too odd.

Emma Forche in person did not disappoint. Tall, stately, and clearly well past her sixtieth year, she was dressed in a sixties-style tie-dyed T-shirt and loose cotton pants. As Rachel entered the reception area to Emma's office, a pair of madly flying lovebirds dive-bombed her. When she ducked her head reflexively, her eyes came to light on a cage which appeared to house several hedgehogs. A huge aquarium with a bubbling hose graced one corner of the room. Art hung on the walls between bookshelves stacked with tomes with titles that appeared to be mainly on the topic of body-mind integration. A whole shelf, Rachel noticed, was devoted to the topic of healing from sexual abuse. Music played softly from speakers in the next room, in which Rachel could see a massage table, ready for the next client to climb on. The room was redolent of warm human bodies, massage oil, and faint incense.

"Thanks for coming, Rachel. Let's sit down." Emma gestured to a pair of overstuffed chairs next to the birdcage. "I've got some tea if you'd like. We're going to be a while, I think. Do you like Wu Wei?" Rachel nodded, barely tracking the request, and Emma moved into a small side room where water could be heard running and the beeps of a microwave sounded. At least the woman used a microwave, Rachel observed. Some of these aging hippies wouldn't go near it, forgetting that heat was only a faster-moving molecule. So what if it got faster from microwaves, she thought to herself. She looked around the room again. It was hard for her to imagine Alix Price coming to this place—an alien planet when compared to the environs of William James Hall.

Sitting waiting for the tea to heat, Rachel found herself struck by the older woman's calm certainty. Emma Forche seemed to believe that she knew something unique about Alix. Rachel felt intrigued. Her well-honed skepticism was rubbed thin because of the lack of any useful information that emerged from the psychological autopsy. No one had had anything truly significant to add to the data mix—not Alix's therapist, not her lover, not her colleagues, no one. The columns in the spreadsheet added up to ambiguity, with a slight lean to the suicide side on Rachel's own bad days. She thought it would be nice to hear something new, although she kept her hopes in check. She knew she needed to be cautious, because she could feel herself almost too eager to hear what Emma had to say. It was the same sense of anticipation she had brought to her encounter with Joel Gibbs, and what a huge amount of nothing she had taken away from that one. Emma returned with two cups of hot liquid. More cliché, Rachel thought. The cups were hand-thrown pottery of the sort sold at the solstice fair, glazed in bright colors. She handed Emma the notarized copy of Joyce's authorization form. Emma glanced at it, then set it down. She appeared to take a deep breath, then she spoke.

"I had been treating Alix for probably twelve years, Rachel. She came to me at first because she had heard from some mutual friends that I was excellent at treating certain kinds of neck problems. And as you probably know by now, Alix had had chronic pain and strain in her neck for as long as she could remember."

Rachel tried to stay focused. This was going to be more old news. She was going to go back to Joyce with absolutely nothing to show for a month and thousands of dollars of time except for her own conjectures about Alix's state of mind. Certainly not with the definitive evidence ruling out suicide that Joyce hoped for. She breathed deeply. Emma noticed, and colored slightly.

"I'm not a terribly verbal person, Dr. Katz." The return to formality brought Rachel's attention back on center. "And what I have to say is difficult. So bear with me, please. I want to tell this story from the beginning. I think it will make a difference. Please."

Rachel nodded and leaned forward in her listening position. "I'm sorry, Emma. It's just been a very long road to here. I suppose I was hoping that you'd have something to tell me that would give some clarity of focus to the whole fuzzy picture. Thanks for being patient with me." Emma appeared to relax ever so slightly and continued.

"So I worked on her neck and shoulders using a variety of means. I specialize in acupressure, trigger point work. But with Alix, I used a range of massage modalities, because for a very long time nothing seemed to help her very much. I was surprised that she kept coming.

"Eventually she started to talk to me and to confide in me. Alix Price was one of the most lonely people I have ever met, Rachel." Rachel noticed that they were back on first-name terms again, and inwardly felt relieved. "She had so many lovers, and none of them, not a one of them, did she feel safe enough with to allow herself to really connect. Even though she fed on being attractive, it was as if the moment someone made love to her, she began to detach from them. She would almost throw them away.

"It took her a long time, probably six years after we began to work together, before she told me of her bisexuality. I actually think that if Alix had been less worried about what other people thought and less interested in making it in her man's world that she would have been a lesbian, no bones made about it. She was less frightened of emotional closeness with her women lovers. They were friends, not conquests, and they stayed her friends after the sex ended. She knew I was one—the friends who referred her to me are. It was as if she were surrounding herself secretly with lesbians, to feed that part of her soul."

Emma paused again. Rachel found herself struck by the woman's dignity, the formal nature of her speech and the depth of her caring for Alix Price.

"Anyway, Rachel, probably a year ago, something started to happen during her appointments. When I would be working on certain areas of her body, she would appear to go into an altered state. She shook, she curled up and screamed and cried. I would stop, of course, and reassure her, try to help her to orient herself. It was terrifying to her, but for the longest time she couldn't or wouldn't talk about it.

"Then last summer, she came in for her appointment and wouldn't take her clothes off. And told me that she had begun to have terrible images that she simply couldn't believe were true. That she knew couldn't be true, because she was an expert on memory, and what was happening to her just wasn't possible."

Emma paused, breathed deeply, and took a sip of her tea. Rachel felt herself begin to shake inside, ever so slightly. This story felt like the beginning of so many stories that she had heard from so many women and men who were starting to recall childhood horror. Recollections of the type that Alix Price had fought to deny the reality of. Oh, Alix, Rachel thought, you were one, weren't you? Then she pushed the thought out of her mind. She reminded herself to keep open. She had no idea what she was going to hear. She knew from Joel Gibbs that Alix was dealing with secondary PTSD. Maybe it was that, her borrowed scenes of pain from her accused parents. "Emma, can you tell me anything about what was happening to Alix?"

"Oh, yes. She was having images of her father having sex with her." The words dropped into the space between Emma and Rachel like a bomb. Images of sexual abuse. Not of accused fathers. Of a father doing terrible things, to Alix. Emma went on, slowly, deliberately. "Intercourse, oral sex, pretty much the range of things that one person can do to another. In these images, she was very young—five, six, seven. And terrified, in pain, her neck being pushed into the wall, just at the place where she'd had such terrible pain for years.

"She told me that she had begun to have nightmares around the time that she was having those fear reactions during her massages with me. That she was getting those images more and more during massage, although she had kept telling herself to just push it away. That she couldn't push it away anymore, that she was sure that she was developing some kind of obsession, probably because she had been listening to so many interviews of sexually abused children.

"I tried to get her to see that maybe this wasn't an obsession, Rachel. To reassure her that she wasn't crazy, that I had heard this before from other people. She cut me off that time, told me that the only reason she was telling me this was because she needed me to change what I was doing in her massage sessions, because lately it seemed to be making things worse. That she trusted me, because she had known me for so long, but that she didn't think I knew enough about obsessions to be able to know what I was talking about."

Emma paused again, her face obviously pained. Rachel noticed that she had been holding her own breath and let it out. "Emma, this is very difficult for you, I can see. Do you need to take a break?"

"Maybe just a stretch. Thanks, Rachel. I know that this must be familiar territory for you—I've heard you do a lot of work with incest survivors. And I do, too. But I've never met someone who was so unwilling for so long to take herself seriously and compassionately as Alix Price. That makes this story harder than it ought to be."

Emma rose from her chair and went through a series of stretching movements, walked over to her kitchen area and replenished her tea, then returned to the chair.

"So she told me what was happening and then she shut down the conversation. And I am a massage practitioner, not a counselor. I had to respect her request, no matter how I felt. I even consulted with some colleagues, and they all said the same thing. Back off, do the massage. Which of course I did.

"I knew that she was consulting a therapist. In the fall, she told me that she had found someone who specialized in working with obsessive disorders and that she felt very hopeful that he would help her. I guess I was relieved that she was at least getting some help."

"So what happened next, Emma?" Rachel was trying to control her impatience. She was listening to Emma on one mental track and on another she was thinking about what Joel Gibbs had told her about what he was supposedly treating Alix for. He had never mentioned anything about images of being sexually abused. Who was telling the truth here? What in the heck was going on? It was one thing to protect a client's privacy and withhold details. But it was beginning to look like Joel Gibbs had invented a story out of whole cloth. Which made no sense at all. Alix was dead. Why lie about her pain? What was there left to protect now?

"She seemed to be doing better at first when she began to see this man. Then around the holidays at the end of the year, something shifted. She started to lose weight, and she didn't seem to be sleeping much. She stopped wearing her perfume. She told me that instead of comforting her the way it always had, it seemed to make the obsessions worse. That the minute she put it on the morning she would be, what did she call it, flooded with images of her father having sex with her. That she was getting angry with herself, thinking she would have to give up her line of research because it seemed to be feeding her obsessions, even though she was supposed to expose herself to things that bothered her. When I asked her about that, she told me that this was her therapist's approach, something called—"

Rachel interrupted. "Exposure and response prevention. Yeah, it's the standard treatment for obsessive compulsive disorder. That's what he told me he was doing with her, right. Sorry, Emma, I interrupted you. Please, go on."

"Then there was a period where she just didn't tell me what was happening. The massages were getting more and more truncated. I could work on her hands and feet, sometimes her head. But she needed to keep her clothes on and to be able to tell me to stop whenever what she called the obsessions would show up. Which was often.

"Then in February, somewhere toward the end of the month I think it was, she came in for a session with me and started to cry. I asked her if I could put my arms around her and soothe her, and she let me, so she just cried in my arms for a long time. Then she began to talk.

"I knew that she had gone back to Boston for a family gathering. She told me that when she was there, one of her cousins approached her and told her that there was something she wanted to tell Alix. The something was that Alix's father had sexually abused the cousin when she was seven and eight every time the two families would spend overnights together. And that she remembered him abusing Alix. She saw him raping her in the next bed, in

221

the same room. That she wondered if Alix had dealt with any of this, because she had been in therapy for a while now and was beginning to feel better enough to be responsible to her co-victims, to validate them. That she knew that this might be hard, given that Alix's dad had killed himself when Alix was still pretty young."

The chill inside of Rachel grew. This wasn't a false memory; this was corroboration, from a witness, of abuse that had really happened. How was it possible that Joel Gibbs kept on thinking that Alix's symptoms were all about secondary trauma, about someone else's experiences? Alix had to have told Joel what she had told Emma. Rachel felt grateful that she was sitting down. If she'd been standing up she might have reeled from the shock. Pieces of the puzzle that had previously seemed unrelated began to come together and make a picture, a new picture of Alexandra Price. Rachel forced herself to focus on what Emma was telling her.

"Alix said that she was in shock when her cousin told her this," Emma continued. "Tried to argue with her, told her that this must be something that her therapist had suggested to her, offered to hook her up with the false accusations people for help in getting over this delusion. Her cousin told that this was precisely why she was telling Alix. She knew of her involvement with those folks and the FoFAP crowd and wanted Alix to know that she had never forgotten. That no way was this a false accusation. That she had written about it in her diary, told her mom and dad. They didn't believe her then but could remember her trying to tell them about uncle Alexander, when she approached them a few years ago about their disbelief."

Rachel started. Alix given the female version of her father's name, then incested by him? What a formula for misery.

Emma went on. "She told me that after her cousin, Beth is her name, talked to her, that she went back to her hotel room and cried for hours. And that she was starting to think that maybe this had happened to her. That even though it was impossible for people to forget and then remember like this, that maybe it was true.

Because she liked Beth, had always been close to her and trusted her when they were kids. She knew they had always shared the same room during family get-togethers. And she couldn't believe that Beth would lie to her. That Beth had been there, had seen all the terrible things that were in Alix's mind. Could tell her what her horrible nightmares looked like, even without Alix saying anything. I'm sitting there thinking, hallelujah, thank the Goddess."

Rachel grinned broadly. Even in the midst of telling a story of pain, the aging hippie rhetoric emerged.

"Thank the Goddess," Emma continued, grinning back for a flash of a second. "Alix was finally seeing the light. And now maybe she could get some real help. I was starting to think of all the really good therapists I know, I work with so many of their clients, someone who was really grounded and solid and smart about incest. Because whoever she was seeing wasn't helping her, had been encouraging her in this nonsense that she was having obsessions. Then she dropped the bomb."

Rachel sat up. More of a bomb than Alix believing in her own delayed incest memories? "What bomb, Emma?"

"It was about her therapist. I still don't know his name."

Oh, but I do, Rachel thought to herself. Joel Gibbs, so shackled by his investment in everything being OCD that he practically suggested a wrong diagnosis to his client. What a boob. And a liar. Rachel now realized that Alix wasn't having intrusive images of falsely accused fathers. She was having flashbacks to her own terrifying betrayal by the father she loved. It was likely that Emma was about to tell her about some colossal stupidity that he had engaged in with Alix in support of the OCD hypothesis. That would be no big deal to Rachel. She had seen a lot of therapists who were overly attached to their initial diagnosis and treatment plan, no matter what the facts turned out to be. Heck, she had done that a few times herself, especially early in her career. But why in the hell had Joel Gibbs lied to her about the content of Alix's intrusions? she wondered once more. What was that about? Trying to cover up his part in making things worse for Alix, in leading her to desperation?

The answer was not long in coming. It was not what she would have expected, although in retrospect, in the middle of the night, she beat herself up for not seeing it coming. It certainly explained Joel Gibbs's interest in Emma Forche.

"What she told me shocked me, Rachel. She told me that as she became more desperate, this therapist had told her that she needed to expose herself to the stimuli that evoked her obsession. That because she had stopped having sex with men she was making her problem worse. And that she needed to do this in order to get better, to have sex with a man again. So he told her that she should start having sex with him, so that when she had her obsessions in response to a penis, he could work with her, she said he called it, in something . . ."

"In vivo," Rachel said almost mechanically. This was a bomb, oh my God, yes. A large, ticking, smelly, radioactive bomb. One she knew only too well. Sex with the therapist offered as treatment for the client. This was the in vivo work that Joel had told her about, the reason why Alix was having longer and longer sessions. This had nothing to do with in vivo exposure to the stories of falsely accused men. It was about Alix being revictimized by the very person whose job it was to help her. He was fucking her. Raping her, really. In vivo, my ass, she said to herself. Abuse. This was abuse, pure, plain, and simple. A reenactment of the abuse and betrayal that Alix had suffered at the hands of her father forty years before. Sex with a therapist was incest, replayed on the body of an adult.

"So, yes, in vivo." Emma continued with her narrative, pale and determined. "She said that she told him that she thought it was a really bad idea, that she had fucked a thousand men and that had never helped her one bit. That maybe she was done with men. And that he told her that she had come to him for his expertise in treating obsessive disorders and that he knew from experience that this was going to get her done with her problems very quickly. That since he couldn't make her have sex with other men, and he certainly wouldn't want to watch her and do interventions as needed, that he was offering to take the risk with her. Since she was a colleague. Since they were equals and peers. Since neither of them believed in transference."

Rachel shuddered. What was it with these guys? The scripts rarely deviated from one case to another. She had heard those lines so many times. Maybe therapists who sexually abused their clients were stupid in other ways, lacking creativity in the rationales they presented to their victims. Sex with the therapist as treatment. Sex with the therapist as desensitization for sexual problems, as a way of gaining mastery over old abuse. Lies, all terrible lies. And the nonsense about them being peers. Rachel knew that this was especially likely to be spouted by therapists whose theories didn't include a human unconscious. The cognitive behaviorists who "didn't believe in transference." Even, sometimes to her greatest personal horror, feminist therapists who mistook the concept of empowering clients and twisted it into the myth that the client could be powerful by having sex with her therapist. And here it was again—Joel Gibbs, reading off the script.

"So she did have sex with him. She told me that she avoided it for weeks and that he finally wore her down. That was the words she used, 'he wore me down.' She told me that he fucked her the way her father had. That everything she had told him, he used to make fantasy scenes. That it sickened her. And that now she was feeling much, much worse. The nightmares and flashbacks were constant. She could barely hold herself together to teach or go into the lab. She hated having sex with him, and she felt trapped. She was turning to me, she said, because she didn't know what to do or who to believe anymore. And that I had always been good to her and careful with her."

Rachel sat perfectly still and waited for Emma to continue. Her mind was anything but still. It raced, overstimulated by Emma's disclosures. It took all of her years of training to remain silent, receptive, listening to what came next.

"So, after I heard this from her I knew I had to intervene. I've talked to people before whose therapists hurt them like this. I even turned in another massage therapist for it, years ago. It's like incest, Rachel. Well, you know that, I'm preaching to the choir according to what I've heard about you around town all these years. I was horrified. Poor dear Alix. This man had taken a wounded woman and wounded her worse." Emma's color was high, her voice no longer calm. Rage coursed through it.

"I told her that what he was doing was wrong, period. That there was no justification for it. That I was certain that the law didn't allow for any exceptions. I told her that she had to stop it, that her body was telling her how bad it was. She cried and cried, she was so afraid that if she tried to stop it she would get worse. I tried to reassure her, to let her know that stopping with this man was the only way to get better. That it would be empowering to finally say no to a sexual abuser. That she could turn him in. I told her I'd heard that these guys are like sex offenders, they do it again and again, that there were other women to protect. And I asked her if there was anyone she trusted who she knew would know about this kind of thing.

"That's when she mentioned your name, Rachel." Rachel sat up. Oh, shit, oh my God, Rachel thought, this was what Alix had called her about. "She said that she knew you from the field, that you weren't exactly friends, but that everyone knew that you'd testified in cases that had to do with sex by therapists. That she could call you up for a consultation. She said that she respected your opinion. She seemed so relieved to have thought about you. I could tell it was going to help. We talked for a little while about her options. Should she turn him in to the psychology board? Should she sue him? She was afraid that it would get out, what had happened to her. That her professional reputation would be ruined. I told her that she really should talk to you, that it sounded like you knew the answers to some of her questions. That all I knew was that this was wrong and hurting her.

"I saw her one time after that. She seemed a little calmer. She told me that she had canceled her appointments with the therapist. That she told him that he was in trouble. She told me that she felt scared and shaky. I was worried, because I was about to go on a vacation for a few weeks. She didn't look great, but she seemed one step back from the edge.

"The next thing I knew I was getting a call from the police. A very nice young woman, Andrea something. Said that she was investigating the death of Alexandra Price and that my name and phone number were in her appointment calendar. I could barely believe it, Rachel. I was so upset. She had been in pain, but she was alive and vital and energized when she left my office that last evening, more than I had ever known her to be. Telling the truth and saying no were setting her free. I still can hardly believe she's gone. Maybe I would have believed it was suicide if I hadn't seen that spark come back into her, felt the life force returning. But I can't. I was so glad when I heard that someone had engaged you to look into her death."

Emma sat quietly, apparently at the end of her recitation. Rachel's mind continued to reel. Suicide was looking like a huge possibility here. She tried to pull herself together to ask some questions.

"Did Alix say anything to you, ever, about thoughts of killing herself, Emma?"

"Actually, no. I thought about this quite a good deal, as you might imagine. I know that incest survivors are often suicidal. I've had enough clients in that position, after all. And Alix was certainly doing badly, what with being raped by that man, her therapist. But her spirit seemed to be holding up through this all. She knew enough to talk to me, after all, to trust whatever little piece of her gut hadn't been silenced by her father and that man. She had plans when she left here. She had shut off that man. She was going to call you. She had confronted her rapist, called him to account."

Rachel nodded. "And she did call me. We had an appointment set for a few days after she died. She never told me what it was about. I had no idea, until this moment. She was right, you know. I was the person to talk to about this. But what was this about confronting her therapist?"

Emma frowned. "She was pretty angry at him anyway. Said he was a careless, selfish fucker who hurt her physically. Not to speak

227

of that she finally understood that he was raping her. She told me that she told him that she had talked to me, that she had gotten professional advice. That he might be in trouble for what he had done. I tried to dissuade her, to slow her down. But I don't know if you knew Alix. Once she got an idea in her head, there wasn't much stopping her."

Rachel nodded. Another way in which she and the dead woman shadowed one another, she thought. They were both persistent. Rachel had seen this in survivors before. The oppressive mantle of fear lifted, and all of the paralysis of years burst into a flurry of activity. Sometimes people did incredibly foolish things during that first intense flush of feeling free. And it seemed as if Alix Price had been no exception. Confronting an offender was a common fantasy, and Alix had apparently done just that, damn the consequences. No wonder Joel Gibbs had lied so thoroughly and completely to her.

Rachel turned to Emma. "Did Alix say anything at all about how her therapist, whose name by the way is Joel Gibbs, responded to her confrontation? Because I talked to him, Emma, and he couldn't have been nicer about her. Of course, he also lied through his teeth about what was troubling her." Rachel realized that she hadn't for a moment stopped to wonder whose story of Alix was more credible. Emma had to be telling the truth, she thought. No wonder Joel had tried, no matter how feebly, to throw her off the scent of the massage practitioner. He knew that she knew and that Rachel would hear this story. And know that he had pushed Alix over the edge. He wants to do damage control, she thought to herself. As if. As fucking if.

"She said that he was upset. That he asked her to think about her own reputation. And that he got angry, called me something she didn't want to repeat. Told her again that he was the expert in treating these things, that I was just something else unrepeatable who didn't know what she was talking about. That he'd be glad to find her references about how the sexual treatment was helpful. Sounded like he got sorta rabid, which is no surprise. I was raped as a young woman, and I went to court and testified against the man.

He was furious at me for turning him in. Maybe this therapist, this Gibbs man, reacted in the same way. You know, Rachel, I guess I was a little surprised that she kept on believing me. But maybe she just believed herself. Sex with him hurt her. I helped her."

The wisdom of the body, Rachel mused. Even with overly heady Ph.D. types, sometimes the truths of one's guts cannot be forgone. Sometimes even we can't ignore that we know what we wished we didn't.

"So he was mad and upset and defensive," Rachel continued. "Sounds pretty normal for these cases. These guys can't seem to believe that their little sex puppets have suddenly grown minds and wings of their own and are about to fly away. But I want to get back to Alix. What else did she tell you?"

Emma sat, thinking. One of the birds flew onto her shoulder, and she reached up to hold it in her cupped hands where it sat quietly, allowing her to stroke its ruby-colored wing feathers. This woman radiates goodness and nurturance, Rachel thought. No wonder Alix finally trusted her.

"Not a lot else. At least not about him. A lot was happening in her life, and most of it was hard. She had a cat, a sweet old girl, who she'd had to put down a few months ago." Ah, thought Rachel, that fills in that loose end. Poor Alix, losing her pet. "We were talking about me helping her to adopt a new baby. You might have noticed." She gestured around the room "I'm very connected to furry creatures. She was coming to terms with being a lesbian, I think. That was hard for her. She'd fought it a long time, and she still didn't quite trust herself about it. This lawyer, Joyce Romanksi, the one who signed this release?" Rachel nodded. "She talked a lot about her. About what a missed opportunity she was, how Joyce was her soul mate, and she hadn't let it happen. That maybe when all of this was better, she was going to give it another try. She was terribly afraid that she'd lost her chance. About the young woman she was involved with at the time of her death, realizing that it was not such a good thing to be lovers with her student. And she talked about her father. About how much pain she was in, what an enormous loss she was experiencing. That she had never known how much she had needed him to be the good, loving daddy she had always believed in. She was hurting."

Rachel sat, bemused by the irony. Joyce Romanski, who had gone into therapy to deal with her feelings about Alix, never knowing how much Alix was wanting and missing her. Tragic. Send in the clowns, it was so tragic. So many missed possibilities here that could have been made right. If only, thought Rachel, if only Alix hadn't been so wedded to the impossibility of remembering incest. If only she had gone to see anyone except Joel Gibbs, anyone who would have recognized what was happening and gotten her the help she needed instead of digging a knife into her guts and twisting. Alix might be with us, and there might have been a happy ending. Rachel could have kept on hating her and would have had to find some other way to avoid spending time with Anna.

The two women sat in silence for several minutes. Rachel finally spoke up. "Emma, this has been incredibly eye-opening. I wish I had begun with you, would've saved a lot of work and time. I wish Alix had stayed alive long enough to get to me and talk to me. I feel so sad just now."

Emma put a hand on Rachel's shoulder. She noticed, because she was unable not to, the incredible tension in the younger woman's muscles. She knew instinctively that Rachel was carrying around her own burdens. "Rachel Katz, I can't say I'm glad you came. But I feel at peace now. I didn't know if anyone else knew the truth about Alix. And now you do, and Joyce will. And maybe Alix can rest."

The remainder of the brief encounter was taken up with the minor social exchanges of farewells. Rachel asked Emma for her card, "for referrals, just in case the need comes up," she said. Rachel actually had herself in mind because she thought she could use some time with this woman. She bundled her things into her carrying bag and headed out the door.

Chapter Sixteen

Rachel was surprised to see that it was still light when she emerged from Emma Forche's quiet, dark office. She had experienced that attenuation of time that occurs when a person is in shock. Alone with herself again, her mind chewed frantically on what she had heard. Alix Price an incest survivor. Alix Price experiencing terrible memories, the kind of memories she had fought in public to deny existed. Alix having the memories confirmed. Alix unable to pretend to herself that this was anything but the truth. Alix with her world split open. And then, Alix Price having sex with Joel Gibbs. Sex with her therapist, coerced, presented as necessary treatment. Alix learning that she had been abused again. Today's revelations put an entirely new face on the psychological autopsy.

It became increasingly undeniable that Alix had killed herself. So many incest survivors were so fragile when the memories swept over them. It was hard enough to deal with the world overturning when it concerned the father you had always loved. Discovering that sort of profound betrayal shook the foundations of reality for everyone and anyone who was forced to stand and confront the truth of incest in their life. But to have something happening that also destroyed everything one had stood for professionally as an adult, to be having the kind of memories that you had told the world simply could not be true? And to have those memories confirmed, conclusively, by the only living witness to the horror? Poor Alix. No wonder she was vulnerable to Joel's crap. She might have been angry and defiant when she left Emma's office, but that never lasted long, in Rachel's experience. The pain would be too huge to keep at bay with anger for very long.

And what about Joel? Rachel realized he must have been lying to her all along. That shithead, that utterly evil man, Rachel thought. Having sex with a client was destructive even to people who were relatively resilient and put-together, not that many of that kind of person ever walked into a therapist's office. But Rachel had seen a number of women in her forensic work over the years with a list of characteristics that were sounding more and more like Alix Price—incest survivor, recent recovery of memories, abusing alcohol, unstable relationships, physical illness or pain—whose response to sexual exploitation by their therapists was to make serious, almost lethal suicide attempts. Andrea Cole had made three of those, after all, before she got to Rachel, and there were at least a dozen others Rachel could think of from her years of practice.

Oh, Joyce, Rachel thought. She was going to be so sorry to have to tell her this. That her beloved Alix probably did kill herself after all. But only because her shit of a so-called therapist pushed her over the edge by screwing her. Rachel bet he was the guy that Ed Barnes saw going to her home that night. He must have said or done something that made it impossible for her to hold on. She wondered if the estate could sue him.

Rachel realized she had wandered over to her car, where Mr. Piggy was curled up on his cushion, snoring. As she came up to the door, his ears waggled, followed by his tail, and suddenly an entire

232

bull terrier body was vibrating with joy. "OK, OK, I'm happy to see you, too. I see you drank up most of the water I left you. Good thing you didn't come with me into that office—all kinds of bull terrier snacks wandering around in there. It would have been quite the feathers-and-fur-flying experience. And I really needed to be concentrating this time, Mr. Piggy. So, doggy-dear, I think I'm gonna take you for a walk. Waddaya say we go to Gasworks?"

The little brown body leaped with enthusiasm. He knew these sounds, they meant lots of lovely goose poop to try to eat. Rachel needed to take a walk, no matter what the dog felt like doing, to clear her mind and consider everything that Emma had just told her. To digest it before she called Joyce or jumped to any conclusions. She was so immersed in her musings about Joel Gibbs and his possible role in driving Alix to despair that she barely glanced at the cars around her. Another oversight for which she would roundly castigate herself in many middle-of-the-night self-criticism sessions. She never noticed the black Mercedes coupe two cars behind her.

She and the dog had just come down the side of the hill in Gasworks Park along the water and were walking to the embankment beneath the old gasworks where she had sat with Anna a few weeks earlier when a man stepped out of the recessed seats along the wall. It was Joel Gibbs. His arm was outstretched. Rachel was taken aback to see him there. Again, she thought. What was this with going to Gasworks and encountering Joel? Then she shuddered. In his outstretched hand was a gun. Pointed at her. She looked down at it. It wasn't a water pistol, she thought. It seemed to be a real gun, aimed at her gut.

"Well, Rachel, you had to go and do it. I tried to dissuade you, but no, you fucking nosy bitch, you. You had to go talk to that other fucking meddling old woman."

Who was this person spewing venom out of the mouth of smarmy Joel Gibbs? Something was terribly wrong with this picture. It was one thing to hear that he was a slime case who fucked his client. But a gun? Rachel frantically tried to review in her mind her training in hostage negotiation. Except she was about to become the hostage. What was she supposed to do? Oh yeah, be calm and talk reasonably with the hostage-taker. She tried not to look at the gun and to focus in on her seemingly deranged colleague.

"Uh, Joel, uh, seems like we have a lot to talk about. Do you think that you could maybe put that thing down, you know, not escalate things for yourself? You're not in any trouble yet. It's not as if a dead woman is in any position to bring a complaint."

"Oh just shut up, stupid bitch. Or would you like me to shoot that stupid dog of yours?" He pointed the gun down at Mr. Piggy, who was confused that this man didn't seem to want to make friends with him and was pointing something strange at his mama.

Rachel froze. Somehow the notion that anyone would harm her dog drained her of all of her self-protectiveness. Mr. Pig came first. She was so taken aback by Joel's behavior that she could barely think straight. Why was he pointing a gun at her? None of what happened called for such drastic measures. Yes, Joel had done an incredibly shitty destructive thing, was probably responsible for Alix's suicide. But this was a bit much. She tried again. "OK, Joel, what do you want from me?"

"What I want is to shut you up. Is for you to walk right next to me, here, like we're sweethearts. What a joke, that anyone would think I'd be interested in a fat dyke like you. But hey, stranger things have happened. And you're gonna act like you're my sweetheart, nice and close so no one can see my gun. We're gonna walk right out of the park together, to your car. And then you're going to drive us to your office, where you're gonna kill yourself. Just like poor dead Alix, now it's gonna be poor dead Rachel. A real epidemic of dead psychologists." He laughed at his own sick joke.

Rachel's shock deepened. Suddenly an entirely new hypothesis emerged from the muck, one that had never even entered the picture until this moment. Suicide or accidental death were not the only possible solutions to the riddle of Alexandra Price. She took a conceptual leap, let it out loud. "So she didn't kill herself, did she, Joel?"

"I thought you had the brain capacity to figure these things out, Ms. smart-ass feminist forensic psychologist. Damn straight she didn't kill herself. I killed her. Me. You really got fooled, didn't you? I fooled you. Me, Joel Gibbs. I know you think I'm not very smart, you and that dyke friend Alice of yours, but I fooled you. I've fooled a lot of people, you can hardly begin to imagine, you stupid fool. All those idiots in the behavior therapy association who think they're such hot shit. I fooled them, too. Think you know so much about so-called sexual misconduct. Fucking expert on transference, you were so busy following your stupid expertise, you walked right into this, didn't you? I know what you wrote." In a high-pitched mock whine, he recited a quote from one of Rachel's articles. 'Victims of therapist sexual exploitation are at increased risk of suicide.' Where was that, in *Professional Psychology*. Fuck, who the fuck cares?"

Gibbs laughed, nervously. "What a pleasure to bring you down, too. Fucking bitch was going to blow the whistle on me, thanks to that fucking bitch of a massage hag. Turn me in to the licensing board. Told me the massage dyke told her she had a responsibility to other clients. Such bullshit. And that could not happen. You know, well you know, you helped pass the damn law. It's a felony for a psychologist to have sex with their clients now. I would have been labeled a Goddamned sex offender. Would have to go to those damn groups and write apology letters." Rachel groaned silently. How had she suddenly become the bad guy in Joel Gibbs's paranoid delusions? Her anxiety led her to blurt out what came next to her mind.

"So, what, you set her up with the overdose?" Rachel figured she had nothing to lose by getting Joel to talk to her. And if he thought she was going to be dead, he might just avail himself of the opportunity for a little catharsis. Or a little bragging, narcissistic murdering bastard, she said to herself.

"I gave her the choice. Nice of me, wasn't it? She could die pretty and drink up the lovely cocktail I'd mixed for her, or she could die ugly with her hand around this gun. Stupid woman probably thought she could wake herself up, she was such a fucking drunk already. All of these women, whining about incest, fucking drunks. Anyways, you're gonna have the same choice. Although no one would call you pretty, fucking dyke bitch."

Rachel had entered some kind of altered state of consciousness in which she felt incredibly calm and clear. Her clinical mind had begun to click, becoming an observer, noting and assessing what was happening to the woman frozen in fear at the end of her dog's leash. She noticed that Joel was revving himself up and becoming increasingly out of control. His use of language was becoming more primitive and impoverished. He was caught up in an emotional firestorm of hate and fear, knowing that he was exposed now. The research was that therapists who had sex with their clients actually hated and despised them. That hate was dripping out all over Joel, dropping like acid on Rachel. Dangerous. Very, very dangerous. She needed to avoid provoking him. He was getting gratuitous in his insults. That was really sloppy, Joel, she thought to herself. A fear-frozen Rachel told herself to keep her wits about her. Her life depended on it. She had to let him think that what he was saying mattered to her. She had to be nice, not her smart-mouthed self. He had a gun. He had killed Alix Price. Rachel was in mortal danger. She knew that the best predictor of future behavior is past behavior. She had to act like a normal person who has a gun pointed at her, whatever the hell that was.

"Joel, you don't have to kill me. Really. I mean, what do I really know? Only some uncorroborated suspicions, you're clearly upset . . ."

He cut her off midsentence. "Come on, don't try to play with me. I am not stupid, I told you that. You know and I know that you've got enough information now to put all the pieces together. And I've just told you what I did, since you were stupid enough to ask. Like you're gonna say this was just a bad hallucination brought on by too many hours with that witch? I don't think so. Sorry Rachel, well, not really sorry actually, but you've got to go. So let's just do it quietly. No need to perturb people. Everyone knows how distraught you were about your girlfriend buying it, so why will this be a surprise?" Rachel was taken aback by this comment. She had no idea how widespread had been the news of Sarah's death and her subsequent withdrawal from the world. "No one's gonna be poking into the circumstances of your demise, I'll bet. One less dyke bitch in the world. Fucking dykes, all of you, Alix, that Joyce bitch, the student, that fucking quack body-worker." The last words were said with even more of a sneer, if possible, than the rest of his hate-filled litany. Joel Gibbs clearly knew a lot more about the women in Alix's life than he had let on in their office meeting. "Take the fucking dog and come on. Now."

Rachel glanced around. The park was characteristically empty at midafternoon—no one around to help her if she yelled. And then there was Mr. Piggy to worry about. The dog had no survival instincts where people were concerned. He had never met a human being whom he didn't want to have as his new best friend, and Joel was only confusing him, not egging him on to attack. The dog had to be protected.

In the car, he jammed the gun into her side. "Now drive to your office. Slowly, like a normal person. No weaving or anything like that." Rachel suppressed the urge to wisecrack that she had never done anything like a normal person. Not the time for humor, Katzie, she admonished herself. She drove in silence along Northlake Way, past the shipyards and marinas and the stands of blackberry tangled everywhere, beginning to flower. Everything stood out in stark clarity. Rachel forced herself to keep thinking. How in hell was she going to get herself out of this one? She had to. Letting this idiot kill her was unthinkable. She would miss safer sex class with Anna, damn it.

Gibbs seemed emboldened by having managed to capture his prey. He kept rambling loudly as Rachel drove, filling in the silence that she created. "You know, if she only hadn't had to talk to that damn massage therapist, everything would have been fine. She was just confused, you know. That bitch cousin of hers trying to convince her that these obsessions were really memories. Drove me crazy after she came back from that reunion, all she wanted to do was talk, talk, talk about that. Pretty fucking obsessed, that's what she was. And then she had to go and spill the beans to that woman who put it into her head that there was something wrong with me fucking her. Stupid bitch. There wasn't any transference, you know that. But the fucking state doesn't know it. So she had to die. And you have to die. Like those other ones died."

Rachel shuddered. Other ones? Did this have something to do with Joel's other clients who had killed themselves—or maybe hadn't killed themselves? A serial killer psychologist—just what she had always needed to encounter among colleagues. Her luck to have the first observation of this previously unknown specialty.

Her attention turned back outward in time to hear Joel say, "because I am not going to lose my license or go to jail. I am not. No fuck is worth that."

Yeah right, Rachel thought silently to herself. He should have considered that before he unzipped his pants. He must have counted on Alix's pride and her ability to keep secrets so long and so well to protect him.

They arrived at her office on the east side of Lake Union too quickly. Joel's eyes darted around. "All right, bitch. Who else is in the building now? And don't bullshit me. I can shoot your dog, you know."

"Uh, OK, it's Friday, right. No one else sees clients on Friday afternoons as far as I can remember. So it should be pretty empty." Joel seemed to calm slightly at this news. This was good. Keeping him calm was important. It gave her more time to figure out what to do. She got out of the car, making encouraging noises at Mr. Piggy, who seemed completely bewildered by the turn of events. One minute they had been in the middle of a nice walk, then the man came, and now they were back at work. His brown eyes looked beseechingly at her. Rachel almost lost her composure and began to cry. How would he survive if he lost her, too? She took a deep breath. She would figure this out. She was a smart woman.

The words resonated through her head. The voice of Fern, her nurse practitioner. "Jeez, Rachel, I thought you were a smart woman. But no safe sex equals a whole lot of nasty medicine. Just remember not to drink anything, and I mean nothing on this drug. Or you'll be one very sick smart woman. Remember, Flagyl on top of booze will make you barf." Rachel would have begun to giggle with relief at this sudden recollection, except that she knew that it would make Joel suspicious. Sure. She'd drink his stupid cocktail, because she would toss her cookies all over the office as soon as he left. So she let him see her tear up looking at the dog. That would keep him focused on his power over her and that would let her be in control. One hell of a time to be a control freak, my girl, she said to herself. She just had to keep paying attention. Fern didn't guarantee that she'd get nauseous on alcohol on top of the Flagyl. She just threatened her with it. So she had to keep paying attention.

Gibbs pushed the gun at her. "So let's get going. I have a date tonight with a real woman not one of you goddamned whiners and dykes. Jeez, I don't know why I go to the trouble of fucking these women, then I have to do this thing. I want this over and done with soon. Your office. Now. No fooling around."

His face was red. She noticed that his pupils were dilated with excitement. Not good, Joel, not good. She breathed deeply, felt the calm wash over her again, and walked up the stairs. "Now Joel, I just have to reach into my pocket to get the key out. And then punch the code into the alarm so that it won't go off." He nodded. She blessed the day that she had had the system put in over the protests of her office-mates, who had worried about what kind of impression the security system might make on fearful clients. She hit the combination of keys that meant that she was being held under duress. That was supposed to make police come. One hell of a time to find out if the alarm company's promises of a quick response to the duress code were real, but she was glad to have that as a fallback if the Flagyl didn't make her vomit up his vile brew.

In the office he shoved her into her chair, and with his gloved hand picked up a pen and paper from her desk. "All right, let's write a nice suicide note. You know, something about how investigating Alix's suicide made you realize that she had made the right choice. How you missed what's-her-name . . ."

"Sarah," she broke in, losing her grip on her control.

239

"Yeah, whatever, how you miss her and can't live without her. Write something about the dog, who's gonna take care of the dog. That'll make it sound real authentic. Oh hell, you know what's in a real suicide note, you're the great expert on this crap."

Rachel took the pen. She noted with irony that it was the engraved token she had received from the state psychological society when she was honored as psychologist of the year. How utterly and wonderfully appropriate, she thought. She knew that if Joel succeeded, the very fact that she had handwritten something would raise suspicions among her friends. Everyone knew that Rachel never wrote by hand. She'd barely touched the pen since it was given to her. She began to write.

When she finished, Joel snatched the paper up. "Jesus, bitch, I can't read a word you wrote. What are you trying to do?"

Rachel suppressed a smile. "You know, my handwriting is lousy in the best of circumstances. At least no one will think that I was feeling happy and composed."

"Fine. Here, drink this, and get it over with. I'm not planning on standing here chatting with a corpse all evening." He pulled a sports bottle like the one she used at her health club out of his pack. It reeked of alcohol. Even the smell made her ill. "Drink up, come on. It'll be better than way."

Rachel held her figurative nose and gulped the mixture down. Her stomach felt queasy, and she burped. She could feel the alcohol absorbing quickly through her stomach lining. Was she feeling woozy already? She fought to keep her mind in focus. "So just out of curiosity, I mean, Joel, I'm gonna be dead anyway, what are you killing me with? I've always wondered what would be necessary to successfully pull off this method of suicide."

"Yeah, right. You are one amazingly stupid bitch, Rachel. But as a dying wish to you, sure, I'll tell you. It took me a couple of tries to get this really right, you know. First one I had to do with a plastic bag after she couldn't keep it down."

First one, thought Rachel through the increasing haze in her brain. Oh my God. He is a serial killer.

Joel went on, proud of himself. "So I finally figured out this mix. One hundred proof alcohol, about forty Seconal, and some Compazine to make sure you keep it down. Of course with Alix I used some of her downers, saved me the hassle of trying to get the drugs."

Rachel felt her heart drop. Compazine? Oh, shit. Compazine was an incredibly effective anti-nausea drug, in addition to being a central nervous system depressant. The damn duress alarm had better work, because Flagyl or no Flagyl, she wasn't very likely to throw up the concoction. She could feel her head spinning.

"I have to sit down, Joel. I'm feeling really sick."

"Oh, poor baby. Sure, sit, lie, I don't care. You'll be good and dead—you should be comfortable, right?" The sarcasm was so thick that it seemed to drip off the walls like slime. The kind of slime that Joel Gibbs was, she thought to herself. Why wasn't she throwing up. Where are the damn police? She began to wonder if she had punched in the right duress code. Or if the promise of quick police attention was all an alarm company scam. She shivered. The dog, who had been huddled in the corner sensing something terribly awry, came over and laid his head on her knee. She absently reached down to pet him. She could feel herself beginning to fade. This wasn't right, she thought, damn it. She was not ready to be dead yet. She still hadn't made love with Anna Sigurdson.

That thought shocked her. As her defenses dissolved under the barrage of the toxic cocktail, unguarded feelings came to the surface. She could feel tears rolling down her face. She was going to die without ever telling this woman that she liked her a lot. And Joel Gibbs would get away with killing another woman. The shithead.

Through her fading vision, Rachel saw Gibbs turning to leave. "Good-bye, Rachel Katz. It's been a pleasure killing you. Too bad you're too ugly for me to fuck. It's kind of interesting to have sex with a corpse. Did it with Alix, you know. Condoms, what a great invention, no trace of me left behind."

Rachel felt foggier and foggier. She fought allowing her eyes to close or her head to drop down. She forced herself to breathe deeply. Then it happened.

Her stomach did a flip-flop. And then another. She swallowed hard. She was going to vomit. Rachel hated to vomit. The Flagyl had overcome the anti-nausea effects of the Compazine. Puking was better than being dead, she told herself.

She made a choking sound, and then a barrage of foul-smelling liquid flew out of her mouth and into a puddle at her feet where it lay, reeking of cheap booze and stomach acid. The dog, curious, began to sniff. Gibbs turned from the door at the sound, his nose twitching with distaste at the odors. He yelled at her.

"Now what in the fuck did you have to go and do that for, you stupid bitch. Now I'm going to have to shoot you. Fuck, I'm going to get puke all over my shoes."

He began to rummage in his pack for the gun, which he seemed to have tucked away as he was heading to the door. At that moment, an arm burst through the door, police special outstretched, followed by a booming female voice.

"Put the gun down NOW. I said NOW." Rachel noticed from her chair where she sat retching and wretched that two police officers had burst into the room. The first, a tiny woman, blond hair in French braids, had her gun drawn on Joel Gibbs. The second, an Asian man, rushed over in the direction of Rachel Katz, stopping only when he saw Mr. Piggy's head turn up.

"It's OK officer," Rachel somehow found the strength to croak. "My dog loves police officers." She dimly noticed through the fog of her consciousness that Joel Gibbs was holding his gun limply at his side, while the other officer continued to bark, "Put the gun down, sir. Now, sir."

The sequence of events that followed stayed in Rachel's memory only in bits and pieces that came together over the succeeding days and weeks. There was a flash of Joel Gibbs dropping the gun on the floor and then being thrown into the vomitous mess by the police officer who had drawn on him. Rachel remembered thinking what a loud voice such a little woman had. Another quick image was of the paramedic team hovering over her. She remembered crying, holding on to Mr. Piggy as someone was taking him away, weeping as if her heart would break. Later, she could remember, too, thinking that she was going to lose her beloved dog forever, feeling like a confused small child. Her throat hurt from the vomit. That wasn't hard to remember, because it got worse from the tube that the medics put down her throat. She would have to remember this for suicidal clients, she thought at one point. How much it hurts to have your stomach pumped.

The ambulance ride to the University Hospital emergency room was brief. She kept popping into sleep, and finding herself rudely awakened by one or the other of the medics, who seemed intent on keeping her eyes open. Then there was a period of brief, troubled unconsciousness, filled with images of Joel Gibbs laughing maniacally at her, of Mr. Piggy lying dead, of Alix Price dancing in front of her, nude. Of Sarah, fading into the distance.

When Rachel next was able to track the world coherently, she found herself looking up into the frightened face of Cori Diaz. The face brightened at the sight of Rachel's open, apparently comprehending eyes.

"Babe, are you OK? The attending said that you should have come out of it before now. So we've all been doing little neuropsych assessments on you. Say something, will ya, hon?" Cori's Texas twang became more pronounced in such moments of worry, her speech more cluttered.

Rachel tried to sit up and fell back down. She swallowed. Her throat burned. She tried to talk. "My piglet?" Tears rushed into her eyes. "Pig, where's Pig?"

"Oh, Rachel." Cori dissolved in a mix of tears and laughter. "You're OK, you must be. Mr. Piggy is fine." Her words came out in a rush, Rachel straining to track. "One of the cops at the scene is a friend of what's-her-name, who used to be your client." Rachel nodded, unable to speak well enough to put Andrea's name into the sentence. "I think she'd told everyone about that dog in your office. So that woman, Andrea I guess her name is, they called her and she came and got him. Has him at her place with her dogs. He's fine, don't worry. Oh jeez, girl, I'm so glad to see you back. You had us all very worried. I gotta call Alice to get her butt over here. And your stupid father. Stupid man, what a really inconvenient time for him to decide that he's forgiven you for living. Practically threatened me if I didn't call him the minute you woke up."

Rachel's mind felt slow, almost frozen. How long had she been here, wherever here was? Oh yeah, Joel Gibbs. Told me he killed Alix. And some other woman. Tried to kill me. I'm in some hospital or another. Threw up. Yuck.

"Cori?"

"Yeah sweetie, what is it?"

"Joel Gibbs, he . . ."

"I know. He tried to kill you. Cops came charging in on him. What did you do to make him so mad, girlfriend? I mean, I know you can be annoying, but kill you?" Cori's attempt at humor actually helped. They don't know about Alix yet, Rachel thought. No one has any idea. She struggled to sit up, leading to mass beeping of machines and the appearance of a perturbed-looking nurse, whose frown left upon seeing the cause of the beeping, an almost upright Rachel.

"Dr. Katz, back among the living. We've enjoyed having you as our guest here at the ICU, but I believe that checkout time may have come."

Rachel coughed, and started to cry, causing Cori to turn and glare at the nurse. "That was not funny, Paulette, look at her, she's a mess, still."

"Cor, it's OK," Rachel wheezed. "No problem. How long?"

"Have you been here?" Rachel nodded. "Two days. Apparently you threw up some but not enough of what he fed you. Absorbed enough to depress your breathing pretty badly. It's a good thing you had that alarm system, babe. You've been off the vent for most of the time, breathing nicely on your own, but you sure were zonked out." Cori's attention focused on Rachel intently, still assessing cognitive function and alertness.

Rachel turned to the nurse, straining to read her name tag, and realizing that part of why the world was fuzzy was that she was missing her glasses. "Glasses?" she croaked.

Cori and the nurse looked at each other and shrugged. "I guess they got misplaced in the shuffle. Or maybe they're with your stuff. I hope you didn't like that top too well, they had to cut it off you," Cori said, gently.

"Oh, fuck. Stupid Joel. Extra glasses, in my nightstand, top right drawer." She started to cry again. Why am I crying? she thought. I seem to be alive. She struggled to put a longer string of words together, but syntax kept eluding her.

"Joel, he, Alix, he . . ." Rachel ran out of steam.

"Listen, babe, don't try to talk just now, OK? We just want to know you're back among the truly living, ya know, people who talk? The whole crew has been a little frantic, don't cha know? Driving the poor resident out of her mind, all of us flashing our doctor titles at her. But you're gonna be OK."

Rachel stopped listening and fell asleep again. The noise of the machines being unhooked woke her up again. Cori was gone. She had no idea how long she'd been out this time. There were no windows to the outside world in the ICU. No wonder people get psychotic in here, she thought. Nothing to orient with. She chuckled a little at the thought. She guessed she wasn't brain damaged if she was thinking about ICU psychosis. She looked up and said to the white blur who was unhooking the machines, "Hi. I'm very nearsighted, so I can't see your name plate. But I'm awake now." She surprised herself at her verbal coherence.

A sweet, low voice responded from the blur. "I'm Paulette, you know, the one who wants to kick you out of here. Which is what we're about to do. Gonna send you and that pack of groupies down to the med-surg unit for a night until we're sure you're OK."

Rachel brightened. That meant that people could visit. And the dog. She piped up, her voice rusty but her syntax apparently back online.

"Uh, Paulette, what's the hospital's policy about service dogs?"

Paulette let out a whoop of laughter. "Your friend Dr. Diaz told me that you were pining for your dog. Service dog, huh?"

"Yeah. He used to work in my office. With trauma survivors. So what's the rules?"

"I have the distinct feeling that whatever the rules are, you'll get to see him sooner than you think." The nurse finished unhooking the various monitors. "Here, let's get you up and into the chair and you can take a look."

Rachel tried to rise, but fell back, woozy. Paulette came over and expertly got her transferred into a chair. She then plucked a pair of glasses out of one of her pockets and stuck them on Rachel's face.

"We found those with your stuff. I believe this should take care of the myopia." She smiled.

Rachel breathed a sigh of relief. She could see. She ran a hand through her hair. It felt matted. "Can I get a mirror? And a comb? Please?"

"That'll have to wait until you get downstairs. We specialize in keeping people alive here, and looks don't matter much. But the way this crowd of yours acts, I don't think they'll care what you look like. It's nice to see a patient who's got such a support system. And such a well-behaved support system, too."

"Well, they are mostly psychologists, you know. Except for the jerk who got me in here, we're pretty nice people." Paulette finished unhooking her and attached the IV, still in Rachel's arm, to a pole on the wheelchair. She got behind it and rolled Rachel out of the cubicle, out of the ICU, and into a curtained waiting area.

She had made it out of there. Rachel smiled and as she did so, the door opened and a small black nose, at knee height, poked through, followed by an ecstatic bull terrier, straining at his lead. Mr. Piggy jumped into Rachel's lap and began to thoroughly cover her with dog kisses. She wrapped her arms around him and began to cry hard. "Oh piglet, baby boy, I thought he was gonna kill you." She petted the dog hard, repeatedly, her arms crushing him into her.

When the reunion had been accomplished and the dog snuggled into her lap, Rachel looked up to see Andrea Cole on the other end of the leash, furiously grinning at her. She was dressed in her uniform. "I just held up the badge and said that the dog and I were on police business. I figure, who's gonna say no to a cop, right? Rachel, I'm so glad you're OK. You cannot imagine how glad I am that nut didn't succeed."

Rachel took a deep breath. No one knew about Joel Gibbs. They just thought he'd gone crazy and gone off on her. Someone had to know, and this was the right someone. Alix was her case, after all. "Andrea, Joel Gibbs. The guy who tried to kill me. He's not just a nut. He was Alix Price's therapist. She was remembering incest." Andrea drew in a sharp breath of shock, understanding dawning on her face. Rachel went on. "He forced her to have sex with him." Andrea's face colored. "The evil fucking bastard," she muttered quietly.

Rachel went on, in a flat voice, reciting the facts that had almost disappeared with her. "She was going to make him stop and turn him in. So he killed her. He told me that he did the same thing with her as me. Held a gun on her, what did he say . . ." Rachel shuddered and shook, the memories returning vividly. "That he told her she could drink the alcohol and pills and die pretty or have him wrap her hand around the gun and shoot her and die ugly. That I would have the same choice. That Alix wasn't the first."

Andrea stood, silent. Cori's face appeared over her shoulder. She had come into the room and apparently heard much of Rachel's accusation. She seemed more shocked than Andrea, Rachel noted dispassionately. Maybe cops are used to hearing about people killing people. Cori spoke up.

"Babe, are you sure about Joel? I mean, I know he's a slime case, but these are some very serious accusations you're making. Maybe you don't remember right . . ."

Rachel interrupted her. "You know, Cori, just right now I don't

247

even remember what I was wearing that day. But, oh, girl . . ." Rachel began to cry again. "I think I'm just labile as all get out, listen to me, big words. Disoriented, I'm disoriented. And see my pup. He's here, he's OK. But that I know, oh my God, Cori, he was gonna kill Mr. Piggy. He killed Alix Price. I remember that right."

The words hung in the air. "You're sure of this," Cori whispered. It was a statement, not a question. Andrea stepped back, pulled out a Palm Pilot, and took notes. Rachel kept talking, needing to get the nauseating knowledge out of her brain and into the light of day.

"Joel Gibbs. He was her therapist. He was fucking her. She was gonna turn him in. So he killed her. Same way as me. I think he killed some other ones, too. He knew the law. Sexual assault now, you know. He knew I knew, from Emma. Would turn him in. He'd be busted. So he wanted to kill me. Make it look like suicide."

"Oh my God. He really did want to kill you. I just thought the man snapped." Cori whispered, "Who's Emma, babe?"

"Easier to think he was crazy. But he's not crazy. He meant this. He meant to kill Alix. Cori, he told me how he learned to kill. How he had to do 'the first one' with a plastic bag. Alice, Alice told me he had clients suicide. Not suicides, Cori. Women he fucked, then he killed them." Rachel's eyes filled with tears again. "I didn't wanna believe it. He had a gun on me, I didn't wanna believe it. He's a psychologist for God's sake. One of us. We don't kill people." The tears trickled down her chin.

Cori reached down into the wheelchair to embrace her friend, who was holding tight to her dog as if to a lifeline. "You know, girlfriend, you've gotta stop hanging out around those psychologists. Dangerous characters, all of us. Oh girl, I'm glad you're back. Sounds like the old cerebral cortex didn't take too much of a beating after all. But my God, girl, this is horrifying stuff. It's not like he's a pillar of our community, but murder? If I hadn't been watching you lie here for two days, I wouldn't be able to believe it." She turned to the cop. "You heard this?"

248

Andrea nodded, grim. "Yes. I heard it, damn him. If you two don't mind, I have to get out of here and get on the horn to my lieutenant. We have a case we have to reopen. I'll come by later to get the boy, OK?" She reached down and squeezed Rachel's shoulder, then headed out, an air of determination surrounding her. This case cut way close to home for her. Someone running around raping and murdering incest survivors was at the very top of Andrea Cole's shit list, and she had the power to do something about it.

Cori spoke again into the silence. "Look, do you mind terribly if I do call some people? You know, Alice, people at the state association, your dad . . ."

"Not my father." Rachel was struck with the coldness in her voice. Odd that it had stayed in her brain, Cori telling her that her father had re-owned her. "Not him. He doesn't deserve to be on the list. He thought I was dead to him all these years. Fine. Keep it that way for now. Call Alice, OK? And Joyce Romanski, tell her I have the answer to her questions. The synagogue."

Rachel stopped for a moment, her brain becoming more awake and alive. Anna Sigurdson. Should Cori call her? Was she close in enough yet? Then Rachel remembered her thought in the office while Joel had her under his gun. Her grief at the idea that she would die before Anna and she made love. A person should pay attention to that kind of thing, she thought.

"Cori, there's one other person who should know I'm OK. Anna, the woman Alice introduced me to? You can probably get her number from Alice, she's—"

"Been here most of the last two days. They wouldn't let her into ICU, I'm the only one who actually got in, and that's 'cause I'm your power of attorney, remember? I saw her when I went out for a few minutes, I think she's probably still out there. Nice woman. I got a chance to know her when the staff chased me out so they could do stuff to you. Do you want me to go look and see if she's still there?"

Rachel was dumbstruck. Anna here? This was just a beginning flirtation, what was Anna doing keeping vigil outside the ICU? She started to cry again.

"Did I say the wrong thing, babe? Do you want me to tell her to go away?" Cori moved quickly to reassure Rachel.

"No. Not the wrong thing. The right thing. And no, please don't ask her to go away. Could we get me out of here, like, now, please? So I can see her?" Cori smiled. Her friend was alive, and there was a woman out there who seemed to care a lot about her.

"I'll go out and tell Anna that she'd better go home and spiff up a bit. Wouldn't want to have her scare you back into passing out with that hair of hers all wild." Cori laughed and headed out the door.

Rachel slowly laid back down. She was alive. Her dog was safe, asleep in her arms as if he had spent the entire time apart awake, pining for his mother. She had reported her story of Joel Gibbs to the cops. And Anna had spent two days in the waiting room. Oh God. That was as much as she could digest. She fell asleep again, the dog in her lap, glued to her as if he would never leave.

Somewhere during this bout of slumber Rachel and her wheel-chair ended up in a room with a view out to the stadium and the lake. When her eyes opened, she was facing the window. The day was gray, the lake placid. The new green of spring was on the trees. April was almost done. She felt empty, calm. Mr. Piggy was lying at her feet, tail batting against the floor as if in welcome.

This time she noticed how sore her body was. Ribs hurting, pain in the crooks of her elbows. They must have done CPR on me, she thought. No wonder she was so sore. She pulled up a sleeve of her hospital gown. The IV was gone, but blackening bruises decorated the insides of both arms. She didn't get the chance to tell anyone how hard it is to get a vein on her, she thought. Oh, well.

She sensed a presence in the room and turned around slightly in the chair. Anna Sigurdson stood at the edge of the curtain that separated the two beds in the room. Her face was drawn. Dark circles accentuated red-rimmed hazel green eyes. Rachel noticed that her hair was slicked back, wet. I guess Cori got her to go take a shower, she thought to herself.

"Can I come in?" Anna seemed for the first time in all of their encounters tentative, uncertain of her place in Rachel's hospital room.

"Please." Rachel's eyes filled with tears. "I heard about you . . ."

"Acting like the complete idiot? Yeah, I guess Cori told you. I guess I couldn't stand not knowing what was going to happen to you. Rachel, dear, what did you get yourself into?" Anna's wise-cracking tone began to insinuate itself back into her voice.

"Don't ask," Rachel wisecracked back. "You know, all in a day's work for us forensic psychologists. Interview people, get held at gunpoint . . ." She suddenly started to cry again. Anna walked over and put her arms around Rachel's shoulders, holding her while she sobbed. This time the tears flowed for a long time, Rachel finally allowing the full ration of terror to course through her. She was safe enough to notice how close she had come to dying.

When it seemed as if her tear ducts had given their last and the latest in a large mound of tissues had been filled with snot, Rachel lay back with her head against Anna's chest, her breath still shuddering and uneven. Anna stroked her hair and forehead, saying nothing, allowing Rachel the time and space. Rachel broke the silence.

"Anna, I nearly died. And I want to tell you this, because I just had an up-close-and-personal encounter with the fact that life is uncertain. When I was sitting there fading out from the stuff he fed me, before I threw up, all I could think about besides my dog was that we hadn't made love yet. That I didn't want to die before we made love. I guess that says something."

She fell silent. Anna's arms tightened around her. "Well, I had been thinking that this was one hell of a way to get out of that safer sex lesson."

Anna hooted with laughter. "I've had women reject me before, Rachel, but no one go to such lengths. So I'm glad, like, way very glad, to hear that this was only a rain check." She bent down and kissed Rachel's cheek. The smaller woman's arms came up and pulled Anna into an embrace, dragging mouth to mouth, tongues clashing, touching, all the emotion of the past few days distilled into the one point of contact. Ambivalence might return to Rachel. But for the moment, she knew precisely where she wanted to be. In Anna's strong arms, that was where.

Chapter Seventeen

The women sat in Joyce Romanski's office. Rachel Katz, thinner and still pale from her close encounter of the almost fatal kind, held all eyes as she spoke. Andrea Cole continued taking notes on her Palm Pilot. Ilona Hegevary sat, quietly crying. Joyce perched on the edge of her own desk, hands clenched on the edge, controlling her breathing as Rachel spoke. Emma Forche was the only person in the room who seemed at peace.

"Alix was such a private person, which worked to Gibbs's advantage. He knew that it was very unlikely that she would ever tell anyone what was happening to her."

Joyce interrupted. "Plus, she made sure we didn't know who each other were. I mean"—and she turned to the Hungarian—"I knew you existed, Ilona. She mentioned she had a research assistant from Hungary. But that you were her lover? Not in a million years."

"Right," Rachel interjected. "Alix kept the segments of her life completely disconnected from one another. Emma, you were the only one who knew more than a little slice. And of course, you were bound by confidentiality. You couldn't say anything to anyone."

Emma sighed. "My dear, even if I hadn't been bound, I have great faith in people's ability to know how and when to share parts of their lives. Alix was just beginning to learn about telling her truths. If she'd lived, I think she would have been tickled to see us all here together. But she was only on the edge of that, you know. And I don't push people. I simply accompany them on their journey."

Rachel continued with her recitation. "It appears that when Alix confronted him about his abuse of her, Joel Gibbs began to plan how to kill her. Funny thing is, every time I do one of these therapist sex cases, the victims tell me how terrified they are that the therapist is gonna kill them for turning him, or her, in. And I've been reassuring everyone that therapists don't do that, that I'd never heard of any offender therapist going that far. Well, I guess Alix wasn't afraid of Joel. And he turned out to be that old exception proving the rule. Andrea, I think here's where you come in."

Andrea looked up from her Palm, turning from her latest notes to her portion of the narrative. "Right. You know, when we busted Gibbs at Rachel's office, he went into this crazy-guy mode. Got himself put on suicide watch at the jail, the whole nine yards. Until Rachel came to, we had no idea that we had anything on our hands except a shrink who'd gone completely nuts.

"Then, Rachel, after you woke up, well, everything changed. He still was playing crazy. I guess it's not hard for him to do that, because he's pretty crazy anyway. Just not the way that gets you off in court, don't cha know? The guy didn't do his research on dimcap." Andrea chuckled. The diminished capacity, known as "dimcap" to the law enforcement crowd, and insanity statutes in Washington State were tightly written. Not just any old crazy person qualified for compassion under them. Joel Gibbs had apparently avoided checking into the details of the laws before making his stab at getting away with attempted murder. "But once I had your statement, Rachel, I got Alix's death formally reopened."

Rachel chimed into the story again. "And that's when I told you about the panties in her bedside table. I was lying there at home, you know, when I first got out of the hospital, just going back over the whole thing, wondering what I'd missed. And those damn stinky panties flew into my mind."

"So we went out and got them. Surprise, surprise, it's Joel Gibbs's DNA. Because until then, the man was claiming that you'd gone crazy, hallucinated maybe. Had suddenly saned himself up and selling us this routine about how you were trying to kill yourself, and he was trying to make you stop. Like we were gonna buy that line of bullshit. Everyone knows that you'd never do that, Rachel." Andrea beamed at her former therapist.

Rachel was silent for a moment. Oh, girl, you have no idea how close I got to that decision last year, Rachel thought. Joel Gibbs had been dead-on about the fake motive for her suicide note. The invisibility, the sense of disconnection, the profound weariness— all of those things had pushed her a lot closer to the edge of that particular cliff than she ever cared to think. But that was not information she was about to share with Andrea. Or maybe with anyone, except a therapist. It was time, she had realized in the aftermath of her brush with final exit. Her life needed a little examination, some fine-tuning. She shifted her focus back to the room and to Andrea's continued narrative.

"So, there we were with his DNA from the semen on her panties. He had a damn hard time trying to explain that away. And then there's Ed Barnes's ID. Gibbs is who he saw going into Alix's house the night she died." While Rachel was in the hospital, the Barneses had come forward with Ed's story.

"We aren't sure yet we can get him for more than the third-degree sexual assault. But we've gotten exhumation orders on the other two women who died in his practice, and the department will be reopening both of those investigations. Between the sexual assault charge on Alix Price and the attempted murder on you, Rachel, the man is going to be visiting lovely Walla Walla for a very long time, I'd say."

Andrea sat back. Ilona and Joyce were both crying by the end of the recitation. Emma got up and gave each one, in turn, a hug, then looked across the room at Rachel. "Shall I tell her?" she asked the psychologist.

"Yes, I think so." Get it all out now, Rachel thought. Trying to pull the cover off this wound slowly was not gonna work.

Emma turned to Ilona first. "Ilona, Alix spoke of you to me frequently. She was beginning to realize that her relationship with you would hurt you deeply." Ilona began to protest, but Emma held up her hand for silence and continued. "Not just because you were the student and dependent on her. Because she knew that you were a bright shining star, that's what she called you."

At this revelation Ilona's sobs started back up again. Emma waited quietly until Ilona had cried herself out again, the other three women watching in various stages of pain and compassion themselves. Emma began again. "She said you were this bright star. That you would have made your professional reputation on your own, no matter what. That being linked to her was going to hold you back, and that you deserved someone who could love you fully, commit to you completely. That wasn't going to be her, Alix knew that. She cared for you very much, almost as much as she admired you. She knew that you were just putting it on about being OK with her screwing around."

Ilona's head slowly nodded. She's been in therapy just long enough, Rachel thought.

Emma went on. "And her heart wasn't with you."

She turned to Joyce. "It was with you." Joyce started, paled, and gripped the desk harder. "Joyce, she told me that you were the love of her life. She was so afraid that she had missed her chance with you. The last time we talked, she told me that when she had worked more through the incest materials, she was going to seek you out. Ask you to forgive her, to have her back. She was ready to

256

make a commitment to you. I'm so sad to be telling you this now. It should be Alix here, alive, to do that. But if you hadn't been so loyal to her yourself, Joyce . . ."

She left the rest unsaid. If Joyce Romanski hadn't doggedly refused to believe in Alix's suicide, then her killer would have waltzed off, free to rape and murder another vulnerable woman.

Joyce's eyes glittered, but her composure held. Damn, she's good, Rachel thought. Alice is about to have a whole hell of a lot of extra work to do, that's for sure. Her heart went out to Joyce. Was it worse to know that someone had loved you so dearly who you would never see again, or to never have known? Rachel couldn't have made that choice if she had another gun pointed at her, she realized. Love, hard-fought and hard-won love, love out of the trenches and thorns of abuse and violation, growing tall past the barriers of hate that came between two women or two men, that kind of love was too precious to not know. And too painful to have missed. Joyce had her answers, and then some. She would not have wanted to stand in Joyce's place, Rachel realized.

Emma spoke again. "Rachel, there's something I have to tell you, too." Rachel looked up, startled. She thought she was done with new revelations, that she was here only as the narrator of the story. "You know that Alix admired you. You didn't know that she felt she owed you a huge apology. I'm not sure you need to hear this, but she was getting ready to let you know herself. I wasn't sure until the last few days that it was you she was talking about, but the more I've learned about you, the more sure I am.

"So, here's what she told me. That she had had an affair with a woman, oh, maybe six years ago. The woman's lover was also a psychologist. She told me that she broke it off when she realized that this woman was only having sex with her because she, Alix, was such a thorn in her partner's side. Alix said that she respected the woman's partner, that she was one hell of a forensic psychologist. That the other woman had died in a car accident. I remember her coming into my office telling me about it when it happened. That was the only woman lover she hadn't kept some kind of friendship ties with, when she realized that the woman had seduced her to hurt her partner. Who Alix didn't like much, I could tell, but respected a lot.

"So during those last few times with me, when she was having these epiphanies bursting all over her, she told me that she had an apology to make. That it was going to be hard to do, but that she owed it to the other psychologist. And Rachel, I'm pretty sure that's you."

Rachel sat in a state of shock. Just when she thought she had sustained all the loss she could, just when she was ready to bury Sarah for good, her ghost rises up out of the grave to torment her. Six years ago—she strained to think what was happening then. Sarah out at meetings a lot for several months. Sarah taking up racquetball. Oh, fuck. Racquetball and coming home from the club freshly showered. Racquetball, one of Alix Price's codes for sex. Rachel could not encompass this. She was just going to stick it in a file folder somewhere.

Rachel looked up. "Thank you, I think, Emma. I needed to know about the apology. The rest, well. Sarah's been dead a while now. I can't break up with her ghost, can I?" Her voice sounded hollow. The rest of the room felt distant. She was having a little dissociative episode, she thought to herself. Oh. She avoided eye contact with the other women in the room, who were looking at her with various expressions of concern on their faces. She glanced up and waved them aside.

"Look, everyone, I'll be fine. I didn't just lose my lover. I just lost a little bit more of my illusions, and they've been getting removed from life support for a while now." Rachel retreated behind her sardonic stance, determined to move the focus away from herself. The others in the room caught the scent of fleeing psyche and backed off. An uncomfortable silence fell.

Joyce Romanski broke it. "I want you all to know that the estate will be suing Joel Gibbs for the limits of everything he's insured for and everything he ever owned. Which, Ilona, is germane in your case. You're in the will, you know. You, too, Emma."

Ilona shook her head. "No, what? In the will, what?" She looked confusedly around the office, her English deserting her momentarily. Emma looked as surprised as Rachel had ever seen her. Neither woman had expected this, Rachel could tell. Joyce went on.

"I asked Rachel to fill me in on insurance policies for psychologists. Turns out that there's a damages cap for sexual misconduct. But no mention of a cap for murder." She grinned wolfishly. "I think I can undo that other cap, too. I talked to someone in town, what's his name, Rachel . . ."

"David Summers," Rachel intoned, still in her faraway place. "He's the expert on sexual misconduct. Did all the cases that came before me. Great guy. He's been going after the sexual misconduct cap for years."

"Right. I talked to Summers, and we're going to do a full-court press on this. The estate deserves every penny it can get from this man." Rachel could see the fire building in Joyce. This case would be her memorial to Alix Price, her transformation of grief. So much easier to lose your lover this way, she thought. Clean, tragic, but clean.

The meeting broke up shortly after Joyce's revelation. Rachel stayed behind for a few minutes. "Joyce, how do you want to settle the bill on this one?"

"You know, Rachel, if I had had any idea . . ." Joyce's voice trailed off. "I wasn't trying to get you killed."

Rachel made a feeble attempt at laughter. "I know, Joyce. You need me too much for court. Here's what I think. I'd like to bill you for whatever part of the hospital costs that my insurance and victim's compensation doesn't pick up. For the cleaning costs to my office, and to replace that top I was wearing." She got a wistful look in her eyes. "I really liked that top, too. Wore it specially because I wanted to get into the Fremont spirit, don'tcha know? So, anyhow, how do you feel about that? I won't bill you for my unconscious time." She laughed again, a shade more heartily.

"You can bill me whatever you want, is what I think." Joyce's freewheeling response was out of character. "I've lost Alix, but you gave her back to me, Rachel. You gave her back in some ways I can never repay, OK? So send me a bill for whatever you think is right. And do bill me for the days you were out, or whatever other down time you had to take."

Joyce then surprised Rachel even more by coming around from behind her desk and grasping her in a tight hug. She held on for a long time, saying nothing. When she let go, she stepped back and looked at Rachel, whose face still bore the remoteness that had fallen on it as Emma related the story of Sarah's perfidy.

"You know, I'm probably speaking out of turn, and you know this anyway, but Rachel, if you're not seeing someone, get into therapy, please. You know how dead-set I was against it. Well, Alice is going to save my life, and change my life. If it helps me, for goodness's sake, it's going to help you. And you've had a whole bunch of body blows lately. Even us uptight attorney types can worry about our friends. I'm worried about you. So, take your own advice, will you, please?"

Rachel felt the tears trying to come through the cold metal at her core. "Thanks, Joyce. Actually, I have an appointment set up with someone. Nearly getting killed is a little hard on a person. But thanks. Not out of turn."

Rachel walked down the corridor to where Mr. Piggy sat at Luanne's feet. Lu and Joyce had reconciled in the wake of Rachel's near death. The relationship was not the same yet, but Lu was determined to stay and work with Joyce. "Come here, baby boy." The dog scrambled to his feet, nails clicking on the hardwood floor. "Lu, thanks again for watching him." She hooked up the leash, ready to leave.

"Thanks, yourself, Rache. You don't know how glad I am that Ed didn't do anything bad. Are we gonna see you around here again sometime soon?" Luanne inquired.

"You know, Lu, I don't know. I think I have a little career rethinking to do here, don't you agree?" She gave the receptionist a hug and headed for the elevator, dog in tow.

Out in the street, Rachel was aware of her persistent feelings of disorientation. Now, she thought. She could disappear now. Run away with her dog, never go home again, never allow herself to face this last betrayal by Sarah. Never allow Anna one millimeter further into her heart. Just get on the ferry and go.

The slight tug at the end of the leash brought her back out of her self-preoccupation. The dog had sighted a friendly human. Emma Forche stood across the street. The light changed, and she walked over to Rachel and the dog. "I thought you'd need some company. I was sorry to be telling you that, but it needed to be said. Truth being one of those scalpels that lets the poison out. So will you walk with me?" She tucked Rachel's arm into the crook of her elbow and took Mr. Piggy's leash in her other hand. "Come on. Let this old woman take a little care of you."

Rachel returned home in the early evening. It was May, she thought. A month since Andrea showed up at her door. A month since Anna came into her life. The month of Passover. She had barely found the time to attend seder this year. Alice and Liz had dragged her to a women's seder where she had sat, impatient for the proceedings to finish, unable to immerse herself as she normally did in the powerful, uplifting story of the liberation from Egypt. So she didn't pay attention to the liberation story, she thought to herself, and here she was, like her ancestors, wandering in a wilderness. How appropriate, that here it is the month after Pesach and she was wandering in a wilderness of unknown terrors. Take me back to the fleshpots of Egypt, she thought, echoing the plaint of the freed Hebrew slaves. Back to Sarah, to the well-known misery she had with her, to the lies they kept, to the familiar bonds. Free her from this freedom that scared her so much. She shivered. Maybe Joel Gibbs should have succeeded. She would not be left with her life stretching in front of her, feeling so hard and rocky and arid.

Anna's timing could not have been better or more necessary.

Her appearance at the door was not entirely unplanned, but it shocked Rachel out of her reverie of self-pity. Anna knew that something was terribly wrong. Rachel seemed a million miles away, drawn tight inside of herself.

"Babe, are you OK?" She stepped through the door and put her arms around the other woman, who seemed at that moment smaller than ever. Dear lord, she thought, what's happened now? Rachel's body seemed empty of soul and spirit.

Rachel resisted for a moment, then allowed herself to sag into Anna's comforting frame. "It's s a bit of a story, Anna. I'm sorry, I'm not really here, am I? Come on in. Sit down."

Anna steered Rachel up the stairs to her sitting room. "You're shivering, babe. Come on, let me wrap you up." Anna pulled blankets off the bed in the other room and circled them around Rachel, who was sitting on the couch, still somewhat oblivious. Anna came and sat next to her, wrapping Rachel in her arms. "Can you talk?"

Rachel nodded. Her voice was flat. "You know, we had that meeting at Joyce's office, to fill everyone in on the story. Emma Forche was there. She kinda dropped a bomb on me. Seems Alix had an affair with Sarah. My Sarah. About six years back. Alix never said it was me, but the facts fit, so Emma told me. And the facts do fit. So Sarah screwed me, more than I knew. I don't know what to believe about her anymore. I feel like someone just tore out my insides all over again. Like someone new died. I'm sorry, Anna. This isn't what you came here for." She stopped as if someone had turned the switch, her face turned away to the window.

Anna shuddered. She was glad that Sarah wasn't alive for her to shake senseless, she thought. How could someone have been so cruel to this kind little person that she held in her arms? She didn't know. She tried to hold Rachel closer, but noticed that as she did, Rachel stiffened.

"Anna, this kinda, how do I say this? It changes things for me. I just don't feel like I have anything to give to a new relationship. You're very dear to me. And I'm just dead inside now. Deader than when Sarah died. I don't even know if I want to come back. I was feeling so high to be alive, and now this. I think you'd better go."

Anna felt punched in the gut. She had held on, persisted, kept vigil, watched Rachel open up her heart. And now this, again, still? This was supposed to be the uncomplicated relationship, she thought to herself. With a nice, sane, smart, funny grown-up. Here she was with another wounded birdie, but this one didn't want Anna fixing her wings. She wants to limp away.

"Rachel, dear heart. I don't think I'm gonna go just now. No strings, OK, but I think you need someone to hold you right now. And I'm here, and willing. So let me stay, please."

Rachel shrugged. She lacked the energy to push Anna away. Some part of her yearned for what this woman was offering her. Maybe she could live from her desires and not her fears, she thought. Her body loosened a notch, and she allowed herself to lean into Anna's embrace.

It was that night that the questions started. Rachel found herself wide awake. She squinted at the clock. Three a.m. Beside her, fully clothed, on top of the covers, Anna Sigurdson slept. She must have been holding Rachel when she conked out, the dog nestled next to her. Rachel crept out of the bed and downstairs to her study.

So what if I hadn't taken this job, she thought. What if? Rachel was still sitting there frozen as the sky lightened into another gray Seattle morning, then startled into life at the sound of Anna's footsteps coming down the stairs.

WHEN LOVE FINDS A HOME by Megan Carter. 280 pp. What will it take for Anna and Rona to find their way back to each other again? 1-59493-041-4 $12.95

MEMORIES TO DIE FOR by Adrian Gold. 240pp. Rachel Katz, a forensic psychologist, attempts to avoid her attraction to the charms of Anna Sigurdson. Will Anna's persistence and patience get her past Rachel's fears of a broken heart? 1-59493-038-4 $12.95

SILENT HEART by Claire McNab. 280 pp. Exotic lesbian romance.
1-59493-044-9 $12.95

MIDNIGHT RAIN by Peggy J. Herring. 240 pp. Bridget McBee is determined to find the woman who saved her life. 1-59493-021-X $12.95

THE MISSING PAGE A Brenda Strange Mystery by Patty G. Henderson. 240 pp. Brenda investigates her client's murder . . . 1-59493-004-X $12.95

WHISPERS ON THE WIND by Frankie J. Jones. 240 pp. Dixon thinks she and her best friend, Elizabeth Colter, would make the perfect couple . . . 1-59493-037-6 $12.95

CALL OF THE DARK: EROTIC LESBIAN TALES OF THE SUPERNATURAL edited by Therese Szymanski—from Bella After Dark. 320 pp. 1-59493-040-6 $14.95

A TIME TO CAST AWAY A Helen Black Mystery by Pat Welch. 240 pp. Helen stops by Alice's apartment—only to find the woman dead . . . 1-59493-036-8 $12.95

DESERT OF THE HEART by Jane Rule. 224 pp. The book that launched the most popular lesbian movie of all time is back. 1-1-59493-035-X $12.95

THE NEXT WORLD by Ursula Steck. 240 pp. Anna's friend Mido is threatened and eventually disappears . . . 1-59493-024-4 $12.95

CALL SHOTGUN by Jaime Clevenger. 240 pp. Kelly gets pulled back into the world of private investigation . . . 1-59493-016-3 $12.95

52 PICKUP by Bonnie J. Morris and E.B. Casey. 240 pp. 52 hot, romantic tales—one for every Saturday night of the year. 1-59493-026-0 $12.95

GOLD FEVER by Lyn Denison. 240 pp. Kate's first love, Ashley, returns to their home town, where Kate now lives . . . 1-1-59493-039-2 $12.95

RISKY INVESTMENT by Beth Moore. 240 pp. Lynn's best friend and roommate needs her to pretend Chris is his fiancé. But nothing is ever easy. 1-59493-019-8 $12.95

HUNTER'S WAY by Gerri Hill. 240 pp. Homicide detective Tori Hunter is forced to team up with the hot-tempered Samantha Kennedy. 1-59493-018-X $12.95

CAR POOL by Karin Kallmaker. 240 pp. Soft shoulders, merging traffic and slippery when wet . . . Anthea and Shay find love in the car pool. 1-59493-013-9 $12.95

NO SISTER OF MINE by Jeanne G'Fellers. 240 pp. Telepathic women fight to coexist with a patriarchal society that wishes their eradication. ISBN 1-59493-017-1 $12.95

ON THE WINGS OF LOVE by Megan Carter. 240 pp. Stacie's reporting career is on the rocks. She has to interview bestselling author Cheryl, or else! ISBN 1-59493-027-9 $12.95

WICKED GOOD TIME by Diana Tremain Braund. 224 pp. Does Christina need Miki as a protector . . . or want her as a lover? ISBN 1-59493-031-7 $12.95

THOSE WHO WAIT by Peggy J. Herring. 240 pp. Two brilliant sisters—in love with the same woman! ISBN 1-59493-032-5 $12.95

ABBY'S PASSION by Jackie Calhoun. 240 pp. Abby's bipolar sister helps turn her world upside down, so she must decide what's most important. ISBN 1-59493-014-7 $12.95

PICTURE PERFECT by Jane Vollbrecht. 240 pp. Kate is reintroduced to Casey, the daughter of an old friend. Can they withstand Kate's career? ISBN 1-59493-015-5 $12.95

PAPERBACK ROMANCE by Karin Kallmaker. 240 pp. Carolyn falls for tall, dark and . . . female . . . in this classic lesbian romance. ISBN 1-59493-033-3 $12.95

DAWN OF CHANGE by Gerri Hill. 240 pp. Susan ran away to find peace in remote Kings Canyon—then she met Shawn . . . ISBN 1-59493-011-2 $12.95

DOWN THE RABBIT HOLE by Lynne Jamneck. 240 pp. Is a killer holding a grudge against FBI Agent Samantha Skellar? ISBN 1-59493-012-0 $12.95

SEASONS OF THE HEART by Jackie Calhoun. 240 pp. Overwhelmed, Sara saw only one way out—leaving . . . ISBN 1-59493-030-9 $12.95

TURNING THE TABLES by Jessica Thomas. 240 pp. The 2nd Alex Peres Mystery. *From ghosties and ghoulies and long leggity beasties . . .* ISBN 1-59493-009-0 $12.95

FOR EVERY SEASON by Frankie Jones. 240 pp. Andi, who is investigating a 65-year-old murder, meets Janice, a charming district attorney . . . ISBN 1-59493-010-4 $12.95

LOVE ON THE LINE by Laura DeHart Young. 240 pp. Kay leaves a younger woman behind to go on a mission to Alaska . . . will she regret it? ISBN 1-59493-008-2 $12.95

UNDER THE SOUTHERN CROSS by Claire McNab. 200 pp. Lee, an American travel agent, goes down under and meets Australian Alex, and the sparks fly under the Southern Cross. ISBN 1-59493-029-5 $12.95

SUGAR by Karin Kallmaker. 240 pp. Three women want sugar from Sugar, who can't make up her mind. ISBN 1-59493-001-5 $12.95

FALL GUY by Claire McNab. 200 pp. 16th Detective Inspector Carol Ashton Mystery. ISBN 1-59493-000-7 $12.95

ONE SUMMER NIGHT by Gerri Hill. 232 pp. Johanna swore to never fall in love again— but then she met the charming Kelly . . . ISBN 1-59493-007-4 $12.95

TALK OF THE TOWN TOO by Saxon Bennett. 181 pp. Second in the series about wild and fun loving friends. ISBN 1-931513-77-5 $12.95

LOVE SPEAKS HER NAME by Laura DeHart Young. 170 pp. Love and friendship, desire and intrigue, spark this exciting sequel to *Forever and the Night.* ISBN 1-59493-002-3 $12.95

TO HAVE AND TO HOLD by Peggy J. Herring. 184 pp. By finally letting down her defenses, will Dorian be opening herself to a devastating betrayal?
ISBN 1-59493-005-8 $12.95

WILD THINGS by Karin Kallmaker. 228 pp. Dutiful daughter Faith has met the perfect man. There's just one problem: she's in love with his sister.   ISBN 1-931513-64-3 $12.95

SHARED WINDS by Kenna White. 216 pp. Can Emma rebuild more than just Lanny's marina?   ISBN 1-59493-006-6 $12.95

THE UNKNOWN MILE by Jaime Clevenger. 253 pp. Kelly's world is getting more and more complicated every moment.   ISBN 1-931513-57-0 $12.95

TREASURED PAST by Linda Hill. 189 pp. A shared passion for antiques leads to love.
ISBN 1-59493-003-1 $12.95

SIERRA CITY by Gerri Hill. 284 pp. Chris and Jesse cannot deny their growing attraction . . .   ISBN 1-931513-98-8 $12.95

ALL THE WRONG PLACES by Karin Kallmaker. 174 pp. Sex and the single girl—Brandy is looking for love and usually she finds it. Karin Kallmaker's first *After Dark* erotic novel.
ISBN 1-931513-76-7 $12.95

WHEN THE CORPSE LIES A Motor City Thriller by Therese Szymanski. 328 pp. Butch bad-girl Brett Higgins is used to waking up next to beautiful women she hardly knows. Problem is, this one's dead.   ISBN 1-931513-74-0 $12.95

GUARDED HEARTS by Hannah Rickard. 240 pp. Someone's reminding Alyssa about her secret past, and then she becomes the suspect in a series of burglaries.
ISBN 1-931513-99-6 $12.95

ONCE MORE WITH FEELING by Peggy J. Herring. 184 pp. Lighthearted, loving, romantic adventure.   ISBN 1-931513-60-0 $12.95

TANGLED AND DARK A Brenda Strange Mystery by Patty G. Henderson. 240 pp. When investigating a local death, Brenda finds two possible killers—one diagnosed with Multiple Personality Disorder.   ISBN 1-931513-75-9 $12.95

WHITE LACE AND PROMISES by Peggy J. Herring. 240 pp. Maxine and Betina realize sex may not be the most important thing in their lives.   ISBN 1-931513-73-2 $12.95

UNFORGETTABLE by Karin Kallmaker. 288 pp. Can Rett find love with the cheerleader who broke her heart so many years ago?   ISBN 1-931513-63-5 $12.95

HIGHER GROUND by Saxon Bennett. 280 pp. A delightfully complex reflection of the successful, high society lives of a small group of women.   ISBN 1-931513-69-4 $12.95

LAST CALL A Detective Franco Mystery by Baxter Clare. 240 pp. Frank overlooks all else to try to solve a cold case of two murdered children . . .   ISBN 1-931513-70-8 $12.95

ONCE UPON A DYKE: NEW EXPLOITS OF FAIRY-TALE LESBIANS by Karin Kallmaker, Julia Watts, Barbara Johnson & Therese Szymanski. 320 pp. You've never read fairy tales like these before! From Bella After Dark.   ISBN 1-931513-71-6 $14.95

FINEST KIND OF LOVE by Diana Tremain Braund. 224 pp. Can Molly and Carolyn stop clashing long enough to see beyond their differences?   ISBN 1-931513-68-6 $12.95

DREAM LOVER by Lyn Denison. 188 pp. A soft, sensuous, romantic fantasy.
ISBN 1-931513-96-1 $12.95

NEVER SAY NEVER by Linda Hill. 224 pp. A classic love story . . . where rules aren't the only things broken.   ISBN 1-931513-67-8 $12.95